Valen

Felicity Heaton

GUARDIANS OF HADES SERIES

Ares
Valen
Esher – Coming in 2017

Find out more at: www.felicityheaton.co.uk

CHAPTER 1

Whoever she was, she wasn't being subtle.

Valen had first noticed her when he had stepped out of his apartment building and into a nearby square right in the heart of Rome, and a jolt had run through him, a hot bolt of electricity that had lit up his senses until they had been singing a symphony, a cantata all about his little assassin tail.

Gods, had he missed her?

After his brothers, Ares and Daimon, had sent a message to their enemy by cutting down the daemon known as Trickster, everything had fallen quiet rather than imploding as Valen had been hoping. He had bet his left bollock to his eldest brother, Keras, that the death of one of their ranks would draw the rest of them out of hiding, allowing him and his brothers to see just how many they were dealing with as the calamity the Moirai had foreseen centuries ago finally kicked into action.

The dumb bastards had done the opposite, showing just what weak-spined pathetic limp fucking wastes of blood and bone they were.

Fuck, Valen had wanted a fight, had craved war with every drop of blood in his body, so fiercely that it had taken him weeks of hunting and dispatching daemons in Rome to finally find some balance again and master his power.

Electricity arced across his fingertips, illuminating his hands as he strolled across the long square towards a narrow road at the southern end of Piazza Navona, luring his little friend with him.

His thoughts returned to her, senses honing in on her location, easily pinpointing her despite the masses of mortals that moved around the popular tourist attraction, milling around the illuminated fountains and snapping photographs of each other in front of the elegant buildings, all of them taking advantage of the more clement weather as spring finally showed the first signs of warming up the city.

The tiny bolts of lightning that leaped between his fingertips chased upwards and burrowed into his skin beneath his long black cotton coat, and his eyelids slid to half-mast as warmth suffused his flesh and sank deep into his bones.

Sweet gods, it felt good.

Always did. Always would.

He let his power flow through him, coaxing it to chase along his skin just beneath the surface, cajoling it into doing his bidding in order to have that momentary high, that sweet, sweet buzz that he had come to crave ever since he had been banished to this fucking hellhole known as Earth, kicked from his home in the Underworld by his father.

All because of the motherfucking Moirai.

He turned his head to his right and spat on the worn stone paving slabs. The Moirai would know it was aimed at their ugly bitch faces.

The lightning dancing just below the surface of his skin grew in intensity, until it lit up every nerve ending and became the one who coaxed him.

Cajoled him into surrendering to it.

He wanted to. Gods did he want to.

Fucking Keras and his other brothers would come down on his head if he let loose around so many mortals though. Hell, they would tear him a new one if he so much as stepped in front of a human, teleporting away and leaving a vapor trail of darkness behind him.

Some bullshit about not being allowed to reveal there were such things as gods.

Valen snorted, not quite a laugh but as close as he ever came to one.

As if he had ever given a damn about the rules.

His steps slowed at the junction in the road and he stopped without realising it, arrested by his own thought.

Rules?

He snorted again. Maybe he did give a fuck about those. Hell, he wasn't turning his tail into mincemeat in front of all the petty little mortals now, was he? Rules were the only reason he hadn't killed her yet, making an example of her to whoever had sent her to kill him.

Weren't they?

She drew closer and he turned his head to his right, until the scar down the left side of his neck and jaw pulled tight and irritated the fuck out of him. He felt her still and then slink deeper into the shadows of the buildings, attempting to blend in with a group of mortals. Good luck with that.

She couldn't hide from him.

He slid his right hand inside his long black coat and shuddered as his fingers found the cool metal of his black blade and tiny sparks of electricity leaped from their tips to the knife, warming it beneath his touch.

He had been aware of her the moment she had stepped from the shadows to follow him, had been leading her on a dance all night without her knowing it. She had tailed him all across the city and into his favourite nightclub, Heavenly Body. He had pretended to chat to the women there, and a few of the men, but the whole time his focus had been on her where she had sat in a dark corner of the bar, her face in shadow as she spoke with two men, acting as if she had gone there to meet them.

His little assassin probably thought he was unaware of her, blind to her dogging his every step.

She was good, but not that good.

In the short time he had been aware of her tailing him, before she had disappeared on him for three long months, he had grown attuned to her, as if she had burrowed beneath his skin just like his lightning to become a part of him in a way.

It was the only way he could explain how he reacted to her without truly being aware of her.

He was always watching for her even when he didn't know it. He didn't need to put his mind to it at all now, not as he had at first. No. Awareness of her was constant. Permanent.

She was branded on him.

Stamped on his black soul.

He knew the moment she was near him, because she lit up his veins as fiercely as his lightning and made his body buzz just as addictively.

Gods, he *had* missed her.

Keras would call him sick if he knew, but Valen didn't give a fuck what his brother thought. He didn't give a fuck what any of them thought, and he hadn't for a long time, not since they had stopped giving a shit about him.

Valen shoved his arsehole brothers out of his head and focused on her where she lingered in the shadows, until she was all that he knew.

Whoever she was, she was human.

A little mortal.

No trace of daemon in her.

Did she know what she had gotten herself into or was she oblivious to what he was—a god?

He wanted to turn around and ask her, but then the game would be over and where was the fun in that?

Someone had hired her to kill him. He had zero doubt that she was a professional, and she was probably very good at her job when her target was a lowly human, without his heightened senses or abilities.

Had she been hired by the same people who had sent a daemon to take down his brother, Ares's, gate to the Underworld in New York?

He would find out soon enough.

He moved on, taking the road to his left and then banking right, and smiled when he sensed her following. He crossed the small square in front of the church and glanced at the ice cream parlour that was closing up for the night, the elderly owner bringing his signs into the shop. It was tempting to stop for a gelato and see what she would do. The weather hadn't been nice enough for ice cream, but now the cold crisp morning air often gave way to a warm afternoon and that heat bled into the evening before the cold stole in again. It was almost gelato weather.

Gods bless the Italians. They knew how to cook.

Gelato, pasta, pizza, and desserts. They made the best damn food. He glanced at the ice cream parlour again, sorely tempted to grab a cup to go, but managed to resist. Once he was done playing with his little assassin, he would find somewhere to indulge his new craving.

That was the other thing he loved about Rome. The clocks were striking midnight around him, but he knew without a doubt he would be able to find somewhere to eat well into the morning hours.

Valen forced himself to move on, taking the next right and then banking left, heading down a narrow street between the old buildings, leading his tail onwards to their final destination.

The streets were growing quiet now. By the time he reached where he was heading, they would be in that strange period of emptiness between the tourists heading to bed and the clubs kicking everyone out.

What would his little assassin do then?

The corners of his mouth quirked. He really wanted to know.

He headed left again, down another narrow street, slowing his pace to allow time for the square ahead to empty. He could see it just in the distance, the rear of the circular building still illuminated by yellow light. Beyond that, the huge open square would be quiet, the restaurants and cafés closed for the night.

They would be alone.

Electricity coursed through him at just the thought, sending a pleasant hot shiver over his skin.

He wanted to pick up the pace, wanted to reach the square and finally meet his little assassin, but somehow kept his steps slow and measured, the thought of arriving there and not finding the piazza empty because he had rushed tempering his urgent need.

He didn't want this moment spoiled.

He wanted it perfect.

His mother's words rang in his mind, a warning she had issued when she had visited him months ago.

She is a storm born of the earth, bearing the name of an angel but the skill of a devil.

Gods, how many days since he had heard those words had he lain awake thinking about them.

Thinking about *her*.

He was sure his mother hadn't meant to make the assassin sound alluring, hadn't meant to weave an image of her that teased his imagination, but she had and he hadn't been able to stop thinking about her since that day.

It had been hell when she had disappeared. At first, he had been convinced it would be only a day or maybe two without her familiar presence in his life as he patrolled Rome's streets. When she hadn't shown up after three, he had told himself it would be only a week. And then two weeks. Then a month.

Three had passed.

Now part of him wanted to confront her and ask her where the fuck she had gone.

How the fuck could she leave him alone for so long?

He snorted at that, this one filled with self-contempt. Idiot. She was an assassin. He was nothing to her. A mark. A contract. A pay-day. That was all he was, and it was stupid of him to think any differently. It was foolish to let her sink this deep into his skin, burrow this far into his black soul.

He had learned his lesson about what happened when he succumbed to such behaviour long ago.

Had even vowed that it would never happen again.

Yet here he was, casually strolling down the slope into the Piazza della Rotonda, following the graceful curved side of the Pantheon, being a fucking fool all over again.

Valen closed his eyes, gritted his teeth and shut down that weak part of himself, slamming the door shut on it and locking it back inside where it belonged.

When he opened his eyes again, he was passing the three rows of thick towering Corinthian columns that supported the triangular pediment at the front of the Pantheon. He cast his gaze over them as he walked around towards the front of the ancient building, acting absorbed in their majesty even as his senses shifted back to his assassin. She had slowed, lingering in the shadows again, hiding from him.

He would know her face.

She would know his.

It was the last thing she would see.

He pulled the two sides of his long black cotton coat back, flashing the gold lining that matched his eyes, and jammed his hands into the pockets of his equally dark combat trousers, careful to keep his blades hidden from the few stray tourists that were leaving the square. Their paces quickened as they caught sight of him, their eyes darting to his scar and widening before they leaped away and their owner hurried in the opposite direction to him.

He had that effect on people.

Valen shrugged it off and stopped in front of the fountain in the centre of the quiet square. He scanned the old, shuttered buildings that surrounded him, feigning interest in their pale blue, terracotta orange and cream façades as he made sure he was alone with his little assassin now. The last of the tourists slinked away into a side street and he waited until his senses said they were far away before turning around, resting his backside against the curved marble base of the fountain, and staring at the columned façade of the Pantheon.

He sighed.

It was beautiful, and older than he was.

That was the greatest thing about Rome. Most of it had been stuck on Earth for longer than him, and half of it outstripped his tender eight hundred and forty-four years in age by at least a thousand more. The crowded city centre overflowed with such places, a mixture of old Roman buildings and ancient sites dedicated to a pantheon of pathetic gods.

Movement to his right snagged his attention and he dodged left, and frowned as something zipped past his head and splashed down in the water behind him. He glanced over his shoulder at it and his frown hardened, his lips flattening as he spotted the small feathered dart sitting in the bottom of the fountain.

What the fuck?

No.

No way she was going to try and drug him from a distance when he had lured her to this square in order to finally come face to face with her and find out what she wanted.

No way in the fucking Underworld was he about to let that happen.

His golden eyes snapped to the little assassin where she lingered in the shadows of a small side street to the right of the Pantheon. He caught a flash of something metal and threw himself forwards into a roll across the cobblestones as his senses blared a warning. Another dart zipped past him and he growled through clenched teeth as he came onto his feet into a dead run at her.

He sensed her alarm, heard the spike in her heartbeat as she hastily reloaded the dart gun.

She fired again and he dodged each bolt with ease, ducking beneath the first and side-stepping to evade the second, closing in on her the whole time. The gun shook in her hands as she was forced to reload again.

His right hand went to the curved black blade sheathed against his hip and he did the one thing sure to piss his brothers off if they heard about it.

He stepped.

Darkness embraced him, cool and comforting, and then the lingering warmth of spring in Rome met him again as he emerged from the teleport.

Right in front of his little assassin.

Her gasp was sweet music to his ears as he introduced her throat to his blade and she froze in place.

A second later, she recovered, raising her gun and aiming it at his stomach.

Valen clucked his tongue, grabbed the gun with his left hand and twisted it out of her grip, earning another delicious gasp from her. He curled his lip at the weapon and tossed it away from him, not bothering to look where it landed as it clattered across the dark grey cobblestones.

His little assassin had the whole of his attention.

Luminous blue eyes like tropical waters stared up into his, wide and beguiling, surrounded by dark make-up that accentuated their striking colour and framed by long black lashes.

Crimson full lips parted to reveal straight white teeth and the tempting hint of a soft pink tongue.

Short dark hair caressed her neck and swept across her forehead, streaked with blue that matched her eyes.

Fuck, she was beautiful.

He swallowed his pounding heart and tried to remember what the hell he was meant to be doing. His eyes dropped from her pouty red lips to the blade he had poised against her throat. That was right.

He was meant to be getting answers, not getting a hard-on.

He had let her have her fun with her gun. Now he was going to have his own brand of fun.

"My turn." He pressed the blade harder against her throat.

She snarled and kicked him in the shin, her knee-high boot connecting hard with it. He was behind her before she could catch him with a second strike and he snagged her right wrist and took her arm with him, twisting it behind her back. She whimpered as he pressed it against her leather jacket and he barely suppressed the hot shiver that rushed through him on hearing the sound leave her lips.

Sweet gods.

Everything about her was sexy.

Sinful.

His wicked little assassin.

As addictive and seductive as his power, everything he had dreamed she would be and feared she wouldn't.

Valen released her wrist and stepped closer to her, so their bodies touched, and his breathing quickened at the same time as hers. He swallowed hard, desperate to wet his throat, and lowered his eyes to the smooth curve of her throat and the sharp edge of his black knife. So provocative. So tempting.

An ache started deep in his belly, a hunger that was always there, lurking and waiting, born of darkness.

He moved the blade closer to her throat, eliciting another delicious whimper that cranked up that hunger, made it fiercer, gave it substance and strength. He could easily kill her. Part of him wanted to do it. He traced a finger down her neck, shuddered in time with her as his lightning crackled between them, energy that lit him up and pulled him deeper into his power's seductive embrace.

She trembled in his arms, her head tipping up so the back of it brushed his chest. Such a petite little thing. He wanted to drop the blade and fist his hand in that silken black-and-blue hair of hers, wanted to hold her head back while he introduced her to all the ways his power could pain her.

Or pleasure her.

He barely bit back the groan that rumbled up his throat at that thought, but he didn't manage to steady his thundering heart and quiet the trembling in his limbs.

His golden eyes slid to her face. To her lips.

Kill her.

Or kiss her?

She tensed and he clucked his tongue again, chastising her for thinking about making a move to break free of him. She had brought this upon herself. She should have stayed away, but she hadn't. She had walked back into his life, and she had tried to drug him.

He looked down to his left, to the gun that lay on the cobblestones a short distance away, and the hunger coursing through his blood transformed from a need to kiss her.

To a need to kill her.

Electricity arced from his fingertips and she gasped and jolted backwards, pressing harder against his body. He growled into her ear and traced his hand over her arm, feeling the leather of her short black jacket, heating it with his power as it tried to insulate her from it. The way she trembled and shook in his arms said it wasn't doing a good enough job.

"If you answer me honestly, I won't kill you." A lie, but she didn't need to know that.

He skimmed his hand over her stomach, smiled as he felt the unmistakable outline of more weapons beneath her leather jacket. He lifted his hand and she tensed as he found the tag of the zipper by her throat and started to pull it down.

Another whimper escaped her.

This one sounded distinctly unlike fear.

He had bedded enough females to be able to distinguish the sounds of fear from pleasure, and the noise his little assassin had just made sat firmly in the latter's range.

Valen slowed, easing the zipper down, his eyes falling to the smooth pale mounds of her cleavage as he exposed it to the cooling night air. The dark halter-top she wore cut low, revealing far too much skin. He frowned, wanted to growl at the thought of her parading around like this, on show for every wretched male out there.

Fool.

He shoved that stupid need out of his head and focused back on his task, rougher now as he tore at the zipper and opened her jacket. He took her other gun from the holster beneath her right arm and tossed it across the square. A knife followed it.

She wriggled as he patted her down, his blade still hovering close to her throat. When he reached her thighs, she stilled and the scent of desire on her was unmistakable. It called to his own need, ratcheting it up higher, and he slowly rose behind her, his eyes locking on her lips again.

Kiss her.

Or kill her?

She wanted him.

He snorted at that, the sensible part of his brain still functioning despite the lack of blood flowing to it.

She had probably been getting off with someone in that dark corner of the nightclub.

"Answer me honestly," he husked into her ear and she trembled.

Such a beautiful reaction.

She nodded.

"You don't want to die?" He wasn't sure why he had to ask that, but he needed it out there. He needed to know it.

A shake.

It was careful, restrained. She swallowed, her throat working slowly against his blade.

She didn't want to die.

Kill her.

Or kiss her?

He spun her to face him. Her wide eyes leaped to his and he saw himself reflected in them.

Saw black eyes staring back at him.

Evil. Darkness incarnate. Just like his fucking father.

Only this darkness emerged for one reason and one reason only. It was born of the hunger to hurt and the terrible need to unleash his power.

He would.

But not on her.

She didn't want to die.

He smoothed his left hand over her cheek and stared down into her beguiling eyes, losing himself in their tranquil blue depths. The hunger to kill her battled the need to kiss her, to know how soft those rosy lips were and how she would taste. He lowered his eyes to her mouth, lost himself there too.

As he entertained the thought of kissing her, and imagined the myriad of ways she would respond, the hold his power had over him waned and the urge to kill faded with it. He breathed out slowly, wondering if she was aware just how close she had come to seeing the blessed isles tonight, sent there by his hand and his blade.

"Who sent you to kill me?" he whispered, eyes still fixed on her cherry red lips, and a new ache started.

A need to hear her voice, to complete the picture of his little assassin.

"I got a call," she said, her voice unsteady at first, but then it gained strength. Confidence. Sexy, alluring, confidence. "I don't know anything about them."

There was bite in her words, delivered wonderfully by her thick Italian accent. A local then. She sounded Roman, right down to the way she could curse at him without saying the words.

He shifted his hand against her face and her blue eyes slipped closed for a heartbeat before they snapped open again. The way her pupils dilated almost fooled him into believing she felt something when he touched her.

Something other than disgust.

Fool. Fucking idiot.

She was an assassin. It was all an act. A lie as much as her words had been. She was trying to play him to make sure he didn't kill her, all so she could kill him.

He pressed the knife harder against her throat, so it nicked her golden skin and she gasped, a friendly reminder that he was the one with the blade and the one who decided her fate. No amount of her acting would change that. She could fuck him and he would still be the one in control.

"Give them a message." He leaned down towards her, so she had to tip her head back to keep her eyes on his and was aware of just who had the power in this relationship.

She nodded.

"If they want to kill me, send someone more competent."

He stepped to the roof of the Pantheon and crouched in the darkness, wrapped in shadows as he sheathed his blade and watched her.

She turned in circles in the square below, her eyes darting around.

Who was she?

He flexed the fingers of his left hand. The feel of her was branded on them. Impossible to forget. Soft skin. Warm. Pulse ticking steadily. Trembling.

The sight of her was branded on his black soul.

Calm blue eyes. Crimson lips. Wild black and blue hair. A body made for sin.

And the way her eyes had flashed in that moment before he had teleported. Anger.

Sweet gods, he bet she had a temper to match his own.

He was counting on it.

His words had insulted her and she had looked ready to fight him, despite the fact he had a blade and she had been unarmed.

His gaze tracked her as she gathered her things, including the spent darts, clearing away all the evidence. A strange hot sensation went through him and his head snapped around to his right, eyes leaping south over his shoulder towards the gate to the Underworld. Bastards could wait.

He looked back down into the square and frowned, the heat within him giving way to cold.

His little assassin was leaving.

He rose onto his feet and lifted his left hand to his face, breathed in the lingering scent of her on his skin, and smiled as he watched her go. The second she was out of sight, he teleported to the Rome gate, heading in the opposite direction to her.

He didn't need to worry.

And he didn't need the bastard Moirai to tell him he would see her again.

He had made sure of that himself.

He had set fire to her temper, had issued her a challenge, and she would take him up on it.

She would come at him with guns blazing.

Valen grinned as he appeared at the gate.

Bring it on.

CHAPTER 2

Stronzo.

Eva idly rubbed her right thumb across the front of her throat as she sat at the grotty bar of Heavenly Body, head pounding from the music and eyes constantly scanning everyone who moved around the dimly-lit basement nightclub. She hadn't seen *him* in two nights.

Her body tingled with the memory of the way his hand had roamed over her, skilfully plucking her weapons from her, somehow making it seem sensual and seductive, when she should have found it alarming. Disturbing. Threatening.

She muttered another ripe curse, aimed it at him with all the venom she could manage.

Two nights, and she couldn't get him out of her mind.

Sure, it was her job to think about him, to get every scrap of information she could on him. Or at least, that *had* been her job. What was meant to have been a simple intel gathering mission had somehow turned into something else a week ago when her client had called her again out of the blue and told her she wasn't done.

He wanted her to drug him.

That unsettled her now as much as it had then, playing on her mind as badly as the man who was her target.

Why had her client changed the mission parameters?

It didn't bother her on a professional level. It wasn't the first time she had been hired to kill someone after all. Years as a hired weapon had taught her to keep herself emotionally detached from her marks and what she was doing.

So why didn't she feel emotionally detached this time?

She had done everything by the book, hadn't strayed from the rules she set out for herself, yet something about her mark had stirred dangerous feelings in her.

Her eyes slipped shut as an image of him that night played out in her mind, a broken replay of him gracefully dodging every bolt from her dart gun, and suddenly appearing before her, towering over her with a slight tilt to his lips that had spoken of amusement rather than fear or fury.

He had been toying with her.

It grated on her last nerve, fraying it more than it already had been, rousing the same potent burst of anger she had felt when he had dared to insult her by insinuating she wasn't a good enough assassin to take his arse down.

"Stronzo," she muttered as she looked down at her shot glass, watching the colourful lights that rotated above her dancing across it and her hands, and reflecting off the wet rings left behind on the black counter by the other patrons of the club when they took their drinks with them to their corners of the busy room.

She lifted it to her lips and downed the vodka in one.

The bartender smiled at her as he stopped in front of her, snagging her attention. His dark eyes twinkled with his amusement, and an image of the man flashed over him, a vision of the way *he* had smiled at her.

Who the fuck was he?

She had done her best to gather information on him, had asked around at every place she had seen him over the two months she had been tailing him in Rome, and had even continued trying to find out more about him in the three her client had pulled her off the job. Nothing she had heard had even hinted at him being skilled in fighting, and the way he had moved, and the blade he had stuck against her damned throat, pointed towards him being in her line of work.

Another assassin.

Was it possible?

Did her client know what he was?

Eva saw another flash of the way he had moved like lightning across the square, sat by the fountain admiring the Pantheon one second and right in front of her the next. Her heart pounded as it had that night, galloping in her chest, flooding her veins with adrenaline as her fight or flight instincts kicked in.

She should have known he was dangerous.

He had the look of a killer, so why not the skills to go with it?

She grunted in frustration and clawed her fingers through her short hair, pulling the blue-streaked black strands away from her face.

The bartender slid her another shot and said something she ignored. He had been hitting on her the past few nights, a new addition to the usual crew who served at Heavenly Body, and while he was handsome, and ripped judging by the way his standard-issue white shirt hugged his powerful body, she just wasn't interested in him.

Her mark flashed across her mind again, standing in the open square with his hands jammed into the pockets of his black combat trousers in a way that pulled them tight across muscular thighs and drew his coat back to reveal a black t-shirt that sat like a second skin over a torso packed with honed muscles.

She shivered as she remembered how that body had felt pressed against her back as his blade sat poised against her throat.

Hard.

Hot.

Eva screwed her eyes shut and downed the shot of vodka, hoping to kill whatever part of her brain had become fixated on him since that night.

He was dangerous.

The darkness that had been in his eyes when she had faced him. She had never seen anything like it. It was as if his golden eyes had turned black as night. It must have been a trick of the light, because they had been gold again when he had lifted his face enough for the streetlamps to shine down on it.

Another hot shiver wracked her, heating her blood with a memory of his hand against her face this time.

That heat turned to the flames of anger as his lips moved, spewing an insult that stoked the fire inside her and had her itching for a rematch even when she wasn't sure she would win.

But she was damned if she was going to allow a man to degrade her like that, making out she was useless, incompetent.

Not worth their time.

Eva slammed the empty glass down on the tacky bar top with enough force to make the man next to her jump out of his skin. She ignored his comments as she pushed away from the bar and slid off her stool, and clawed her way through the heavy Saturday night crowd, heading for the exit.

He wasn't coming.

Now he was wasting her time.

She pushed her way up the steps and shoved the metal door at the top open. Cool swept over her and she breathed deep of the crisp night air, using it to soothe her anger and wash it away.

Just as she had found some calm again, the sound of her phone ringing broke the silence. It buzzed in the back pocket of her black jeans, sending vibrations down her right leg. She snatched it and frowned at the screen.

Damn.

Her client.

Not what she needed tonight.

Eva debated not answering it, even when she knew it wasn't an option or a path she wanted to take. She'd only had a few meetings with the man, but he had given her the impression right from the moment she had met him that he wasn't the sort of person you disappointed and lived to tell the tale.

That was the only reason she had agreed to drug the mark when her client had called and acted as if he had never told her she had done her job and the contract was fulfilled.

She swiped her thumb across the screen to answer it and lifted it to her ear.

"We need to meet." Her client's deep voice rang through the speaker before she could even utter a greeting, his tone brooking no argument. A demand, not a request. She was sick of hearing that tone coming from a man. He was the same as the rest of them, thinking that because he had hired her, he owned her arse. "Come to the villa immediately."

He hung up.

Eva lowered the phone and scowled at it. Stronzo. The king of them.

But it seemed he was also the king of her until he decided to release her from his rule, and that meant she was going to have to drive all the way out into the countryside to his villa just to see what the fuck he wanted at such an ungodly hour of the morning.

She huffed and pocketed her phone, placing it in the inside one of her leather jacket this time. She zipped the black leather up as she walked, following the maze of narrow streets back to where she had parked her scooter, and tried not to think about how her body had lit up when her mark had dared to frisk her for weapons.

When she reached the small black and silver Vespa, she looked along the wider street in both directions, scanning the parked cars and the few people moving around it. She wasn't sure what she was looking for, but the hairs on the back of her neck had suddenly stood on end and for a ridiculous moment she had been sure someone was watching her. She brushed it off and unlocked the chain on her scooter, and dumped it into the storage beneath the seat. She pulled her helmet out of the same box and tugged it on, fastening it beneath her chin, and slung her leg over the bike.

A shiver raced through her and she paused with her hand on the ignition key. Looked around again.

No one was on the street now. No one was watching her. She inhaled and blew out her breath. She was just being jumpy. The combination of her client's call and waiting for her mark to leap out of the shadows and kill her had made her jittery.

She started the engine, switched on the lights, kicked up the stand and pulled out onto the empty road. The weird sensation faded as she sped through the streets of her beloved city, leaving the centre behind and heading for the outskirts. Bright streetlamps soon gave way to total darkness as she hit open roads. The warmth of the city gave way to cold at the same time, and she huddled down into her jacket as the chilly night air sapped the heat from her bare hands and face.

Eva kept her focus locked on the road ahead of her, following it as it snaked through dark countryside, her Vespa struggling over the hills that surrounded Rome. She should have brought one of her cars out with her tonight, but it was easier navigating the small streets of Rome on a scooter.

She looked across at the city as she reached the top of one of the hills and rounded a bend. It sparkled below her, a warm sea of stars in the night. She always had loved the view of the city from up in the hills. It looked so peaceful, even when she knew it was far from quiet.

Even in the dead of winter the tourists flocked to Rome.

Lured by its magic, its beauty, and its history.

The Eternal City.

The road twisted again and she reluctantly turned her back on the city and lost track of time as she drove, passing small villages and long cypress-tree-lined driveways that led down to farms and villas.

She slowed as she neared the tree-lined avenue that would take her up another steep hill to her client's enormous three-storey mansion and caught a glimpse of the illuminated palatial yellow-ochre building in the distance as she turned into the driveway.

She hated this place.

Even at night it reminded her of her old home, the one she had lived in before turning her back on her family.

Eva pushed those memories to the back of her mind as she approached the villa. The two men dressed in black patrol fatigues at the gate nodded as she slowed her scooter and passed them. Whoever her client was, he took his security very seriously. Every time she had come to the villa, she had seen at least two men on the gate and another four in the grounds, and further men inside.

All armed.

She parked her Vespa beside a black Lamborghini and kicked the stand down as she switched off the engine. As she dismounted, she shoved her keys into her jacket pocket, keeping them close at hand in case she needed them. She was armed beneath her leather, but a quick escape was preferable to a shoot out if things went badly. There was no way she could out gun so many men, not even if she could get her hands on a few of their weapons.

The golden gravel of the driveway crunched under her knee-high black boots as she walked, removing her helmet as she approached the grand villa from its side, her eyes leaping over the rows of windows, skipping the ones that glowed with golden light and focusing on the unlit ones. She caught movement in some of them.

She was being watched from all angles.

Her client was always this cautious, even with her. It seemed he had serious trust issues.

Or he was waiting for someone to launch an assault on him.

She could easily imagine there were people out there who wanted him dead, rivals who wouldn't think twice about attacking him at his stronghold.

The gravel gave way to sandstone slabs as she entered the enormous patio that spanned the long façade of the grand house, edged with a delicate stone balustrade to her right, where the hill dropped off and the view was stunning even in the darkness.

Rome shimmered in the distance, a golden glow that illuminated the night sky and challenged the stars.

She dragged her eyes away from it, focusing back on her destination. The elegant columned porch jutted out from the building, perfectly manicured topiary framing it and making it look like any other Italian mansion when it wasn't anything like the innocent family homes or farmhouses in the area.

A killer lived here.

She was as certain of it as she was her name was Eva.

Killers recognised their own kind.

She stepped past the man on the door and into the bright foyer of the villa. Light danced around the room from the crystal and gold chandelier, reflecting off the white marble floor and pale yellow walls.

Her heartbeat ticked up and she drew in a slow, secret breath to steady it as another man watched her closely, unwilling to let him see her nerves.

What the hell had she gotten herself into? She should have been suspicious of her client from the start, would have been if she had first met him here rather than in a public location in the city. With so many men in his employment, he hardly needed her to spy on his target, and he definitely didn't need her to drug him or kill him, or whatever the fuck she was meant to be doing to him now.

Something was wrong with this whole situation. Something that set her on edge and had her wishing she had unzipped her coat and unclipped her gun.

The security guard narrowed his eyes on her and she shot him a smile as she casually swept her fingers through her blue-streaked hair, neatening her appearance, hoping the man would think fixing it so she looked good for his boss was the only reason she hadn't moved from the foyer.

When the man raked his dark eyes over her, a slight smile tilting his broad lips, she flashed him a wink and sauntered towards the two staircases that curved elegantly upwards to the first floor, a little swing in her hips to keep him off guard. She looked back at him as she walked between the two staircases and took a right, heading beneath them. The guy grinned at her, practically slobbering as he stared at her arse in her tight jeans.

He disappeared from view as she hit the corridor and her walk lost all swagger and turned all business, her expression following suit. Her blue eyes fixed on the wooden door at the end of the long pale green corridor. She would smile for the bastard on the other side, would play her role as his obedient assassin to perfection to appease him, but the whole time she would be on alert, because she had quickly learned he wasn't the sort of man you let your guard down around.

She had swum with sharks, had worked for the worst of Italy's underground bosses, but she had never met a shark like her client.

He ate the other sharks for breakfast.

The door opened a second before she reached it, swinging back to reveal an enormous black-walled office with a pale grey marble floor, and the biggest ebony desk she had ever seen in the centre of it.

Leaning against that desk, dressed in a crisp black suit with a white shirt opened at the collar to reveal a hint of defined muscles, was what she could only describe as a man most women would call sex-on-legs. Blush pink full lips curved a little as his stunning emerald green eyes met hers and he pushed onto his feet, coming to stand at least six-feet-six in front of her. The tailored suit hugged his trim figure to perfection, accentuating every curve, and sure, she wasn't immune to his charms.

No matter how fiercely she tried to be.

She prepared herself every time she was about to face him, shut down every feeling and locked them in place, putting herself firmly in control of her emotions.

Yet every time he turned that smile on her, those feelings broke her hold and defied her.

"My angel," he said, the smile curving his sinful lips reflected in the deep baritone of his voice. A voice made for melting panties.

She hated it when he called her that. In the underground world, she was *the* angel. She was not his.

She cleared her throat, wishing she could clear her head just as easily, and nodded. "Signor Benares."

His smile grew wider and he shoved long tanned fingers through his wild sun-kissed blond locks, something he always did whenever she called him that, as if her tacking on an honorific set him on edge for some reason.

"Just Benares, my dear." Another panty-melting factor about her client. The guy was British, and said everything with a regal edge that she was sure many women would find seductive.

Eva was too busy pondering his words to be affected by the manner of their delivery and his accent. She had tried at least twice to get him to expand on why he was just Benares.

Like, he had no other name?

Her Italian stock had shackled her with around a million names, so the thought of someone only having one was completely foreign, and ridiculous, to her. He merely smiled if she asked, so she had given up.

She yawned, hoping to make a point about the hour without saying it, and he leaned back against the ebony desk, canting his head as he raked those jewel green eyes over her.

"Tired, my dear?"

She wished he wouldn't call her that, as if she belonged to him. My angel. My dear. It made her skin crawl.

Eva rolled her right shoulder, gunning for casual. "It's been a late few nights."

"Since you failed?" A female voice echoed around the room, a sharp snap to the British accent that was at odds with her client's more melodic one.

Eva frowned at the blonde woman as she sashayed around the desk to her client's right, a short black dress hugging her incredible figure and tall stiletto heels making her already long, lean legs look even longer. A sleek fall of golden hair cascaded around her shoulders and down to the small of her back, and eyes the colour of summer skies locked on Benares.

Beautiful didn't seem a good enough word to describe her. Eva was sure that if this woman walked around in Rome, every red-blooded male would be following her, calling after her and wanting her. No man on the planet could be in the same room as her and not be affected.

Eva glanced at Benares.

His eyes hadn't left her.

The blonde's blue eyes didn't stray from him. They held an expectant edge, one Eva could easily read. She wanted Benares to look at her. When she halted close to him, and his eyes still remained on Eva, her beautiful face darkened, her rosy pouty lips compressing into a vicious line and fine eyebrows dipping low.

Eva had never met the woman before, but the way she looked at Benares, and then turned that black scowl on Eva, left her with the impression that she was something to her client and she didn't appreciate the way he was looking at Eva.

A lover?

"Jin," Benares whispered softly, tenderness in it, and the woman looked back at him. He still didn't take his eyes off Eva, not even when he shot his right hand out and grasped the woman called Jin by her throat. She gasped and bit her lip, as if his touch had been one of pleasure not violence, and looked as if she might melt into a puddle at his feet as he hauled her towards him, causing her to bump against the desk. He turned his face towards her, bringing his lips close to her cheek, but his eyes still remained locked on Eva's. "Temper."

He shoved Jin backwards, away from him, and she stumbled a few steps before catching herself and glaring at him.

Jin turned that glare on her. "You failed."

Eva held her ground and glanced at Benares, wanting to see his opinion on what had happened, hoping that she hadn't made a grave mistake by driving to a very private estate in the middle of a huge tract of land in the dead of night.

It wasn't going to end here. Now. She told herself that on repeat even as she took stock of all the possible exits in the room and recounted every escape route she had planned without taking her eyes off Benares.

The blonde's face darkened again and she took a hard step forwards, towards Eva. It caught Eva's attention but not his. His green eyes remained firmly rooted on her, perusing her from head to toe at a leisurely pace as Jin took control of the meeting.

Eva wasn't sure what the hell their relationship was, but she wished he would stop looking at her as if she was someone he wanted to bed, because the more he stared at her with interest in his eyes, the darker Jin's mood turned and the more the woman looked as if she was considering killing her.

It seemed Benares wasn't the only shark she was swimming with this time.

Jin was in on the plan, client number two, and Eva had the sinking feeling that disappointing her would result in the same bloody end as disappointing Benares.

Death.

She knew that the game she played was dangerous, had always been aware of it and the fact that every job might be her last, but it was all she knew. It was her life and she didn't know how to live it any other way now. She had stepped out of the light and into the darkness, and there was no going back.

There was only going forwards.

"Failure was not an option," Jin snarled, flashing straight white teeth, and her blue eyes seemed to brighten with her fury.

"Perhaps if you had given me all the information you already had on him, I wouldn't have failed," Eva shot back, maintaining the behaviour Benares would expect from her from all their meetings and telephone calls.

She wasn't meek. She was dangerous, took no prisoners, and certainly didn't let anyone push her around. She was an assassin, and she was damned good at what she did. Although, she wished she had chosen to add a little meekness when she had decided what sort of personality she was going to have with him. A dash of meek might have gone some way towards placating Jin at the very least.

Although the heated look in Benares's eyes said that he liked the headstrong, sassy and hot-blooded personality she had chosen that was much closer to her own real one.

Eva squared her shoulders, planted her hands on her hips, and glared at both Jin and Benares. "Maybe if you had mentioned that he had skills... the same skillset that I have... I would have been prepared."

Benares casually rested his hands on the desk on either side of his hips. "True."

So he had known that her mark was a killer. An assassin. Stronzo. She wanted to throttle him for that, even when she knew it would be suicide.

"We will give you a second chance," he said and the look Jin shot him conveyed everything Eva needed to know.

That hadn't been the plan.

Benares had called her all the way out to the secluded villa in order to kill her. What had changed his mind?

He raked his eyes over her again, a slow slide from head to toe and back again, and smiled when his emerald green gaze met hers. Jin continued to glare at him, looking for all the world as if she was also considering throttling him.

"You fought him," Benares said, his smile holding. "You survived. I am sure you could do it again."

He raised his right hand and Jin obediently strutted to the other side of the desk and squatted there. She opened a cupboard, closed it and rose back onto her feet. Eva frowned at the seven-inch-long black rectangular case she held in her hands.

A weapon?

Eva tensed, preparing herself.

Benares sighed. "Always so distrustful. That is the problem with your breed."

He held his hand out to Jin but rather than taking the case from her, he motioned for her to give it to Eva.

The woman approached her, her pretty face still locked in a scowl, one that screamed of anger at Benares, and jealousy. Again, his eyes remained rooted on Eva even when Jin was in his line of sight.

What game was he playing? Was he trying to get his lover to kill her?

She wanted to tell him to quit staring at her, but held her tongue instead and focused on the ominous black case on Jin's upturned palm as the woman held it out to her.

"Since you can fight him, and he does not seem interested in killing you, then you get a second chance." Benares nodded towards Jin.

She bowed her head and opened the case.

Eva's eyes went wide.

A glass syringe sat nestled in black velvet within the box.

Her gaze shot to Benares. His smile widened the smallest amount but it didn't reach his eyes. They were cold now, impassive and diamond hard.

"Do not fail again, my angel."

A hypodermic needle? Was he serious? She hadn't exactly fought her mark and survived, and the bastard knew that. He knew that the mark had shut her down before she had even had a chance to start fighting.

He knew everything.

Which meant he had people watching her every move.

Why?

Jin snapped the case shut, startling her out of her thoughts, and Eva's gaze leaped to her.

"It is rare. Do not squander it this time." Jin shoved the case into her hands.

Eva wanted to ask what was rare—the drug she was meant to administer to her mark or a second chance from Benares?

She kept her mouth shut and clutched the case instead, heart pounding as she considered what they were asking her to do.

They wanted her to drug her mark, and this time they wanted her to do it up close and personal. No dart gun. Just a syringe.

Eva eyed the case.

"What is it anyway?" she said with as much confidence as she could muster, holding on to her mask so Benares didn't see through it to the fact that she was scared, afraid of him and thinking twice about going through with his request.

Running the hell away from Rome was starting to look good. She could disappear, lay low and keep her head down somewhere remote. Maybe South America.

The coldness in his emerald eyes warned not to try it, that he could already see through her carefully constructed façade and knew what she was thinking, and that it wouldn't end well for her. How powerful was he? Every honed instinct she possessed said that he was too powerful, that he could easily track her down and kill her if she dared to disobey or tried to flee.

"A means to an end," Benares said.

An end.

Poison.

It wasn't her style, but she was hardly in a position to say that. What the client wanted, the client got.

Although she did find it strange that she had been hired to tail her mark and learn about him, and now her client was asking her to kill him. Benares had only ever asked her to gather information, had made it sound important that she did so. Why would he want to learn about someone he meant to kill?

He had made it sound as if he had been looking for a weakness he could exploit.

Now he was asking her to poison him.

Had something changed?

Eva shut down that line of thought before it got her into trouble. She had the feeling that the less she knew, the better off she would be on this particular job. Clients were allowed to have a change of heart.

She tried to shrug it off as she bowed her head and retraced her steps through the villa, but the heavy feeling in the pit of her stomach refused to go away.

She had never been one for guilt before, so why did the thought of what she was going to do with the contents of the case she clutched tightly in her fingers unsettle her?

She caught a flash of her mark holding her, powerful arms caging her, his knife pressed against her throat together with his knuckles.

The press of those knuckles had felt more dangerous than the blade, sending an electric thrill through her, and the way his incredible eyes had held hers, merciless and cold, but at the same time filled with a wealth of emotions just beneath their golden surface, had ignited a spark that had set her on fire.

Eva put it down to the fact he had bested her, pushing aside all the other reasons she could think of for the way she had felt in his arms, desperate to remain professional and maintain her distance.

It had been a long time since someone had beaten her, and that was all this feeling was.

He had brought a spark of excitement back into her dull little life and had reignited something inside her.

A fire she thought had died long ago.

CHAPTER 3

Valen had somehow managed to stay away from his little assassin for three nights, when every shred of his being had wanted to head into Rome and track her down to finish what they had started. He wanted her to come at him guns blazing, with that fire flashing in her stunning eyes. He wanted to tangle with her.

Gods, he wanted that.

He shoved his fingers through his blond hair, raking it back from his face, and gripped it hard, taking pleasure from the pain as it tugged at his scalp. His hand shook, muscles tensed and quivering, trembling with need that was becoming impossible to contain. He was hungry for another shot at her, ached with a need to hear her voice and smell her again, to feel her body plastered against his.

His beautiful little assassin.

He still wasn't sure whether he wanted to kiss her or kill her.

The darker part of himself, the side ruled by his power and thirst for violence, wanted the latter. The lighter part? He wasn't sure that existed anymore, but something inside him wanted the little female in a way he had never wanted another.

Centuries on this godsforsaken plane and not once had he desired a female the way he desired her.

He vaguely recalled bedding some mortals at the start of his sentence, but his interest had waned as his power had grown, becoming more seductive and alluring, and pleasurable, than they could ever be.

His lightning had become everything he needed, both his pleasure and his pain, his joy and his despair.

He wanted for nothing else.

Except her.

Now he couldn't get his mind off her and it was starting to become a pain.

His brothers had noticed it during their last meeting the night after he had let her go. The night after she had returned to him. He had managed to blow them off, spouting bullshit about the Rome gate keeping him busy and all the pain-in-his-arse Hellspawn that kept calling him out to it to open it for them so they could travel between this realm and the Underworld.

He had even tossed in a few daemon hunting reports for good measure, ensuring his brothers had no reason to suspect anything. His brothers were pain-in-his-arse gods, always sticking their noses in where they didn't belong, and they pissed him off more than the Hellspawn who dragged him to the gate at all hours of the night as if he was their personal bitch.

Valen stared at the shimmering gate to the Underworld that formed a pattern of concentric rings filled with glyphs and rested flat like a disc above the ground in the middle of one of Rome's ancient sites in the Palatine Hill.

Keras, his oldest brother, was the worst. Self-righteous prick. The fucker had been looking down at him for the past five and a half centuries, always watching him as if waiting for him to fuck up again.

He spat on the sand beside him.

Bastard.

He idly stroked the obsidian blade sheathed against his right hip beneath his long black jacket, thoughts turning dark as he imagined helping Keras out the night he had decided to cut his own throat in order to see if Ares's new plaything, Megan, really had the ability to heal.

Valen would have gladly cut it for him. A little deeper than Keras had chosen. Of course, the other five pains-in-his-arse would have come down on him and even dear old Dad probably would have got in on the action too. Fuck, maybe even Nemesis herself, although the punishment she normally dished out to him was more pleasurable than having to spend time with his brothers.

Eight and a half centuries he had been putting up with his brothers' bullshit.

The last couple of centuries had been the worst. At least when they had been in the Underworld he had been able to keep to himself, to go away whenever they bothered him too much and roam the various realms, finding some quiet.

Now, he couldn't escape them. They stepped into his apartment all the fucking time, acting as if he needed a bloody babysitter.

He snorted at that, but there wasn't even a hint of amusement in it this time. Not a drop.

Bastards.

The ground beneath his feet warmed and he looked down, frowning at the delicate green stem that pushed from the sand between his black leather boots, growing before his eyes. It formed a bud that opened to reveal a small golden flower.

The light faded as the colourful rings of the gate shrank into a yellow dot and winked out of existence.

Valen stared at the flower. A message.

He huffed and scuffed his boot over it, crushing the delicate bloom into the dirt, and turned his back on the gate.

The ground shook in response.

His father's doing.

He closed his eyes and gritted his teeth, cursed himself for letting his temper get the better of him when his mother had only been trying to soothe him with the flower, a symbol of her love. He issued a silent apology to her and walked away, heading into the darkness and not bothering to send one to his father.

He was ninety-five percent certain that Hades despised him as much as his brothers did.

It was entirely possible that only his mother loved him.

Only his mother *could* love him.

It was safer that way anyway.

He didn't believe what she had said to him three months ago when she had broken the rules to leave the Underworld and visit him when Ares had gone moon-eyed over the mortal female, Megan.

Persephone was a romantic. A fool.

No one could love him.

The curse made sure of that.

A curse he deserved.

His whole fucking life was cursed and had been since that night five and a half centuries ago, but even if he could change the events of that night, he wouldn't do it. He would rather live with a curse on his head than live without taking action against those responsible for what had happened.

He reached the perimeter fence of the site and stepped, teleporting to the other side, and kept walking, heading along the road towards the centre of Rome and leaving a trail of black smoke in his wake. He jammed his hands in his pockets as he walked, his gaze on the pavement, his head whirling with thoughts he did his best to ignore and shut out.

Memories he wanted to forget.

The familiar swirling sensation started in the pit of his stomach, a warning that daemons were nearby. The coppery stench of them hit him a moment later and he stretched his senses out far and wide, tuning into his surroundings and scouring the ruins for the filthy wretches.

His internal radar pinpointed them directly ahead, near to the island that sat in a bend of the Tiber river.

It seemed his night was looking up.

Most days he cursed his father for sending him to the mortal world with his brothers, but never when he was fighting daemons. He lived for times like this, when he could drench his hands in their black blood and send them screaming into the afterlife. The rules of his mission clearly stated he was allowed to use any force necessary to ensure daemons didn't breach the gate between the Underworld and Earth.

Lightning crackled between his fingertips as he withdrew his hands from his jeans pockets.

Valen used all the force of the Underworld at his disposal to eradicate them, never holding back even a fraction of his strength. He showed them no mercy, because they had shown the same to his family. They had attacked his parents once, and then again when Keras had been born, shaking the Underworld with their impudence and forcing his father to banish them from his realm. Now, because of a future the Moirai had seen, an attack on the eight gates that would merge the Underworld and Earth to create a new realm, Hades had banished him and his brothers here to fight the daemons and protect their world.

Daemons had fucked with his family, in too many ways to count.

What they had given, they would receive.

Eternally.

He would hunt and destroy them until either they were extinct or he drew his last breath.

He kicked off with his left foot and stepped, disappearing from the street near the Palatine Hill and reappearing in a small square on the island in the centre of the river.

The three daemons immediately froze.

They looked as human as he did, but their stench gave them away, their corrupted souls bleeding through the skin they wore.

Valen slowly drew his coat back and rested his hands on the hilts of the twin black blades strapped to his hips.

The female of the group tensed. The two males, both slightly older than her and appearing in their late twenties to mortal eyes, which placed them at around seventy to one hundred years old, moved to shield her.

How noble.

He eased the blades from their sheaths and lowered them to his side as he focused on his body.

On his power.

The brunet male's eyes leaped down to the long black curved knives as that power flowed out of Valen on command and arced along the metal, causing flashes of light in the dimly lit square. His paler-haired companion eased back a step, his left hand fumbling behind him and finding the female. He caught her arm and pushed her back with him.

Distancing themselves?

Did they think he was going to let them go?

Valen clucked his tongue, causing the titanium stud in the centre of its tip to crack against his teeth.

"Run," the blond hissed and shoved her hard, and she twisted as she stumbled.

She found her footing and broke into a dead sprint.

Valen sighed. He did hate it when they tried to run. It took the fun out of it.

He idly tossed his right blade into the air above him, slipped his hand into his coat and pulled free two small throwing knives from their holster against his ribs. Lightning danced across their surface as he poured his power into them in the split second it took for him to draw and set them loose with a casual flick of his wrist.

They hit the female in her right shoulder and lower back and she shrieked as she went down hard, her body jerking as his electricity rushed into it.

The brunet looked over his shoulder at her and then back at Valen, and hissed through his teeth as Valen caught his second black blade before it hit the floor.

Actually fucking hissed.

Shapeshifters.

Had to be.

It had been a while since he had fought one. Several of the shapeshifter species had elevated themselves to the rank of Hellspawn rather than daemon by providing thorough charts of their bloodlines and aligning themselves with other Hellspawn breeds united under the banner of his father and pledged to protect the Underworld from daemons.

What species of shifter were these three? Their stench said they were still daemon, still corrupted and twisted by darkness.

He flicked a glance at the writhing female and frowned as she alternated between mortal and demonic in appearance, sprouting horns and wings, and even a lizard-like tail as his lightning continued to ravage her body. Scaly lips peeled off rows of serrated sharp teeth and her yellow eyes watered as she grunted and whimpered.

Not a species that his father had any love for, which meant he had the green light to tear them apart.

He raised his left blade and took aim, targeting the female while she was down and vulnerable.

A familiar sensation went through him and he froze.

Heat warmed the space behind his breastbone, chasing out the cold calm he was used to and not only during a fight when most warriors found themselves detached from everything, a creature of logic not emotion.

His little assassin.

She would choose now to return to him.

He snarled and hurled the knife at the female, but took no pleasure from her scream as his blade sank deep into her side.

Damn meddling mortal.

Fighting was only fun when he could use his power and while he normally didn't give a shit what sort of chewing out his eldest brother would issue if he broke the rules, or the potential punishment handed down from on high, he found himself playing by the book.

Acting mortal.

Because of her.

He eyed his remaining two opponents. If he snuck a little lightning into his blades while fighting them, would they go bat shit crazy like the female had?

Valen wasn't sure whether daemons revealing their existence to a mortal because of something he did was grounds for punishment.

Ares had fought Trickster in front of Megan, revealing the existence of gods and daemons to her in the process, and hadn't been punished.

But then Megan was a Carrier, a mortal with Hellspawn blood in her family tree and a power of her own.

Damn it.

"Fucking little assassin," he grumbled and the two daemons frowned at him.

He shot them a glare, letting them know his words hadn't been aimed at them and they shouldn't have been listening. Fuck, he wasn't even sure if they had been aimed at her, or his own pathetic desire not to stir the pot this time and cause trouble.

A desire to fit in.

What was the point in that?

It wouldn't change a damned thing and he knew it. Every fucker on the planet would still despise him because they had already made up their mind about him and there was no way to alter it for the better. Nothing he did could redeem him now.

The ground warmed beneath his feet.

Valen scuffed it with his boot.

Not now, Mother.

One of the idiot daemons rushed him. They never did learn. Every daemon in this world thought they could be the one to claim the glory of bringing him to his knees. Morons.

He was a god.

He grinned and power raced through him, lightning that warmed his bones and lit his blood. He kicked off, propelling himself right at the hapless dimwit. There was a flash of panic in his eyes, a momentary twitch as he tensed, as if regretting his actions already, and then he broke right.

Valen kept running, aiming for the brunet now that his companion had cleared the way. The daemon looked ready to piss in his pants, but he pulled his shit together just as Valen reached him and blocked his right blade with his forearm.

Instead of the expected scream and stench of black daemon blood, his blade bounced right off the bastard.

Scales emerged from beneath the male's black jumper and rippled over his hand.

That was cheating.

Valen spun on his heel and brought his left blade around in a deadly arc, aiming it for his throat this time. The black knife struck. Bounced off scales again. Fucker.

The male slammed a fist into his kidney and he grunted as he staggered forwards from the blow. Fine. Maybe these two weren't as weak as most of the daemons he fought. He wasn't going to complain. It had been too long since he had been able to go all out and have a good brawl.

The feel of his little assassin's eyes on him reminded him that he couldn't go all out now either.

He grumbled another string of curses aimed at her and focused on his two opponents. The female was still down, leaking blood at a rate that said she wasn't going to be getting up anytime soon. If at all.

The pale-haired bastard landed a blow in his stomach and Valen knocked him back with a right uppercut of his own. He went to follow with a blow with his left blade to see whether this one could do the impenetrable scales trick too, and the brunet grabbed him from behind, locking his arms under Valen's and restraining him.

His friend grinned.

Victoriously?

Was he serious?

This was little more than a brief inconvenience, a pause in the build up to what was going to be a very bloody, very beautiful fight that would end in only one way.

With him grinning victoriously at their corpses.

Pale-haired idiot approached, cracking knuckles like some cliché out of an action movie.

Valen reared back as he came within striking distance, forcing his captor to bend backwards with him and allowing him to bring his legs up. He slammed his right boot hard into the pale-haired one's skull, heard bone crack beneath the blow, and followed it with a left kick to the chest. He staggered backwards, lost his footing and landed on his arse in the small square.

Brunet struggled. A useless endeavour.

Valen's boots hit the deck again and he kicked upwards once more, propelling himself over the head of his captor. He landed behind the bastard and the wretched worm tried to run, so Valen stuck a knife in the back of his left thigh.

He screamed, somewhere between a hiss and a shriek, and limped away while fumbling with the blade.

Valen wanted it back. It was one of his favourites.

He kicked off again, shouldered the guy in his spine and sent him sprawling across the flagstones, landing on top of him and tearing a pained grunt from his lips. He shoved a knee hard into the daemon's back, reached over and yanked the blade free of his thigh. Another hiss-scream tore through the night and he swore little assassin gasped from her perch in the shadows.

A boot came out of nowhere, slamming into the side of Valen's head and knocking him sideways, off the brunet. He growled, his head throbbing and darkness pouring through his veins in response. It coaxed his power, drew it to the surface, and by the gods he wanted to unleash it all on the fuckers.

He wanted to make it rain lightning until only ashes remained.

He raised his hand to do just that and both daemons flinched, tensing in preparation for the strike.

Damn it.

Unleashing enough voltage to blow his enemies to pieces would also put the assassin in danger, and he was damned if he was going to ruin his perfect track record of not harming mortals.

He called his black blade to his hand, using another of his powers to rip it out of the dead female daemon. It shot into his palm and he closed his fingers around the bound leather hilt, slowly rose onto his feet and faced the two males.

Both of whom looked somewhere between stunned and relieved.

Their lucky day. He was going to have to kill them the old-fashioned way.

He reached beneath his coat and palmed another two of his throwing knives. He couldn't risk imbuing them with electricity, not with the assassin watching, but they could still do their work. They could still slow down the daemons for him. All it would take was a well-aimed blow and the Moirai being nice to him for once by not letting scales get in the way.

Brunet staggered onto his feet. Black blood pumped down his leg, soaking into his jeans and making them shine under the street lights.

It stank.

Valen curled his lip at the male.

Darkness coursed through him in response, growing stronger, rising to consume him as it often did. His father's gift to all his sons, born of his blood in their veins. A dangerous, often undeniable, hunger to destroy.

Valen loved it.

He knew the second that darkness manifested, shifting like a malevolent shadow across his features and turning his eyes black, because the daemons glanced at each other and looked ready to bolt.

No. Not on his watch.

His teeth ached, canines sharpening, and the darkness gripped him tighter, squeezing the light out of him. Just the way he loved it.

Brunet turned to make a break for it.

Two throwing knives put an end to that, the first slamming to the hilt in his right calf and the second burying deep into the back of his skull, dropping him like a sack of bricks onto the ground.

Blondie turned wide fearful eyes on his dead companion and then slowly looked back at him.

"You're next." Valen grinned.

Movement on his senses was the only warning he had before the soft fragrance of roses and sin hit him and knocked him off kilter.

Threw him right off his game in fact.

He pivoted on his heel and blocked the knife little assassin had aimed at him, ripping a startled gasp from her and knocking her backwards. She recovered quickly, coming at him again, her blue eyes flashing with determination. Another thrust of the blade. This one he blocked a little harder with his forearm, enough that it was probably going to leave a bruise.

He frowned as she regrouped and came at him again, and he realised it wasn't a knife she held.

It was a syringe.

What the actual fuck?

Why the hell did she keep trying to drug him?

He clucked his tongue and stepped, closing the short distance between them in a heartbeat, his face twisting into a sneer as he reached her.

Wide blue eyes hit his and she blinked hard, the only outward sign that he had startled her again.

He towered over her. Such a little thing, but so fierce and fiery. Even faced with him as he was now, consumed by the darkness, hungry for blood and violence, she stood her ground and was recovering her wits. He could see it in her eyes as they slowly narrowed, could almost hear her rapidly considering every move she could make and every consequence of that action.

"That for me?" he murmured and jerked his chin towards the glass syringe she gripped in her right hand.

He half expected her to shake her head, had met enough mortals and fought enough daemons to know how most of them would respond given the situation.

She nodded.

Her fingers twitched.

In a lightning fast strike, he caught her hand and squeezed it.

She cried out as the glass smashed under the pressure and staggered backwards as he released her, clutching her bleeding hand.

Valen smiled. "We all have our little problems."

Panic lit her eyes.

He turned away from her and hurled his remaining blade at Blondie, because the damned idiot was standing in the middle of the square gawping at him and the assassin and he should have been running, or taking advantage of Valen's distraction to at least attack him as he had anticipated.

It seemed everyone was bent on doing the opposite of what he expected tonight.

The blade nailed him in his left pectoral and Valen frowned, anger with the assassin and the daemons condensing into anger at himself for missing his target. Six centuries of playing with knives and not once had he missed the exact spot he had intended to hit.

Rather than watching the daemon writhe in agony as he clutched the blade protruding from his heart, Valen had to go all the way across the damn square to recover it. He stomped over to the daemon, ignoring the way his little assassin went into full meltdown behind him, muttering some not very complimentary things about him in her native tongue, pulled the blade from Blondie's chest as the daemon blankly stared at it, and ran it across his throat.

And, yeah, he might have put a little lightning in it, because the bastard went down shaking like a leaf in a hurricane.

He glanced back over his shoulder and found the assassin too preoccupied with her predicament to notice the way the daemon was switching back and forth between mortal and scaled monstrosity.

He took a few steps back towards her, the black haze lifting as his body got the message that the fight was done. Over before it had really begun. Disappointing as always.

The assassin lifted her head, skin pale as snow and eyes as round as saucers. He hazarded a guess that she wasn't sure what had been in that syringe, but that she thought it was lethal.

Not his problem.

So why was he finding it hard to leave?

Why did he want to go to her and check her hand, and see if he could figure out what the bastards had given her to use on him?

He shut down his softer side and shoved it back into place where it belonged.

If he felt any need to find out what poison had been in the syringe, it was because he needed to meet with his brothers later and he could report it to them, together with how persistent her client was getting.

It had nothing to do with her.

He edged back a step, distancing himself, and she swallowed hard. Her blue eyes turned glassy as she wavered on her feet, whatever drug had been in the vial already affecting her.

Was it going to kill her?

Was it wrong that he didn't want it to?

She was out to kill him, which should have been enough for him to want her dead, yet he couldn't bring himself to end her.

He couldn't bring himself to watch her die either.

He turned away from her, focused on his apartment and stepped.

Something grabbed him from behind and fell away as he landed in his apartment, hitting the tiled floor with a hard thump and a muffled grunt.

Valen looked down at the assassin where she lay at his feet, breathing hard, her skin flushed now and pupils rapidly switching between wide deep pools of alluring darkness and pinpricks.

What the fuck had been in that syringe?

Whatever it was, he wasn't sure it was killing her.

He bent over and pulled her onto her feet and she didn't try to fight him. She melted into him, a limp little thing in his arms. Fragile. Delicate.

"Who sent you?"

Fear crossed her beautiful face and he had the impression it wasn't the drug making her scared now. She was afraid of her client.

"No one can find you here. I'll keep you safe." He frowned. Blinked. Had he just said those words?

He struggled to focus as his head became heavy and a deep hunger began to burn in his gut.

A dangerous hunger.

What the fuck?

He blinked again and looked down at her hand and then manoeuvred her so he could see his own. Blood stained it. His blood. He squeezed his eyes shut as the throbbing in his head grew worse and then opened them and peered down at his hand.

Something glimmered in the overhead light.

A splinter of glass.

Fucked.

Royally fucked.

"Why?" she murmured, and gods, it was the sweetest thing he had ever heard, lit up his blood like a sultry whisper and made the burning inside him grow hotter, fiercer.

Damn. Not a poison meant to kill. He laughed, and she frowned at him. He knew it was an inappropriate response, but she would probably find it hilarious if she knew what the fuck her client had just given to her.

She wriggled in his arms. "I tried to kill you."

Her question made sense now. He wasn't one to hold grudges. Not really.

Well, maybe a little.

"Who sent you?" he said again, but couldn't get his damn voice above a whisper now, just as she couldn't.

It was already fucking with his head.

He set her down on his black leather couch and ripped the splinter of glass from his hand. A pointless endeavour. The drug was already in his system. It was a waiting game now. Sooner or later he would purge it.

He glanced at the assassin as she wilted on his couch, slumping so her top half was lying on the seats and her legs dangled so her sexy little knee-high black boots hit the floor.

Valen told himself not to do it, fought for control, but his eyes betrayed him and roamed up those kinky boots, over tight black jeans and the sinful curve of her hip, to her leather jacket. It had spilled open, revealing another wicked little number, this one a red halter-top that barely held her breasts in as she lay on his couch.

In his apartment.

Alone with him.

He rubbed a hand over his mouth, groaned as he smelled her on it, but not only her.

The sweet poison she had managed to hit him with filled his nostrils too.

The throbbing in his head roamed lower, mingled with that intoxicating needy heat in his gut and kept going, flames licking downwards. He groaned and resisted rubbing a hand over another part of his anatomy.

This wasn't good.

"Who sent you?" He tried to make it sound demanding, but he sounded out of breath, on the verge of panting.

Valen sucked down a deep breath and held it, and almost laughed at himself again. As if that was going to make a damned difference.

The assassin rolled onto her back, flinging her right arm above her head, and gods, she had to stop doing shit that made her look so damn tempting.

At least until his body purged the drug.

"There was a woman this time," she murmured, her eyes slipping shut, and slowly lowered her right hand.

"This time?" His eyes narrowed on her. At least she was being more talkative, giving him information he could use.

"Was a guy before… working together." She toyed with the black lengths of her hair, twirled a blue strand around her fingers, and sighed.

He damn near came in his pants.

"Up," he snapped and when she didn't budge, he stalked over to her, grabbed her right arm and yanked her onto her feet.

She crumpled into a heap on his floor, shaking so hard he thought she might rattle something loose.

He bent to pick her up again. The second he wrapped his hand around her arm, electricity bolted through him and the way she gasped said she had felt it too. Not his power though. This was something else. Something a little too dangerous for his liking.

He pulled her up and she fell into him, her hands pressing against his chest, scalding him through his t-shirt even though she was freezing.

"What's happening to me?" she whispered as she looked up at his face.

"You got a taste of your own medicine." He gazed down at her, fighting the hazy warmth that crept up his arm from his palm and the words it whispered to him.

Kiss her.

Her eyes dropped to his mouth as if she had heard that same demand, but her shaking worsened and her skin paled further.

This wasn't good.

"I'm going to die." Her face twisted, pain filling her eyes and driving out the desire, fear that called to him.

Valen cradled her closer and closed his eyes, losing his fight against the drug.

"Don't let me die," she whispered against his chest.

Gods, that tore at him.

He wrapped his arms around her. "I won't let you go."

This wasn't good at all.

CHAPTER 4

Valen lifted the assassin into his arms and stumbled through the huge living room of his apartment, heading towards the bathroom. He bumped off the dark wooden wall of the corridor and she moaned, curling up in his arms. He murmured an apology and held her closer, a trickle of panic running through him.

Was she going to die?

He shouldn't care. He really shouldn't.

So why did it feel as though his heart was being torn apart all over again?

It was the drug. It was fucking with him. He shook his head to clear the hot haze from it and walked onwards, staggered really. This wasn't good at all. The fog in his head turned into a strange sort of lightness that made the hallway spin in front of his eyes.

He tried to shake it off.

That only made the room spin faster.

Fuck.

He shut his eyes and used his senses to guide him to the bathroom. By the time he had passed the two bedrooms to reach it, his head felt heavy again. Almost normal. He risked opening his eyes. The hallway remained mercifully still.

Valen shoved the wooden door to the bathroom open and carried the assassin inside. He had to get her warm.

A voice at the back of his mind said what he had to do was call his brothers. He was in deep shit and he knew it.

"No," he bit out and she looked up at him, blue eyes hazy but questioning him. "Wasn't talking to you."

She remained staring at him, teeth chattering and lips almost as pale as her cheeks. Damn it.

He set her down on the floor, afraid to risk putting her on the closed toilet seat in case she fell and hit her head, and went to the claw-footed tub. He twisted the taps and paused as water thundered into the empty bath.

What the hell was he doing?

He looked back at her where she sat by the door, clawing at her clothes as if she wanted to rip them off even though she was freezing.

He wasn't sure why he was helping her. Fuck, she wanted to kill him.

He eyed her hand. Although he wasn't sure the drug was meant to end him. The way she was squirming as he stared at her, her eyes fixed on his and imploring him, echoed everything that was boiling up inside him.

Gods, he wanted her.

Craved her.

Needed her.

"It's the drug," he said, more to himself than to her, needing to fill the room with the sound of something other than her soft whimpers. "It'll wear off in a day or two."

At least he thought it would. He really needed to call Marek at least. As the brains of the bunch, his older brother was sure to know what had been in the syringe.

But that would mean bringing Marek here to her.

When she was under the influence of the drug.

He snarled at the thought, darkness rising in his blood to obliterate it. Never. None of his brothers were coming near this place, near her, when she was like this.

His growl rumbled through the room as he stalked towards her, and rather than being afraid of him on hearing the inhuman sound, her eyes grew darker, hungrier, as if he had thrilled her rather than frightened her.

He caught her wrist and pulled her onto her feet. She didn't protest as he shoved her leather jacket off her, or even when her holster followed it, her guns hitting the white marble floor tiles with a loud crack. If anything, she writhed harder, and the way she tried to press against him, gods.

Some part of his fucked up brain was still functioning though, because he managed to ignore the urge to surrender to her and scooped her up into his arms instead. She looked pleased, her blue eyes dark with her desire, and threaded her arms around his neck in a way that maddened him, pushing him right to the edge.

He dumped her in the bath, ripping a shocked shriek from her and splashing water all over the tiles.

She floundered, tossing more water over the side, and he caught her shoulders, shoved her back against the white tub and glared at her.

"Stay." Because he was having a hard enough time controlling himself when she was in a position where he couldn't really get at her.

If she left the tub, he wouldn't be able to resist her.

He glanced at his hand and bit out a ripe curse.

When she was well again, he was going to find whoever had sent her after him and fuck them up.

They had done this on purpose.

Valen sank to his knees beside the tub, not giving a damn as water soaked into his jeans, his hands still clutching her bare shoulders to keep her in place in the hot water.

He rested his chin on the curved top of the bath and breathed slowly, trying to bring himself back down and muster some control over his body.

She stared at him, stunning blue eyes bright in the light that reflected off all the white tiles surrounding them, calm and tranquil, oddly distant.

A little colour returned to her cheeks.

Her lips grew rosy again.

He wanted to kiss them. Needed to taste them. Taste her.

He closed his eyes. How the fuck was he getting out of this one?

Did he even want to get out?

Valen opened his eyes, locking them straight on hers. She was beautiful. Breathtaking. Water dripped from the tangled strands of her short hair, rolling down the black and blue to leave trails down her cheeks that he wanted to wipe away. His hands felt too heavy to lift though, too good against her bare skin, feeling her warmth as it returned to chase the cold away.

She blinked slowly, shuttering those eyes that he wanted to stare into for eternity, never looking away. He wanted to drown in them.

The drug was something from the Underworld if he had to guess. It felt similar to the tonic some of the Hellspawn bars added in small doses to their brews to provide their patrons with a relaxing buzz that really took the edge off, something which he had indulged in from time to time. It would make sense that a daemon might know how to make the same drug, and how it would affect him.

What didn't make sense was sending her to deliver it.

Unless this was all part of the plan.

If it was, was she in on that part?

No. His gut said that she wasn't. She had thought the drug would kill him, had been terrified when he had crushed the glass container in her hand and exposed her to it.

She didn't know it was an aphrodisiac.

The hungry look in her eyes and the way her cheeks flushed as she raked her gaze over him said she was beginning to get the message though.

He rubbed his thumbs across her bare shoulders and she shivered, but not from cold. Her skin was hot beneath his hands now, but she would get cold again if he didn't get her dried off and into something warm before the water temperature dropped.

His bed sounded like a good place to put her, and then he could get into it with her and into something warm, somewhere he hadn't been in too long.

He shook that thought away and focused on lifting her from the tub and getting her dry. Water sluiced from her clothes as he set her down on the tiles and she slipped, her boots skidding on the slick surface. He probably should have removed those before putting her in the bath.

He bent to remove them now and her hands came down on his shoulders, heating him through his coat. He tried to ignore how good her touch felt, how that heat seeped into him right down to his bones. Tried and failed.

He really had to call his brothers.

He growled and she froze. A little shiver wracked her and then she moaned and brushed her fingers through the short hair at the back of his head.

Valen swatted her hand away and went back to her boots. It didn't stop her. She pushed hot little fingers through his hair, curled them around the longer lengths on top, and surprised him.

By yanking his head back so he was staring up at her.

Sweet gods.

Hot lust bolted through every inch of him in response, a hunger the magnitude of which he had never felt before.

She towered over him, her wet red halter-top clinging to her breasts and her stomach, revealing everything to him. Her nipples beaded and he bit back a groan, ached with a need to rise up on his knees and suck on them through the material of her top.

Her blue eyes dared him to do it.

Water rolled down her chest, between the valley of her breasts, and his breath shortened as he followed a drop, cock ached as it hit the triangular cups of her top and soaked into the material.

Temptress.

"Fuck," he barked and forced himself to pull her hand from his hair and shove it away.

He wasn't sure how he managed to do it, or to return to removing her boots as if nothing had just happened, she hadn't just issued him an invitation to do wicked things to her.

It was the drug.

She placed her hand on his head again, smoothed her fingers over his hair and stroked the curve of his right ear.

It was just the drug making her do this.

He savoured it anyway, soaked it all up like some pathetic sap, even though it was a bitter pill to swallow.

She wouldn't touch him, wouldn't want him if she was in control. The drug was affecting her and it was affecting him too, and he couldn't let that happen.

He wouldn't.

He finally got the damn fucking zippers on her boots down and pulled them off, tossing them a little too harshly across the room judging by the sound of splintering marble. Temper. It was taking a nosedive as he worked to get her out of her wet clothes, touching parts of her that he shouldn't be touching.

Her hips as he undid her belt and her jeans.

Her thighs as he shimmied the wet material down her legs.

Gods help him.

He tried not to look as he revealed them, but he wasn't a saint. He was as sinful as they came.

She moved, shattering the fragile hold he had on his control, and he looked up at her as he reached her ankles with her jeans, and couldn't bite back the groan this time.

She pulled her red top off, and he ended up on his arse, stunned by the sight of her.

Seduced.

Her top hit the floor with a wet slap but he couldn't rip his eyes away from her. He couldn't breathe.

He had never seen anything so sensual, so alluring.

His eyes dropped to her left leg, to the start of a black and violet ink artwork that mesmerised him. A point above her knee grew into a scaly tail that snaked around her thigh before sprouting two legs with clawed feet that gripped her above her hip on her stomach and just below it. The tattoo disappeared around her back, before reappearing on her right where claws penetrated her hip and a long neck gracefully curved over the flat plane of her stomach to end in an ornate dragon's head that sat with its open jaw on either side of her navel.

Between the dragon's teeth, in the sensual hollow of that navel, sat a diamond that looked for all the world as if the dragon was holding it.

Sweet gods.

Valen swallowed hard.

She skimmed her hands down over her chest, cupping her bare breasts, and stared at him with that challenge back in her eyes.

He wanted to take her up on it.

Really wanted to.

She had to know that, had to see it in his eyes as he waged war with himself. He had never been honourable. Never been a good man.

Why the hell was he starting now?

She bit her lip, teasing it with her teeth in a way that told him to forget reforming himself and just give in to her.

He couldn't.

Gods, why couldn't he?

What the fuck was wrong with him?

It wasn't real. That's what was wrong.

All of it.

It was the drug.

That tossed a bucket of ice water on his libido and gave him the strength to get onto his feet, pull off his coat and sling it around her, removing the tempting sight of her from his eyes.

She frowned and tried to wriggle out of his coat.

Valen growled at her, flashing teeth, and held it tighter, refusing to budge. He had it together, but he wasn't sure how long he could hold it that way. It wouldn't take much for him to be back on his arse, on his knees, panting for her, and he wasn't sure he would be strong enough to claw back enough control and resist next time.

He pulled her back into his arms, carried her out of his bathroom and took a left into the first bedroom.

She scowled at him as he crossed the tiled floor in the pale-yellow-walled room and dumped her on the huge wooden bed. He grabbed the blanket and tossed it over her.

"Sleep." Even as he said it, he knew it wasn't going to happen.

She had that look in her eyes again.

Moonlight shone through the two windows beyond the bed, illuminating her where she lay in it, highlighting her smooth skin as she shirked his black coat and writhed beneath the thin white covers. Gods, they did nothing to hide her from his eyes, seemed to cling to every dangerous curve as she moved in a sensual dance, one designed to lure him to her. She had to know what she was doing.

Fucking temptress.

He had to call his brothers, let them take over, question her or something while he pulled his shit together.

He reached into his jeans for his phone.

She reached a hand out to him.

Valen paused, torn between calling his brothers and answering her call.

His little assassin made his decision for him by shoving the pale covers aside, getting onto all fours and crawling towards him across the king-size bed.

He shook his head, his fingers trembling against his phone as he silently begged her not to push him. He wasn't a fucking hero. He didn't have that sort of willpower.

Everything good in him said to back away as she reached him, but his feet wouldn't cooperate.

She fisted his black t-shirt in one hand and then the other, pulling herself up and pulling him down at the same time.

Move.

He had to move.

Her right hand slid around the nape of his neck and it was game over as she dragged his mouth down against hers.

Roses and sin.

She tasted as delicious as she smelled.

He groaned, slanted his head and claimed her mouth, thrusting his tongue past the seal of her lips and seizing all of her. She moaned, arched against him and held him tighter, clung to him as if he was her saviour not her damnation.

His hands shook, the temptation to grab her and lay claim to all of her almost overpowering him.

He shoved those hands into his pockets, but even that wasn't enough to stop him from aching to touch her, to weigh the firm globes of her breasts in his palms before he devoured them with his mouth.

The feel of her hand on the belt of his jeans had him jerking backwards.

He staggered away from her, only stopping when his back hit the wall of his bedroom, and shook his head, warning her to keep her distance.

She held her hand out to him again.

It was bleeding.

Valen couldn't stop himself from walking towards her, drawn by a need to take care of her that he couldn't understand.

He took her hand, felt it shaking in his, trembling with the same need that coursed through him. He lifted it to his lips and licked the shallow cuts, groaned and shuddered as he tasted her blood and the drug.

It was potent, instantly washing away all his doubts and his fears, allowing need to master him once more.

He lifted his eyes to hers and found them dark and inviting as she watched him, her lips parted and rosy from his kiss.

On a snarl, he tossed her hand aside, claimed the nape of her neck with his left hand and seized her mouth with his own. She moaned and melted into him in the most delicious way, and he swore he could feel her need pounding in his veins, beating in his heart.

He didn't stop her when she reached for his belt this time. Couldn't.

His will to resist had shattered the moment his lips had touched hers and now he was as shackled by need as she was, a slave to this deep craving blossoming inside him, this dark urge to lose himself in her.

He tore his mouth away from hers only long enough to rip his t-shirt over his head. When he went to seize her mouth again, her hands on his bare chest stopped him in his tracks and the way she looked upon him set his blood on fire until it burned like an inferno.

He wasn't sure anyone had ever looked at him like that.

As if she wanted to eat him up, devour every inch of him.

Mercy.

She caught him off guard, springing from the bed into his arms and knocking him back into the wall. He grunted as his back hit it hard and she swallowed it in a fierce kiss. Her lips meshed with his, tongue sweeping across them one moment and teeth teasing the next. Her bare breasts plastered against his chest, her heart pounding with the same staccato rhythm as his.

Out of control.

He groaned into her mouth and grabbed her backside as she wrapped her legs around his waist, pressing her hot core against his aching erection. Her fingers tangled in his hair, ploughing through the long lengths on top, and he gritted his teeth as she yanked his head back.

Damn. Some fucker out there had made her for him.

Words swam at the back of his mind, a hazy warning about curses that dissipated as she went to work on his jeans, fumbling around between her legs, driving him crazy with need.

Her lips were hot on his throat, scorching a trail down it as she pulled his head back further, forcing him to obey. He groaned and held her closer, palmed her backside and drank every drop of pleasure she sent blazing through his body.

Her hand found his hard cock and he shuddered, an involuntary whimper escaping him that he pretended not to hear because thankfully she didn't seem to hear it either. She was too busy stroking him, teasing the blunt head with masterful fingertips that had his knees turning to jelly and legs ready to buckle.

He reached between them and pulled her hand away before she did any permanent damage. No fucking way this ended with him spilling all over her panties.

She moaned, writhed harder, and yanked his head down. Her lips claimed his again, her kiss hard and demanding, pressing him into turning the tables on her. She wanted it rough. He growled as she snagged his lower lip between her teeth, sending a sharp lance of pain down his jaw, and tugged on it.

Damn, he would show her rough.

He turned with her and slammed her against the wall, and she moaned in response. Wicked little assassin.

She rocked against him as he kissed her, seizing control of it and dominating her with every stroke of his tongue along hers, not letting her have her way. She tried to bite him again and he caught her by her jaw, clucked his tongue and held her fast as he kissed her. She moaned, writhed and wriggled, pressing her damp core against his aching erection.

Too much.

He pinned her to the wall with his body so he could use his hands, and tore her panties away, groaned as his throbbing shaft was suddenly exposed to the slick warmth of her.

She moaned louder, rocked harder.

Valen gave her what she wanted.

He eased back, grasped his cock and shifted it down, running the blunt head over her clitoris, teasing her with it. She leaned her head back and grasped his shoulders, constantly moving in his arms, as if she couldn't keep still, as if need mastered her just as it mastered him and she was a slave to it, wouldn't be able to stop moving until it was satisfied.

He could do that for her. He could satisfy both of their needs.

He buried himself in her in one hard, unforgiving stroke, driving her into the wall.

She cried out, the sound born of pleasure rather than pain as he filled her, stretching her around his cock, making her take all of him. Her nails pressed into his shoulders and he grunted as she clawed at him, her face screwed up in bliss.

He seized her mouth as he withdrew and plunged back into her, claiming her body. She clung to him, her legs wrapping tight around his waist, holding him to her as her nails raked over his shoulders, leaving her mark on him just as he ached to leave his mark on her.

She would never forget him.

He kissed her hard as he drove into her, giving her everything she wanted, everything he needed. She was hot, tight. Heavenly. He grunted and thrust deeper, long hard strokes to make her feel every inch of him, to claim every inch of her.

She released his right shoulder and he moaned as she clawed at the wall, rocked and writhed in his arms, lost in the moment.

He was right there with her.

His little assassin.

He frowned as he thrust back into her.

Tore his mouth away from hers, much to her disapproval judging by the way she grabbed his neck and tried to pull him back to her.

He tensed, not letting her have her way, but kept pounding into her, unable to stop now that he had started, not until he felt her shatter around him.

"Name," he uttered and she frowned at him as if he had gone mad. Or had at least forgotten English. If she expected him to string a sentence together when he was screwing his brain out, she had another thing coming. "Your name."

She threw her head back as he plunged into her. "Evaaa… god."

He frowned now, thrust harder as she tensed around him, her breasts bouncing with each meeting of their bodies as they strained together, reaching for release that promised to be mind-blowing.

"Eva?" he rasped, strangled and hoarse as she clenched him, showing him just how tight she could go and almost making him choke.

"Uh huh." She nodded and then her fine black eyebrows shot up as he angled his hips and drove deeper. "Oh ho… oh… *oh*!"

More like it.

Valen buried his face in the curve of her throat, breathed in her subtle scent of roses, sin and sex, taking her all in.

Eva.

"I could drown in you." He kissed her neck and she tilted her head, let him at it as she clung to him. He held her tighter, pinning her breasts against his chest. "I could die right now and wouldn't care."

Her hands came down on his back, but she didn't claw and scratch him. She stroked him, almost tenderly.

And then she bit his shoulder.

"I'll die along with you." She licked the place she had bitten, as if she wanted to soothe him, but her words had sent him shooting too far out of his head for him to feel any pain.

She would?

He growled, a possessive and hungry snarl that vibrated through every inch of him, born of his entire being—body, heart and soul.

He drove deep into her and she cried into his ear, going taut for a heartbeat before she trembled in his arms and around his cock, body quivering and milking him. He grunted and moved faster, deeper, hungry to find his own release as she found hers. It came upon him in a swift, blinding flash, almost sending him to his knees as he spilled inside her. She moaned with each hard throb of his cock, the sounds of her pleasure music to his ears as he stood frozen against her, immobilised by the force of his release.

Eva stroked his shoulder, peppering it with soft kisses between quiet whimpers as her body continued to spasm. He rested his head on her shoulder, pressed his forehead against her neck and held her up by her backside, breathing hard as he tried to settle his pounding pulse.

A sinking, cold feeling filled his chest, pushing out all the heat and light.

A sensation that he would never be the same again, that being with Eva had been his greatest mistake yet, because it had altered something fundamental in him, something he had been guarding closely his entire life.

His heart.

It beat hard as he held her, feeling her trembling in his arms, her body quivering around his and little pants of air escaping her as she struggled to come down from the high of her climax.

Something awakened inside him. Something fierce.

Dangerously possessive.

Whatever her plans had been, he was changing them now.

No more fighting.

Just this... this craziness and passion.

That was all there was going to be between them now.

Sparks.

They skittered over his skin, burrowed deep into his flesh and seemed to bring him to life, rousing the dark side of his blood, the part of him that had come from his father and cried out to brand her with his name, to make sure that she was his.

He pulled free of her and carried her to the bed as she rested her cheek on his shoulder. He pressed his right knee into the mattress and laid her down on it, and placed his hands on either side of her ribs as he drew back with the intention of kissing her and starting round two.

She was out cold.

He canted his head and studied her, absorbing her beauty as she lay beneath him. It wasn't her naked body that held his attention though, or the sensual way her dragon tattoo curled around her curves and the jewel in her navel sparkled in the moonlight.

It was her rosy kiss-swollen lips and the way her long black lashes rested against her flushed cheeks.

She looked content.

Satisfied.

And he had been the one to do that.

He couldn't remember the last time he had made someone happy.

Valen lifted his right hand and brushed his knuckles across her cheek, feeling her warmth and her softness, mesmerised by all of her.

She truly was beautiful.

That beauty was only made more devastating by what he knew about her. She was a fighter. A warrior. Gods, it shouldn't be a turn on but it was. It made him burn hotter for her. She knew what it was like to walk in his world, to face insurmountable odds and be the victor, to battle hard to live to see another day.

His hand shook and he shoved it back against the bed, ashamed of how weak she made him, how uncertain and pathetic.

Would she be alright now?

The haze that had come over him, the urge to lose himself in her, had faded the moment he had climaxed. Was it the same for her?

He hoped so.

He went to press his hand to her forehead to check her temperature.

His phone rang.

"Fuckers," he muttered, knowing exactly who it would be on the other end of the line.

Only his brothers had his number. They would choose now to bother him, when he wanted to be alone with her.

Just a little while longer.

He glanced at the clock on the wooden bedside table to his left.

Cursed when he saw it was well past the time he was meant to have shown up at the mansion in Tokyo for their meeting. He was lucky they had only called him and hadn't popped into his apartment to get an eyeful of him and Eva.

Eva.

Not the name of an angel.

Unless it was short for something.

Had to be the case. His mother's visions were never wrong when she consulted nature. The name of an angel and the skill of a devil.

He smiled and stroked Eva's cheek. There was more devil than angel in her.

He dipped his head, pressed a soft kiss to her lips, and then pushed away from her.

"Won't be long," he whispered as he covered her.

He fastened his jeans, grabbed his t-shirt and pulled it on, and focused on the old mansion in Tokyo.

Darkness swirled around him, comforting him as he steeled himself. His brothers were going to be pissed, but then that was nothing new. They were always upset with him about something.

He appeared in the middle of the main living space of the old Japanese building and silence descended.

"What's up?" He shot for casual and hit irritating judging by the looks Keras, Ares and Daimon gave him.

Just the three of them.

He glanced around, expecting to find his idiotic fellow-blond youngest brother somewhere in the circle of comfortable armchairs and couches, blowing the shit out of something in a video game. It seemed Cal was either late or had left already, and Valen bet his left bollock it was the latter.

Marek, the brunet smarty-pants of the group was missing too, together with their somewhat deranged older brother Esher.

Now that was unusual.

Valen might have understood Esher's lack of appearance if Megan had been with Ares, because the sight of them mooning over each other sickened Valen too, but it wasn't like Esher to be absent from anything, especially when it was taking place in his home. Esher was insanely protective of the mansion, and Valen could understand why. Even he found this place calming and beautiful now. It hadn't been the case when he and all of his brothers had lived here, but now they had their own spaces, and he was normally here when everyone but Esher was absent, it had a certain appeal to it.

He glanced to his left, to where someone had slid back the wooden-framed white screens to reveal the courtyard in the middle of the three sides of the single storey mansion, and the garden beyond. So much nature. He wished it would soothe him now, but his hackles had gone up the second he had realised he had been left alone with the three biggest dicks in his family and there wasn't enough calming nature in the fucking world to bring them back down, not when he could sense a confrontation coming.

"He out at the gate?" Valen peered over his shoulder and leaned left a little so he could see into the kitchen at the opposite end of the long room to the TV area, just in case the only other brother who had ever fought in his corner was in there.

Nope.

He was shit out of luck.

Keras calmly closed the book he held on his knees, set it down on the low wooden coffee table in the middle of the couches, and rose onto his feet. His eldest brother's green eyes hardened like diamonds, reminding him of their father.

They both had that regal, too-handsome bone structure and pitch-black hair.

Valen had tried to adjust that bone structure and rearrange that hair a few times in his life. Unfortunately, Keras was irritatingly good at fighting and healed just as quickly as the rest of them.

Ares stood behind Keras and folded his muscular arms across his broad chest, causing his black t-shirt to pull tight across them, accentuating his build. Boy needed to shop for a bigger size, but Valen didn't expect him to get that. He always had been more brawn than brains. Keras's little guard dog.

The fiery edge to Ares's dark eyes said not to test him.

Daimon sighed dramatically and shoved black-leather-clad fingers through his softly spiked white hair, his pale blue eyes shifting between him and Keras. If he wanted to make a point, he was going to have to be blunter than that.

"Yeah, I'm late, I get it. Yeah, we're going to fight, *again*. No need for the theatrics, Brother." Valen stuck his hands in his jeans pockets. "I was busy."

"So the same excuse as always?" Keras took a step forwards.

Not a hard one. Just a light step. But it was enough to convey the same amount of anger and irritation that a hard one complete with a stamp of the foot would have. His brother had that sort of talent.

"It's the truth. My little friend is back." Boy, was she back.

He almost grinned, but schooled his features so his brothers couldn't see his amusement, because they would probably mistake it for something else and tear him a new one.

"What have you learned, Valen?" Ares actually had the balls to emerge from behind Keras, coming to stand beside him. It seemed his second eldest brother was getting bolshie since falling in love. It had only taken him close to a thousand years to grow a pair.

Valen mulled over what to tell them. Keras's green eyes demanded everything, and said he wouldn't be satisfied with an answer short of that, and Valen did want to get back to Eva as soon as possible.

So for once, he didn't bother to lead his brothers on a dance designed to piss them off.

"She's an assassin. I think daemons hired her. She's tried drugging me twice now." And succeeded once. Okay, so he wasn't going to tell them everything. He paced a little towards the open doors to the garden, feeling everyone's eyes boring into him as he searched for a sense of peace in all the flowing water, stone lanterns and green moss. He glanced back at his brothers where they had remained in the far end of the enormous rectangular room. "She's human."

Shock rippled across their faces. Very satisfying.

"You killed her?" Keras said and Valen got another pleasing round of horrified looks when he shook his head.

He shrugged and turned his back on the garden, pacing back across the pale-golden tatami mats that covered the floor. It was only then he realised he was still wearing his boots.

In his haste to get to the meeting and back again as quickly as possible, he had teleported straight into the mansion rather than to the porch outside.

He looked at the wooden door opposite him, suddenly glad Esher wasn't around because his brother would have lost it. Esher was a sucker for rules, traditions, that sort of shit. Not removing his shoes outside and placing them on the rack probably would have earned him a going over, and Esher was the one brother he hated fighting.

While he was usually immune to his own power, something about Esher's ability to manipulate water turned his lightning against him, conducting it in a way that fed it back into him. Sure, normally it was only mild pain.

Sometimes a little burn or two.

Sometimes it was worse than that though.

Sometimes he ended up having to grow shit back.

He flexed the fingers of his left hand and shook away the image of them charred, flesh blistered and peeling in some places, and completely melted away in others, leaving only blackened bones behind. Bile rose up his throat and he swallowed it hard. It had taken him over a week to heal that injury. A week of Esher's guilty looks and his other brothers' merciless teasing about having a damn skeletal hand.

Valen closed his eyes and focused on the present. Eva danced across his dark vision, the bright blue streaks in her hair shining as vibrantly as her dazzling eyes.

"I have her captive, and I will question her." He snuck a glance at his phone. He had already been gone over twenty minutes. He wasn't sure when she would wake, and he didn't want her to wake alone.

"Bring her in, Valen." Daimon this time, and wasn't it just like him to want to play by the rules to please their self-appointed boss?

Valen shook his head again. "No. My captive, my rules."

"I can just go and get her myself." Those words might have been the biggest mistake Keras had ever made.

Valen snarled at him and lightning raced down his arms, crackled across his fingers and arced between them and the tatami mat floor of the building, snapping as they struck it and leaving black scorch marks behind.

"Dare," he barked and glared at his brothers. "She is my business. Not yours."

Keras calmly took another step forwards. "*Our* business. If she works for the ones who targeted Ares, she is a direct link to the threat to our gates… *our* world, Valen."

He knew that, and he knew the right thing to do, but neither of those things stopped him from raising his hands and taking aim at his brother.

Eva was his.

Keras took another step, his green eyes darkening, shadows building in them that warned he was close to getting a reaction out of his older brother for the first time in a long time and he wouldn't like it when it happened.

"Bring her in now, Valen!"

"Go to Hell. It's my business." Valen threw his hand forwards, but managed to stop himself from unleashing his power as he pointed to Ares. "You let him deal with his shit alone, and that means I get to deal with this alone. You come near Rome… I don't think I need to say what will happen."

He stepped before any of his brothers could respond, but rather than returning to his apartment, he landed on a grassy hilltop overlooking Rome and slumped onto his backside on the dewy grass.

He was pushing his luck.

Keras might give him a day to cool down, but his brother would come knocking, and Valen couldn't blame him. He was right after all. Eva was a direct link to those who had targeted Ares, those who wanted to destroy the gates they protected.

Rome flashed between the current world and the one to come, what he and his brothers had termed the otherworld.

The yellow pinpricks of light that illuminated the beautiful mix of buildings and ancient archaeological sites became fire that spewed from the broken ground, and fault lines intersected the city, some as deep and wide as ravines, threatening to swallow it all. The Colosseum had shattered in half at the edge of one yawning abyss, the remaining stones ravaged by lava and crawling with black specks. Beasts. Things not of this world nor his one, born in the fires of destruction wrought by the daemons.

Screams tore apart the waning night whenever the otherworld flashed over the current one, and he closed his eyes against the sight of his city burning, but couldn't shut out the terrified wails of the mortals as they were hunted and killed.

Fucking Moirai.

They had foreseen this event, and Hades had sent him and his brothers to protect the gates spread around the world, to guard the Underworld and everyone in it from such a terrible fate, and at the same time protect the mortals.

To keep them loyal to their mission, the Moirai had 'gifted' him and his brothers with the ability to see the future of their city should they fail.

It was more of a curse.

All of them felt it. They all hated seeing the city they protected falling into ruin, seeing their failure whenever they gazed upon it. It pissed Valen off, because it made him feel he had already failed, that there was no way of stopping what the Moirai had seen from passing, and he knew his brothers felt the same. It didn't drive them to work harder, because none of them could work harder.

They had busted their balls for two centuries, never straying from their duty, waiting for their unknown enemy to emerge.

It seemed that time was now.

He opened his eyes and looked down at his city, watched as the sky lightened in the distance, signalling the start of a new day.

He had never felt that so keenly as he did now, with Eva waiting for him to return.

He needed to go back to his apartment.

Not so he could question her about her clients. Not yet.

Right now, he just needed to see her again.

He needed to hold her in his arms.

CHAPTER 5

Eva stretched and yawned, a strange warmth curling through the entire length of her body, a sensation she wasn't sure she had ever felt before and couldn't quite describe. Contentment? She had never been content, and couldn't think of a reason why she would feel that way now.

In fact, she couldn't recall much beyond heading out on a mission to make another attempt at delivering the drug to her mark.

She slowly opened her eyes. Everything around her was hazy, a blur of brown, yellow and bright white. She blinked rapidly, but her vision was slow to come into focus.

When it did, she gasped and launched backwards, hit something hard and scrambled for the covers when she realised she was naked.

In a strange bedroom.

Her gaze leaped around, charting everything from the tiled floor, to the pale yellow walls and the wooden wardrobes that filled the space opposite her at the foot of the enormous bed, to the two huge windows to her left that allowed light to flood into the room and revealed a stunning view over Rome's rooftops. Her head throbbed in response to the sudden movements and the information overload, and she clutched it and buried it between her knees.

She closed her eyes.

What the hell had happened?

Her mark flashed across her dark eyes, a distorted replay of him fighting two men.

She snapped her head up and stared down at her palm, at the shallow healing cuts on it.

Fuck.

It all came flooding back.

He had shattered the syringe in her hand, and then he had shattered her.

The satisfied hum in her body made sudden, dreadful sense.

The result of what she could only describe as mind-blowing sex.

Eva groaned and slumped back against the hard wooden headboard. What had she done?

She raised her hand in front of her, sighed as she stared at the lacerations and slowly pieced together everything that had happened, from the moment she had tried to take her mark down to the moment he had taken her.

She groaned again and wished she could blame it all on him or the drug, but she dimly recalled he had tried to resist her and the drug had only worked to loosen the hold she had on the desire she already felt for him.

It was tempting to bury her head in her knees again, so she shoved the covers away and leaped into action instead, intent on salvaging some of her dignity. She was damned if he was going to find her in his room when he came back.

Her feet hit the cold tiles and her knees gave out, turning to jelly beneath her. She clutched the mattress to stop herself from hitting the floor and pulled herself back up onto it. Damn. She needed a moment. The humming in her body grew stronger, sending a pulse through her, a hot wave of pleasure that rolled through her like an aftershock.

Stronzo.

She had avoided physical contact since becoming an assassin, but she could remember sleeping with men and none of them had ever left her this way.

She cursed him, and then added a few more on top when she remembered that she had given him her name. Another first since stepping into her current line of work. She always kept everyone in the dark about her as much as possible.

Even her clients only knew her by her alias—the angel.

Now her enemy knew her name.

This wasn't going to end well.

She looked at the door, intending to listen for him and see if she was alone. Instead, she caught a wicked flashback of being pinned against the wall beside it, his hard body driving into her as he gave her everything she had wanted.

She had ached for him so badly last night, had needed him to the point where she had honestly felt as if she would die if the desire that had been blazing inside her hadn't been sated.

By him.

Eva bit her lip as another aftershock rolled through her.

Stronzo.

She was better than this. Stronger than this. She pushed onto her feet again and refused to let her legs give out beneath her as she hurried across the room to the wardrobes. Relief blasted through her as she yanked the wooden doors open and found them full of clothes. She grabbed a t-shirt and a pair of combat trousers, both in black, and pulled them on. They were too big, dwarfing her despite her mark's athletic frame.

Eva held her trousers up as she padded quickly across the tiled floor to the door. She eased it open, peered both ways along the wood-panelled corridor. It was quiet. Either he was sleeping it off somewhere, was sitting in wait, or he was out. She prayed it was the latter and looked off to her right. The bathroom.

A flash of him undressing her in there leaped across her eyes.

She raced along the corridor, silent in her bare feet, and breathed a sigh of relief as she spotted her holster and leather jacket on the white marble floor in the bathroom, together with her boots. She quickly tugged her boots on, grimacing as she discovered they were damp and cold, and then slung her holster across her shoulders.

God, the weight of her weapons felt good.

She shrugged into her leather and turned to leave, paused as she saw the black bathrobe on the back of the door.

She pulled the belt free of its loops and used it to hold her trousers up, tying it tightly around her waist.

She paused again at the door and looked back at the claw-footed tub that was still full of water.

A flash of him watching her while she had been in that tub, of his handsome face awash with concern, crashed over her and she couldn't breathe as she struggled against the invisible tide, fighting the questions and the desire they stirred—a need to remain and see him again.

She wanted to know why he had taken care of her.

Eva shook her head, causing her short black hair to sway across her neck. No, she didn't.

What she wanted was to get away before he returned.

To sleep with a man was a mistake.

To sleep with her mark was beyond unacceptable.

She had to leave now, while she had the chance.

She had complicated things enough.

She was meant to be killing him, not giving him a joy ride.

Eva crept along the hall, keeping as quiet as she could in case he was hiding ahead of her, waiting for her to emerge. She reached into her jacket and drew her gun, and the weight of it in her right hand helped steady her nerves as they rose with each step closer she came to the end of the corridor.

Those nerves settled as she reached the open wood-walled room. She quickly scanned it, not bothering to take in any of the details, focused on ensuring that her mark wasn't home. Good.

She turned right, towards a door that had a peephole. It had to be the exit.

Eva hurried towards it, picking up speed now, and holstered her gun. The last thing she needed was someone in the apartment building seeing her with a weapon and calling the police.

She stopped short of grabbing the handle as something shimmered across the wooden door.

A trick of the light flooding the room from the windows behind her?

She turned to look at them.

Her mark stood right behind her.

She moved in an instant, launching into action on instinct, her right fist flying at his face.

He easily caught her hand.

Golden eyes shifted to it, his handsome face cold and devoid of emotion as he studied her hand. He released it and she snatched it back, considered going for one of her weapons and then thought the better of it when she caught the challenge in his striking eyes, the dare to do it.

"Leaving without a goodbye kiss?" he husked and her damned knees weakened again, her heart pounding a hard rhythm as her eyes betrayed her and fell to his lips.

Lips that had mastered hers, that had seared her flesh and set her on fire.

"Stronzo," she bit out and reached for her weapon, no longer caring about the odds being against her.

He was on her in a flash, his hand grasping her wrist and shoving it against her chest, pinning it there so she couldn't draw her weapon from its holster. Those lips she had been fantasising about curled, flashing canines that seemed unusually long.

He pushed her backwards, pinned her to the door, and she struggled against him, refusing to let him dominate her. He made a low growling noise in his throat when she managed to get her fingers around the grip of her gun and pressed her wrist harder against her chest, so hard it was difficult to breathe.

Those golden eyes issued a demand.

It took her a moment to remember he had asked her a question.

"Kiss?" She gave him a confused look and darkness flashed in his eyes, almost stopped her in her tracks but she pushed on, playing it cool and praying she was going to somehow get away with her life. She was done with this mission, and this man. It was too dangerous. She was going to run. Benares might find her, but he might not, and that was a chance she was willing to take. "What are you talking about? Why would I kiss *you*?"

Maybe she had put a little too much venom into that word, because his expression darkened, a storm brewing in his eyes that set her nerves alight and had her pressing back against the door. Fear. She had felt it plenty of times in her life, enough that she should have been able to control it as she did with most of her emotions, but it was too powerful, shoving at that control, filling her with a need to escape and run, and she wasn't sure that it stemmed from her current position.

She wasn't sure this fear had anything to do with her mark at all.

His face softened, lips curling into a slight smile as he lowered his eyes to her mouth and released her arm. She tensed as he raised his hand, bracing herself for a blow. His palm touched her cheek and she flinched even though it was a light caress not a hard strike, unable to stop the reaction her body had decided upon before he had even made contact.

He frowned.

"Because of last night." He smiled again, smoothed his palm across her cheek and down to her jaw.

His touch was feather-soft, but she was aware of his strength, knew he could snap her neck in a heartbeat if she said or did the wrong thing. She trembled as he caressed her, stirring heat in her veins and pulling memories of last night to the front of her mind again. Desire rushed through her on a wave of electric tingles, tinged with panic she couldn't quite shake.

Her gaze slipped to his lips and then shifted to the scar on the left side of his face. It started low on his jaw and ran down his neck to his collarbone, the skin ragged and distorted, as if someone had burned his flesh away.

It both frightened and fascinated her.

Everything about him screamed danger, but she felt no pressing need to move and escape him.

She didn't fear him. Not after last night.

What she feared now were the sparks that leaped between them, intense and seductive, and the air of power and danger that he emanated, uncontrolled and wild, undeniably alluring.

He growled and closed his hand around her throat, shoved her back against the door by it, but there wasn't any strength in his grip. He wasn't trying to hurt her. She lifted her eyes to his, caught the brief flare of pain in their incredible golden depths before he extinguished it. He had startled her to stop her from staring at the scar, because he hadn't liked it.

If he didn't want people to see it, why did he wear the long lengths of his blond hair down over the right side of his face and not the left? It would have covered the scar on his jaw and part of his neck.

The pressure on her throat lessened as he eased back.

"You don't remember last night?" he said, his voice as soft as his expression now, almost docile and affectionate.

"I tried to kill you last night," she countered and pushed his arm, moving his hand away from her. He eased back another step. A bonus she hadn't expected. "I don't know how I ended up here, but I'm leaving."

Blond eyebrows dropped low over golden eyes that brightened and locked on her, fixed so intently that she shivered under their scrutiny.

"You don't remember making love?"

Making love? If what had happened between them had been making love, then she wanted to see what raw, hungry sex with him was like.

"The drug must have affected you too, because I don't recall fucking you."

His hand closed over her cheek again. "You don't remember?"

His thumb grazed her lower lip and her breath left her on a sigh that she couldn't hold back as she stared up into his dazzling golden eyes and slowly shook her head.

Somehow, she stopped herself from melting against him and found the strength to keep up her charade. "I want to kill you. Why would I fuck you? I would never fuck a mark. I would never sleep with you."

Those dangerous eyes darkened again and his demeanour changed in a blink of them. He caught her jaw and tilted her head back, his eyes scouring hers. His were cold now, empty of the storm that had been building in them a moment before.

He grabbed her arm and yanked her away from the door, and had it open and her out of it a second later. She hit the wall of the corridor hard, grunted as the impact sent fiery sparks rushing through the bones of her right arm and across her upper back.

"Never… ever… come after me again. The next time I see you, I *will* kill you. Do you understand?"

Eva looked across at him.

He slammed the door in her face.

Stronzo.

But she had the feeling that word should be directed at her this time. She wasn't sure why.

She sagged against the wall and waited for the pain to pass. The one radiating from her arm faded, but the one in her chest lingered as his ultimatum rang in her ears.

She had already made up her mind that she would never see him again, so why did that ultimatum cut her like a blade?

Eva clutched her right arm, looked back at the door and lingered for a moment before forcing herself to walk away.

She was going to walk away from all of this. Disappear.

She was going to get out of Rome, drive to her small villa in the north, and get her head straight. She needed space to get some perspective, and not only about him.

Every instinct she possessed screamed she had been set up.

The drug she had been given hadn't been poison. It had been some sort of aphrodisiac, which meant Benares had wanted her to end up sleeping with her mark.

Why?

The cold gnawing in the pit of her stomach said she knew the answer to that question.

Benares was using her to get to the man. Her mark was an assassin like her, a master of his emotions, and a loner as far as she could tell from the months she had been tailing him and learning all about him. Benares had already known those things about her mark, she was sure of it now, and he had chosen her because they were alike.

It had been his first step in bringing them together, a common ground they shared that would make it easier for his plan to come to fruition.

That plan was turning her into her mark's weakness.

She could see that now and was damned if she was going to allow it to happen.

Benares had chosen the wrong woman for the job. She wasn't a whore. She was an assassin.

She reached the bottom floor of the apartment building and stepped out into the street. A quick scan of her surroundings placed her far from the last place she recalled—the island in the Tiber river. She couldn't remember how she had come to be in his apartment. Everything between the square and his bathroom was a blur that refused to come into focus.

Eva rubbed her aching head, soothing her temples with her fingertips.

She really needed to get her head on straight.

That need only grew when she caught herself looking back up the height of the cream-rendered building to the floor where his apartment was, harbouring a ridiculous hope that he would be leaning out of his window, framed by the green shutters and watching her.

Damn him.

Damn Benares too for messing with her head and throwing her life into turmoil.

Eva turned her back on the elegant old building and charted a course towards a main road, hoping she would find a taxi there. She was a long way from her own apartment, across the other side of the city in an area that had money stamped all over it. Her mark had to be good at his job to earn enough money to live in such a fancy area.

She ignored the whispered urge to look back the way she had come.

She was never going to see him again. That was final. She valued her life.

The main road was quiet, still in the early morning, and she strolled along it, desperately trying to shut out her thoughts about her mark and what they had shared. He had been so different with her. Intense. Passionate. Full of emotion.

He had been a complete contradiction to the man she had tailed, blowing all of her research apart in one wild, explosive moment together.

She managed to hail a taxi, regaining awareness of the world for as long as it took to give the driver directions to her apartment and then losing herself in her thoughts. She mulled over everything, trying to piece her mark together but failing dismally.

Maybe it had been the drug. It had affected them both.

She came out of her thoughts again as the taxi rattled over cobblestones and pulled up outside her apartment building in a small square. She handed the driver his money, stepped out of the cab and walked up the gentle slope towards the entrance to the pale grey rendered building. She punched in the code to unlock the smaller rectangular door set into the large arched wooden double doors. It clicked and she pushed it open and stepped over the threshold, into the cold shadowy broad tunnel that joined the square to the courtyard of the building.

It was quiet.

Eva ran through her normal checks, halting in the shadows to scour every inch of the courtyard from her yellow Ferrari, black Maserati and white Fiat 500 in the centre of it, to the covered walkway that ran around the four sides where the ground floor of the four-storey building had been set back to provide shelter.

She shifted left and right to see past the arches and columns that supported the upper three floors of the building, making sure no one was hiding behind them. Satisfied she was alone on the ground floor, she scanned the dark windows of the upper floors. No sign of movement there and none of the alarms hidden around the courtyard had been triggered. She flipped a silver panel on the right hand wall of the tunnel down, punched in another code to turn off the motion sensors, and then flicked the panel closed again.

Normally, she would turn on the lights in the courtyard when returning home, but not today. Today she wanted to get in and out unseen, so she stuck to the shadows in the covered walkway, heading to the opposite side of the building.

She would pack a bag and get away from Rome, away from the madness of Benares and her mark.

Maybe she could even use some of her contacts to help her.

Plenty of them owed her a favour, and she was sure some of them could hold their own against Benares.

She unlocked the door to the building and quickly moved up through the silent levels.

Or maybe she could kill him herself.

Security would be a problem, but there was a chance she could slip into his villa while he was sleeping and take him out.

Eva almost laughed at herself for even considering it.

She reached the floor she had chosen to live on in the building. Her building. It had cost her a small fortune, but it was better than sharing one with others. She wasn't sure how her mark did it. How could he live surrounded by so many people?

She paused at the door to her top-floor apartment.

Or did he live alone in his building just as she lived alone in hers?

She wracked her brain, trying to remember whether she had seen or heard anyone when she had been leaving his building.

She hadn't.

Eva shook her head. It had been early, barely dawn. It was possible everyone in the apartments had been asleep, or she had missed hearing them because she had been so preoccupied with getting away from him after he had kicked her out.

Kicked her out.

It felt as if he had done just that, that if she had acted differently he would have kept her around, even when he knew she had been hired to kill him.

Or whatever Benares had hired her to do.

She pushed the solid metal door open and stepped into her apartment. A quick scan revealed everything was right where she had left it and none of the motion sensors had been triggered. Good.

Eva turned to close the door.

And almost jumped out of her skin.

Jin curled a crimson-painted lip at her surroundings.

How the hell had her client found her? No one knew where she lived. She had made sure of that, had covered her trail relentlessly, ensuring that her base of operations remained hidden from her clients.

Yet Jin was standing on her doorstep, looking for all the world as if she wished she wasn't.

"You did well," Jin said, coldness in her British accent that had Eva wondering whether she was being sarcastic, or whether everything really had gone as Benares had planned last night.

Eva ran a glance over the woman and frowned. Combat fatigues. The black long-sleeve roll-neck top hugged her incredible figure, and tight trousers had been tucked into rubber-soled leather boots. Even her blonde hair had been tied back into a neat ponytail.

Why was her client dressed as if she was going on a special-ops mission?

It dawned on Eva as she spotted something sticking out of the woman's pocket, something that resembled a balaclava.

There was a reason Jin had known where she lived, and had known the moment she had returned to her apartment.

Jin was the one following her, reporting her every action to Benares.

She had tailed Eva to the square last night, and from there to her mark's apartment, and she had seen her leave this morning and had followed her to her apartment building.

Eva curled her fingers into fists at her sides and cursed herself, and her mark too. It was his fault she had failed to notice her tail this morning. She had been too preoccupied with thoughts of him. Stronzo.

Damn him to Hell.

How much did Jin know and how much was she piecing together from Eva's appearance?

She was dressed in her mark's clothing after all. She huffed and cursed again. She should have squeezed back into her damp things. Her shoulders sagged a little.

It wouldn't have changed anything. She had still been spotted leaving his apartment building in the morning after she had been there all night.

Her eyes widened in horror. The windows. Rooftops. A groan escaped her. Just how much had Jin seen?

Eva wanted to bury her head in her hands and scream in frustration. Instead, she tipped her chin up and rolled her right shoulder as casually as she could manage.

"I was just doing my job." It sickened her to say that when in part it was the truth.

She knew without a doubt now that Benares had hired her to seduce his target, her mark.

Her stomach rolled, but she held her shit together.

"We want you to go to Valen one more time."

Anger lanced her as those words reached her ears, making her blood come to a boil in her veins. No damn way. She knew exactly what that meant. She was done with this job. She was done with Benares and Jin, and her mark.

Valen.

Was that his name?

In all the months she had been working the job, she had never uncovered it. Wherever he went, he used a different name, so many that she had grown tired of asking people what it was and had settled for leaving it a mystery.

What had he done to deserve Benares coming after him like this?

Why was it so important to Benares that she continue to seduce him?

The greater part of her wanted to tell Jin to go to Hell, but there was a small piece of her that wanted to question the woman so she could learn why Benares had hired her and could uncover his end game.

That desire disappeared with a sharp pop as Jin leaned towards her, blue eyes eerily bright in the dim light, and smiled.

"You enjoyed it didn't you?"

Eva scowled at her. "No. I've done my part. I've done what you asked. I'm an assassin, not a whore. This isn't what I do, so I'm done. Understand?"

Jin sighed and leaned back. "Benares will be disappointed. He does not like it when people renege on a contract with him."

Eva held her ground, planting her hands on her hips and keeping the frown on her face, hiding the sudden spike of nerves that shot through her together with images of her lying in a ditch somewhere, beaten and dead.

"I'm not reneging on anything. Benares withheld information from me, something I don't like, and I did what he asked. I got intelligence on this Valen character for him. I did what I was hired to do."

Jin's smile turned cruel. "I do not recall your contract stating what it was my brother had hired you to do."

Brother.

Eva's mouth flapped open and she quickly snapped it shut. Benares was Jin's brother? Her stomach turned again, revulsion churning it this time as she caught a flash of the way Jin looked at him, desire written plainly across her face. What sort of sick relationship was happening in that mansion?

She barely suppressed the shudder that went through her.

On the heel of a deep desire to vomit came a realisation that rocked her to her core.

The demented bitch was right.

Her contract with Benares didn't state what it was she had been hired to do. None of her contracts did. It was hardly sensible to put in writing that she was going to kill someone.

Damn. She should have been specific this time though, since Benares had only hired her to gather information on Valen. Now she was trapped by her own damn contract, and stupidity.

"So you will do as Benares desires?" Jin moved closer, that twisted smile holding, a glimmer of satisfaction in her blue eyes that told Eva she liked seeing her squirm.

Why? Because her brother had a twisted thing of his own for her?

Did Benares even want her to sleep with Valen again?

A voice at the back of her mind whispered that it was probably Jin who wanted to see it happen, that the woman had a motive of her own and it was born of jealousy, which had grown into a desire to ruin her in her brother's eyes so he would no longer want her.

Both of them were sick.

"If I do this, I'm done?" she said, going against every instinct that screamed at her to slam the door in Jin's face, pack a bag and run as far as she could before she was pulled deeper into their twisted world and whatever game they were playing.

Jin nodded. "If you get the result we desire, then yes, your contract will be fulfilled."

The result they desire.

That was just another way of saying she wouldn't be done, that Benares wouldn't release her from her contract and he would keep changing the rules, using her in whatever way he saw fit. She would never escape them.

But running wasn't the answer either.

Benares would find her.

There was only one way to be free of him.

She bit back a smile as a plan came to her, one that was dangerous but might be her only shot at saving herself.

She was going to play her mark against her client.

CHAPTER 6

Valen glared down at Rome, watching it flicker from the present to the possible future between lightning strikes. Black clouds boiled overhead, the rain cold on the nape of his neck as it hammered down, turning the grass beneath his backside to mud.

Eva.

Another white-purple bolt lit up the sky and ravaged the earth, tearing it up just twenty metres to his left and shaking the hillside. He growled through clenched teeth, fury mingling with hatred in his veins, tangling together so tightly they sucked all his other useless emotions into the blackhole they created.

Valen let them go willingly, didn't give a flying fuck about anything as the rain poured down on him and his beautiful lightning ripped apart the sky and shook the ground.

The storm raged before his eyes as fiercely as it raged within him, savaging everything in its path, so violent that it was bound to draw attention from Mount Olympus.

He didn't give a fuck about that either.

He shoved onto his feet and raised his face to the sky, held his arms out at his sides and let the storm build within him, coaxed it and fed it, pushed it to its limit. Lightning struck all around him, the thunder so loud it hurt his ears, and car alarms screamed in the distance. Each rapid strike only served to fuel the fury mounting inside him, and in turn it served to quieten the pain.

Power raced along his bones, through his veins and lit up his nerves. He embraced it and let it flow through him, let it carry him away in the hope it would burn everything in its path—all of his feelings.

His memories.

Her.

The rain grew heavier, pelting him like shards of ice, but still he didn't move.

He kept feeding the storm, even when he could feel the fear in the air, hear the terror of the mortals far below in the city.

A city he had vowed to protect.

That made him want to stop, but he couldn't now. He couldn't. Not until the storm had burned away whatever this fucking idiotic feeling was inside him, this feeling that shouldn't exist.

This weakness.

Another flash of Eva denying she had slept with him tore a scream from his throat and had lightning striking hard all around him. The smell of earth and ozone flooded the chilly air, but it didn't comfort him today. Not when her words taunted him.

She would never fuck a mark. She would never sleep with him.

He knew what she had been trying to say. She had driven her point home hard enough that it had pierced his chest, but hadn't quite hit its mark.

Valen finished for her, hammering it into his own stupid head. She wouldn't fuck a mark. Meaning something without feeling, something detached and methodical. Fair enough. She wouldn't sleep with him. Meaning she felt no desire for him, was repulsed by him, would never even consider him whether he was or wasn't her mark.

He laughed at that, but it was a broken hollow sound, one that only stoked the fury in his veins until it blazed so hot he couldn't control it.

He snarled and snapped his head down towards his city at the same time as he brought his hands forwards. Lightning struck across Rome, hitting every single one of the two hundred plus rods he had painstakingly placed on the buildings to protect them. The entire city shook from the force of the blow.

He didn't give a damn what she thought.

It bounced off him just as the rain did, washing from his body and rolling away from him.

His power rose again, another bolt charging, making his blood hum and bones warm. Gods, it felt good.

It was beautiful.

The only beauty he needed in his dark world.

There was nothing as addictive as his power. Nothing as seductive. Nothing as pleasurable.

It was all he needed.

It was all he would ever need.

He pressed his middle finger and thumb together in front of him and clicked.

The lightning rushed to obey him, a white-purple blaze shooting from the black sky to split and split again, creating a branching pattern above the city before each tiny fork connected and the earth responded, sending electricity racing up the branches and thickening them as thunder boomed across Rome.

The otherworld flashed over the city, a vision of fire and horror, filled with the screams of mortals and the choking stench of death. It was growing worse again.

He needed to deal with the assassin, and whoever had sent her.

It was the only way to restore some balance to Rome and the world, and stop the otherworld from looking so crappy.

But to do that, he would have to see her again.

He growled and raised his hand to conduct another lightning strike, and snarled again when his hand shook, weakness invading his body and making it difficult to move his fingers. He had pushed too hard again, had let his power take too much from him. He lowered his hands to in front of him and stared at his upturned palms. They trembled violently and he struggled to form fists, fighting the cold ache that started in them and seemed to travel through his body, sweeping the last of his strength away.

Fuck.

He threw his head back and roared at the sky, unleashing his anger in the only way he had left.

Fury at himself this time.

He shouldn't have gone all out. He had a city to protect and he was no use to it if he couldn't use his power.

Valen looked down at Rome, barely able to see it through the haze of the rain.

A city he had just terrified.

He sank to his knees on the slick grass and let the storm fade, let it all flow out of him and calm replace it, filling him up and stealing away his emotions. The rain lightened and then gradually stopped, revealing the city to him. Relief swept through him. It was fine. Still in one piece.

Which was more than he could say for himself.

The black clouds parted, allowing the sun to shine through and hit his back. It instantly warmed him, as soft and comforting as a caress, and he sat on his knees and let it soothe him and chase away the cold.

When his hands stopped shaking, his bones no longer trembling, he pushed back onto his feet and trudged down the slick hillside towards the distant road, skidding in places and having to fight to retain his balance. His punishment for using too much of his power. He was going to have to walk all the way back to his apartment, a distance of at least five miles.

He couldn't even step that tiny distance now.

What use was he to his city when he was like this?

No use at all.

He shoved his hands into the pockets of his black jeans and huffed as his soaked black t-shirt tugged against his skin, irritating him. He hadn't wanted to bring his coat, even when he had known it was going to end up pissing down on him.

It smelled of her.

By the time he reached the city outskirts, his feet were sore in his boots, souring his mood further. He cursed Eva's name with each step, and that only dragged his mood deeper into a dark mire.

His brothers were right.

He needed to deal with her.

At the very least, he had to locate her and bring her to his brothers so they could question her.

He growled at that thought.

He didn't want Keras anywhere near her.

She would probably fall head over heels for the bastard.

She was his.

He laughed under his breath at that and hardened his heart again, pushing her out of it as he turned a corner.

The scent of lilies hit him.

That heart softened to mush.

Valen froze and dragged his eyes away from the pavement, fixing them on the woman standing before him in the alley, shadowed by the elegant buildings that surrounded her.

A ray of light in the darkness of his world.

She held her slender pale hand out to him, her smile lighting up her face as it curved her soft shell-pink lips. Her luminous green eyes sparkled with love and understanding, a stunning contrast against the earthy red of her wavy hair that curled around her bare shoulders and brushed the black layers of her corseted dress.

Valen went to her as she desired, unable to refuse her.

She carefully lifted her hand and smoothed her palm across his cheek.

"I felt your anger and your hurt, and Hades gave me leave to see you." Her melodic voice danced around him, as comforting as an embrace from her would have been, and he sank into it and let it push all of his heavy thoughts away, replacing them with only her.

He had figured Mount Olympus would feel his fury. He hadn't banked on his father feeling it all the way in the Underworld too.

"Can we go to your home to speak?"

He instantly shook his head, his insides growing heavy and dragging him back down. He didn't want to take her there because he wasn't ready to face it yet. He didn't want to think about Eva right now.

"To another place?" Persephone said with a bright spark of hope in her soft voice and he nodded.

"I know somewhere." It was hardly suitable for her, but it was nearby and it would hopefully be quiet at such an early hour.

The sun was still peeking above the horizon, not quite ready to bid goodnight to Rome.

His mother nodded, and the fact she had come to him again sank in as he led her through the streets, struggling to stop himself from growling at every male who looked at her. She was off limits. He would kill anyone who even thought about speaking with her, let alone looked as if they might try it.

He turned down another smaller alley a short distance from the Pantheon and pushed a plain metal door open, holding it for her.

She thanked him with a gentle smile and stepped inside, and he grimaced as he noticed she was barefoot.

At least flowers weren't sprouting around her feet as they normally did.

He glanced back along the street in the direction they had come, relieved to see she hadn't left a trail of blooms in her wake.

Valen followed her into the building and up the concrete steps to the bar. It was mercifully quiet, with only a few people hanging out at the round tables and the long black bar. The female bartender, a slight brunette, nodded at him and he led his mother to a booth in the corner of the room, away from everyone else.

She eased down onto the padded black leather.

Gods, she couldn't look more out of place.

She would have been more at home in Heavenly Body, his favourite club, because Hellspawn frequented that place, but it never opened until darkness had fallen. This bar opened throughout the daylight hours too, and the downside to that was the fact it only attracted mortals.

Which only seemed to trigger a response in his mother that made her seem even more out of place.

Her bright green eyes darted around, taking everything in, abject fascination shining in them. When the mortal female came for their order, he thought for a moment that his mother would start questioning her, her excitement about being out in the world and surrounded by humans too much for her to contain.

She didn't get out much.

Her deal with her mother and her role as a goddess meant she was allowed to leave the Underworld from spring to summer, but since having Keras she had turned into a stay at home mum and rarely left her husband's side.

Hades was a jealous and possessive bastard.

It ran in the blood.

Valen was surprised he had allowed Persephone to come to him.

"Why are we not at your home?" she whispered and reached across the round black table to him.

He sighed. "I just don't feel like being there right now."

"Is the reason you tried to destroy Rome the same reason you will not go home?"

"That's a little harsh," he snapped and then regretted it when her fine dark eyebrows pinched together and she sat back, distancing herself. He huffed. "Rome is still in one piece."

"Is it the female?"

He folded his arms across his damp chest. No way he was going to answer that.

Her small smile said she already knew the answer anyway. The bartender arrived with his drink and another one for his mother. He waited for her to leave, watching his mother closely so she didn't surrender to her urge to question the mortal.

Persephone's brow crinkled as she eyed her drink.

"It's just juice." He stirred the colourful plastic stick in his, mixing the grenadine with the fruit juices and causing the ice to clink against the sides of the tall glass. "It looks better than drinking water."

Since he wasn't allowed to drink booze like a normal person.

His brothers preferred water. Water was boring. But then so were his brothers.

"Dad got over Ares dating a Carrier yet?" Valen was sure that was going down well with their father.

Megan was barely one step away from a daemon. The only difference being her power to heal came from Hellspawn ancestry, one of the breeds that Hades deemed alright.

There were plenty of mortals out there like her who had dormant powers that came from daemon blood though, and if Megan had been from one of those families, Hades would have flipped his shit.

"I am not here to speak about Ares and Megan."

The fact that his mother was allowed to use her name, and that she said it in such a warm way, went a long way towards telling Valen that Hades was already getting used to Megan being involved with Ares.

Boring.

"Tell me about the female."

He really didn't want to do that, but his mother was giving him that look that said she wasn't going to leave until he confessed everything, or at least something.

No way he was telling her everything. There were some things his mother didn't need to know about him.

"You were wrong about her name." Could he leave it at that?

It struck him that he was fishing, and that had him pissed all over again. Hadn't he decided to capture Eva, hand her over to his brothers and forget about her?

Persephone smiled at him over the rim of her glass. "I was not."

He casually leaned back into the leather seat and toyed with the stirrer in his drink. "Were too. She's called Eva. That isn't the name of an angel."

"Evangelina."

Valen's stomach dropped, plummeting to the depths of the Underworld, and his heart gave a hard beat against his chest.

Evangelina?

It certainly sounded heavenly to him.

Sweet gods, he could easily imagine whispering it against her neck, pleading her to have mercy on him.

His senses lit up, sending a shower of sparks skittering through him, and his eyes darted to the door as the lights there stuttered. His breath left him in a rush as he recognised the wicked curves of the woman before she stepped into the lights of the bar, flooding him with the same fierce hunger he had experienced last night in her arms, and the scent of roses and sin hit him with the force of a tidal wave.

Evangelina.

His angel.

CHAPTER 7

Eva needed a drink. A stiff one. Maybe two. Three. Who knew? She had spent the past few hours locked in her apartment, debating what to do. Run, or fight?

As it always would with her, it had come down to fight, but she still wasn't sure who she was going to make her target.

Benares or Valen?

She parked her black and silver Vespa in a side street, pulled her helmet off and put it into the box beneath the seat as she mulled over her options. Her fingers worked automatically as she took the thick chain and locked the wheel of the scooter, and she sighed as she straightened and stuffed the key into her black jeans.

Valen had threatened to kill her if he saw her again.

Would he carry out that threat even if she was bringing him information?

She wanted to say that he wouldn't, but some part of her knew that he might still go through with it. With her current run of luck, it wouldn't surprise her if he killed her right after she told him everything she knew.

Benares viewed him as a weak link.

A weak link in what chain though?

She tipped her head back and sighed again at the darkening sky. Going in circles like this was going to get her nowhere. She had to make a decision, and although she feared Valen as much as she feared Benares, she was going to stick with her original plan.

Whether he killed her or not.

She palmed her gun through her leather jacket, the feel of it there if she needed it soothing her and steadying her nerves.

She would have one drink to keep those nerves in check and then she was going to drive to Valen's apartment and put her plan into action. Hell, maybe she would catch Valen by surprise and gain the upper hand in the situation.

A bullet in his thigh might give her that.

It would certainly slow him down enough to give her time to make him listen to her.

She smiled to herself as she walked along the street, heading towards the small bar she often visited when her thoughts were weighing her down, imagining shooting Valen in the leg and trussing him up while he was preoccupied by the pain. If he was as good at his job as she was, he would find a way out of the ropes or whatever she tied him up with, but she would be long gone by then.

Would he come after her, or go after Benares?

Only time would tell on that one.

She scanned the street, checking for the millionth time that she was alone. When Jin had left her, Eva had followed the bitch to the edge of the city and had only turned back when Jin's car was a speck in the distance on the road to the mansion.

Hopefully Benares was keeping his little spy occupied.

Eva shuddered at the thought.

Even if he had another tail on her, all they would see was her doing as he had bid, finding Valen and taking another shot at him.

Not that she was going to seduce him.

She would do her best to make it look as if she was though, just in case someone was watching her.

The guy standing guard outside the bar nodded as she approached and pulled the metal door open for her. She thanked him with a smile and a sway of her hips, enough to appease his appetite, and didn't punch him in the face when he smacked her on the arse as she passed him. Her smile dropped off her face, a scowl taking its place as she walked up the concrete stairs, the blue overhead lights hurting her tired eyes and making it hard to see ahead of her.

She hated that.

It always felt as if she was walking into a trap.

As an assassin, she relied heavily on all of her senses, and having one dampened always set her on edge.

The light gave way as she reached the top of the steps and left the corridor behind, allowing her to scan the room for any potential threats. She swept the room from right to left, seeing nothing out of the ordinary.

Eva froze as her gaze hit a booth on the left of the room.

She recovered an instant later, before his eyes landed on her, and casually strolled towards the bar, pretending she hadn't seen him.

Valen.

His gaze tracked her, burned into her despite the distance between them, but she shut him out as her heart pounded hard against her chest and the nerves she had come here to quash rose to new heights, making her limbs stiff. She eased into a stool at the bar as smoothly as she could manage and secretly blew out her breath as his eyes left her.

Eva flagged the bartender, getting the guy. He smiled at her and she shot him one back, because it didn't hurt to flirt. She glanced at Valen while the man took her order for a shot of vodka. Especially when he was with a woman.

A very beautiful woman.

His lover?

Deep red hair curled around her slender shoulders, brushed the black strapless dress she wore and seemed to glow against her pale skin. Warmth washed over her soft delicate features as she spoke, an undeniable air of grace surrounding her, making her appear almost too perfect to be real. She looked like a damn fae, something from another world.

A goddess.

She was certainly holding Valen's attention.

He was staring at the woman with heat and tenderness in his golden eyes, a look she had never witnessed in them before.

One that said he was close to the woman.

They were around the same age, and she was stunning, even more beautiful than Jin. She had to be his lover. No man in his right mind could be with a woman that beautiful and not want her.

Eva downed her shot and ordered another, trying to keep her eyes off Valen and his female friend, because the way he was looking at her, and she at him, was stirring all kinds of feelings inside Eva, ones she didn't want to examine too closely.

She didn't care if he had a girlfriend.

If he loved someone.

Last night meant nothing to her.

She swallowed the second shot of vodka, and the bartender poured her another and leaned his left elbow on the bar. His muscles bunched, causing his white shirt to tighten across them, and she tried to listen as he talked to her, the sparkle in his dark eyes saying he was flirting with her. She managed a few responses, even touched his arm, causing him to suddenly look there.

Valen's gaze burned into her.

She shut him out.

Laughed at something the bartender had said.

The feel of Valen's eyes on her grew more intense, heating her and making her heart pound, filling her head with images of last night and how fiercely he had kissed her, and how rough and possessive he had been with her, and the things he had said.

He could have died right then and wouldn't have cared.

She drew her hand away from the bartender's arm and nursed her vodka shot.

It had been the drug speaking. He felt nothing for her. He meant nothing to her.

A little voice taunted her, whispering that if he meant nothing, why was she drowning her sorrows while thinking about him?

Why was she jealous of the woman he was talking to again now, his eyes bright and flooded with warmth, the complete opposite to the way he had looked at her?

She downed the third vodka, hoping to kill the brain cells that were fixated on him.

Glanced at Valen.

The warmth in his eyes was gone.

Darkness crossed his face as he stared at the table that separated him and the woman, and then he lifted his gaze to hers. Pain. It was there in his eyes, written in every handsome line of his face.

The woman said something.

He shook his head and bowed it, shoved his fingers into the longer lengths of his blond hair and clawed it back. The muscle in his jaw popped and he ploughed his fingers through the shorter hair around the sides of his head. His shoulders sagged and his eyes closed.

What had the woman said to him?

Whatever it had been, it had hurt him.

Eva tried to drag her eyes away, guilt crawling through her. The conversation was clearly intimate, and she was invading their privacy. She had just found the strength to look away when the woman reached over the table and touched his left cheek, feathering her fingers over the scar there and then down his neck, unafraid to touch it.

Valen raised his head and looked at her through eyes that held an incredible depth of love.

Eva looked away from him, her chest tight and aching, and focused on her drink instead. The bartender had kindly filled it for her again. She turned the small glass back and forth in her fingers, telling herself on repeat to leave. Being here was only hurting her.

She needed to speak with him though.

He hadn't killed her yet, so there was a chance if she approached him now and told him everything, he would take the bait and she would live to see another day.

She glanced back at them.

The woman covered Valen's hand with her own and held it. His expression didn't change, the emotion that had flooded it remaining even as she spoke to him and he responded.

An emotion that surprised Eva.

Vulnerability.

It was the final straw.

Everything she thought she knew about him turned on its head and she saw him in a different light.

He had proven himself a killer, someone without a shred of emotion. She had spent hours following him and not once had he shown any hint of softness. Everything about him had been hard and cold, his emotions locked down in a way that she had envied.

And then last night had happened.

At the time, she had been convinced that the passion and need, the desire and tenderness he had revealed to her had been a reaction to the drug, just as her behaviour had been.

Now, she knew it had been real.

He wasn't a man without feeling. He wasn't a merciless and cold killer.

He was something else.

She didn't fully understand him yet, but she wanted to know him. She wanted to know this side of him so she could complete the picture of him.

Impossible.

He had made that clear to her this morning when he had thrown her out of his apartment.

If she went to him, the walls would come up, the emotions locked down again, held beyond her reach. She couldn't blame him.

If last night had been real, then she had wounded him by denying remembering it. He struck her as the sort of man who reacted viciously when wounded, would do anything to protect himself from further hurt, and didn't forgive easily.

Eva frowned as the woman stood and wished she could hear what she was saying to Valen, because the way he tipped his head back and looked at her made Eva's heart break for him. Thumping music made it impossible to hear their conversation though, leaving her with only his reaction. The woman bent over and he closed his eyes as she embraced him, her slender arms wrapped around his shoulders and her lips pressing against his forehead.

When she pulled back, he opened his eyes again, locking them straight on hers. The woman swept the long strands of his hair from his forehead, the action tender and filled with love, and said something, an anxious edge to her expression.

He nodded and the woman left.

Eva watched her go, waiting until she had disappeared into the crowd gathering on the dance floor before turning her focus back to Valen. He stared at the table in front of him. No. He was staring at the woman's empty glass, a distant look in his eyes, one laced with hurt.

She blew out her breath.

This was going to end badly.

She flagged the bartender. "Two shots."

His right eyebrow shot up and then he frowned across the room at Valen, muttered something and went to work. He slammed a second glass down beside her one, filled them both and didn't wait to take her money. He walked away from her. She thought about calling him back, and then shrugged it off and picked up the two glasses.

What did she care if a man was in a mood with her because he thought she was interested in someone else?

She was probably going to be dead in the next five seconds anyway.

Eva pushed out of her stool, dragged in another deep breath to steady herself, and marched to her doom.

Valen tensed when she slammed the glass down on the table in front of him, arched an eyebrow and then glared up at her.

"You look as though your girlfriend just dumped you." She shot for cocky as she flicked her hair out of her face and stood a little taller, hoping he couldn't see through the mask she wore to the truth lurking beneath.

He scared her a little.

Just a little.

He had threatened to kill her after all.

Cold golden eyes narrowed on her, empty of the tender emotions she had seen in them just minutes ago.

"I thought I told you never to come near me again?" He pushed the drink away, leaned back into the black leather seat of the booth, and folded his arms across his chest, causing his defined muscles to flex.

Eva ignored the hot bolt of desire that blasted through her and casually took the seat opposite him, doing the opposite to everything her instincts were screaming. She was not going to run.

She slid the drink back across the circular table to him. "If you want, I'll kill your woman for free."

He scowled at her. "My woman?"

She jerked her head towards the door behind her. "The one that was just here."

His golden eyes shifted to it. "My mother."

He had to be joking.

"Leave." His expression changed abruptly, darkening around twenty degrees, and he pushed the drink back at her again. "Last warning."

Eva wished he would look at her with the same consuming fire that had been in his eyes when he had stared at the woman. There was only ice in them, as thick and impenetrable as a glacier.

As much as she was beginning to want to leave, she couldn't. Not until she had done what she had come here to do.

"The people visited me."

His face lost some of the darkness at least, gaining a glimmer of curiosity. It lasted all of a second before the veil descended again. He picked up the shot glass and glared through the clear liquid at her.

"So it's poisoned then."

Eva glared right back at him. "Poison isn't my style."

He laughed, a mirthless and dark sound. Fine. She had drugged him and at the time she had been convinced it had been poison in the darts and in the syringe.

"It's their style. I do what the client wants." She wasn't sure why she felt the need to defend herself with him.

Did she want him to approve of her? Would he think less of her if she was the sort of assassin that employed poison as a tool rather than choosing a more intimate method of dispatching their marks?

She remembered how confident he had been with only a blade, that all the times she had seen him fight he had only ever used a knife. Never a gun.

Never a drug.

He sniffed the shot glass, looked as if he might drink it, and then held it away from his lips again.

"It's just booze. I thought you needed it. You looked as though you were breaking up."

He slammed the glass down with a sharp bang. "She's my mother!"

A few patrons looked her way and she smiled at them all, hoping they would go back to dancing and drinking, leaving them alone again.

Was he serious?

"Leave," he bit out and shoved the shot glass towards her, spilling more of the contents. "Final warning."

He was fond of issuing those, but he didn't seem inclined to act on them. At least not with her.

Eva might have obeyed him this time, but when he had shouted at her he had revealed something about him that she had never noticed before, and she felt pretty damn sure she should have given the fact that tongue had been in her mouth, rasping over her flesh, just a few hours ago.

There was a stud in it.

A plain metal ball right in the centre of the tip.

How the hell had she missed that during their little make-out session?

Her pulse pounded in response and she wrestled with the sudden flush of desire that rushed through her, somehow managing to get a lid on it and remain in control.

There was something terribly sexy about it, something wicked and alluring that tugged at her and made her want to crawl onto the table and kiss him, but at the same time it rang warning bells in her head.

Was he a player?

It was the sort of thing such a man would have. Plus, he had looked very close to the woman who had just left, yet he hadn't turned Eva down last night when she had been all over him. She wasn't buying his line that the woman was his mother.

His golden eyes burned into her.

Maybe it was his step mother?

"She's really your mother?" She had to ask, because it was beginning to get weird. First Jin talking about Benares being her brother, even though the bitch clearly had a thing for him. Now Valen was speaking about a woman he had looked more like a lover to than a son being his mother.

He sighed, and she had never had a man sigh at her in a way that clearly screamed he wanted to reach over the table and choke her with his bare hands.

"She's my mother," he gritted out and rubbed the bridge of his nose. "She doesn't come to see me often, only when she can leave home. Dad misses her too much so she never stays away long, not like the old days when she would spend the whole of summer in Greece."

His eyes snapped to her, so fierce and sharp that she tensed.

"Why the fuck am I telling you this anyway?"

She wasn't sure, but she wasn't going to do anything to make him stop. She had followed this man for months, and never uncovered any personal information about him. Now he was telling her about his family. Although, she still found it hard to believe that the woman who had just been sitting with him was his mother. Even if she was his step mother, she still looked too young to have been spending summers in Greece away from his father. Valen had made it sound as if he was talking about a time decades ago, and the woman had looked around the same age as him, barely into her thirties. No way that woman could have been married to his father back then.

"Unwind. Have a drink." Because she was beginning to need one of her own.

She lifted the shot glass to her lips and awareness of his eyes on her, tracking her every move, had her slowing down, savouring the way he followed her hand and the way his gaze drilled into her mouth. His golden eyes darkened, something shimmering in them, heat that had been there the night he had fought her in front of the Pantheon and had shone in them again last night when he had been fighting to resist her.

God, he had fought it.

She had given into the haze of lust so easily, but he had tried to be a gentleman.

It hit her hard and she knocked the drink back, needing it now more than ever.

He muttered something she thought might have been 'temptress' and looked away from her.

Eva pushed his drink back towards him. He frowned down at it.

"You drink it." He tried to push it back but she kept hold of the glass, refusing to let him do it.

His fingers slipped on the glass and touched hers and she gasped as lightning arced up her arm, heating her bones and setting her body on fire.

He snatched his hand back.

Had he felt that?

"I don't drink." If he had felt it, he masked it well, hiding it better than she had.

She had felt sparks for a man before, back in her youth, or at least she had thought she had. What she had experienced with that man, it was nothing compared with how Valen could light her up with nothing more than a brief brush of his fingers across hers.

It was nothing compared with how he could set her on fire with just a look.

His golden eyes met hers, igniting an inferno in her veins as they held hers, steady and unwavering, dark with desire that called to her own, giving it a stronger hold over her.

"Drink it," she murmured, not quite with the world as she lost herself in his eyes.

He shook his head. "No."

"If you drink it, I'll tell you all about my clients. Everything I know." It had been the plan all along to tell him everything she knew, but suddenly it felt like a desperate move on her part, born not of a desire to unleash him on Benares so she would be free and more of a desire to make Valen stay.

To make him talk to her.

That wasn't like her at all.

What the hell was wrong with her? What was it about him that had her going against every instinct she had as an assassin?

"If you drink it, I'll tell you what they told me."

His eyes darted between hers and the glass, turning hard and cold one second and filled with conflict the next, as if she was asking him to do something terrible.

"I can't." There was more emphasis on it this time. "There will be repercussions if I do."

Repercussions?

It was only a drink.

"Your loss." Eva took the glass.

He grabbed her hand, sending another thousand volts screaming up her arm. His fingers were warm against her, that heat oddly comforting, rousing a fiercer need to make him stay. He held her firm and she lifted her eyes from his hand to his face.

He stared into her eyes with such force, such intensity, that it shook her, and his voice was a low whisper, laced with something akin to fear or possibly even remorse.

"If I drink this… I don't know what will happen."

Eva smiled. "I'll give you information… that's what will happen. Live dangerously."

He grinned and her heart stuttered.

"Always do."

CHAPTER 8

"If I drink this… I don't know what will happen." Honest words, ones that would chill a lesser man to his bones, especially if they knew what he did—that the unknown reaction to the drink his little angel offered could be anything from a mild buzz to the complete annihilation of Rome.

That little angel smiled like the devil she really was, always leading him into temptation. "I'll give you information… that's what will happen. Live dangerously."

He grinned.

"Always do."

And wasn't that the crux of his problem?

Sense waged war with a deeply rooted need that he had never been able to kill, no matter how fiercely he had tried.

A need to please his brothers and redeem himself.

A need that drove him to do stupid things that would probably only end with them hating him even more than they already did.

If that was possible.

He was about to find out.

Valen closed his eyes and necked the drink.

It went down hot, burning his throat, and he could feel it spreading tendrils through his body, fiery fingers that worked their way outwards from his heart until they gripped every inch of him. A tremble started in the pit of his stomach, vibrations that rumbled through his bones and he gripped the table in front of him with both hands, desperate to anchor himself.

Light exploded in its wake, blasting through him and filling all of him, blinding him to the darkness that rose up behind it, a shadow of doom.

He sank short claws into the wooden table top and growled through his gritted teeth as hunger poured through him, a ferocious need that pounded in his blood and mastered him, rending holes in his strength until it leached from him and he swore he could see it pouring from his flesh like blood.

Valen tried to scoop it up, desperately pressed his hands to his chest and stomach, fighting the hold of the hunger. Black shadows flowed from between his fingers, swirled and disappeared into the light, and nothing he did stopped them from leaving him.

The light around him faded and he stilled as he faced the shadow that loomed before him, a flickering silhouette of destruction and damnation.

Horns rose from its head like a crown and talons tipped the fingers of the hand it extended to him, mirroring his own movement as he reached for it. Crimson eyes glowed from the black abyss of its face, edged with gold, blazing in the darkness as it called him to surrender to it.

Give up the fight.

Give in.

Valen pressed his palm against the shadow's outstretched one.
And surrendered to it.

CHAPTER 9

Eva reached for Valen as he shook before her, gripping the edge of the table with such force that it rattled between them. What was wrong with him?

His eyes snapped open before she could touch him and she gasped as they glowed in the low light, liquid pools of fire, golden and shifting like an inferno.

A dark shadow crossed his face and his wide pupils narrowed into pinpricks.

Tiny sparks skittered over his bare arms.

The shot glasses on the table smashed.

Eva gasped.

"What are you?" Her voice shook as violently as the rest of her as she shrank back into the seat, mind racing and heart pounding, both sending her spinning as she tried to grasp what she had just seen.

A memory hit her.

How she had travelled from the square on Tiber Island to Valen's apartment. In the blink of an eye.

His glowing golden eyes narrowed on her. "The stuff of dreams and nightmares."

He locked his hand around her wrist before she could take that in and hauled her out of her seat. She stumbled along behind him, struggling to catch up and comprehend what was happening. He dragged her into the middle of the busy dance floor and whipped her into his arms.

Lightning rushed through her again as his hard body met hers and his hands claimed her waist, one sliding low to cup her backside.

She trembled in his arms, thoughts pulling her in a thousand directions, all of them screaming at her to get away from him.

Those thoughts fled as he began to move, starting a slow, sensual dance that worked his body against hers, filling her head with wicked images of them. She tried to hold it together, to retain some sense so she could figure out what was happening, but it became impossible when he went to war on her, lowering his head and kissing her neck. A hot shiver danced down her throat to her breasts as his tongue stroked a line up her neck and she felt the cool, hard bead of his tongue stud pressing into her flesh.

She had to stop this. She wasn't sure what was happening, didn't understand why her mind was screaming this was a bad thing, that she had made a dreadful mistake by convincing him to drink that shot of vodka, but she had never ignored her instincts before and she wouldn't start now.

No matter how tempted she was to surrender to him.

Eva tried to push him back but his right hand clamped down on her backside and hauled her back against him, and his left hand wrapped around her throat. He pressed his thumb against her jaw and tilted her head back, devoured her throat with hot wet kisses that worked to undo the strength she had found, making it bleed out of her and replacing it with an aching need to give in to him. She wanted to give in.

She wanted that passion they had shared last night, that madness.

He groaned against her skin and worked his hands into her leather jacket as he danced with her, a slow grind that was at odds with the pounding fast beat of the music. His body rolled against hers, all hard muscle and strength, power that had her knees weakening and body straining for more. She lost the fight against the desire he stirred in her when he skimmed his hands across her stomach and they met her guns.

And he moaned low in his throat.

Shuddered in her arms.

As if finding her armed had thrilled him.

God.

Eva swallowed hard, closed her eyes, and desperately tried to muster the will to resist, the strength to break away from him and do what was right—getting him back to the booth and talking to him.

His mouth seized hers.

Hot. Hard. Demanding.

Intoxicating.

Eva melted into his arms as he wrapped them around her, pinning her to his chest and bending her backwards.

Bending her to his will.

She moaned into his mouth as his tongue brushed hers, unable to hold it back. He groaned in response, as if he had heard the quiet sound of supplication over the thumping music and it pleased him. He kissed her harder, mastering her as he had the night before, and she was powerless in his arms.

He shuddered when she stroked his lower lip with her tongue and his mouth froze against hers, a sense that he was waiting for something filling her. She smiled as it hit her and licked his lower lip again, and then sucked it into her mouth, pressed her teeth into it and tugged hard on it, surrendering to the same wicked need that had rolled through her the last time she had been in his arms.

Valen growled and claimed her mouth again, plundering it with his tongue, the stud clacking against her teeth. She wanted to feel that stud on her flesh again, imagined the places he could use it and trembled against him as a new hot wave of desire flashed through her. He moaned and kissed along her jaw, nipping it hard in places, sending sharp bolts of pain down her neck to mingle with the pleasure building within her.

He wrapped his lips around her neck and sucked, ripping a husky groan from her throat as she clutched his head. A few people stopped to look at her but she shot them all glares and they went back to dancing. Sense reared its head again, whispered that she had to stop this now, before it went any further.

It seemed Valen didn't possess the same niggling voice.

His palm met her crotch and she shuddered as he rubbed her through her jeans, teasing her and winding her tighter, until she was fit to burst or scream. His mouth worked magic on her throat, his left hand seizing the nape of her neck and sending shivers tripping down her back and chest. Her nipples tightened, aching for his attention even though she was aware of their location, of the people surrounding them. Valen's right hand grabbed her backside and he wedged his right thigh between hers, and she bit back a moan as it pressed against her core, rubbing it with each sway of their bodies, sending her spiralling closer to the edge.

She needed him to kiss her again.

Eva tunnelled her fingers into the longer lengths of his golden hair and yanked his head back.

The look on his face stopped her dead.

Golden eyes held hers, a glimmer of affection shining in them, directed at her this time.

She loosened her hold on his hair and fell into those eyes, her awareness of the world around them fading as he looked down at her, hiding nothing from her now. She lowered her hand to his face, wanting to touch it as the woman had, to show him that she wasn't afraid of him either.

Someone touched her shoulder.

His eyes turned jet black and snapped up to lock on the person behind her.

She gasped as he disappeared.

A muffled grunt, and feminine shriek, and a low growl had her whipping around on her heel in time to see Valen send a brunet man to his backside in the middle of the packed dance floor. Her eyes shot wide. The woman who had screamed ran. The man stared in disbelief at Valen, blood streaming from his nose.

As for Valen.

He let out another inhuman growl, his shoulders shifting with each hard breath he drew.

They were shaking.

Eva eased a step closer to him, drawn towards him by an urge to comfort him that she didn't quite understand. Was it because she wanted him to know that she had no interest in the man he had punched, or because of something else?

The way he had looked in the moment before he had disappeared flashed across her eyes. So much darkness. So much fury.

She leaped back when he suddenly bellowed and clutched his head, bending forwards as he yelled at the floor.

The dance floor broke into pandemonium, people pushing for the exit while others scrambled back towards the tables, heading for friends or their belongings.

"Valen?" she whispered, her hands shaking as she reached for him, her instincts blaring a warning at her that she refused to heed.

He wasn't going to hurt her.

She hoped.

The man with the broken nose spoke as he pulled himself onto his feet, muttering it beneath his breath but the music ended abruptly just as he said it, the DJ deciding it was time to join everyone else in trying to get away from the fight.

"Woman that hot is wasted on you. I just wanted to see if she would trade up."

Eva wanted to hit him herself for that one.

Valen beat her to it.

With a feral growl, he launched himself at the man, tackling him back to the ground. The entire room froze as they went at it, exchanging punches as they rolled around, kicking at each other. She didn't like the man's odds. Valen landed twice as many blows as they brawled, and the man was clumsy in his attacks, obviously untrained.

She needed to do something or he was going to end up dead.

She grabbed Valen's arm when he went to swing another punch at his foe.

He froze and slowly turned his head towards her, his golden eyes turning darker than black as he looked at her hand where it gripped his arm, stopping him from hitting the man.

Eva realised her mistake around a second before he shoved to his feet, grabbed the man by his throat and threw him across the room as if he weighed nothing.

She had defended the man.

"It isn't what you—"

Valen shoved her aside and she grunted as she hit the black bar, pain shooting outwards from her back. She bent forwards and gritted her teeth, eyes watering as she struggled to shut down the pain and push it out of her body. The sound of glass smashing, the cries of women, and pained groans and muffled grunts of a fight surrounded her, blending in her ears into one cacophony.

She had been in bar fights before.

Eva lifted her head and looked around her.

But none of them had been like this.

None of the fighters had been like him.

Valen didn't even flinch as several men attacked him, striking him with broken glass bottles and chair legs, trying to beat him down. He fought back against them all, never surrendering even an inch of ground to them, taking each blow he couldn't block and still managing to land some of his own.

Another man flew across the room to land at her feet, his face a bloodied mess as he wheezed.

She looked from him to Valen, her eyes going wide again as he slammed his fist into a table one opponent shoved at him and the thick wood shattered as though it was made of flimsy tinder.

A man came around behind him and Valen spun on his heel, and she gasped as she saw the state of him.

Lacerations covered his chest, long rips in his black t-shirt exposing them to her eyes, and a thick gash darted up the right side of his neck and over his jaw, the cut deep and bleeding heavily.

The fear that had been gripping her disappeared, blasted away by the sight of him.

She had to stop him before he got himself killed.

Eva shoved away from the bar.

And collapsed to her knees, shock rocking her as five tall men appeared around Valen and a sixth just poofed out of nowhere a few metres away, this one bringing a woman with him.

What the ever living fuck?

She stared, slack jawed, as the five men worked to contain Valen, unable to compute what she had just witnessed, even when it backed up what had dawned on her when her memories of last night had completed themselves.

People could teleport.

Valen snarled and growled like a wild thing, fighting the men as they tried to overpower him, and an urge rushed through her, commanding her to rise onto her feet and help him. These men all out-muscled and outweighed her, but she was damned if she was going to stand by and let them treat him so roughly when he was hurt.

She shoved onto her feet.

Someone grabbed her arm and held her back, their grip fierce and unrelenting.

"Do not interfere." A man. She looked up at him and found kind dark eyes watching her and a rough yet handsome face warmed by a smile that seemed out of place in the current situation. Unruly dark waves caressed his forehead and curled against his neck, brushing sun-kissed skin. "Valen just needs to calm down."

They knew him then?

"Dial it back, Brother," the one with long blond hair said and held his hands out in front of him, palms facing Valen as Valen turned on him with a snarl.

A white-haired man eased around behind Valen, and one with overlong black hair that was similar to Valen's in style but hung over the left side of his face and had been shaved neatly around the sides, not hacked, moved in from the other side. They were flanking him. His eyes darted between them all, shifting to whoever had moved last, but kept returning to the one nearest to her.

A tall man with a physique that matched Valen's, wild short black hair, and sideburns that reached low on his cheeks and came down at an angle, tapering to a point that accented his sculpted cheekbones. A long black coat hugged his slender frame, flaring from his waist to almost brush the heels of his polished black shoes.

Valen's eyes narrowed on him and his right hand went to the thin black braid around his left wrist.

All six men tensed.

"I would not do that, little brother." The tall black-haired man's smooth voice held a note of warning, a thinly veiled threat that things would get bloody if Valen disobeyed him.

Valen pulled on the band.

The man disappeared into a swirl of black smoke and reappeared behind Valen, his left hand landing on Valen's shoulder and his right hand catching Valen's to stop him from snapping the band.

"You need to sleep it off," the man said.

Valen's face twisted in disgust.

He collapsed.

The man caught him and gently lowered him to the floor. The same floor that felt as if it was pitching and rolling now, unstable beneath her trembling legs. She struggled for air, sucked down breath after breath that did nothing to stop her head from spinning.

What the fuck was happening?

Who the hell were these people?

Who the hell was Valen?

His words rang in her twirling mind.

The stuff of dreams and nightmares.

Her legs gave out. The man's hand on her arm stopped her from hitting the floor. He pulled her back onto her feet and shifted his grip to hold her upright.

The black-haired man looked from Valen to her, the concern that had been filling his green eyes disappearing in a heartbeat, turning them as cold and hard as emeralds.

"How long can you hold them, Keras?" the white-haired one said to him and something dawned on her.

The other people weren't moving.

She stared at everyone else in the bar, cold crawling over her skin beneath her clothes, fear that trickled into her blood and turned it to icy sludge.

Everything was frozen in place.

Not just the people as they stood like statues, some running for the exit while others reached for objects they could use as weapons.

Those objects too.

A broken bottle hung suspended in the air just behind the white-haired one, levitating there.

God, she was losing her mind.

The one the man had called Keras pinched the bridge of his nose and frowned. "I do not know. Long enough, I hope."

Long enough for what?

"Get to work," Keras barked and they all burst into action, moving between the frozen people and pressing two fingers to each of their temples.

Even her guard left her.

Eva eyed Valen where he lay on the floor in the middle of the room, blood trickling from his wounds, torn between going to him and running like hell.

She didn't want to leave him with these men, but if they were his brothers, they would take care of him. There had been concern in Keras's eyes when he had been looking at Valen. She had to believe that he wasn't going to hurt him.

She had to because if she stayed here, she was ninety-nine percent certain she was going to pass out just like Valen had, but without any assistance from his magical, god-only-knew-what, brother.

Eva sidestepped.

Keras's green eyes snapped to her.

Damn.

He stalked towards her, his long black coat flaring around his ankles in a way that looked unnatural. Eerie.

She backed away and hit the bar. Trapped.

"Do you have any idea how difficult it will be to remedy this?" he snapped and something flashed in his green eyes, something that reminded her of how Valen had looked before he had turned into a raging, savage and dangerous beast bent on destroying everything and everyone in the bar.

No.

The darkness in Keras went far beyond what she had seen in Valen's eyes.

"Tone," someone muttered.

It might have been the brunet who had appeared with the woman.

Keras scowled in his direction anyway.

When he looked back at her, the darkness in his eyes was gone, and it struck her that he was as stupidly handsome as Benares. Probably just as dangerous too. What gene pool had they crawled out of?

She looked past him to Valen and her heart kicked up a notch, beating harder against her ribs. Blood had pooled in the cuts on his face, and formed a line across his cheek from the left corner of his mouth, but even with all the bruises and blood, and the scar, he was still more handsome to her than Keras or Benares.

He made her heart pound.

Keras cleared his throat and her gaze zipped back to him.

"What happened?" he said, his tone softer now, and she was sure the one who had muttered before about his tone praised him for it.

"I told him to have a drink and unwind... I didn't know—"

"Fuck," someone cut her off.

"Fuck indeed," another replied.

The built-like-a-body-builder brunet with the woman grimaced. "We're in trouble now."

"He did make a mess." She felt small when they all turned to glare at her and shrank back against the bar.

"It is not the mess." This time it was the one who had held her arm.

He seemed far nicer than the others, that smile still in place, warming his rough features. He had the build of the other brunet, but he wasn't wearing a coat like that man and the others. A pale linen shirt hugged his broad chest, hanging loose over a pair of dark linen trousers, and his toes poked out of the end of his sandals.

"We are not allowed to drink alcohol." Keras. He looked as if he meant it too, which caused a cold feeling in the pit of her stomach. "He knew better."

"He always knows better... never stops him though, does it?" The white-haired one again, and the look he threw at Valen made her want to scream at him that she had made him do it.

Valen had told her how many times that he couldn't drink it? She had practically forced it down his throat.

The look on all of their faces said they had made up their mind though. They thought Valen had done it on purpose. He had. But not to get any of them or himself into trouble. He had done it for information.

The blond man who looked the youngest of the group at barely thirty and the one with black hair styled similar to Valen's picked him up off the floor, holding him between them.

Keras turned his back on her and looked at the other three men. "Make it quick."

"What are you going to do?" Eva lunged forwards, afraid they were going to hurt Valen.

She ran straight into Keras's arm and grunted as it slammed hard against her chest, knocking the wind from her. He turned glacial green eyes on her.

"Memory alteration." The way he said that, his voice dark and cold, devoid of any emotion, sent a shudder through her and had her easing back a step and looking for the nearest exit.

She had seen enough strange things in the past twenty-four hours to believe these men were capable of such a thing.

He stared down into her eyes and slowly shifted to face her, and the ice in her veins grew thicker.

The frozen people in the club weren't the only ones about to get their brains meddled with.

She swallowed hard.

He was going to mess with hers too.

Eva blurted the first thing that came to her.

"I have valuable information."

The body-builder stopped halfway through saying something to the petite brunette he had brought with him and looked across at Keras. "She the girl?"

The girl?

"It would seem so." Keras ran a glance over her, and then looked back at Valen where he hung between the two men. "What have you gotten yourself into now?"

"Will he… will he be okay?" Her voice was small, but it seemed loud in the silent room. Everyone stared at her, shock written across their faces this time. Even the kind brunet looked surprised.

"As far as we know, you have tried to kill our brother several times," Keras snapped, his eyes flashing dangerously as he closed in on her. "Why the hell do you care if he will be alright?"

She didn't have an answer to that.

"I shouldn't. Right?" She wasn't sure why she was tossing that question out there, as if they could tell her at what point she had lost her mind and gone completely off the rails, undoing years of self-discipline and training, and tossing all of her instincts as an assassin aside. She looked back at Valen, her chest warming at the sight of him, even as fear for him flooded her veins. "But I do."

The six men all exchanged a look.

"What are you going to do to him?" She bravely met Keras's cold eyes.

She wasn't sure she could take him in a fight. Something about him warned her not to even try, but the rest of her was ignoring it and gearing up for one, her mind sharpening and instincts firing as she secretly assessed everyone in the room, trying to discern their weaknesses.

"You should be more concerned about what we might do to you."

Her gun was in her hand in a flash and she had it aimed at him before he could react.

When he did react, it was nothing more than a slight quirk of his right eyebrow.

Not quite what she had expected.

Someone chuckled.

"She has fight. I like her," the woman said and received a round of chastising looks from the men.

The big brunet slung his arm around her shoulders and tugged her against him. "You would. She takes after you. Waving a gun in my brother's face to protect one of us."

79

Eva was tempted to look at the woman and see whether she had done just that, but kept her eyes locked on Keras. His face remained impassive and her nerve started to crumble as he just stood there and stared at her, as if waiting for her to make her move.

"You're not going to hurt him." She pulled the hammer back.

Keras took her statement as a question.

"Of course not. As annoying as he can be, he is our brother. Why in our father's good and gracious name would we hurt him?" He shook his head and turned away from her.

Eva frowned at the back of his head. Wait. She did have a gun, didn't she? Yes, there it was in her hand, aimed at him, ready to fire. Why the hell wasn't he reacting? Why was he acting as if she posed no threat to him at all?

"You're not going to hurt me either, Stronzo." She squeezed the trigger.

He disappeared.

She gasped as a hand materialised out of thin air and knocked the gun up just as it fired, sending the bullet blasting into the ceiling, and another hand grasped her throat, fingers pressing into it and sending pain radiating through her bones.

Those fingers shifted, closing over her jaw, and Keras pulled her head down as his lips found her right ear.

"See him," he whispered into it, his voice a dark menacing snarl that sent a cold shiver down her spine as she looked at Valen. "He is the only reason you are still alive. Not the information you have in this head I could pick apart in seconds, or that pathetic weapon in your hand. *Him*."

"Why?" That question trembled on her lips.

"Because something tells me alcohol is not the reason he just tried to destroy this bar."

The black-haired one holding Valen's arm scowled at her, his blue eyes eerily bright in the low light.

The blond one on the other side of Valen looked across at him. "Let's take him home, Esher. Everything is good here."

They disappeared in a cloud of black smoke.

Eva stood frozen to the spot, fear like acid in her veins, her hand shaking hard against the gun.

Keras whispered into her ear, his words the most sinister and terrifying thing she had ever heard in all her years as an assassin.

"You have a lot of explaining to do."

She read between the lines to the threat hidden within.

If he didn't like what she had to say, she was a dead woman.

CHAPTER 10

Green splashed across his vision. Black intersected it. Gold made it shine.

Crimson stained it.

Twin orbs of that dreadful scarlet hovered before him, trembling against the hazy backdrop of emerald, obsidian and sunshine.

Light that had left this world.

But wasn't destined for the next.

Cold stole through him, numbing his flesh, chilling his bones. It took everything from him at first, washing it all away, leaving nothing.

Nothing.

Crimson.

It wavered before his eyes, out of focus, suspended above the dying light.

A light that had left *his* world.

Plunged it into darkness.

Fire began in the hollow pit of his chest, born of the fragile emotions piecing themselves back together. Piecing him back together.

But in a new way.

The male they constructed from the scattered remnants her departure had left behind knew nothing of the light. He embraced the dark, the violence and the fury.

The desperate need for vengeance.

They had taken her from him.

They had failed.

The scarlet orbs grew smaller, seemed to burn brighter, gold streaks swirling around them now. The scattered pieces gathered faster, racing to finish their dark work.

The god they constructed had no light, no love. Not a single drop left for this world or those in it.

Because this world had taken everything from him.

It had taken her.

It had failed him.

The green, black and fading gold dropped away and darkness swallowed it, leaving only the burning crimson and the harsh swift arcs of lightning that chased around them.

They would pay.

White burst into life around him, chasing back the darkness, but it wasn't light. It wasn't her.

She was gone.

He blinked slowly as he pivoted on his heel and everything came into focus.

The white glistening marble columns that enclosed him in a circle. The dazzling green fields that surrounded it. The endless blue sky. All things she would never see again.

The dais in front of him. The three females huddled there. The blood on his hands.

Her blood.

Soon it would be theirs.

Because they had failed her.

Darkness poured through him, oily and thick, consuming all of him and driving out the last of the light. There would be only darkness on this day.

Only death.

The youngest female crawled forwards, fear written in her blue eyes as she reached a hand out to him, the white robes she wore pooling around her, cinched with gold at her waist.

Gold.

He despised that colour now. It no longer had the lustre or brought the light he had once enjoyed.

Now it was the colour of death.

"Please," she whispered, hoarse and broken. Weak.

They never should have been allowed to protect her.

Their favour meant nothing.

He turned his gaze away from her and shut out her cries for mercy, her pathetic whimpers, and stared off into the distance, to the point where green fields met blue skies. She should have been somewhere like this. She should have been allowed to go to the blessed isles.

She should have been allowed to live.

"You decided your fate when you decided hers." He flicked his hand towards Clotho and her scream rang in his ears, echoed around the mountain and sent deep pleasure rolling down his spine.

The sharp tang of his power filled the air, charged it as he unleashed it all on her.

A swift death.

The other two wouldn't be as lucky.

His mercy had just run dry.

Lachesis made the mistake of trying to escape.

He was on her in a heartbeat, driving her into the ground and tearing at her with claws he didn't recognise, mind pounding with a dark urge that controlled him, stole away any command of his body, refusing to release him until it was satisfied. Crimson splashed across white and gold, his vision turning hazy as he slashed at her flesh.

She had to pay.

Her struggle ceased and he canted his head and frowned down at her, confused. He shook her, growled as he realised she was dead, and turned to face the remaining fate.

She stood in the middle of the temple, robes fluttering in the breeze that tousled her snow-white hair. Worn, creased hands folded gently in front of her, and her dim grey eyes held his, showing no fear.

Only acceptance.

"Valen," she murmured, her voice thin and reedy. "It was not our doing."

He knew that.

But someone had to pay.

He rose to his feet and came to face her. Crimson rolled down the hard plates of his chest piece, soaking into the black leather and tainting the gold trim. The leather of his right vambrace creaked as he moved his arm and closed his fingers over the hilt of the sword hanging from his left hip. The sound of metal sliding against metal broke the silence as he drew the blade, felt the weight of it in his grip and it was the weight of his responsibility, a heavy burden to bear but one he would shoulder nonetheless.

For her.

His eyes stung, vision blurring again, and he blinked, frowned as twin streaks of heat formed on his cheeks and realised that it hadn't been rage blinding him when he had sat with her lifeless body, or when he had killed Lachesis.

It had been tears.

He rubbed the back of his left hand across his face, not caring when the black leather plates that protected the back of it caught his nose and hurt, because nothing could eclipse the pain that now lived in his heart.

Eternal.

He flexed his fingers around the hilt of the sword, felt it vibrate with his power as it became part of him, and stormed towards the remaining fate.

Atropos bowed her head and held her arms out to him.

He roared, unleashing all the pain and fury inside him, stepped and appeared right in front of her.

Her cloudy eyes widened. Her lips parted on a shocked gasp.

Valen caught her as she slumped and gently laid her down in the middle of the temple, numbness rushing in to dull the fierce pain and his anger, leaving him hollow inside.

"He will not allow this," she whispered.

He bowed his head, his golden hair sweeping forwards to brush his cheeks. The mark on the left side of his face and neck burned, as if warning him that the one she spoke of was already aware of what he had done.

"I know," he murmured. "But it had to be done."

Her breath left her on a sigh.

Silence fell.

He stood slowly, grimacing as his sword grated against bone and slid back through flesh, turning the air thick with the stench of blood.

He stared down at the old fate where she lay, crimson pooling outwards from beneath her and blossoming on the front of her white robe. He carefully cleaned his blade and sheathed it, the dull feeling in his chest growing heavier as he gazed upon her.

"It had to be done." He turned away from her, pivoting slowly on his heel to face the opposite direction, his gaze falling on the mountains that rose in the distance to pierce the endless blue sky. "It has to be done."

Someone had to pay.

The Moirai hadn't been the only ones to fail her.

The dark urge returned, a cold blast that stole the last of the heat from him, filling him with only ice and pain, and a terrible need for vengeance. It wasn't sated.

Wouldn't be until it was done.

He stalked forwards, his long strides gaining pace as he closed the distance between him and the mountain.

It had to be done. Even when he knew it would only end in his death.

The agony churning inside him, the pain and the fury, the despair, all reached boiling point as he left the temple behind and sprinted across the velvet green grass towards Mount Olympus. It was too much. It swallowed him, stole control and made him a slave to it, to the dark and terrible need, the all-consuming desire for revenge.

On a violent bellow, he stepped into the darkness of the Underworld and out into the temple that topped the mountain, looking down on everything. Everyone.

The temple of his uncle.

Zeus.

Valen glared at him where he stood in the centre of the temple's grand hall, his thigh-length white robes crisp and perfect beneath his gold armour, while Valen's own armour bore her blood and that of the Moirai, his skin stained crimson. While Valen struggled to breathe, was consumed by emotions that bombarded him, Zeus's worn face was set in an expression that revealed no shred of feeling, his golden eyes emotionless as they watched him from beneath the delicate twisted band of his crown.

How could the bastard be so calm?

How could he stand there and do nothing?

Valen clenched his hands into fists at his sides, squeezed them so tightly his arms shook as he wrestled for control, tried to claw back some sanity and drive back the darkness that pushed him to attack. His chest heaved with each hard breath he drew as he fought the pain that threatened to tear him apart.

It was no use.

That pain scattered the pieces of himself he had clawed back together and the lure of the darkness was too powerful to resist. Rage boiled in his veins, stoked by seeing his uncle unaffected by her death, so fierce now he felt he would burst if he didn't let it out, didn't let it consume him and control him.

He needed it out.

He unleashed a war-cry that echoed around the huge temple and threw his right hand forwards, launching a white-purple bolt of lightning at his uncle.

Zeus easily deflected it with a casual sweep of his left hand, sending it shooting towards the row of thick white marble columns to Valen's right.

That only served to infuriate him even more.

He shot another bolt and then another at Zeus, and again his uncle deflected them as if they were nothing. If he couldn't land a distance attack, there was only one thing he could do. He blinked away the tears and ran at his uncle.

Zeus's golden eyes widened.

Valen slammed his right shoulder into the bastard's gut before he could move, grunted as the gold armour he wore over his short white robes sent fierce hot pain rolling down his arm and back, and gritted his teeth against it as he drove forwards. If Zeus was going to deflect everything he threw at him, he would just have to get close enough to him that he wouldn't have time to defend himself.

Zeus grunted as his back hit one of the towering marble columns and Valen roared as he pressed his hands to his uncle's chest and unleashed everything he had. Lightning shot from his palms, spreading in sharp jagged tendrils across the gold plates of Zeus's armour. The bastard finally reacted, throwing his head back and bellowing as lightning tore through him.

He would make his uncle feel the same pain as he did, wouldn't stop until he felt as battered and broken inside.

Valen gritted his teeth and pressed harder against Zeus's chest, unleashed more of his power, not relenting even when his head turned and limbs shook. If it took everything he had to make his uncle pay, then he would give it. He would keep giving it until it killed him.

For her.

Something firm pressed against his chest.

He looked down, frowned at the sun-kissed skin of the familiar hand plastered against his breastplate.

Screamed as he was sent flying backwards so fast the world was a blur, and then it erupted in pain. White-hot agony. Every inch of him blazed with it as he smashed through a column and hit the floor, sliding across it. The heavy top half of the column broke away from the ceiling and struck the marble floor, shaking it just as he came to a halt. He clenched his jaw against the pain pulsing through him like a wave of lightning strikes and fought to get it back under control so he could finish what he had started.

When it had dulled to a more manageable level, he grunted and rolled onto his front, grimaced as he pressed his hands into the cold white marble floor and every part of him ached in protest, another thousand hot needles pricking his skin.

He pushed through the pain and eased up onto his knees.

Froze when he saw white leather boots in his vision, the elaborate gold plates affixed to them reflecting his face back at him.

His eyes were black.

His canines little more than fangs.

He shook away the fear that gripped him and steeled himself.

Even if the darkness consumed him entirely, he wouldn't stop.

He looked away from his reflection and sat back on his heels.

Zeus towered over him, his golden eyes ablaze and narrowed on him, the soft waves of his dark brown hair curling around the nape of his neck and brushing his forehead, slipped from his delicate gold crown that formed a band around his head.

"Will you stop?" His uncle's deep voice boomed around the temple.

Valen shook his head.

He couldn't, even when he knew his uncle would kill him, was too powerful for him to defeat. The pain was too much, burned too fiercely in his soul, blazing in his heart. It demanded retribution.

It demanded blood.

It demanded that others suffered as much as he was.

"There has already been enough suffering… wrought by your own hands, Nephew."

"Get out of my head!" Valen sprang at him and slammed his right fist hard into his jaw, snapping his head to his right.

Zeus shifted his right foot back to brace himself and that was the only reaction Valen got from the bastard.

He didn't understand how Zeus could be so calm. His niece was dead. Why didn't it rake at him as fiercely as it killed Valen? Didn't his uncle give a damn about her?

Clearly not.

Zeus had stood by and allowed her to die after all. He had let it happen. He had stood there and had done nothing.

It was his fault too.

Valen snarled, all the darkness of the Underworld pouring through him, bleeding from his hands and his skin, mingling with his lightning as it sparked from his fingers.

He screamed and flew at his uncle, lost to the pain and the darkness, a slave to his need to satisfy them both. He lashed out with his right hand, catching Zeus with a whip made of pure lightning. It snapped and cracked as it struck Zeus's chest, knocking him backwards. Zeus's face darkened, his golden eyes flashing brightly as power sparked from his hands.

Lightning to match Valen's.

Zeus drew his hand through the air and golden arcs of lightning struck all across the temple. Valen hurled himself forwards as one shot from the ceiling directly above him, rolled across the white marble and came onto his feet. He snarled and lashed out with his white-purple whip again, sparks flying from it as it cut through the golden bolts crashing down all around him. The blazing arc of his own power hit a sheer wall of crackling gold before it could strike Zeus down.

Zeus flicked his right hand towards Valen.

Valen stepped, dodging the attack, and appeared on the other side of the temple just as the golden bolt struck the wall where he had been and shards of marble exploded outwards, raining down in a misty haze of dust.

He grinned and swept his left hand up in a fast arc. White-purple bolts of lightning shot up from the marble floor, growing larger as they neared Zeus, racing towards him in a wave. Zeus turned and sidestepped, and Valen growled as the attack rolled straight past him.

That growl was short-lived.

It became a roar of agony as a bright streak of gold struck him in his chest and sent him flying across the room again. The scent of singed leather filled his nostrils and he cried out again as fire seared his chest, the metal of his breastplate burning against his bare skin. He hit the wall hard, grunted and dropped to the floor, landing face first on the cool marble, breathing hard and crippled by pain as he desperately clawed at his chest piece, trying to get it off him. The scent of burning flesh joined that of the leather.

He fumbled with the first clasp.

Arched forwards and screamed in pain as another bolt seared him, striking hard from above and sending electricity pouring through his body.

The tinny taste of blood flooded his mouth. The odour of it filled his nose.

The lightning abated.

Valen wheezed through burning lungs, shaking on his side on the floor, sparks of electricity skittering over his skin and snapping at his flesh as his body fought to purge the lightning strike.

His ears rang, the sound oddly watery, and heat ran from his left ear, trickled and tickled and then dripped to the floor.

That same liquid threatened to fill his battered lungs, crawled up his throat and past broken lips.

Boots appeared in his hazy vision and he trembled as he tried to look up at their owner. He had to move. He had to finish this. He gritted his teeth and growled in despair as he found he couldn't, his body refusing to respond to his command, disobeying the dark need that still poured through him and urged him to destroy.

He managed to lift his eyes to his uncle's face.

There was no mercy in those golden eyes.

No shred of pain.

Zeus didn't care if he died, just as he didn't care that she was gone.

Tears burned Valen's eyes, hatred blazing in his veins, directed at himself now, stoked by the anger that flowed through him and screamed that he was weak.

He had failed.

He hadn't been able to make those who had failed his sister pay their due. It was going to end here for him.

It was going to end before he could see her safely home to the blessed isle where she belonged.

Zeus raised his right fist and a golden bolt appeared in it, crackling and sizzling as he held it fast.

It was going to end here.

Now.

"Zeus!" The female voice rang around the damaged temple, in Valen's broken ears.

A flicker of light appeared in the darkness within him.

Small at first, nothing more than a pinprick in the inky black, but it grew as her voice reached his ears, and his heart, soothing them both.

"I beseech you... do not take Valen from me too."

Zeus looked across at the female, a flicker of hurt finally showing in his eyes.

"Forgive him," she whispered and moved closer, near enough that Valen could feel her warmth and bathed in her light, and the desperate need to destroy gave way to a fierce need to see her.

She stepped into view, hair the colour of blood tumbling in soft waves around pale slender shoulders, her skin drained of its usual colour, turned to snow. Dark circles shaded her normally luminous green eyes. Black framed her delicate body, as if she had been wrapped in darkness, the same darkness that burned inside him and fought back against the light.

A stark contrast to the pale green and white robes she usually wore.

The colour of mourning.

Pain filled him again, fiercer than ever, and he ground his teeth and cried out, desperate to unleash it, desperate for his broken body to respond to his commands, to his burning need to avenge his sister.

Persephone turned tear-filled eyes down at him and that need only grew stronger, but in turn his body seemed to grow weaker, unable to bear the exertion of his desire to move let alone fuel such a thing.

A tear slipped onto her cheek, a pure diamond, and she looked back at his uncle.

"Forgive my son." She clenched her hands in front of her chest and her fine eyebrows furrowed, her rosy lips trembling as she spoke. "He is angry. He is hurt by the loss of his sister. We all are… but Valen is so passionate… so much like you. He cannot hold back that pain as the others can. It is in his nature to unleash it, and that is all he has done."

Zeus's golden eyes turned cold. "What he has done is murder the Moirai."

"And that is something you can undo," she said without inflection, without a single shred of anger in her voice, but Valen could see it in his mother. She was seething, burning with pain just as he was. She stepped closer to Zeus, her green eyes darker than Valen had ever seen them, and brambles grew from around her feet, twisted black vines of thorns that spoke of her pain. Her suffering. "But you will not be able to undo the damage you will cause if you take Valen from me too. If you take him from Hades. There will be no coming back from that."

The darkness in her voice and in her eyes shocked Valen.

What had become of the gentle creature he loved so deeply?

She had transformed into a warrior carved from the same material as he was, hardened by grief and determination.

Zeus stared at her.

Second stretched into minutes, and then into an eternity.

His uncle lowered his hand and the bolt faded from it.

It was over. Valen had failed.

Zeus would restore the Moirai, and everything Valen had done would be for nothing. His sister was still dead and no one had paid for that crime.

His uncle shifted his gaze down to him.

"Love drove you to this, so it is love I will take from you." Zeus eased down to crouch beside him and Valen flinched as he pushed him onto his back and placed his hand against the left side of his face. "You will never know it again."

Valen screamed as fire blazed down the left side of his face, unable to move as it seared him and the acrid stench of burning flesh filled his lungs once more. The flames spread, consuming his neck, eating away at him, and darkness threatened to rise and swallow him.

Zeus's words rang in his ears as he stared up at him and saw only malice and hatred in his uncle's eyes.

"Not even those who once favoured you will love you now."

Valen shook his head, silently pleading his uncle not to do it, not to take that from him. He had been wrong.

Someone was paying for what had happened.
He was.

CHAPTER 11

Valen shot up in bed, breathing hard, his hand pressed against the left side of his face and his neck.

Where his favour mark had once been.

His racing heart slowly steadied, panic and pain gradually flowing from him and restoring his balance, and the world came into focus around him.

He frowned at the row of wooden wardrobes that took up the entire wall opposite him, and then across to his left at the windows that punctuated the pale yellow wall and revealed a rainy day in Rome. His bedroom. He was home.

Not on Mount Olympus.

He hunched forwards, pulled his knees up beneath the white sheets and buried his head in them as he breathed, narrowing the world back down so he could settle his tumultuous feelings and calm his body and mind.

The scar on the left side of his face throbbed as if it had just happened and he held it, willed his body to shut down the pain faster because he couldn't deal with it right now.

He hated the nightmares.

The memories that refused to leave him.

They always made him feel like shit.

A niggling voice at the back of his mind said the nightmare he had just lived through wasn't the only reason he felt as if someone had just dragged him through the river Acheron by his ankles.

He tried to recall what had happened before the nightmare.

Groaned as it came back to him and held his head, squeezing it hard. If he was lucky, it would burst under the pressure and he wouldn't have to deal with the inevitable fallout.

Voices travelled into the room from the corridor to his right, ripping another low moan of despair from him. Seemed he didn't even have time to gather his shit before the storm hit him. His brothers were here, probably waiting for him to wake up so they could tear him a new one or two.

Maybe even disown him entirely this time.

Valen flopped back on the bed. He was damned if he was going out there until he was good and ready, or they came to get him. He didn't need a confrontation right now, when his head was pounding and his emotions were all over the place, his bastard mind finding it funny to keep hurling snippets of his nightmare at him whenever he started to calm down, throwing him back into turmoil.

He caught a flash of Zeus staring down at him and his scar burned hotter.

He rubbed at it, frowning at the ceiling and cursing his uncle.

The debate grew more heated, and he tuned into it because he figured he might as well hear what they were yelling about him. It was always good to prepare for battle, and what better way to prepare was there than knowing exactly what was going to get thrown at you?

It was certainly a good way to kill the time it would take them to decide to check on him and bring the fight to him.

"It could have been worse. It could have been speed, or coke, or whatever that shit is that mortals love putting in their bodies." Ares sounded more angry than usual. Megan clearly wasn't seeing to his needs enough to bring all that testosterone down to a manageable level.

Keras snapped back. "It is bad enough. A city without its guardian is a vulnerable one. We need to know what we are dealing with here."

Valen cringed. He was in deep shit. Deeper than normal. Keras sounded ready to kick him back to the Underworld for an audience with their father.

Or teleport him to Mount Olympus.

Zeus's words rang in his ears, a continuation of the punishment he had thankfully woken up in the middle of only to find himself plunged into another nightmare situation.

I banish you from Mount Olympus.

On penalty of death.

He listened harder, trying to detect just how pissed Keras was with him. He didn't think his oldest brother would go so far as to dump him on Mount Olympus, a place he wasn't allowed to go under any circumstances, but he wasn't one hundred percent certain.

Which sucked.

Love drove you to this, so it is love I will take from you.

A familiar female voice pierced his heart, coming from the other room, rising above his brothers' argument.

You will never know it again.

Valen snorted at that. As if he needed the reminder. He lived with it every day, every second he was awake and even in his sleep. He was bone-deep aware of the curse his uncle had placed on him.

No one could love him.

Not even her.

"And I've told you a thousand times... I will only speak with Valen."

She would only speak with him.

He wished his stupid chest hadn't warmed in response to that. What it contained clearly hadn't received the message she had thrown at it loud and clear the other morning. She wasn't interested in him.

"She just isn't going to change her tune." Ares again. "There's no point in pressing her."

Marek's warm, deep voice joined the din, a touch of amusement in it that had Valen straining to hear what he was saying. "... Clever. I'll give her that. What better way to ensure her survival than to make us wait until Valen is awake?"

That wasn't amusement in his voice.

It was admiration.

Valen flew from the bed, tossing the covers across the room, and dragged his black jeans on. He buttoned them as he stormed into the wood-panelled corridor, darkness swirling through his veins, pouring into his soul.

A snarl curled from his lips.

The room ahead of him fell silent.

His mood plummeted faster when he scanned the room, registering Ares, Marek and Keras all standing on the left side of it near the bookcases that lined the wall between the windows and the fireplace, and then Eva opposite them on the black leather couch in front of him.

Guarded.

Her guard was Megan, but it was still a fucking guard.

He supposed it was better than finding one of his brothers sitting with her on the couch. He would have lost his shit if he had seen that. As it was, he wanted to kill Marek for daring to speak about Eva with admiration in his fucking voice.

He snapped his focus to the brunet bastard.

Marek eased a step back and held his hands up at his sides, causing the rolled up sleeves of his charcoal linen shirt to tug back against his toned, tanned forearms. "Easy."

"Fuck easy." He stormed towards him, unable to contain the urge rolling through him, a dark desire to acquaint his brother's head with the wall.

Keras stepped in front of him. "I should have known you would be the same after you woke up. Always looking for a fight. Do you never consider the consequences of your actions?"

Valen glared at him. He wanted to say fuck the consequences too, but Keras had that look in his green eyes, that one Valen knew meant trouble. They were empty. No trace of feeling in them.

It was like looking into a void.

A carcass without a soul inside it.

It moved, spoke, and acted like Keras, but something was wrong with it.

Something dangerous.

He backed off a step, turned his glare on Marek so his brother got the message, and then scrubbed a hand over his hair, shoving the irritating lengths out of his face.

He glanced over his shoulder at Eva. Her wide blue eyes ran over him, back and forth, up and down, heating him by degrees until he was burning inside. There wasn't a trace of desire in them though, not as there had been on the dance floor. The only emotion he could read in their incredible tranquil depths was surprise.

He couldn't blame her.

He remembered enough about what had happened back at the bar to recall that he had been injured, some of those cuts severe in mortal terms, and now those wounds were gone, not even a scar remaining.

Keras sighed.

Valen braced himself.

"Do you have any idea the damage you might have caused?" his brother said, that calm tone setting him even more on edge. Valen looked back at him. A flicker of darkness crossed Keras's green eyes, a brief shadow, the only hint that he was feeling anything in there—that there was still a soul left in his body. "If we hadn't arrived when we had… gods, Valen… what in our father's good and gracious name were you thinking? Were you even thinking?"

Valen waited, could see it coming, brewing on the horizon in his brother's eyes. Those emotions his brother kept in check so well were boiling now, writhing and seething, slowly breaking free of the hold he had on them.

"No excuses?" Keras bit out and his eyes finally brightened, molten emeralds flecked with gold and silver. "Just like you I suppose. You do something rash... something stupid... and expect us to clean up the mess. We end up being the ones who have to piece everything back together again because you do not give a damn what happens. You do not give a damn about anything."

Valen held his gaze, refusing to look away, even when he wanted to.

He deserved his brother's wrath, because he had well and truly fucked up this time. He would take it like a champ, but no amount of harsh words would be punishment enough for his crime.

Part of him wished Keras would lose it too, would turn this battle of words into one involving fists, but his damned brother was in control today.

"I had information and—" Eva cut herself off when Keras turned cold eyes on her.

She had information and she only wanted to give it to Valen.

He found that oddly pleasing, as if she trusted him. Gods only knew why. He was the last person in the world anyone should trust.

He was the last person in the world anyone *would* trust.

Keras made that clear as he laid the accusations at his feet, and his two other brothers joined in.

"It was stupid, Valen, and you know it. You know the rules." Ares this time, and Valen wanted to fly at him but he held his ground, clenched his fists at his sides and kept taking it.

"Stupid does seem to be his middle name at times, but I think we should—" A brave attempt by Marek to calm the situation, exactly what Valen expected from him but he could have at least not insulted him at the same time.

"Not stupid," Keras interjected. "He knows what he is doing when he does it. He knew the reason we are not allowed to drink alcohol. He always knows exactly what he is doing, and what the consequences will be and he does it anyway."

His oldest brother stared him down.

"You act without thinking." Keras stepped towards him, black bleeding across his irises. "You always have... and look where it gets you. You break the rules and we all pay for it. You are the same now as you were back then. Gods, some days I am glad Calindria is not in the blessed isle to see what you have become."

Ares gasped. Marek stared at Keras in disbelief.

Valen staggered back a step, heart racing, blood pounding in his ears, his eyes wide as he took that verbal blow to his chest, a knife that his brother seemed to take pleasure in plunging into his heart.

He flicked a glance down at Eva and caught the fury in her blue eyes as she glared at Keras, but another emotion overshadowed it as she shifted to look at him.

Disappointment.

He took another step back, unable to breathe as she twisted the knife in his heart. It was too much.

She already looked at him the same way as his family did.

His mother was wrong.
He *was* cursed.
No one could ever love him.
He closed his eyes and stepped.

CHAPTER 12

The fact that Valen had just disappeared in a black swirl of smoke should have freaked Eva out, but she was too angry with his brothers, too riled by the verbal barbs they had thrown at him, and a little mad at Valen too for not defending himself and telling them the truth.

She shot to her feet, her legs shaking as Keras's impassive green eyes landed on her, awareness that he could easily kill her despite all of her training rushing through every inch of her. Anger pushed all fear to the back of her mind though and gave her the strength to give him a piece of it.

"He drank it because of me!"

Ares's dark eyebrows shot up. Marek looked equally as surprised.

Keras's expression didn't shift to show a single jot of emotion.

She made a low growling noise and paced around the couch, trying to work off some of her energy before she did something stupid like unleash it on him. Valen deserved a good smack around the head too.

Why hadn't he fought his brothers? Why had he let them say all that shit about him to his face without putting up a fight or setting them straight?

She looked at them where they formed a rough line, their backs to the windows that revealed a rain-swept Rome.

They hadn't exactly given him a chance to defend himself and they had cut her off when she had tried to help him. Maybe they were always this way with him and it was easier for him to take it.

Or maybe he felt he deserved it.

"If he drank it because of you, why did he not say that?" Keras broke the thick silence and she glared at him, itching to snatch her guns off the side table where he had placed them after taking them away from her and stick one where the sun didn't shine.

"You didn't give him a chance!" She almost took a step towards him, reined herself in at the last second and clenched her fists instead. "You had already made up your mind about him, hadn't you? Anything he said wouldn't have made a shit of difference."

She shook her head as she thought about how he had looked, the pain that had been in his eyes when he had glanced at her. He hid it well, had taken all their abuse without flinching, but Keras had managed to strike something locked deep within Valen and he had struck it hard.

He had hurt him.

His own brother.

Memories flickered in the back of her mind, a dim past she didn't want to recall, an argument that echoed in her ears and then faded as she mastered her emotions again. Her past was just that. It was over. What had happened then meant nothing now. Her family were gone, left in that dim memory, and she was glad of it.

They had only caused her pain.

Just as Valen's family only hurt him.

Her fists shook at her sides, the pain of her past mingling with the present, blurring together to stoke her anger to a dangerous new level, ratcheting it up until she was perilously close to losing her temper.

She stared at Marek, and then Ares, and finally Keras, hoping her words hit their mark.

"You act as though he's fucked up... if he is... then it is all your faults. You don't know him at all. You don't see the hurt, do you?" She narrowed her eyes on Keras and bit out, "You don't see his pain."

She turned on her heel and stormed away, heading for the exit.

Someone grabbed her and she caught their hand, twisted it off her and shoved, sending him staggering backwards into the side of the couch. Marek. He huffed and tried to grab her again.

"Let her go."

He froze as Keras's command rang through the room.

Eva looked back at the bastard. Maybe she had been wrong. Keras took the crown from Benares. He was the king when it came to arseholes.

He sighed, raked long fingers through his wild black hair, and actually dared to look genuinely sorry.

"I will find Valen and bring him back... if you will stay."

Eva shook her head, almost laughed at that. He only wanted her to stay because she had information. He didn't really care about her, or Valen.

"Don't bother. Leave Valen alone... I'll find him myself." She snatched her leather jacket from the back of the couch, strode away and paused at the door with the handle in her grasp. She didn't look back at him. "Some brothers you all are. You make me glad I no longer have a family."

She yanked the door open and slammed it behind her, and broke into a dead sprint before any of them could think to stop her.

She took the steps quickly, heart wrenching up into her throat when she missed one and almost fell. She grabbed the banister and managed to stop herself, and sank to her backside on the steps as it dawned on her.

She wasn't sure where to start looking for Valen.

She couldn't go to the bar as it had been closed off by the police, and the club he normally frequented wouldn't be open. She thought about the hill where she had seen him a few times while she had been tailing him to gather information on him. Would he be there?

She didn't want to think too hard about the things she had seen, because she felt as if she was going mad whenever she tried to make sense of them, but if someone could theoretically teleport, would there be a limit to the distance they could cover?

Could he have teleported to the hill?

Her stomach turned and she rubbed it, trying to get it to settle, and vowed not to think about teleporting people and bizarre powers any more today.

Even if he could magically zip from one place to another, she couldn't.

If she was going to get to the hill, then first she needed to get home.

It was a starting point, and she badly needed one right now, needed a direction so she felt as if she was doing something, moving forwards rather than standing still.

Moving closer to him again.

She pushed onto her feet and made it to the foyer of the building, and then out into the street. Rain poured down, saturating her in seconds. The weather had been atrocious since they had brought Valen home over a day ago. Her stomach turned again, the memory of how she had gotten there making her want to vomit. She pushed it out of her mind and told herself she had imagined it.

One of them hadn't grabbed her and teleported with her.

She flagged a taxi and slid into the back seat.

A whole damn day she had sat in that living room with his brothers watching her. The woman, Megan, had been kind, taking care of her and making sure she ate something. The men had just glared at her and discussed Valen.

Eva sighed and rested her head against the window of the cab, watching the streets fly past.

They had been so different.

There had been concern in their voices, even in Keras's. Where had those feelings of warmth gone when Valen had woken up and come into the room?

They had given her the impression they cared about their brother, and then they had shown her just how wrong she had been about them.

They were just like every other family.

Just like the one she had left behind.

Full of betrayal and false feelings.

The sensation that had been growing inside her from the moment she had started on her mission and first set eyes on Valen came into focus, revealing itself to her at last.

Kinship.

The feeling that he had a similar soul to hers, a similar story behind his journey into the darkness.

That they were one and the same.

The urge to find him grew stronger, pressing at her, and she quickly exited the taxi as it pulled up outside her apartment building and hurried across the cobblestones of the square to it, intent on finding him and letting him know that no matter what he thought, he wasn't alone.

Eva punched in the code on the silver box beside the arched entrance, waited for the buzz and pushed the small gate set into the huge arched wooden doors open. She stepped over the threshold and went to close it behind her.

Blinked.

Valen stood in the middle of the square, rain rolling down his bare chest, a distant empty look in his golden eyes.

"You promised me information." Those words had a hollow ring to them too, as if he wasn't quite with her.

Was it because of the things his brothers had said to him?

Who was Calindria and what had happened to her?

The hurt she spied hidden beyond the emptiness in his eyes told her not to ask, because that spot was still sore from Keras's attack on it.

"Did you track me here?" She leaned out of the entrance and looked around the square.

No sign of his brothers.

"I wouldn't leave you alone with them." Because he didn't trust them with her. It was all there in his eyes for her to read.

He had come flying out of his bedroom to attack Marek, and she wanted to ask why, replayed what his brother had said just before he had appeared and found no reason for him to have reacted to it. Marek had merely sounded impressed that she was savvy enough to know having Valen around when she gave them all the information she had was a wise thing to do, a way of stopping them from disposing of her when she was no longer useful to them.

Or was it because Marek had sounded impressed with her that Valen had launched that attack?

His eyes narrowed on her from across the small square, heating her in the way she feared they always would when he looked at her like that, as if she belonged to him.

"You followed me," she whispered, a little breathless.

Because he had wanted to protect her. He had wanted to protect what he viewed as his.

"It wasn't difficult. Far too easy in fact. You owe me information." He walked up the slight incline towards her, his bare feet silent on the dark cobblestones, and stopped close to her, towering over her in a way that forced her to tip her head back to keep her eyes locked on his. His golden eyes darkened, heating her outwards from her chest, and she secretly sucked in a breath to steady herself. He lowered his head, until his mouth hovered barely an inch from hers, and whispered, "I want it now."

Eva swallowed hard.

He wanted it.

She felt like an idiot when he moved back a step and it hit her what *it* was.

Information. That was all he wanted from her. Nothing else.

His eyes were cold again, the heat that had been in them erased, as if it had never existed.

Was any of this real, or was she dreaming it all? It felt more like a nightmare, one that was twisting her in knots and getting stranger by the second.

She never should have taken the job.

She looked up at Valen, into golden eyes that shone in the low light, a fierce possessive fire lighting them up again as he gazed down at her.

But then she never would have met him.

Eva lifted her hand without thinking and lightly feathered her fingers over the left side of his face.

He scowled and knocked her hand away, and distanced himself, the darkness back in his eyes, the heat destroyed by her carelessness this time.

She should have known he wouldn't allow her to touch that part of him, not as he had the other woman—his mother.

He looked off to his right.

Panic lanced her.

"Wait."

His golden eyes slid towards her and his eyebrow rose. She had surprised him with that outburst and command.

She had surprised herself too.

It wasn't like her to act this way, to let her emotions control her like this. She had spent years honing her skills as an assassin, including the ability to keep her heart shielded and feelings in check, distancing herself from the world so she could do her job.

Valen had undone all of that in a matter of days.

In a single moment.

The very second she had come into contact with him that night in front of the Pantheon.

He looked as though he might leave anyway, as if he felt as uncomfortable as she did, out of sorts and traversing unknown waters. Dangerous waters. She wasn't sure how to process what was happening either, but she wasn't going to run away from it.

She wasn't that sort of woman.

She also wasn't the sort of woman who made a deal and then backed out of it.

"I owe you information." It was a reasonable excuse for wanting him to stay. She frowned as a group of women eyed him as they walked past and began talking amongst themselves, whispering things that she couldn't hear but could guess at. It wasn't difficult. He was standing bare-chested in the middle of the square, every inch of his delicious honed torso on view. It was bound to draw attention from female eyes, and stir desire in some of them. A dark urge to grab his arm and yank him into her apartment building, away from the eyes of other women, rushed through her and she barely tamped down that desire. "Come inside."

It was better than grabbing him, but he reacted much the same, both eyebrows snapping up and his golden eyes going wide as he looked from her to the building and back again. His pupils dilated, but the desire that shone in them lasted barely a second before he had it under control and crushed out of existence.

"Fine," he snapped and sauntered towards her, a sensual, almost predatory gait to his step. Her body heated, skin flushing beneath her clothes, and her mind raced forwards, conjuring images of him gathering her into his arms and kissing her as he had back in his apartment. He stopped right in front of her, looked down into her eyes, and the coldness in them hurled her out of her fantasies and back to cruel reality. "I thought you wanted to let me in."

She did, and not only into her apartment. A foolish endeavour. They were assassins, born to lead a lonely life, and getting involved with him would only make it more difficult on her. Remembering the nights she passed in his arms before he inevitably left her, the stolen moments they had shared, wouldn't bring her comfort when she was alone again.

They would only torment her.

Eva stepped aside and let him past, and closed the door behind him, shutting out the women with their prying eyes.

She turned around and found herself face to face with Valen.

In the low light, his eyes seemed to glow as he looked down at her, a softness to them that hadn't been there a moment ago and was gone when he blinked.

"It's probably best we do this in my apartment." She wasn't sure it was the greatest idea, not when his eyes widened slightly, and not when they followed that by narrowing on her in suspicion.

God, she couldn't make sense of him. He sent her in circles, had her spinning so quickly she wasn't sure what was up and what was down. One second he was looking at her as if he might die if she stopped kissing him, if she distanced herself, and the next he was looking at her as if she might be the one to kill him and he felt nothing when he was around her.

She pushed her unruly emotions back down, brought up her guards to form a wall around her heart, and crossed the courtyard, heading for the door into the building.

Valen tailed her, threatening to undo all her hard work to control her feelings and slip into a more business-like gear when he raked his eyes over her and she felt it, that hot zing that went through her whenever he looked at her. It followed the path of his gaze, forming small lightning strikes over her curves.

Eva had half a mind to turn on him and tell him to stop.

She couldn't do this. She wouldn't.

She was an assassin.

She wasn't just another woman for him to bed and leave either. She never had been able to play that way. Ever since she had first awoken as a woman, had her first kiss with a boy at the village near where she had grown up, she had been deadly serious about relationships, falling deep and hard for the object of her affection.

Even when she had known it would only end with her heart being broken.

This time, she felt that more keenly than ever, but Valen wouldn't only break her heart. He would tear it from her chest and take it with him when he left.

She unlocked the door and moved swiftly up the floors, a desire to get this over with and let him leave brewing inside her as her thoughts led her down dark paths.

She didn't bother to check if he was following her, and didn't slow, practically running up the stairs to the top floor. She opened the door to her apartment and stepped inside the large open plan space. One of the first things she had done on moving in had been removing the walls, creating no place where an enemy could lay in wait for her.

She kept the door to the bathroom open at all times, giving her a clear view into the space beyond her bedroom on the left side of the expansive room. A low wall separated her bedroom area from the living area in the centre of her apartment, and to her right a long island formed the barrier between it and the kitchen. Beyond the kitchen, set into the right wall, was another door. That one she kept closed because there wasn't enough room in the shallow closet for anyone to hide there. It housed her arsenal of weapons.

She crossed the room, the wooden floorboards creaking under her slight weight.

When Valen started to follow her, the noise grew louder and then suddenly stopped. A few squeaks of wood rubbing followed it and she looked back at him from the kitchen island to find him testing the floor with his bare right foot, pressing down and lifting it again, a frown on his face.

He lifted his golden eyes to meet hers. "You might want to get the floor fixed."

She smiled and shook her head, causing her short hair to tickle the nape of her neck, sensitising her skin and making her want to shiver in a good way. Or maybe that was Valen's presence and the way he was staring at her, setting her body alight and making her hyper-aware of him where he stood in her apartment, his defined chest exposed to her and stirring wicked hungers, needs that were impossible to deny when she was around him, no matter how hard she tried to control herself.

She struggled to tamp down that reaction to him and kept walking to the end of the wooden kitchen island.

"It's intentional. I picked up the idea in Japan. They call them nightingale floors. It was so they could hear any intruders who tried to enter the castles and deal with them before they could attack." She picked up the t-shirt off the pile of clothes stacked on the black granite worktop of the island, turned and tossed it across the room to him, hoping he would put it on and cover the glorious distraction that was his chest. He caught it, frowned at it and then at her. "It's yours."

He opened it up and held it out between his hands, his eyebrows rising. "You stealing my clothes now?"

She shrugged. "Mine were wet."

His eyes met hers over the top of his black t-shirt, sending a hot shiver tumbling down her spine and sending her awareness of him shooting into the stratosphere. They were dark, desire pooling in them, stirring it in her.

Was he thinking about that night?

Her breathing shortened as memories popped into her mind, replays of how he had taken care of her, and how she had repaid him.

He snapped his gaze back down to the t-shirt and put it on, covering all that wicked, alluring flesh just as she had needed him to. He muttered something and when he looked back at her, that desire was gone again.

Erased.

Was it because she had denied remembering what had happened that night?

She opened her mouth to ask him, but remembered how his brothers had treated him and the way he had acted, and other words came out instead.

"Why didn't you tell your brothers the truth?"

His golden eyes turned glacial. "I didn't come up here for this shit."

"You should have told them… but you just let them say all that crap about you… why?"

He turned his back on her. "It's none of your damned business. If you're just going to start on me, then I'm leaving."

Did he always run away from confrontations? No. She knew the answer in her heart, and with it came a realisation that hit her so hard she had to lean on the worktop for support.

He thought she was like them.

The things they had said to him had reeked of disappointment, and now she was saying things that were giving him the impression she felt the same way—that he had disappointed her.

"I just figured you would at least kick their arses like they deserved." She hoped he would look at her again, because she wanted to say something to him and he needed to see in her eyes that she wasn't lying.

He remained with his back to her.

If he wanted to do this the hard way, then she could do that, because he deserved to know the truth about his brothers.

"They're arseholes." She walked towards him, the floorboards gently creaking beneath her with each step. "Complete stronzi."

He tensed as she came up behind him, his back going rigid as her hand ghosted over it, ridiculous fear stopping her from touching him when she wanted to because she knew it would give him comfort. Hopefully her words would give him what she was too afraid to offer with a touch. She moved around him and he looked at her, a flicker of hurt in his eyes that remained when he blinked, and warmth suffused her, spreading outwards from her chest.

He wasn't hiding his feelings from her.

"They're arseholes... but they were worried about you."

The light that had been in his eyes disappeared, the warmth leaving with it, and coldness swept in as they brightened.

Not the reaction she had expected.

She had thought he would be pleased to hear that, but it hadn't gone down well at all.

He huffed and backed off a step, and she could almost see the barriers coming up, shutting her out again. "You don't know a fucking thing about my brothers. They don't give a fuck about me. Deep inside, they're probably pissed I'm not being punished or I didn't end up getting myself killed."

That was a harsh thing to say, and her heart went out to him when he looked away from her, staring off to his left towards the windows, and she realised she believed it. Every word.

He thought his brothers hated him.

"Just give me the information."

She frowned at his noble profile, cold stealing through her as he folded his arms across his chest and closed his eyes, completely shutting her out.

Very well.

Eva rubbed the sore spot between her breasts, trying to soothe the ache building there. Her stomach felt heavy again, weighed down by guilt as she pieced together everything she knew about him and built that clearer picture.

And it revealed that she had been a bitch.

She had hurt him.

He was convinced his brothers despised him, and she had the feeling that it went beyond just his family. He thought everyone hated him. Even her.

The things she had said to him had wounded him. She had denied sleeping with him and had told him in no uncertain terms it would never happen with him, that she didn't want him. She had rejected him, just as his brothers did, but just like his brothers the things she said to his face and how she felt inside were two very different things.

And just like his brothers, she was a damned bitch for behaving that way, showing him only coldness and none of the warmth he made her feel.

Making him feel as if no one could love him.

"Ares took care of you. Marek too," she whispered, afraid to say it any louder in case he turned on her and lashed out.

He was hurting, and delivering the truth to him gently would be more of a balm to his heart than hurling it at him. He might listen to her rather than rejecting her words outright. She remembered the way his mother had handled him, how gentle she had been.

Valen needed that sort of touch.

He was used to receiving the opposite though.

He frowned, his nostrils flared and he sighed. Was she getting through to him? Or was he about to explode and lash out at her?

"They care about you."

He tensed and she decided to back off, to let it go and not press him any more. Small steps. It was better to deliver it gently and slowly than make him take it all in at once. Maybe he would believe her then.

I care about you.

She kept that one to herself.

He definitely wasn't ready to hear that. She didn't need to see his eyes to know his mood was degenerating, turning dark and vicious again.

Before he could snap at her that he wanted information and that was all, she decided to give it to him.

"Benares is the man who hired me," she said and Valen opened his eyes and looked back at her, a steadiness in his gaze that soothed her nerves. Small steps. He had taken in what she had said to him about his brothers, and he believed her even if he wouldn't admit it. The hurt that had been in his beautiful eyes was gone now, but he hadn't killed it or hidden it from her. She had eased it. "Jin is… apparently his sister, which if you saw how she acted around him, you would find as stomach-turning disgusting as I do."

He almost smiled. The corners of his lips twitched, as if he wanted to do it, but his mouth remained flat and unyielding. Holding on to his anger towards her? A childish thing to do, but he was a man. Her years as an assassin had taught her that no one could hold a grudge like a man.

"I'm listening." He walked away from her, his bare feet leaving marks on her floor as their damp soles hit the warm wood.

"I have trousers," she said and he frowned over his shoulder at her. She pointed towards the end of the kitchen island and he looked there. "I borrowed those too."

"*Stole.*" He glanced at her and she didn't deny it.

Her gaze tracked him as he crossed the room and picked up the black combat trousers.

"The bathroom is—" Her words died on her lips as he shoved his wet jeans down right in front of her, giving her a glorious view of long, lean legs and damp black trunks that clung wonderfully to his crotch.

Her eyes widened as those trunks followed his jeans, revealing all of him to her.

He paused and frowned at her. "Stop staring."

She folded her arms across her chest. "This from the man with no modesty?"

He shrugged, stepped into the combat trousers and tugged them up.

His eyes locked with hers as he buttoned them.

His wicked smile set her heart on fire.

"I figured it was nothing you haven't seen before."

That heart pounded erratically against her chest and she cleared her throat and convinced her eyes to escape the hold his had on them. She hurried into the kitchen, to the refrigerator, and yanked the door open. She shoved her head inside and almost moaned as the cold air cooled her burning cheeks. Damn him. She had to stop letting him affect her so easily.

"Drink?" She poked her head out of the refrigerator.

He wasn't at the end of the island anymore.

"No thanks. Last time you offered me a drink... it didn't end well." His voice came from behind her and she looked over her shoulder.

He slumped onto her worn cream couch, stretched his arms along the back of it and kicked his bare feet up onto the glass coffee table.

"I'm still not entirely sure what happened," she said and the light left his expression again, turning his handsome face dark.

"I'm not entirely sure you want to know. Let's leave it at that." He was closing up again, shutting her out.

Protecting himself.

She was entirely sure she wanted to know. She wanted to know the answers to the thousand questions causing a riot in her mind, a thousand questions that were all centred around him.

The stuff of dreams and nightmares.

More nightmare than dream.

But she still wanted to know.

She wanted to know him.

He didn't want her to know though. That much was clear to her, together with his reasons. He thought that if she knew about him, about all the craziness that surrounded him, it would drive her away.

Eva grabbed a bottle of water, closed the refrigerator and crossed the room to him. His gaze tracked her, head tipping back as she came to stand over him.

"I'll leave it at that... for now," she said, letting him know in no uncertain terms that they weren't done on that subject.

She would know about him.

She would complete the picture.

"This Benares bloke," he said, and she wanted to smile at the way he had let her know that he was fine with her proposition, changing the subject rather than shutting her down, "and his sister... what did they hire you to do?"

Eva sat on the coffee table near his legs. "Tail you and give them all the information I could get on you. Habits, movements, people you knew and anything personal I could find out."

"You're really going to tell me all this?" His frown spoke volumes, and she sighed.

"You're only just trusting me?"

He rolled his right shoulder. "Is this another thing they want you to do?"

Eva shook her head. "No. They want me to sleep with you again."

His eyes widened slightly and then narrowed as he smiled, and she realised what she had said.

Again.

She had just admitted that she remembered sleeping with him the first time. Not only that, but she had said *sleep with*, not fuck.

He looked as if he might prod a little into that but then relaxed into the back of the couch, slumping further in the seat, looking altogether too at home in her apartment.

As if he belonged here with her.

Ridiculous.

Yet it warmed the colder parts of her heart.

"So you're telling me this why?" He looked her over again, scrutinising every inch of her, as if he could spot an ulterior motive in her body.

Or maybe he just wanted to look.

She shirked her leather jacket and tossed it onto the couch next to him.

His eyes darkened, desire flaring in them together with something else as he dropped his gaze to her chest.

Anger.

"You show too much flesh all the time."

Eva laughed at that and pointed at him. "You're one to talk. I wasn't the one parading around Rome topless."

"I'm male. It's allowed."

Meaning wherever he came from, women showing a little skin was frowned upon. He had awfully outdated sensibilities for a man who looked little more than thirty years old.

She looked down at her black low-cut t-shirt. She wasn't even showing that much cleavage.

She glanced at Valen and caught him staring again. The look in his eyes, the hunger that echoed in them, made her feel as if she had her breasts out and bare, completely exposed to him.

She cleared her throat and he looked away from her, gazing off to his left again.

A touch of colour climbed onto his cheeks.

She had figured him for a player, liable to use and discard women, always on the hunt for pleasure, because of his tongue stud. Had she been wrong?

Was he more like her than she had ever imagined possible?

Someone who fell deep and fell hard, and found it impossible to do anything without feeling and therefore remained at a distance from everyone to protect themselves?

"Why am I here?" he whispered.

Because he wanted information from her.

Because he wanted to be with her.

Her heart tore her between those two answers.

Fear made her choose the safe option.

"I promised you information, and got you into trouble… and my reason for giving you this information is to get you into trouble again."

He slowly turned his head towards her, and she didn't look away when his eyes locked with hers, because she wanted him to see the truth in them and she needed to see the truth in his when he responded.

"I want you to kill Benares."

A frown flickered on his brow and he sat up, bringing his feet down onto the wooden floor and resting his elbows on his knees as he leaned towards her, his eyes searching hers.

"Why?"

She fought the urge to glance away, to lie and make up some other reason to cover her weakness.

His eyes softened. "Why, Evangelina?"

God, no one had called her that in a long time.

Not since her mother had passed away.

Fear hit her hard, her strength stripped away by the gentle look in his eyes and the concern in his deep voice.

"Because I'm not strong enough… and his security is too tight for me to do it alone… and because… he's going to kill me if I don't kill him first." She closed her eyes when Valen growled, a sound that was more beast than man, a feral animal both vicious and wild, out for blood. "I know it. He called me to his villa to do it the other night, after our fight outside the Pantheon, but he gave me a second chance."

She tensed when warmth pressed against her cheek, steady and strong, flowing into her, and opened her eyes and looked into his. They were dark, colder than they had ever been, but in their depths there was more heat and light than ever too.

"I won't let him kill you," he whispered and smoothed his palm across her cheek, and she almost surrendered to the need to lean into that touch and steal more comfort from it. "Have you heard from them since?"

She nodded. "When I came back here after leaving you the other morning, Jin tailed me. She gave me an order to seduce you again. I saw in her eyes that once they have what they want, it's game over for me. I've worked for powerful people, dangerous people, but they've always respected me. They've never…"

"They're not going to kill you," he murmured again and she wished she could believe that. The conviction in his eyes and in his voice this time told her to do just that, but it was still difficult. "I'll kill them first."

She pulled away from him, pushed onto her feet and paced across the room, hating the way she felt as her legs trembled beneath her with each step and her heart pounded. Pathetic. She was an assassin. She knew the game she played was dangerous and that one day it would come to a bloody end.

She had always been fine with that. She had never feared death.

Until she had met Valen.

Now all she could think about was how badly she wanted to live.

It was ruining her.

She shoved her hands through her hair and pressed them against the sides of her head.

"Eva," he whispered and she shook her head, warning him not to come to her, not right now.

Not when she was weak.

She was liable to fall into his arms again and it would only chase away this nightmare for a short time, until her head cleared and the questions started again, tearing her apart.

Had she slept with him because she wanted him?

Or because she wanted to live and hoped Benares would allow that if she did as he ordered?

"Do you think they follow you everywhere?" Valen's deep voice curled around her, a gentle embrace that kept her grounded and drove some of the panic away.

She nodded. "Jin watches me and reports to Benares."

"Even now?" He was closer.

She nodded and turned to look at him.

His lips claimed hers, strong arms banding around her like steel and pinning her to his chest. She pressed her hands to his pecs, shivered as she felt hard muscles beneath her palms and the thunderous beat of his heart. She didn't have the strength to push him away. She needed him too much.

He skimmed his hands down her back to her bottom and clutched it as he kissed her, his tongue teasing hers, the pleasure that rolled through her in response chasing away her fear, filling the world with only him. She moaned and wrapped her arms around his neck, and clung to him, kissing him back with every drop of desire that burned in her veins, all of the need that hummed in her bones and blazed in her heart.

Valen groaned against her lips, slanted his head and deepened the kiss, leaving no part of her untouched.

His shoulders shook beneath her hands as she caressed them, and she felt humbled by his reaction, by how fiercely she affected him as she kissed and touched him.

As deeply as he affected her.

He broke away from her lips, pressed his forehead against hers and breathed hard against her lips, his hands trembling against her backside.

"Seduce me."

CHAPTER 13

Eva moaned at that proposition, shook with the force of the need to do exactly as he wanted and seduce him.

Fear clawed its way back into her heart though.

If she did this, would it be because she wanted him, or because she wanted to live?

Would it be real, or a moment of make-believe designed to fool anyone who might be watching from the rooftops beyond the windows?

One look into his eyes answered those questions for her.

It would be because she wanted him as fiercely as he wanted her.

It would be real for them both.

She pulled herself up his body and captured his lips, and he moaned as she delved her tongue between them. An electric sizzle chased over her backside where he gripped her and he broke away from her lips and released her. She frowned and tried to get close to him again, but he held his hands up between them.

"One second. Just one." He breathed hard, sucking in each breath before expelling it on a sigh. "Maybe two."

He looked at his hands and she looked there too. Blinked. She had to be imagining those tiny sparks chasing along his fingers.

He shook his hands, and when he stopped, the sparks she had imagined were gone.

"All good now." He grabbed her, hauled her up against him and kissed her hard.

She wanted to ask what all that had been about but the power of speech left her as he kissed her and she felt his stud teasing her tongue, and imagined it elsewhere again. She had never been with a man with a piercing before.

She clutched his shoulders, pulled him down to her and kissed him harder, losing herself in the fantasy for a moment, shivering as she pictured him between her bare thighs, driving her wild.

He groaned. "Gods, you smell good."

She frowned at that and wanted to ask where it had come from, but he seized her mouth again, silencing her with another kiss.

He turned with her and kissed along her jaw, down her neck, laving it with his tongue and turning her thoughts wicked again. She glanced off to her right, towards the window. Was someone watching?

Her gaze roamed to the bed beyond the low wall behind the couch.

Could she do this while she thought someone was?

She wasn't shy. She worked hard on her body after all. But the idea of being with Valen while someone might be watching everything they did had her cheeks burning up.

He chuckled against her throat. "Trying to set me on fire?"

She eased her cheek away from him so he couldn't feel her embarrassment but he didn't let her get far. He swept his lips up and kissed it, feathered his mouth along her jaw and nibbled her earlobe.

Teased it between his teeth and tugged on it.

She couldn't hold back the moan that rumbled up her throat in response to that wicked, teasing touch, or the reaction it pulled from her.

She caught his cheek, shifted him to face her and kissed him hard, ending it by sucking his lower lip and teasing him with her teeth. He groaned and gripped her harder, pinned her against his chest so the wild beat of his heart reverberated through her.

Seduce him.

He wanted it. She wanted it too.

If this was a seduction, what would she do?

She squeezed her thighs together as it came to her and trembled as pleasure rolled through her, brief but sweet.

Valen glared at her when she moved back a step, breaking contact with him, and reached for her.

She stopped him in his tracks by taking hold of his lower lip, squeezing it tightly between her finger and thumb, and pulling him towards her. He tried to kiss her and she evaded him, earning herself a wicked growl of displeasure that sent another fierce bolt of heat shooting through her and made her want to squeeze her thighs again.

She ignored that need and led him towards the bed, tugging on his lip.

His golden eyes darkened as they leaped to the double bed and then back to her, screaming at her that he wanted to pick her up and carry her to it. She shook her head, silently chastising him, and kept leading him, pulling him along with her.

When she reached the bed, she released him, pressed one hand against his chest and made him take a step back. She took one too, placing some distance between them, grabbed the hem of her t-shirt and pulled it off over her head. Another growl echoed through the room, causing more heat to pool between her thighs.

She squeezed them and tossed her t-shirt onto the wooden floor. Her boots followed it, and then she shimmied out of her jeans and straightened.

Valen stared at her, lips parted and eyes dark, hungry as they roamed over her exposed curves.

She paid him back in kind, her eyes drifting over him, and wriggled her legs again when she spotted the hard outline of his cock in his combat trousers. Another hit of pure pleasure rolled through her in response to the sight of it tenting the black material and the memory of how good it had felt inside her, filling her up and stretching her. Completing her. Her clitoris throbbed and she moaned.

His gaze snapped up to meet hers.

She was too enthralled with his hard-on to look at him.

He moved, whipping off his t-shirt and dropping it on the floor. His fingers made quick work of his fly and he shoved his trousers down, his cock springing up as he freed it, tearing another moan from her. She glided towards him as he stepped out of his trousers, eyes fixed on his hard length, the need to touch it too fierce to deny.

He tensed as she made contact, trembled as she eased her hand down to expose the blunt head, and moaned as she kept going and fondled his balls. His hips jerked towards her, a sign of his hunger that thrilled her.

Eva wrapped her hand around his cock and led him towards the bed. She stepped up onto the cream covers and kneeled on the bed. The front of his legs hit the side of the mattress and he lifted one knee onto the bed. Eva stopped him by bending over and wrapping her lips around the soft head of his length. He groaned and his hand came down on her shoulder, shaking against her as she took him into her mouth.

She pressed one hand against his thigh, spreading his legs further, and then lowered it to his sac. He trembled as she tugged on it and rolled it in her palm, stroked the spot behind his balls and teased him.

"Eva," he breathed and his left hand found her hair, twirled the dark lengths around his fingers and gripped her hard. He grunted as she sucked him, pressing her tongue into the underside of his long cock, and swirling it around the sensitive tip. "Gods."

His balls drew up.

He pushed her back, panting hard, and shook his head when she brought her lips back to him. She smiled and mercilessly licked the head, teasing the crevice with the tip, and he shuddered and moaned, tipped his head back and caused every inch of his body to tense so deliciously that she instantly squeezed her thighs together and rubbed them, swaying her hips to give herself a little hit of pleasure of her own.

She licked up the length of him and flicked her tongue over the head, and he tensed further, delighting her hungry eyes.

The muscles in his jaw popped.

His cock throbbed in her hand.

Any more and he would be climaxing, and what sort of seduction would that be?

She wanted him inside her when he found release.

She wanted to feel it again.

Eva shuffled backwards on the bed, luring him by his hard shaft onto it. When both of his knees were on the bed, she led him to the padded cream headboard, made him turn around and pushed him onto his back.

She sat back and gave herself a moment to admire him as he lay before her, each hard breath straining his muscles, making her quiver with a need to lick and touch him.

Heaven, he was perfect.

His hands shot up to clutch the headboard as she leaned over him and licked his cock from root to tip, and she moaned at the sight of him. She hadn't thought it possible for his muscles to become any more tense than they had been, but he had managed it. His lean, powerful body called to hers, filled her with an urge to have him inside her. She moaned, humming against the head of his cock as she teased it with her tongue, and he shuddered.

That trembling worsened when she shifted to face him, and slung her right leg over his hips. She rubbed him between her thighs, needing a little hit of pleasure before she really kicked her seduction into gear. His hands came down on her thighs, grasped her hips and guided her as he strained, his face twisting in pleasure.

Eva raised her hips and denied him again.

He made a noise that was somewhere between a groan and a growl, but he didn't try to stop her when she crawled up the length of him.

Her gaze zeroed in on his mouth.

She leaned over him, her breasts swaying above his chest, still caged by her black bra, and the need to kiss him gave way to a more powerful one that filled her.

One she surrendered to willingly.

She lifted her right hand and stroked her fingers through the wild, long lengths of his golden hair, brushing it back from his face so she could see all of him. Pools of liquid gold watched her closely, a touch of vulnerability in them that made her want to reassure him that she wasn't going to hurt him. She just wanted to drink her fill of him.

Eva lightly caressed the gentle sweep of his forehead, followed the arch of his left eyebrow and then traced the straight line of his nose. He nipped at her fingertip when she swept it across his lips, teasing them with a touch she knew would make them tingle.

He was handsome, whether he knew it or not. Just the right amount of danger about his looks, in the twist of his lips and the flash of his eyes.

She lowered her mouth and replaced her finger with her lips before she did something foolish like trying to touch his scar again.

He arched upwards to meet her, managed to somehow seize control of the kiss even though she was the one on top. She tugged on his lower lip with her teeth and released it, looked down at him again and resisted the urge to kiss along his jaw because she would choose the left side, the scarred side.

Instead, she flashed him a wicked smile and stroked her fingertip across his lip. "Why do you have a tongue stud?" She stared at his mouth.

His lips curved into a smile. "Not for the reason you're thinking."

"You know that's what they're for though, right?"

He shrugged. "It's for me. Not for you."

"You sure?" She pushed on his shoulders, forcing him down as she rose up onto her knees above him, bringing the apex of her thighs close to his face. "Because it's about to be for me."

He groaned, fire flashing in his eyes as he lowered them to her knickers. He smoothed his palms up her thighs and the fire in his eyes shifted to something else, something that had her slowing down and watching him.

Fascination.

She kept still as his strong fingers traced the tail of the dragon that curled around her left leg, his eyes tracking them, the fascination in them building as he reached her thigh and then her hip, the point where the ink disappeared around her back. His eyes shifted slowly across her stomach, as if he could see the design that danced across her back, and settled on her right side where the dragon emerged, its talons digging into her hip. He lifted his left hand and followed the design again, sending a hot shiver tripping across her skin and making it tingle.

His golden eyes leaped ahead of his fingers and settled on the head of the black and violet beast on her stomach, and she wanted to look down it but couldn't take her eyes off him.

He stole her breath.

A few people had seen her tattoo, men included, but none of them had ever looked at it the way he was, had ever made her feel the design was sensual in some way, seductive and alluring.

Or that she was those things.

He fingered the sapphire-coloured gem nestled in her navel, sending another achy shiver through her as his skin brushed hers.

"You have a piercing too." He glanced up at her, the brief meeting of their eyes making the shiver that wracked her grow fiercer, so powerful it stole her breath just as he did. "It was a diamond before."

He trailed his hands across her stomach, stealing her voice as desire rolled through her in response, and lowered them to her hips. Anticipation built inside her, stoking the need and making her tremble, as his gaze dropped to his hands and he skimmed his fingers along the waist of her underwear.

She gasped as he yanked his hands away from her and the sound of lace tearing filled the room. The deep moan that issued from his kiss-swollen lips obliterated her desire to chastise him, filling it with another.

A desire to hear him making sounds like that while he was inside her.

She loved the sound of his pleasure.

He slid his arms between her thighs, wrapped his hands over them and pulled her down against his face.

Her hands hit the top of the headboard and she gripped it hard, barked out a moan as his tongue stroked her and the hard bead of his stud teased her. Oh fuck. She hadn't been prepared for it to feel this good.

She held on to the headboard, hands and arms shaking as he went to war, laving and teasing her with his tongue, swirling it around her sensitive bud and driving her out of her mind. For each moan she loosed, he answered her with a deep groan, as if the sound of her pleasure thrilled him as much as the sound of his thrilled her. She tried to keep still but it was impossible as he slowed his pace, long strokes of his tongue that started at her core and ended with a flick or a swirl over her bud.

Her thighs trembled against his hands and his shoulders, and she cried out as he dipped his tongue into her core, probed her with the tip and sent her soaring.

His hands shifted, claimed her backside and dragged her against his face, and she couldn't hold back as he probed her again, fucking her with his tongue.

"Valen," she moaned and he stilled.

Damn him.

She rocked against his face and gritted her teeth when he still refused to move.

A shriek left her as he moved so fast the room was nothing more than a blur and she gasped as she found herself sitting in his lap and him facing her, something akin to astonishment in his eyes. It was gone a second later as his mouth claimed hers, fierce now, a demanding press that she surrendered to.

She dug her nails into his bare shoulders and kissed him back, letting him know that she didn't mind that he had changed their tempo and pretending she hadn't seen just how shocked he had been to hear her whispering his name in pleasure, with warmth and desire, and need.

What sort of hard life had he led to end up thinking that no one could love him?

The sort of life she wanted to end right here.

Right now.

She kneeled and he kissed across her breasts, pulled them free of the lacy cups and lavished them with his tongue, swirling it around her tight nipples before sucking them into his mouth and sending sparks skittering across her chest and down her stomach. It pooled between her thighs and she held on to him with one hand in the shorter, roughly chopped hair at the back of his head, keeping him where she needed him.

With her other hand, she reached behind her and grasped his cock. He groaned and sucked her nipples harder as she stroked him, and then stilled as she guided him to her entrance and the blunt tip pressed inside. His breath was hot and fast across her chest as she eased down, savouring every hard inch of him as he filled her.

His hands slipped to her backside again and he held her as she wriggled, making sure every inch of him was inside her, or as much of him as she could take anyway.

Hell, he was hot inside her, so hard and big.

She grasped his hair, tugged his head back and seized his mouth.

He was quick to respond, taking command of the kiss as he moved her, helped her slide up and down his rigid cock. She couldn't do this slow. Her need for him had built too high already, almost at the precipice, and the rough way he grunted into her mouth and thrust her down onto his hard shaft each time she rose off it said he felt the same way.

They both needed the same consuming madness they had experienced in their first time together.

Eva moaned as he drove into her, struggled to keep kissing him as pleasure built inside her, bliss that said it would blow her away again when it came over her. She rocked against him, pressed her free hand against his thigh behind her and rode him hard, fast, delirious with a need to find release. He groaned and gripped her harder, clutching her backside and driving deep into her as his mouth dropped to her chest.

She leaned backwards, groaned and shook as the position placed him deeper inside her, the angle making each long thrust of his cock hit the sweet spot. His mouth claimed her left nipple and sparks shot outwards from it. They skittered over her skin and she frowned as she swore they rushed from the spots where he held her backside too, tiny arcs of lightning that added to her pleasure, lit it up and set her on fire.

"Valen," she breathed and he growled and thrust harder.

It wasn't enough.

A gasp left her as her shoulders hit the bed, her hands falling away from him, and he drove hard into her, stroking her with every inch of his length as he leaned over her, holding her backside above his thighs where he still kneeled on the bed. The angle put him deeper still, so deep that it took only two delicious plunges of his cock to send her shooting beyond the precipice and right over the edge.

She gripped the covers and couldn't stop her hips from rolling as hot pleasure swept through her, her body shaking so fiercely she feared she might fall apart.

"Eva," Valen husked and sucked on her nipple, groaned against it as he thrust hard and deep, riding her climax and stretching it out.

She sagged into him and the bed, breathless and boneless, and he grunted and tensed, jerked hard into her and shook as he followed her, length pulsing and throbbing wildly inside her, sending ripples of pleasure through her.

She squeezed him, moaned and shuddered as the feel of him throbbing propelled her over the edge again with him.

He collapsed against her, his head falling to rest between her breasts, hands still holding her hips, keeping her in place on him.

Eva sighed out her breath.

Damn.

She wasn't sure she could move.

The sound of her phone ringing shattered the silence.

Valen lifted his head from her chest, the haze in his eyes dissipating as the phone continued with its melody.

"Answer it." He sounded groggy, as bone-deep satisfied as she felt, and damn that made her feel good.

She didn't want to, because she knew what he did. It would be her client calling her to congratulate her on a job well done, which meant they had been watching.

Were watching.

She wasn't sure whether she should be acting cool now, or still be playing the role of seducer, ensuring Valen was under her spell.

He rolled off her, flopped onto his back and heaved a long sigh.

She convinced herself to move, getting onto her front and crawling across the bed.

Valen smacked her bare backside.

She frowned over her shoulder at him.

His smile was unrepentant.

She leaned over the side of the bed, fished her jeans from the floor and found her phone, swiping her thumb across the screen to answer the call as she lifted it to her ear.

"We need to meet to discuss your next step."

The phone went dead.

She huffed, sagged into the bed on her front and let the phone drop to the floor.

The soft press of Valen's lips against her bottom pushed the fear that had been trying to creep into her heart back out of it again, drawing all of her focus back to him. He kissed his way up her back, lavishing her tattoo with attention, and over her shoulder, and lay beside her, his back to the window now.

Something she was grateful for.

She didn't like the idea of whoever was watching them getting to see him now that her seduction for their benefit was over.

Especially if it was Jin.

The thought of that bitch seeing Valen naked riled her beyond words.

"Benares?" Valen murmured and idly ran his fingers over her shoulder, his hazy golden eyes following them.

She nodded.

"How did he sound?"

Eva mulled it over. "Pleased, but urgent. He wants me to come to him."

Valen stiffened, his fingers pausing against her shoulder.

His handsome face darkened.

"No."

While she appreciated his concern, she didn't appreciate his tone. "I have to go. If I don't, he will get suspicious."

"He might decide now would be a good time to kill you." The haze drifted from his eyes again, replaced with calm cold. "I said I wouldn't let that happen."

And he had meant it, which touched her.

"I have a theory, a good one, and meeting him might help me turn it from a theory into fact. I can get more information from him." She rolled onto her side to face him. "He wants to discuss the next move."

"Which might be killing you." His eyes hardened and she half expected him to flat out refuse to let her go.

She was beginning to wish she hadn't told him that Benares planned to kill her now.

"I have to do it." She laid her hand on his cheek and surprise flitted through her when he didn't knock her hand away since she had chosen his left one. The skin was rough beneath her fingers, but it was warm. It was him. She smoothed her palm up when he started to look uncomfortable and brushed her fingers through the tangled lengths of his blond hair. "I want to get all the information I can for you."

A question echoed in his eyes, one that pulled a sigh from her.

Yes, she wanted to do it for him.

Someone had done a real number on him, worse than the one her family had done on her.

"I'll go, get all I can from Benares and Jin, and then I'll meet you."

He shook his head. "I'll come with you."

Eva twirled a strand of his hair around her finger and wanted to give in and accept that offer, but she couldn't. "What if they're still watching? They've been following both of us. If they see you following me to the villa…"

His sigh said it all. Benares would definitely kill her.

He caught her hand, and drew it away from his hair, and his eyes were sincere when they met hers. "Just… be careful then. Be quick. In and out. Don't linger.

Get the information and get back to me. I'll be waiting at Heavenly Body, keeping my tail occupied. Meet me at eight p.m. sharp. Don't be late."

Eva nodded. "I'll be there."

Her heart melted a little when he brought her hand to his lips and kissed it.

That same heart went bat shit crazy when he disappeared, leaving wisps of black smoke behind.

She looked around her apartment, desperate to convince herself that he had just moved faster than her pleasure-hazy brain could comprehend.

She was alone.

Even his clothes were gone.

Eva flopped down onto the bed and stared at the ceiling.

She was no longer convinced that she was seeing things.

She was now convinced she had gone mad.

She must have.

She had seen Valen do things that were impossible, including the fact that electricity had definitely sparked from his fingers when he had asked her for a moment, and she had witnessed his brother stop time while the others erased people's memories.

And now she had just offered to betray her client, a man who was as dangerous as they came and liable to kill her if he so much as suspected she was lying to him and was now playing double-agent for Valen.

Eva corrected herself.

She hadn't gone mad.

She had lost her fucking mind.

CHAPTER 14

Valen was not sitting in a dark corner of the heaving nightclub, nursing a drink and constantly staring at his phone. He was not counting the seconds, waiting impatiently until the moment he could see Eva again.

He wasn't.

He tapped the screen, causing it to wake up and illuminate the square steel table and his almost empty drink.

The digital clock shifted to one minute past eight.

Eva was late.

He drummed his fingers on the table, trying to keep his temper under control as a thousand thoughts assaulted him, tearing him in as many directions and stirring emotions he struggled to control. White-purple arcs leaped between his fingers and he grimaced as they forked downwards, striking the table, sending tiny jolts of pain snapping through his bones as they connected.

Who the fuck put steel tables in a nightclub anyway?

It was the one thing he hated about Heavenly Body.

Other than the insane number of possible conductors for his power dotted around the edge of the basement room, it was perfect, a dark busy space where he could be alone with his thoughts and where daemons never bothered him.

Hellspawn frequented it, the daemons' more noble cousins keeping the wretches at bay. While daemons loved to bother him and his brothers, because they were guardians of the gates to a place they desperately wanted to go, a barrier between them and the glory of being the first daemon to enter the Underworld in centuries, they hated Hellspawn and kept their distance from them.

They feared them.

Valen huffed and flicked the stirrer in his drink back and forth as he propped his chin up on his upturned palm.

They should fear him more than the Hellspawn. He was the one liable to butcher them for just breathing the same damn air as him.

His gaze slid to the phone, catching it just before the screen went dark again.

Two minutes past eight.

Where was she?

A cold feeling settled in his stomach and began to grow, tugging at his feelings, prodding them and pushing them to places he didn't want them to go. She would be here. She was just running late.

He glanced at the door, catching glimpses of it through the packed dance floor.

She was.

One emotion popped free, the one he hated most of all.

Fear.

Another emotion latched onto it and pulled free with it, one that he always succumbed to easily despite his best efforts to let it all roll off his back and not be affected by its poisonous whispers.

Doubt.

What if it had all been an act?

She might have been saying everything he wanted to hear, giving him bullshit information so she could get rid of him and make her escape, or worse, so she could do exactly as her client had wanted.

Seduce him.

Had he played right into her hands?

If he had, then she was a better actress than he had given her credit for, because he hadn't suspected a thing. He glared at the glass in front of him. He hadn't suspected anything because it had been his idea. Seeing her afraid of the one she had called Benares had sparked a deep protective instinct inside Valen, and that instinct had told him to go along with whatever her client had planned for her to do so she could look as if she was still working for them.

He had practically seduced himself for her.

He growled and flicked the stirrer so hard that the glass toppled. It cracked when it hit the steel table top and rolled towards the edge. He huffed, picked it up and set it down so fiercely it broke in two.

Gods, he was an idiot.

Her outburst had convinced him that she gave a fuck about him, that she might feel something for him. Clearly, he had been wrong.

He should have known better.

No one could love him.

He checked his phone again. Five minutes late.

Fear that he had been duped morphed into fear something had happened to her and his heart began to pound in a sickening rhythm against his chest.

What if she was only late because Benares had done something to her?

He cursed beneath his breath. He should have demanded that he went with her, he shouldn't have let her convince him to stay away. He should have kept pressing his point until she had crumbled, giving in to him.

At the very least, he should have made her tell him where the bastard's villa was so he could go there now and check on her.

For all he knew, she could be trapped there, held by Benares.

She could be hurt.

He swallowed hard.

Dead.

His heart gave a hard beat and he pushed onto his feet, a desperate need to find her flooding him.

He didn't care if she had played him, if it had all been an act to her, because it was real to him and he couldn't bear sitting here doing nothing, not knowing whether she was hurt and afraid, in mortal danger.

Movement out of the right corner of his eye sent his eyebrows dipping low.

A blonde slinked through the crowd as it parted for her, her red lips curved in a bright, sultry smile as she flicked glances at all the men who panted after her. Her long hair shimmered beneath the colourful lights, swaying against her backside, almost reaching the hem of her impossibly short black dress. Thigh-high leather boots encased long toned legs, four-inch spiked heels making her taller than most of the males around her.

Valen stared at her, couldn't take his eyes off her or remember what he had been doing before she had walked into his life. Something pressing. Something he needed to remember. It gnawed at him but he struggled to pin it down, and the longer he looked at the female, the less important it felt.

The bartender served her a drink, placing her before all the others who had been waiting at the packed bar for longer. No one seemed to mind. They were all too busy staring at her.

She said something, pushed away from the bar and moved through the club, blue eyes appraising every male, earning her their attention even if they were already with a female.

She turned to tease a few of them, giving her back to Valen. He arched an eyebrow at her tiny dress and the fact the damn thing didn't even cover the whole of her backside. Twin curves dipped below the hem of it. If she bent over, she would flash everything at the world.

That was no way for a female to dress.

A flash of another woman crossed his eyes, the creamy swells of her modest cleavage on show, and heat and hunger surged through him.

He looked down at his phone on the table.

He had been doing something.

The blonde moved closer, facing him again, her pouty lips pursed as she fixed her sultry gaze on him.

He had been doing something, hadn't he?

He frowned at his phone and shook his head as it grew hazy and he couldn't remember, and then it felt inconsequential again because the female stopped right beside him.

She gently placed her drink down on his table and her right hand against his chest.

Heat swept through him from the point where she touched and he frowned down at her hand where it rested against his black t-shirt.

This wasn't right.

This hand with its black painted nails and gaudy gold rings wasn't the one he wanted on him.

He growled and knocked her hand away, and she gasped, her blue eyes going wide as she staggered back a step and clutched her arm to her ample breasts.

Those blue eyes weren't the ones he wanted to lose himself in for eternity.

He went to reach for his phone and she placed her hand on the bare skin of his arm, sending a hot wave through him that fogged his mind and pushed thoughts of leaving out of it.

Why had he wanted to leave anyway?

Everything he wanted was right here.

She leaned towards him, tiptoed to bring her lips to his ear, and whispered, "Hello, Handsome."

A shiver ran through him and the haziness building in his head thickened, swamping all of his thoughts. She slid her hand up his arm, groaned low in her throat as she traced his taut muscles, and teased the sleeve of his t-shirt.

"You have the body of a god," she murmured and licked his earlobe, sending another hot cascade of tingles through him.

"Because I am one," he muttered in response, some part of him aware that he shouldn't have said that.

That he was meant to be doing something else.

He was meant to be somewhere else.

Her grip on his arm tightened and the heavy feeling in his limbs increased, pushing those thoughts away again. The only thing that mattered was being here.

With her.

She feathered her lips along the right side of his jaw and he closed his eyes, swayed as heat ran through him from the points where her lips pressed and fingers touched. This was where he wanted to be.

"I need a little taste of you," she murmured against his skin.

He didn't resist her as she pressed her lips to his.

He opened for her, lost himself in kissing her. She tasted… wrong. He couldn't put his finger on it and the thought only lasted a moment before it dissipated, as if someone had pushed it out of his head.

She moaned and slid her arm around his neck, dug her fingers into his hair and pulled him down for more.

Wrong.

Her touch was too light, too gentle.

Where was the roughness he needed? Where was the wickedness he loved?

She nipped at his lip and for a moment it felt right, but then she kissed him again, and the taste of her flooded his senses, stronger this time. Wrong. Something was wrong. But he couldn't stop kissing her, because this was where he wanted to be.

She pulled away and breathed against his lips, her voice a throaty murmur of pleasure and approval, "You have a tongue stud."

A male voice echoed in his head. His own. *Not for the reason you're thinking.*

A female one joined it, her Italian accent teasing his ears, heating that cold space behind his chest. *You know that's what they're for though, right?*

It's for me. Not for you.

You sure? Because it's about to be for me.

Cold filled his chest again and he grabbed the woman's shoulders and shoved her back, glared at her as she tried to get close to him again.

"Leave me alone." Because he had to be somewhere. Wherever the owner of that seductive little voice had gone.

Her blue eyes went wide but the shock in them was short-lived, gone in the space of a heartbeat, and she shoved him into the chair behind him and straddled him. He snarled at her and tried to push her off him, but her mouth descended on his and the haziness rolled back in. He went slack beneath her, lost in the heat of her kiss again, the gnawing feeling in his chest drifting into the distance as the fog built inside him.

"You taste better than I thought you would," the blonde murmured against his lips and licked at them. "I could feast on you for years."

She shook in his arms, moaned as she kissed him again. The haze grew stronger, his body weaker.

Feast on him?

He sat beneath her, those words echoing in his mind, swimming around it in the strange haze.

A different gnawing started inside him.

He growled as it broke through the damned fog in his head.

"Fucking daemon," he snarled against her lips, fisted her blonde hair and yanked her mouth away from him.

She hissed and writhed on his lap, panic filling her blue eyes. He grabbed one of her arms to contain her but she lashed out with the other, scoring her nails across his neck. He growled and gripped her tighter, tearing a satisfied grunt of pain from her treacherous lips as he pulled her head back so hard he thought her neck might actually snap.

She leaned back with it, stopping that from happening, and shoved at him, a wild thing in his arms. A few people stopped to stare. He shot them all black looks that warned them away, and they proved how little backbone they had by leaving and not coming to her aid. Pathetic mortals.

The Hellspawn merely tossed disinterested looks his way, ones that revealed they had realised a daemon walked amongst them and they weren't going to stand in the way of him killing her.

White-purple blazes of lightning crackled around his hands and she flinched as each tiny bolt leaped to her skin. He sucked down a hard breath and clawed back control, because no matter how fiercely he wanted to blow her apart with his power, he couldn't. His brothers believed he flouted the rules, that he constantly ignored them and did as he pleased without thinking about the consequences.

They were wrong.

Eva's words rang in his head, a broken replay of her throwing in his face the fact he had let his brothers come to a wrong conclusion about him and had done nothing to make them see the truth.

She was right. He had let them believe the worst of him, and he shouldn't have, because he hadn't flouted the rules, he hadn't acted without considering the consequences.

He had done it to further their cause, to aid their mission, and they should have been fucking grateful for it.

They should be fucking grateful he wasn't pumping fifty thousand volts into the bitch writhing on his lap too, exposing himself to the watching mortals and inciting the wrath of Zeus and their father.

Gods, he wanted to do that, wanted it so badly he hurt, wanted to throw a massive fuck you at his uncle and watch the mortals quake in fear as they recognised him for the powerful being he was, revered him as they should, bowed and scraped at his feet as their ancestors had, but he was better than that.

Or at least he wanted to be.

So as much as it sickened him, the bitch got to live and the mortals got to carry on oblivious to the fact they were in the presence of a god.

He released her arm, grabbed the broken glass from the table and had it pressed against her throat before she could even move.

She froze, terror lighting her eyes as she tried to look down at the glass where it hovered close to her artery.

Daemons died just as easily as mortals.

"Hurt me, and you'll never see Eva again," she said and he was the one who froze this time.

His blood ran cold.

"Where is she?"

The woman smiled wickedly.

"With my darling brother, and right about now, she's probably falling into his arms and under his spell."

CHAPTER 15

Coming to the mansion alone hadn't been a wise idea.

Eva stood opposite Benares in the sumptuous living room, a place she had never been before and one she never wanted to set foot in again. There was only one exit, and that was the door beyond the couch where he sat. Clever bastard. By being already seated on the gaudy antique sofa when she had arrived, he had skilfully forced her into having to move to the furthest point from the door in order to see him.

He had manoeuvred her into a position where she was at a disadvantage.

Benares gestured to the couch opposite the monstrosity he lounged on, wearing only his shoes and black slacks, his bare torso on full display.

The second sofa was equally as hideous, with dull gold fabric stretched over the solid seat and back, and bright gold on the wooden decorative edges and the claw-footed legs.

Eva shook her head. Again. His handsome face darkened at her refusal.

He sighed dramatically and preened his blond locks. The action caused his biceps to tense beneath his sun-kissed skin and the muscles of his torso tightened with them, shifting in a symphony that drew her gaze down to them.

A trickle of heat ran through her.

She forced her eyes back up to his stunning green ones.

The smile that teased his blush full lips grated on her nerves for some reason.

She frowned, wiping that smile away.

"Signor Benares, I have done what you wanted. My contract is fulfilled?" She hadn't meant that to come out as a question, spoken with a waver in her voice that he heard judging by the way his smile returned.

He liked that he made her nervous.

It hadn't been the case before she had come into contact with Valen. Damn him. He made her weak. She had allowed herself to feel something for him, and now it was working against her. In him, she had found a reason to live, and that had allowed a fear of dying to creep into her heart.

Now she couldn't look at Benares without feeling as if she was looking Death in the face.

Benares casually crossed his legs at his ankles where they rested on the also rather hideous gold and glass coffee table between the couch he sat on and the one she stood beside. He stretched, every muscle on his honed powerful body shifting in response, luring her gaze back down to it.

Another tremor of heat rippled through her.

Eva shook it away but it was harder this time.

She rubbed her forehead as it ached.

He placed both of his hands behind his head and frowned at her, concern in his green eyes. "Are you unwell, my angel?"

She shook her head, mostly because she hated it when he called her that, partly because the ache grew stronger as he spoke, his British accent filling her ears.

"It's been a long day," she murmured, closed her eyes and drew down a deep breath.

The heavy feeling in her head faded a little, but it came back when she looked across at Benares.

He smiled at her, something about it setting her on edge, even though he didn't look any different to how he normally appeared. His green eyes shimmered with warmth, heat that always made her want to leave, to get away from him even as she wanted to get closer.

"Apparently so," he said in a low voice laced with a warm, teasing edge that curled around her. He ran his green eyes over her, lingering on her breasts and her hips, and then lifted them to meet hers. "You had quite the work out."

She frowned at him again. "I did what you wanted. I'm done."

Her stomach dropped when he shook his head.

Her blood ran cold.

This was exactly what she had expected, but she hadn't anticipated the jolt of fear that had run through her on having him confirm that he wanted her to do something else.

He wanted more from her.

She was beginning to fear what that more was.

She was beginning to wish that bitch was present, because being alone with him set her on edge and she couldn't stop her eyes from leaping between him and the door, betraying her nerves.

"You seem… tense," he husked and a hot shiver ran through her, melting some of that tension from her muscles. He sighed and shook his head. "He obviously did not do a very good job. If it had been me in that position, between your thighs, you would have been boneless, my angel. Sated for days."

She schooled her features as fear flooded her and resisted the urge to look at the door again, desperately trying to keep her feelings hidden from him.

Something was wrong.

Off.

This wasn't right.

He was different. Usually he flirted with her, but tonight there was an edge to it, a darkness about him that rang alarm bells in her head.

Was he angry with her?

Or with Valen?

Was he jealous?

She had seen what jealousy did to men. She had witnessed how it drove the weaker ones to do terrible things, to take out their anger on the one they felt had betrayed them and hurt them, believing the object of their desire would only want to be with them then.

Her own father had been such a man. Abusive. Vicious. Jealous of every man who had so much as looked at her beautiful mother. Her mother had been loyal to him, had defended him whenever he had hurt her, had loved him despite his terrible flaws, and because she hadn't stood up for herself, her brother had walked in their father's footsteps, believing it was alright to behave that way, to treat women as if they were objects, possessions.

Slaves.

Anger flashed through her, heating her blood to boiling, and she clenched her fists as memories assaulted her, images of all the times her father had hurt her mother, of all the times her mother had made excuses for his behaviour, and of all the times her father had betrayed her trust. How many women had been his mistress in the years he had proclaimed to love her mother, in the years he had told her how faithful and loyal he was being to her despite how disloyal and unfaithful she was to him by allowing men to just look at her?

Her mother had been a fool, but she hadn't deserved any of it.

She hadn't deserved to be used, hollowed out of all her feelings and slowly destroyed, simply because she had loved someone and they had only pretended to return that love.

No one deserved that.

"My angel?" Benares whispered into her ear and she tensed.

His hands came down on her shoulders, warming her leather jacket, and she went rigid as he closed his fingers over her, the pressure of his grip sending a cold tremor through her. Dangerous. She shouldn't have lost awareness of her surroundings like that, allowing him to move without her knowing it. Damn it.

But she might be able to work it to her advantage.

He had left the couch and now stood behind her, which meant the path to the door was clear.

She shirked his grip and turned on him, backed off a step and placed some distance between them.

Placing her closer to the exit.

He frowned at her, his green eyes darkening, and then smiled. "Are you sure you are not unwell?"

She nodded, brushed her short black hair out of her face and laughed it off. "I'm just tired. Are we done?"

"No," he said, no trace of feeling in his deep voice, and sighed as he looked her over. "You should take more care of yourself. It would not do for such a beautiful flower to be allowed to wilt."

Wilt?

Eva arched an eyebrow at him and glanced off to her left, to the object in the room that disturbed her most.

An entire wall of mirrors.

She had been sure Benares was vain the moment she had met him, but this mirror went beyond vanity and it wasn't there for the sake of making the massive room appear larger.

Ice crept down her spine.

It was there for other reasons.

Reasons she didn't want to think about and that kept her firmly on edge around him, aware that she was in a dangerous position.

She stared at her reflection in the mirror, his voice ringing in her ears. She hadn't bothered to fix her make-up after showering, or dry and style her hair. She had wanted the meeting over with as quickly as possible so she could get back to Valen with the information she had promised.

"It's been a long day," she said with a false smile and turned back to Benares. "Sometimes a woman needs a day off."

He shrugged, bare shoulders rolling in a way that made his pecs dance and reminded her that he was only half dressed. "It is no problem. You are still beautiful... perhaps even more so without the trappings of human nature. I think I almost prefer you in your raw, natural state."

Another shudder went down her spine and the hairs on the back of her neck stood on end.

She glanced over her shoulder at the door.

When she looked back at Benares, he had moved closer to her.

"Is something wrong?" he murmured, concern in his eyes that she wanted to believe was real, even when she felt certain it was all an act, designed to set her at ease around him and make her enamoured with him.

"I'm just waiting for that woman to show up."

"Woman?" He frowned down at her, and then at the wooden door, and then it melted away and he smiled, charming to the last. "My sister? She will not be back tonight."

Eva's stomach turned. Jin hadn't been lying. They were siblings. She swallowed the bile that rose in her throat and barely resisted clutching her stomach as it churned. The way they acted around each other had led her to believe they were lovers, and now they were brother and sister. She wanted to be sick.

Benares pressed his palm to her forehead and she tensed. When the hell had he moved closer? She had to stop spacing out around him or she was going to end up in trouble.

She brushed his hand away and paced the room, her boots loud on the wooden floor that had been polished so highly that it reflected the grotesque golden furniture and red walls.

"You are unwell," Benares said and she didn't bother to deny it this time, because it would be a good excuse for her vomiting all over his expensive Italian leather shoes.

"I think I picked up a cold in the rain," she muttered, hoping it would be enough to get him off her case.

"Perhaps you have been putting things in your mouth that do not belong there and that has made you sick?"

What the hell was that supposed to mean?

She turned to ask him whether he was making insinuations about the things she had done with Valen, and whether Jin had been giving him a blow by blow record of events over the phone, and then thought the better of it. He stood at the opposite side of the room, his arms folded across his bare chest and his handsome face set in a black scowl.

Jealousy.

Her father had looked like that too often, on the verge of losing his temper, fighting the need to lash out.

She didn't want to be on the receiving end of Benares's anger.

The darkness lifted from his eyes and his face softened as he crossed the room to her. "I am not myself today. I apologise."

She didn't stop him when he raised his hand, smoothed his palm across her cheek and tilted her head back, lifting her eyes to meet his, because rejecting him would be the push he needed to shove him over the edge.

Instead, she allowed the caress, allowed him to be this close to her when all she wanted to do was push him away, and she hated herself for it.

She was just like her mother.

Eva broke away from him, unable to bear it after all.

She was stronger than that.

She would never allow anyone to use her that way, to lead her on and use her feelings against her. She wouldn't let someone play her for a fool.

"What is it you want me to do now?" She zipped her leather up, trying to make it clear that they were done and she was going to leave.

Benares stood just a few inches from her, his green gaze locked on her face, a myriad of emotions playing across his eyes, ones she wanted to decipher because she feared they were all about her.

His pupils dilated and his eyes dropped to her lips, and her heart started a slow pound against her chest.

That wasn't what she had meant by her question.

"Am I to seduce the mark again?" She kept her tone level, voice empty of emotion, and schooled her features again to hide all of her feelings from Benares. All business. "Or do you want me to kill him?"

His eyes snapped up to hers. "Kill him?"

Darkness crossed his features.

"As much as I would like it, that is not part of the plan." He curled his hands into fists at his side and she had the feeling he really did want to kill Valen, and he was angry that he couldn't order his death.

Why couldn't he?

"So what is the plan?" she said, more curious than ever.

"Keep him under your spell." There was bite in his tone, anger that she had never heard before, and it compounded the feeling that he wanted Valen dead but it wasn't allowed, that they needed him alive for some reason and it was killing Benares. "Bring him to the villa. You have three days."

So he wanted Valen alive, and unharmed, but under her spell, and she had three days to deliver him. Her curiosity grew and she wanted to voice the questions filling her mind, but held her tongue and kept her cool.

Her heart provided the answer to the question plaguing her the most.

Had this been the plan from the start?

Yes.

Benares had said the drug was a means to an end when she had questioned him. He hadn't meant that it would kill Valen. He had meant that it was the only way to get what he wanted.

He knew more about Valen than she had thought.

He had known that she wouldn't be able to deliver the drug to Valen because he was too strong and far quicker than she was, and that she would end up exposed to it instead, and that Valen wouldn't be able to resist her when that happened.

He had known that Valen would sleep with her, and that it would affect him.

That she would become a weakness he could exploit.

They didn't want Valen dead.

They wanted him vulnerable.

Why?

The answer hit her hard.

Benares didn't only know about Valen. He knew about Valen's brothers too. He knew about the crazy shit that surrounded them and that they were different.

He knew everything, including the fact that Valen already felt like an outcast.

She had realised Valen felt that way when she had witnessed how his brothers had treated him and how he had reacted when she had confronted him about it. He believed they couldn't love him, that they hated him.

Valen was already vulnerable.

Benares was merely using that to his advantage, employing her as a weapon against him, one designed to turn Valen to his side.

She was going to be the instrument of his downfall.

A cold shiver chased through her and she wanted to tell Benares the deal was off, to scream at him that what he was doing was cruel and vicious, and she wouldn't do it. She wouldn't hurt Valen by using his feelings against him.

Benares watched her like a hawk.

Eva pulled herself together and steadied her racing heart. She wasn't going to hurt Valen because she wasn't going to do what Benares wanted. He didn't need to know that though. She needed to keep up the act, and keep her shit together or Benares was going to see straight through her and see that she was playing him.

And then he would kill her.

"I'll do it in two." She flipped her hair out of her face and shot him a smile.

"Three will suffice." He closed in on her again. "My sister will be well fed by then."

Fed?

She must have looked confused, because he smiled.

Calmly said, "You do not want to know."

She didn't but he obviously wanted to tell her, and that meant whatever he was talking about would frighten her.

"Three days it is then." She turned towards the door and gasped when she found him standing right in front of her, blocking her exit.

What the hell?

He advanced on her and against her better instincts she backed away, moving further into the room, towards the wall of mirrors she felt sure served an erotic purpose.

"I'm a little hungry myself." He raked green eyes over her, from head to toe and back again, and strange heat bloomed in the wake of his gaze but quickly turned to cold as it moved on, lifting towards her face. "You seemed pleased earlier, when I said Jin was out."

She hadn't been pleased, wasn't sure where he had gotten that one from. She had been trying to stop herself from throwing up.

He closed the distance between them and towered over her.

"Is it my sister's absence that pleases you… or being alone with me?"

His mouth was on hers before she could respond, fierce and hot, forcing her to open to him. She pressed her hands to his bare chest and he wrapped his arms around her tightly, pinning her against him. His tongue invaded her mouth.

Eva bit down on it.

He growled and reared back, and she shoved at his chest, struggling against him and trying to break free as her heart thundered, fear sending adrenaline coursing through her veins. Fight won this time. She brought her knee up hard between his legs.

He grunted and released her.

She staggered backwards, legs trembling and pulse racing, battling for control over her body and her mind.

Escape.

She had to escape.

She edged sideways, towards the two couches, and the door.

Benares breathed hard, doubled over and clutching himself as he muttered dark-sounding things in a language she didn't know.

She eyed the door again, and then him as she finally gained control of her fear and fury rushed in to fill the void it left inside her. Her memories pummelled her, battering her from all sides, disjointed snippets of how her father had treated her mother.

Eva wiped the back of her hand across her mouth, revulsion sweeping through her on the heels of her anger. "You kiss me with the same mouth you kiss your sister with?"

"Not the same mouth," Benares muttered and slowly lifted his head.

A cold wind blasted through her, chilling her so fiercely her feet froze to the wooden floor and she couldn't breathe. Couldn't believe what she was seeing.

Bright white embers glowed in his eyes, his pupils nothing more than thin vertical slits in the centres of his irises, and the skin around them turned dark and then cracked, forming jagged fissures that shone bright blue. He rose to his full height and seemed to grow even taller as he straightened. Blue markings like lightning streaked over his shoulders and down his arms, caressed his sides and glowed as fiercely as the ones around his eyes. Around those markings, his skin darkened to the colour of ash. The tips of his ears stretched into points and his hair blackened at the roots and bled into crimson at the ends.

His lips flattened, darkened to obsidian, and sharp teeth flashed between them as he spoke.

"This is the mouth I kiss my sister with."

Eva screamed and kicked off, breaking left towards the door.

Benares grabbed her right arm and she shrieked as he pulled it so hard the socket blazed and pain near-blinded her, making her vision wink in and out of the darkness.

He whirled her to face him and she clawed at him as he kissed her, lips fiery hot on her neck. Heat swept through her, carrying away her will to fight as it invaded her flesh and then her bones, sinking deep into her. She wanted this. She wanted him.

No.

She didn't want this.

She didn't want him.

He was a monster.

Eva gathered herself and shoved against him, slapping at his face and his shoulders, and he growled into her neck and held her closer, pressing claws into her sides.

"Get off me." She shoved with all of her might, slamming her palm into his jaw and knocking his head back and his lips away from her. "You disgust me."

She hit him again and managed to break free this time but she didn't get far.

He grabbed her arm and pulled her back to him, and her eyes went wide as his lips came down on hers. Heat flowed through her, driving out the fear and the fury, replacing it with strange calm. She surrendered to it, losing herself.

But then a thought pinged into her head.

It wasn't right.

This wasn't the man she wanted to kiss.

"Get your damn hands off me." She wrapped her hand around his throat and squeezed as hard as she could.

Benares snarled, the sound dark and unholy. "You will give in to me."

"Never." She stamped on his foot and shoved with her hand, pushing him off her again.

She threw a hard right hook, slamming it into his nose.

He grunted, staggered back and pressed his hand to his face. His eyes darkened when it came away covered in black liquid.

The white sparks in them grew brighter.

He turned them on her.

She saw the instant his temper snapped.

Eva made another break for it.

Benares appeared in front of her, his fist connected hard with her jaw and she went down fast.

Pain bloomed on the left side of her head as it struck the edge of the couch.

The last thing she saw was Benares standing over her, violence and hunger in his glowing eyes.

And then everything went black.

CHAPTER 16

Esher stalked through the wet streets of Tokyo, the breeze cold against his cheeks but already carrying the scent of morning.

Time was running out.

He prowled around a corner and looked both ways along the intersection, his honed senses charting several blocks around him as he scoured them for his prey.

Restless hunger gnawed at him, never sated and ever present. He growled through clenched teeth and then pulled down a slow breath, closed his eyes and focused, stilling his body to focus his mind.

The black need abated, but refused to leave him, still held him at its mercy and whispered seduction in his ear, words that promised retribution.

Satisfaction.

He huffed and stepped, appearing on a rooftop above the intersection. The wind was stronger up high, whipping the tails of his long black cotton coat around his leather boots and the jeans he had tucked into them, filling the silence with the sound. He welcomed it, focused on it and his body, and that black need.

A hunger to destroy.

He shifted foot to foot at the very edge of the roof, toes hanging over the drop, mind clear and focused, body honed and ready.

Soon.

The kill would be his soon.

It would satisfy him enough that he could rest and regain his strength for the next night.

For the next hunt.

He eased back so his toes were on the edge of the skyscraper's roof and crouched, resting his elbows on his knees and allowing his hands to dangle between them as he waited.

Waited.

Minutes ticked past and mortals appeared, scurrying around below him like ants. He didn't care where they were going or where they had come from, or which of them was rushing to their death.

For once, they weren't the target of his ever-present urge to kill.

His usual need to make them suffer had been redirected, replaced by a consuming desire to locate the ones behind the attack on his brother, Ares.

The ones who wanted to open the gates.

The ones who had tried to harm his family.

His lips peeled back off his teeth, darkness bleeding through him as rain began to fall. He would find them, and they would pay for their sins.

They would pay for trying to hurt the ones he loved.

The wind picked up, rain lashed his face and his coat fluttered behind him.

He remained still, not moving a muscle and not feeling the cold as he scoured Tokyo with his acute senses, picking out every mortal within a mile radius.

The bright lights and neon shone up from the streets all around him, all across the vast city. He lifted his head and scanned the panorama, studying it.

To his left, Tokyo Tower speared the sky, bright orange against its backdrop of the business district and the river. On his right, a dark swath in the middle of too much light called to him like a beacon, a pocket of nature that surrounded the castle of the emperor.

Back when he and his brothers had first arrived, much of Tokyo had been open space, filled with traditional wooden structures. There had been peace. Now there was so much noise.

He gritted his teeth.

It grated on him, pushed at his control and made him want to either leave or destroy everything in his wake.

Yet, somehow, he remained, and the city remained with him.

It flickered to the otherworld in the rain haze, a city bathed in flames and fighting for survival. Rain fell as streaks of fire and the building beneath him creaked and groaned, the section to his left torn away to leave only twisted metal and chunks of broken concrete that looked as if a huge daemon had ripped it in two. Blue fire dashed across the dark park, chasing something. Screams rose up from far below him, the terrified shrieks of mortals combining with the roars of daemons to ring like music in his ears.

Gods, he wanted them to suffer like that, because they deserved it.

Despicable monsters.

All of them.

Both daemon and mortal alike.

Tokyo flickered back to the present, rain-swept and quiet.

The tower glowed to his left. The park beckoned to his right.

Behind him, the air vibrated with the power of the gate.

He held it open as he had every night over the past three months.

A lure for the daemons.

So far, none had dared to approach it.

But they would.

He could feel it in his bones, could sense it in nature as she whispered to him. The daemons were coming.

Soon he would have the fight he wanted, the battle he needed, and the blood on his hands that he craved.

Soon.

But not tonight.

The only creatures foolish enough to be near him were the mortals below, scurrying around beneath their cheap convenience store umbrellas, absorbed in their lives and ignorant of others.

Ignorant of the damage they did.

Esher looked back at the gate, water rolling off the longer lengths of his black hair and soaking into the pale blue scarf he wore wrapped around his neck.

The colourful concentric rings hovered in a disc flat above the rooftop of the skyscraper, flaring in places as they turned inside each other, twisting in opposite directions. Impatient. Like him. They wanted a purpose, a reason for being here in this world.

He had none to give them.

The symbols between the bands of the circles shimmered in different colours and he closed his eyes, allowing their power to soothe him as they connected him back to the Underworld.

To the only world he cared about.

He turned away from the gate and watched the mortals passing below him.

He despised this world and the foul creatures who inhabited it.

Barely a century ago, the gate had been at ground level like the ones his brothers protected around the world, but the mortals in Tokyo had built and built, never stopping, destroying everything in their path and pushing nature out. It seemed to him that they only knew how to destroy.

They only thought of themselves.

He pushed the sleeve of his black coat back and stroked his wrist, not feeling the obsidian woven band that encircled it.

He only felt the scars.

They burned beneath his cold fingers, irritating him, and he scratched at the band, sneered as he glared down at the mortals below him. Beneath him.

Humans.

He growled through his teeth and tracked them one by one, the darkness rising inside him, writhing and spreading black tendrils through his body, its grip on him growing stronger. His blue eyes darted between the mortals and short fangs pressed against his lower teeth as he ground them together.

They wanted to destroy everything.

Especially when they didn't understand it.

Especially if it was stronger than they were.

The rain around him stopped falling, droplets suspended in the night air, shimmering like colourful pearls as they caught the lights of the gate behind him.

He stared at them, breathed hard and fought to calm himself, chanting in his head in the language of his home, the only world he cared about.

The only world that cared about him.

His fingers rubbed harder, digging into his wrists, and pain built there, fire that licked at his flesh and seared his bones, and he looked down, catching a glimpse of blood before it disappeared, leaving only scars behind.

He growled and the water he held in the air around him vibrated, trembling as if it feared him.

It had nothing to fear.

Water was his passion, his companion, his most precious thing. It was the only thing that was good about this wretched world. His powers had grown stronger, giving him control over more than water, placing any liquid under his command, but it was the water he loved and it was the water he controlled.

It was abundant here, flowed in so many forms. Rivers. Seas. Rain. Tears.

A component of every living thing.

A weapon he could use against them.

He dropped his focus to a lone male as they crossed the road and walked along the pedestrian street opposite him.

Esher narrowed his gaze on the human as the noises of their world broke through the silence of the rain and reached his ears, scratching in them. Car horns blaring. Engines roaring. Traffic crossings speaking as they stopped those cars and mortals twittering to each other as they used them.

The rain suspended around him began to shake.

His mother's voice whispered in his mind, a soothing melody that had him reaching for the pocket of his dark grey shirt.

Whenever it becomes too much, my beloved, find your peace.

He pulled the tiny black noise-cancelling ear buds from it and pushed them in his left ear and then his right, and let the strings of the classical piece wash over him.

She had said other things when she had given him the gift, things he hadn't bothered to put to memory because they had been about the mortals, about learning to forgive and to love humans again.

Impossible.

He would never love a human.

It was bad enough that a mortal, a Carrier, had dared to invade his family and steal Ares's heart. Now a second brother had been targeted by one of their vicious, deceptive kind.

If that mortal dared to harm Valen.

He focused his power.

The water around him exploded.

She would pay for it with her own blood.

CHAPTER 17

Eva started awake, her heart lodged in her throat, head spinning and pulse racing. She blinked hard and a tremble started deep in her core. What had happened?

She fought to remember.

The shaking wracking her tired, aching body grew violent as an image came to her.

Benares.

Only he hadn't been the Benares with the playgirl good looks and sultry smile, oozing charm and seductive promises.

He had been a monster.

He loomed over her, his arm a tight band across her back, glowing white-blue eyes surrounded by obsidian streaked with equally bright lightning that blazed outwards from them and black lips moving soundlessly, flashing sharp teeth.

A monster with hunger in his eyes.

Eva shook so hard that she struggled to push the cream covers off her body.

Tears filled her eyes, making it hard to see, and she blinked them away only to have more replace them. They tumbled down her cheeks as she ghosted her hands over her bare legs and her hips, searching for marks.

Searching for something that would confirm her worst fears.

Bile rose in her throat and she swallowed it down as she reached her stomach, sobs shaking her even as she fought them back and tried to deny them.

She didn't remember undressing.

She remembered the hot feel of his mouth on hers, remembered hitting him and him striking back. She lifted a trembling hand and winced as her fingers made contact with the left side of her head. She remembered hitting the arm of the couch on the way down.

And then Benares looming over her.

Cold froze her blood in her veins and wouldn't thaw, no matter how many times she told herself that he hadn't touched her.

She couldn't convince herself.

Because she wasn't sure.

He had wanted her, and she had been at his mercy.

He was a monster.

Something from a different world, from Hell.

God. She pulled her knees to her chest and rocked as she tried to shut out the image of him, but it was branded on her mind, taunting her with the truth.

Benares was a monster.

She shuddered and buried her face in her knees as she finally heard his words.

He wanted to feed on her.

She wasn't sure what that meant, or whether he had done it.

She wasn't sure of anything anymore.

No.

She was sure of one thing.

She had to get away.

Eva rolled from the bed and gathered her clothes from the wooden floor, pulling them on with trembling fingers. She gave up trying to button her jeans and zip her boots, and fumbled with the black t-shirt. Tears blurred her vision again and she blinked them away as she crawled across the room, fear giving way to determination as her instinct to survive took over. The floor squeaked beneath her, filling the heavy silence together with her panted breaths.

She reached the doors that covered the left half of the far wall of the room, next to the kitchen, and pulled her phone from her jeans. Her fingers shook so violently as she opened the case and slipped the key out of the pocket in it that she almost dropped it. It took her several attempts to slot the key into the lock on the door and turn it.

Relief poured through her when she heard the latch click.

She hastily pulled the doors open. It was dark on the other side, but she didn't need to see to know where her kit bag would be. She grabbed the black duffle and pulled it out of the cupboard, and felt it to reassure herself there were weapons inside.

Everything she needed was in it. Money. Clothes. False identities.

Eva tugged it to the kitchen and used one of the stools to pull herself onto her unsteady feet. Her legs threatened to give out but she locked her knees and shoved fear to the back of her mind.

She could break down later.

Once she had escaped this madness.

The air shifted behind her.

The wooden floor creaked.

Eva screamed and swung her duffle, hit the person hard enough to make them grunt and crumple to the floor. She bolted for the door, grabbing the first set of car keys on her way past the bowl on the kitchen island counter where she kept them, and a black padded jacket from the hook near the door.

She yanked the door open and ran down the stairs of the building, refusing to slow even as her boots flapped around her ankles.

She lost one at a bend in the staircase.

Kicked the other off and kept running.

She hit the door to the building with such force that it slammed against the wall as it opened, the loud crack echoing around the courtyard like a gunshot.

Eva frantically pressed the button on the car keys, blood racing so hard her head spun. The lights on her Fiat 500 flashed and she grimaced. She just had to pick the keys for the slowest damn car in her collection.

She opened the door of the compact white car, threw her bag and coat onto the passenger seat and shoved the key into the slot. The engine started with a reassuring purr.

She had to run.

She had to escape.

Eva put the car into gear and flicked on the headlights.

Her gasp shattered the silence.

Valen stood between her and the exit.

"Don't leave," he shouted.

Hurt flashed in his eyes but she was focused elsewhere.

On the arcs of white-purple lightning that crackled over his hands.

He was a monster too.

They were all monsters.

She gunned the engine.

His hand rose, palm facing her, a gesture for her to stop.

To do as he bid.

She shook her head again. She couldn't. She had to run. He would move. He would move or she would run him over. She had to get away.

She needed to escape this madness.

She needed to escape before it swallowed her whole and there was nothing left of her.

Her bare foot hit the gas peddle.

Move.

She stared, eyes widening, as the car lunged towards him.

Move.

She willed him to do it, because she couldn't stop. Her body wouldn't listen now. She needed to run, before Benares found her.

Because Benares had...

"I said don't leave!" Valen's voice crashed into her head, knocking that terrifying thought out of it.

His hand curled into a fist and he slammed it down into the car bonnet. The back wheels lifted off the ground as the front of the Fiat crumpled under the blow.

Her eyes nearly popped out of her head.

She shrieked as the lights on the dashboard and the headlights flickered, and arcs of electricity chased over the chassis and up his arm.

His eyes glowed bright gold.

The engine stuttered and died.

Her panted gasps filled the silence as she stared at him.

What in God's name was he?

A quiet voice at the back of her mind whispered that she knew what he was—a monster, just like Benares. Another voice issued from her chest, trying to push the first away, telling her that was a lie. He was nothing like Benares.

Even when she had denied it, some part of her had been aware that Valen was different, that the things she had seen him do were real and that he had powers. That had frightened her, but he hadn't.

He had been gentle with her.

He had looked at her with something akin to affection in his eyes, a feeling she had only seen him reveal to his mother and had kept hidden from his brothers and the rest of the world.

His fingers flexed and he looked down at his right hand, drawing her attention there. Blood ran down it, but it was the sparks that chased up his arm, crackling and snapping against his skin, that held her attention.

He wasn't a monster.

But he wasn't a man either.

Her panic slowly subsided, but fear remained, its grip on her so fierce she couldn't shake it, she could only fight it and the images of Benares it kept throwing at her, piecing them together in a way that made her feel he had done something to her.

Violated her.

Tears filled her eyes.

Her hands shook against the steering wheel.

Her foot still pressed the dead accelerator down.

The headlights flickered and a bright bolt of electricity leaped from the bonnet and hit Valen's hand, and chased around his arm.

He didn't even flinch.

He sauntered over to the driver's door and opened it.

"I'll explain later, but right now you're the one who is going to do some explaining," he snarled and she had half a mind to say that was her line.

That aching mind fixated on the first part of what he had said, because the rest confused the hell out of her.

Was he going to explain about what she had just seen him do and the whole crazy parallel world she had fallen into?

She hoped so.

She had seen him total a bar, had seen his brothers pop out of thin air, and seen him disappear in the same manner, and now he had stopped her car with one hand.

That hand caught her arm and he dragged her from the car, and then reached in and snatched her bag and coat. She stumbled as he pulled her towards the gate and she saw the front of the Fiat.

It was wrecked, the white metal twisted and caved in where he had struck it with his fist.

Impossible.

Her knees gave out.

His strong hand on her waist steadied her and a quiet thrill chased through her. A blush touched her cheeks as flashes of the times they had been together filled her mind, bursting into existence for a heartbeat before returning to the darkness.

Memories of Valen became memories of Benares and panic lanced her.

She pulled away from him, for a moment seeing Benares holding her. When she blinked, the vision disappeared, leaving Valen behind. His golden eyes gained an edge of hurt as he slung the strap of her bag over his shoulder and he grabbed her arm again, tugging her roughly towards the gate.

She stared at the front of her car, and then at his hand on her arm, and fear gave way to anger, an emotion she knew how to deal with.

She twisted free of his grip and he looked back at her.

"What the fuck are you?" She didn't mean it to come out so blunt, so harsh, but the words flew from her lips, fuelled by rage that shot her temper straight into the red.

He flexed his hand again, making the muscles in his forearm ripple with hidden strength, and reached for her.

"I said I would explain later. After you've explained yourself."

After she had explained herself?

She frowned at him, head pounding, stomach twisting into knots as she struggled to make sense of that and everything that was happening to her.

"Come," he barked, a sharp edge to his usually mellow deep voice.

He was angry with her.

He walked a few steps towards the door set into the huge arched gate and looked back at her, his eyes narrowing and eyebrows dropping low above them when he saw she hadn't moved.

"I'm not going anywhere with you. I don't know what's going on anymore and I want out. I'm tired of this. I'm tired of everything. I'm just tired."

"I bet you are," he snapped and muttered something beneath his breath.

"What the hell is that supposed to mean?" If he was trying to make her angry, he was pressing all the right buttons.

What had she done to upset him?

Other than hit him with a bag, run away from him and attempt to run him down with her car.

"We must leave here. Come and I will explain." He held his hand out to her again, his eyes bright golden pools of danger that shook her to her core along with that one word.

She wished he would stop saying it.

Heat pooled at the apex of her thighs whenever he told her to come, memories of their time filling her head and her heart, but on the heels of that fire came ice that chilled her to the bone and conjured images of Benares.

"No." She mimicked his empty tone, bone-deep tired of being ordered around and left in the dark.

Tired of being afraid.

Her strength was flowing from her now that she had stopped, now that Valen was here. She wanted to collapse into a heap and break down just as she had promised herself she could.

It wasn't like her, and she didn't like it.

She didn't like feeling this weak, this vulnerable, when she was used to being strong and in control.

She wrapped her arms around herself, squeezed hard and tried to hold herself together.

"I can't do this anymore," she whispered. "I'm so tired."

His face darkened and his words lashed at her, tearing through her fragile defences. "I guess it must get tiring fucking every guy you meet… but we can talk about that later. Right now, I need to get you to safety."

She stared at him, reeling from that blow, ears ringing from the hard hit.

Fucking every guy she met?

Her eyes slowly widened as the meaning behind that sank in.

There was only one way he could have known about what had happened at the meeting, and that was if Jin had gone to see Valen.

What had that bitch said to poison Valen against her?

Or was it not what Jin had said but what she had done?

Benares's deep voice echoed in her mind, sending pain shooting through her chest.

His sister had gone out to feed.

Had Valen fallen for Jin's charms when she had somehow resisted Benares? Had she resisted Benares?

The blood in her veins chilled and she could almost feel the heat draining from her as she stared up into Valen's eyes.

They were dark and hard, as cold as her blood. He honestly believed she had slept with another man, that she would do such a thing.

Had she?

Eva turned her face away from him, looking off to her right, into the shadowy corner at the side of the courtyard, her eyes stinging and heart pounding as she fought to pull herself together and find her feet again.

Valen unleashed a low growl.

He grabbed her arm and yanked her to him, his actions so rough she flinched as pain bloomed in her shoulder. His touch softened and she flinched for a different reason when he brushed the fingers of his other hand over the left side of her head.

It throbbed, hot and pounding in time with her pulse, sending waves of sickening pain rolling over her skull.

"What the fuck happened?" he snarled and she felt his eyes leap to her face, their familiar burn demanding she look at him.

She couldn't.

Not when she was falling apart all over again, torn to pieces by his question.

"I don't know," she whispered and the trembling started again, so badly this time that she felt sure her knees would give out. Tears blurred her vision. She shook her head as she tried to find the answer and those tears skated down her cheeks, hot against her skin.

He growled again, a sound that should have frightened her, fit for a monster, but she felt no fear as he inspected the cut on her temple, his touch light and gentle, his anger visible in the trembling grip he had on her arm.

He was no longer angry with her.

He was angry for her.

And she was stupid because it brought more tears to her eyes.

She rubbed them away, not wanting to cry over something as trivial as him being angry about what had happened to her, even when he was the first man to do that for her. He was the first to stand in her corner and want to fight for her, to avenge and protect her.

It was so tempting to surrender and rely on him like that, to let everything that had happened consume her. Destroy her. But she couldn't.

She was stronger than this.

"I'm going to kill the bastard," he bit out and his fingers shook against her skin.

She slowly lifted her eyes to his, wanting to see that fury shining in them, turning them molten gold.

Needing to see it.

His irises burned brightly, glowing in the low light.

But he wasn't a monster.

He wasn't like Benares.

The fury blazing in his eyes turned to rage as they narrowed on other parts of her face, and her neck, and then settled on her split lip.

"I'm going to fucking kill him." He went to pull away but she seized hold of his arm, fear sending a cold blast through her and her heart screaming at her to stop him.

Not because she was afraid Benares would hurt him.

But because she didn't want him to leave.

She didn't want to be alone.

He stilled, strain written across his handsome face, a war erupting in his eyes, telling her how deeply he wanted to avenge her but also how deeply he wanted to stay as she had silently asked.

He slowly sobered, the rage in his gold eyes dropping from a boil to a simmer, but not leaving them. He had it under control, but it would only take a spark to light it up again.

"Did he—" He clenched his fist and the muscle in his jaw popped.

Eva swallowed hard and shook her head, but she could only move it a fraction of a degree as uncertainty wracked her. "I don't think so."

"You don't think so?" he snapped, his voice loud in the courtyard, that rage rolling back to a boil in his eyes.

"I'm... I'm not sure." Tears streaked down her cheeks. "I hit my head... I passed out."

Her knees finally gave out.

Valen caught her and pulled her into his arms.

"Nothing happened," he whispered into her hair and stroked her back, his caress soothing her ragged nerves and helping to clear her head, driving out the fear that controlled her and allowing her to focus. "If Jin is a succubus, I'm guessing this Benares bastard is an incubus, and... he wouldn't. It isn't in his nature to feed that way."

She nodded against his chest, even though she didn't have a damn clue what he was talking about. Succubus? Incubus? They were just myths, weren't they? Legends of demons made up by people hundreds of years ago.

Was Valen telling the truth, or was he just saying whatever she needed to hear to put her mind at ease?

She drew back to look into his eyes and search for the answer there.

The courtyard spun as if someone had tossed them into a blender and darkness engulfed her.

It parted a moment later, but everything kept spinning around her. She gripped Valen's arms, digging her fingers into his biceps. Her vision stopped whirling but her stomach was slow to follow, still turning and twirling so violently she feared she would throw up.

Valen pulled her against him, his hand pressing into the back of her head and pinning it to his hard chest. His t-shirt was soft against her cheek, his body warm and his embrace comforting. She sank into it, letting him be strong for her.

Another first.

She had never allowed anyone to do such a thing before.

She had never relied on anyone the way she was coming to rely on him.

He sifted his fingers through her hair, and, God, it was soothing, filled her with warmth and light that banished the cold and the darkness.

How did he do this to her?

She wanted to draw back and look at him, seeking an answer to that question this time, but she didn't have the strength to move, because she didn't want this to end. She wanted him to keep holding her like this.

Maybe forever.

"Be quiet," he murmured against her hair and she frowned, hadn't realised she was making any noise.

A low growl echoed around her.

It didn't come from him this time.

She had the sudden sensation that they weren't alone.

Right now, I need to get you to safety.

Valen had come to her because she was in danger.

Her heart started like a jackhammer against her ribs.

In danger from what?

Was it Benares?

Panic sank its claws into her again and she pushed her palms against Valen's chest, shoving him back as a need to run surged through her.

He clucked his tongue and grabbed her as she backed off, his large hand locking tightly around her wrist.

Her left foot hit thin air.

Her eyes zipped to the courtyard far below her and her vision wobbled, her cars and the smouldering wreck of the Fiat zooming towards her and away again.

She opened her mouth to scream at Valen about the fact he had almost killed her by teleporting her to the edge of the pitched roof rather than the apex of it, but her voice died as the courtyard below her stopped doing strange things in her vision.

Cold stole through every inch of her.

It wasn't Benares.

She stared, numb all over, at the things crawling around below her. Some sort of creature. There were four of them, resembling something between a man and a dog, their elongated limbs making it impossible for her to fool herself into thinking they were one or the other. They snapped and snarled whenever they came too close to each other, their sleek black bodies bristling with aggression and shimmering ethereally under the slim light, iridescent like a beetle's armour.

Valen slowly pulled her back towards him, drawing her focus back to the fact she was dangling perilously above them. He eased back up the slope, boots silent on the terracotta tiles.

Eva peered down at the monsters.

"What are they?" she whispered.

Two of them looked up.

Eva shot backwards, bumping into Valen's chest, her hand clamping down over her mouth. She breathed hard, fought to slow it in case they heard her and came after her. Their blue glowing eyes hovered in her mind, sending fear trickling through her numb body, drawing an image of Benares to the surface of her mind.

"He's on to you," Valen whispered and caught her arm.

Benares had sent the monsters?

She looked back at Valen, believing him for a moment, but then another reason for Benares sending demonic creatures after her dawned on her.

It was another ploy.

It was a trick to make Valen fall deeper under her spell so she could bring him to them.

Valen had been quick to save her, and her wounds had drawn out his softer side. Had that been part of the plan too?

She shuddered. No. Benares had wanted to seduce her. He had wanted to feed on her. If there were such things as incubi and he was one, then feeding was a sexual thing. She glanced back at Valen. Had Jin fed from him?

She hated herself for asking that question, and for the tiny seed of doubt it planted in her heart.

"We need to move again." He pulled her back against him.

"Wait." Her stomach did a violent lurch at the thought of teleporting and she shook her head.

If he dragged her through that dark, twisting and turning space again, she was definitely going to vomit.

"It wasn't a request." He wrapped his arms around her.

Someone put the world into a blender again.

CHAPTER 18

Eva kept her eyes squeezed shut as her head kept spinning long after her feet had hit solid ground.

Thankfully, Valen kept hold of her, his hands firm against her side and back.

"Eva," he whispered and she didn't want to open her eyes, not even when his voice was so coaxing and soft, luring her out of the darkness and making her want to see him so she could see how he looked when he spoke to her like that.

One hand left her.

She clamped her hands down on his arms, pressing her fingertips in hard, afraid she might collapse.

He made a soft snorting sound that echoed with amusement and feathered his fingers across her cheek.

"You can come out now."

She knew that. She just wasn't sure it was a wise idea.

She was stronger than this.

Eva sucked down a breath that went no way towards steadying her trembling body, lifted her head towards his, and slowly opened her eyes.

His smiled down at her.

Black wisps of smoke curled around his shoulders, framing him, and her eyes widened when she dropped them and found similar onyx ribbons twining around her arms.

Her stomach rebelled.

Eva shoved out of his arms, almost fell as she twisted away from him but managed to remain upright somehow, and ran down the wood-panelled corridor that led to the bathroom. She hit the door hard with the flat of her hand, sending it slamming against the white tiles, and skidded to her knees in front of the toilet.

"Having a moment there?" The teasing male voice came from the other room just as she threw up.

"Bite me." Valen's reply had more venom than a cobra.

She hadn't realised they weren't alone.

It didn't stop her stomach from lurching.

Eva gripped the toilet bowl and threw up again.

"Are you okay?" A female voice this time.

Megan.

Hell, she was glad it hadn't been one of the men or Valen who had come to check on her.

She nodded and groaned, her cheeks heating as shame swept through her. There went her reputation. Everyone in the other room would always see her as a woman with a weak stomach, a fragile constitution, and not the assassin she really was.

Eva pulled herself up onto her feet, flushed the toilet and turned towards the sink. She kept her gaze firmly away from the mirror, unable to face her reflection when embarrassment scalded her cheeks. She twisted the cold tap, bent over and splashed water on her face. It was refreshing, soothing more than just her burning cheeks.

"It takes a little getting used to," Megan continued and Eva glanced across at the brunette as she moved, pushing her shoulder-length hair out of her face. Her dark eyes were bright, shining with amusement and affection. She glowed. Was it her relationship with Ares that made her glow like that? "It took me at least twenty times."

Eva groaned. Twenty? "I don't think I can handle one more, let alone another seventeen or so."

She hung her head forwards and watched the water roll down the strands of her black and blue hair as she waited for her stomach to finally settle.

Megan seemed so happy with Ares.

He had powers like Valen, and a temper to match judging by what she had seen of him, but Megan was with him, unafraid of him.

Happy.

Could she really be like that with Valen?

She stilled and watched the water swirling down the drain.

Could she?

"Megan…" she started and froze when she looked across at the woman and spotted Valen standing behind her, a dark shadow against Megan's crimson jumper and blue jeans.

Eva's cheeks heated to a thousand degrees again, heart pounding a staccato rhythm as she stared at him and the question she had been about to ask right in front of him rang around her head.

Do you think Valen likes me romantically?

He frowned at her and then looked himself over as if he thought she saw something wrong with him and that was the reason she had frozen solid.

God, what was wrong with her?

What was it about Valen that had her so backwards about being forwards?

She liked him.

That was the problem.

She had never been shy around men before because they had never made her feel the way Valen did. They had never made her *feel*.

Could he like her the way she liked him?

He blinked, seemed to snap himself out of whatever thoughts were running around his head, and glared at Megan. She rolled her eyes and walked away, leaving them alone.

Could he?

Sure, he seemed to enjoy her company, looked at her with heat in his eyes and wanted her, but was it more than that?

She couldn't ask him outright. If she did, there was a chance he would crush her, and she was tired of being weak. There had to be a way for her to tell whether those feelings she caught glimpses of in his eyes at times were real.

He held his hand up.

Her gaze leaped to it.

Lemonade.

"You… uh…" He averted his gaze, staring at the running sink tap. "I saw it on TV once."

He shoved the can of lemonade towards her, a hint of rose climbing onto his cheeks.

"You had a shock."

When she didn't take it, he looked positively mortified.

"Shit. I got it wrong… I thought a sugary drink was good in this situation."

God, he was adorable.

He went to take his hand back.

Eva placed hers over the can, stopping him in his tracks. The blush on his cheeks grew darker as he stared at their hands.

The second she took the can, he snatched his hand back and rubbed the nape of his neck, and then jammed both of his hands into the pockets of his black combat trousers.

"Thank you," she said.

He blushed harder and turned his back on her. "No big deal."

But it was.

With a single action, he had revealed himself to her, letting her see past the barriers and catch more than just a glimpse of his feelings.

He cared about her.

She cracked the can open and his head whipped around, eyes darting to her hands.

"You're going to drink it?"

Eva laughed, the sound out of place in the midst of her tumultuous feelings, making her feel she really had lost her mind. "What did you expect me to do with it?"

He shrugged, rolling those toned shoulders beneath his black t-shirt, pushing all of her fears even further away as he drew all of her focus to him.

She sipped the drink and managed a smile for him. "You did get it right. Sugar for shock."

Her voice lost all the warmth she had tried to put into it and she stared down at her can of lemonade, the reason for him giving it to her sweeping back in to overwhelm her.

"He wouldn't have," Valen whispered and stepped into the room. He hesitated and then placed his hands on her upper arms, and she looked up at him, right into his eyes, seeing the belief in them. "Incubi feed on pleasure. If he knocked you out…"

He ground his teeth and she could see he was finding this as difficult to talk about as she was.

She nodded, letting him know he didn't need to finish. She knew what he was saying.

Benares wouldn't have received any nourishment from violating her, and feeding had been his objective, although part of her still feared that the other reason he'd had for wanting her might have driven him to do things while she had been unconscious.

Jealousy.

He wanted to take her from Valen.

She sipped the drink again and felt better as some of her strength began to return.

Valen placed his palm against her left cheek and brushed the pad of his thumb across her lower lip, his golden gaze locked on it, darkening by degrees as he stared at the cut that darted over it.

"I'm going to kill the bastard," he murmured, and his irises brightened, the softer emotions melting away under the heat of his rage.

It touched her that he wanted to protect her, but it fuelled the feeling that had been lurking in the pit of her stomach, gnawing at her for days.

Damn guilt.

"Valen," Ares called from the other room.

Valen went to turn away from her.

Eva caught his left wrist.

"I've been an arse," she blurted and he frowned over his shoulder at her.

She tried to look him in the eye but hers refused to lift above his shoulders, so she stared at his throat as he turned back to face her.

His head lowered, bringing his square chin and the wicked curve of his lower lip into view, and she knew he was looking at her hand where it held his arm.

Waiting for her to explain.

"I've been an arse," she said again, thinking this time she would be able to get the rest of the words jammed in her throat out into the open.

No.

They remained lodged there, and the longer he stared at her hand, the more fiercely they resisted her. She swallowed and squeezed her eyes shut. She was stronger than this. She had already told him in a way, so she wasn't sure why admitting it was so difficult. He needed to hear her say it, and she needed it out there to alleviate the guilt eating away at her.

She opened her eyes, forced them to meet his, and shoved the words out. "Our first time together blew my mind."

He stared at her, too sober for her liking, completely unreadable.

Her stupid heart started pounding again.

He had to say something.

A glimmer of something warm lit his eyes and then he grinned. "It blew your mind so hard you forgot it, huh?"

She barely heard his words, was too entranced by the sight of him smiling at her. Really smiling. There was nothing forced about it, nothing false. She had made him smile.

She had the feeling that smiling like this was rare for him and she should cherish it.

"Don't sweat it," he said.

She thought he would pull away and go to his brothers, but he pulled her into his arms instead and captured her mouth in a fierce kiss, demanding and delicious, one that melted her. She leaned into it, sought more of it, unwilling to let him give this to her and then steal it away before she was ready. He moaned and angled his head, and kissed her deeper, claiming all of her. The stud in his tongue stroked over hers and she shivered in his arms as a thrill chased through her, memories of how good it had felt against her flesh igniting her desire.

Valen pulled back and pressed his forehead and nose against hers, his panted breaths matching hers as he held her.

"Next time, I'll try to blow your mind so hard you forget your name."

Heat flashed over her skin at just the thought. "I like the sound of that."

He jerked back, surprise widening his eyes before they narrowed on her, blazing with heat and a dark hunger, a need that she knew he saw reflected in her eyes.

"Valen!" someone barked and he flinched, turned cold eyes towards the corridor and glared in the direction of the living room.

The haze of the kiss gave way to the cold that had filled her when she had figured out Benares's plan, and she tightened her grip on Valen's arm, holding him in place and stopping him from going to his brothers.

She had to tell him. He wouldn't like it, would be upset with her for saying it, because he was like her in so many respects and didn't want her to view him as weak.

She didn't.

He was strong.

But he was vulnerable, and it was his family that had made him that way.

So before she allowed him to go into the other room and face that family, she needed to make sure he was aware of Benares's plan. She needed to protect him in the only way she could.

She had to tell him her theory.

Whether he wanted to hear it or not.

CHAPTER 19

"I don't think Benares is on to me... I don't think he sent those monsters to kill me. He did it because he knew you would rush in to protect me... because he wants you deeper under my spell." Eva glanced away from him, sighed, and then lifted her eyes back to meet his. "Benares plans to turn you to his side. I'm supposed to bring you to him in three days. He's using me as a way to lure you over."

The rage burning in Valen's veins, the black need to find Benares and rip him into tiny pieces, stood up to the ice that assaulted him as Eva's words sank in, but it wasn't long before the cold was winning, vanquishing the fire.

Making him numb.

He stared down into her beautiful blue eyes, saw the truth shimmering in them as they revealed her fear and her worry, and how much she hated having to tell him this because she knew it would hurt him.

Her grip on his arm tightened. Her hand shook against him. He glanced down at it, not feeling anything as he silently fought the mocking voice ringing in his mind, laughing at him.

Benares had targeted him for one reason.

The bastard thought he was the weak link.

Feeling began to seep back in, emotions born of the darker side of his blood. Benares dared to insult him?

He ground his teeth and growled through them, filled with a need to deny that he was vulnerable, to show Eva that he was anything but weak.

He was strong.

She hesitated, the concern in her eyes growing as she stood before him in the bathroom, clearly unsure what to say.

An urge to head out into the night, find Benares and destroy him replaced the one to make her see that he was strong. It whispered seductive words in his ears, bid him to listen to it and surrender. He planted his boots to the floor and refused.

If he went after Benares now, the bastard might think that Eva had told him about his plan and might send someone after her. The thought of her being at Jin's mercy, or that of those fell beasts Benares had called forth from some dark corner of this world, left him cold to his marrow.

But he had to do something.

He needed to show that he was strong.

He was.

Eva slipped out of focus as he sank into his thoughts, easily consumed by them and the emotions running riot inside him.

He had always viewed himself as strong, one of the strongest in the group.

Realising that he might have been wrong about something that felt like such a fundamental part of himself was crushing to say the very least.

He couldn't accept it.

Even when he knew it was true.

He even had to admire the bastard for coming up with this plan.

He and his brothers were strongest when they were a united force, an army of gods.

The worst of it was, it wasn't the enemy who had placed them into this position, on the brink of being turned against each other. Not really.

It had been him.

Gods, he was a massive dick.

The enemy were only attempting to accelerate what he had already started.

He had been slowly driving a wedge between him and his brothers, gradually pushing them away and separating himself from them, since Calindria had died.

Since Zeus had taken away his favour.

He pressed his fingers to the scar on the left side of his face. They shook, but nothing he did steadied them, not when the ground was tilting and bucking beneath his feet, about to give out.

"Valen." Eva's soft voice reached his ears and he blinked himself back to her, stared down at her where she stood in front of him, closer to him than before.

He caught the apology in her tropical blue eyes before she dropped them to his chest.

Valen reached out to touch her.

She beat him to it, lifting her hand a second before she raised her eyes back to his, and placing it over his.

Against his scar.

"I know," she whispered, so much feeling behind those two simple words, feeling that seemed to reach into his chest and squeeze his heart. She cast her gaze down again, sighed and bravely met his eyes once more. "I know the path you're taking. I've pushed away everyone I ever cared about... family included. Part of me did it because I was angry with some of them, because I thought I hated them, and part of me did it to protect the others. I was so angry... with my father for how he treated and betrayed my mother, and my brother for following in his footsteps and siding with him... I was even angry with my mother for being so weak. That anger led me to a dark place, Valen, a place where I turned against the world... where I became little more than a weapon for hire."

She did look away from him now, her gaze locking on the tiled floor, and that heart she had squeezed went out to her, but it warmed at the same time as awareness of what she was trying to do steadily filled him.

She was trying to make him feel better by revealing that they weren't so different, that she knew his pain and the darkness he faced, and that was why she needed to stop him from making the same mistake she had.

Her confession was more than all that though. There was a deeper meaning behind it, and that was what touched him.

She had told him without words that she understood him.

That she had seen this side of him and she wasn't going to walk away.

It hadn't changed how she felt.

Whatever the fuck that was.

He wasn't going to probe into it right now, when she was afraid to look at him, because she had revealed her vulnerable side in order to make him feel better about his own. She would bolt. Neither of them liked being vulnerable, both of them reacted badly to it, liable to lash out to protect themselves.

He wouldn't press her.

For once, he was going to do the opposite to what he wanted without protest or being forced.

He shifted his hand, moving it out from beneath hers, and pressed it to the back of her one, bringing her palm into contact with his face. He held it there, absorbing her warmth as he studied her and what the hell they were doing, searching for an answer.

He could only draw one conclusion, and it rocked him to his soul.

His mother had been right.

There was a woman who had been made just for him.

That woman's name was Eva.

"I might vomit." Daimon's deep voice cut into the moment like a knife, slicing it in two, and Valen shifted his gaze to his left, to his brother, and glared at the bastard, leaving him in no doubt of the pain he was about to suffer for interrupting them.

"Your stomach must be weaker than mine." Eva lowered her hand from Valen's face, a snap to her tone.

Daimon scowled at her, his pale blue eyes shimmering dangerously.

Valen chalked it up as a victory for her and ran his eyes over her curves as she walked away from him, a sway to her hips that exuded confidence and that warrior air he found so damn appealing about her.

"Be my guest." He gestured towards the toilet, would have shoved his brother in its direction if this had been the Underworld, where Daimon's power wasn't liable to give him frostbite as a reward for touching him.

Daimon growled, his white eyebrows dipping low above his glittering pale eyes, but Valen wasn't listening. He followed Eva in a daze, transfixed by the difference in her, how she had gone from warm and tender, to cold and hard in a heartbeat, not allowing Daimon to see that softer side of her.

Mine.

That side of her was for his eyes only, belonged to him and him alone.

She stopped in the living room, sank into his black leather couch at the end nearest her duffle bag where it rested on the terracotta tiled floor, and kicked her feet up on the wooden coffee table. They were bare, their soles dirty, and he barely stopped himself from going into his bedroom and finding her a pair of socks to keep her feet warm.

When had he gone from warrior to woman?

He wasn't going to turn into Ares, castrated by his love for Megan, reduced to following her around like a puppy, looking at her as if she was the light in his life, his sole reason for living, and he would do anything for her, whatever she commanded.

Even get her socks.

151

Eva looked up at him and he realised he had been staring down at her, stood beside the couch like a dolt and probably looking as goofy and moon-eyed as Ares.

Gods, it was too late for him.

She had already castrated him.

Her lips curved into a faint smile.

Warmth bloomed in his chest.

He scowled at her and that faint smile became a full blown one.

"Message received." She winked at him. Teasing him now?

Just how well could she read him, how in tune were they?

"What have you discovered?" Keras said from his spot in Valen's favourite black wingback armchair near the fireplace, his softly-spiked short black hair, long coat, shirt and trousers making him blend into it.

Keras absently twisted the silver band on his left thumb around it. His brother played with that ring so much Valen was surprised he hadn't worn it down to nothing over the past few centuries. He would have if it had been made of any other material, but it had been forged from the metal of the gods on Mount Olympus.

A gift designed to last an eternity.

Like the feelings behind it?

Valen had never grown balls big enough to ask that question, or dare to see what Keras would do if it went missing, even though he was beyond curious. Level a city probably. Possibly the entire planet. That ring probably meant more to his older brother than anything else, family included.

Keras's green eyes turned wary as they shifted from him to Eva.

His big brother had no reason to fear her. She was as mortal as they came, near powerless against them, and for once she wasn't armed.

Concern flared in Keras's eyes, gone so fast Valen thought he had imagined it at first.

Keras looked as if he wanted to say something but was struggling with it, which meant one thing. Valen hadn't imagined that concern, and Keras wanted to apologise.

His big brother had always been awkward about such things. Valen wasn't much better at it. He blamed their father. Hades wasn't good with apologies either. Persephone did all the apologising for him.

Valen shrugged, shooting for casual, an attempt to let his brother know it was no big deal and he didn't have to apologise for chewing him out when he had done nothing wrong. Correction. He had done something wrong. He had let Keras say those things without defending himself. They were both at fault, so he couldn't hold Keras to blame.

Not entirely anyway.

"We're up against a pair of siblings. Brother and sister. An incubus and a succubus. They seem old for daemons. Strong, but not really a threat." Valen propped his right hip against the side of the leather couch, sticking close to Eva.

She looked calm on the outside, but something about her warned she was far from it, that she was nervous about being around his brothers again and had been happier when they had been alone.

Gods, he wanted to be alone with her again.

At least Keras had only brought Daimon and Ares with him. It made sense. Marek needed to guard the Seville gates, and Calistos could cover the Paris and London ones in Keras's absence. It was daylight in Hong Kong, where Daimon's gate was, and heading towards evening in New York, the city Ares protected.

Daemons didn't move around during the day, not unless they had a burning desire for a suntan.

The sort of tan that turned their skin crispy.

The only other brother who could leave their gate unattended right now was Esher, and Valen hadn't expected him to come.

Megan had been one mortal too many for Esher, with Eva in the mix too now he was bound to start keeping his distance as much as he could.

Valen couldn't blame him.

Ares rested his backside against the sill of the window opposite him and Eva and crossed his legs at his ankles, his heavy-soled black leather boots clunking against the tiles as he set his right foot down.

Megan moved to his side and he slung his arm around her and pulled her into the shelter of his embrace, tucking her against his black t-shirt. She pressed her hand to his black-jeans-clad thigh and smiled up at him, her dark chocolate eyes a contrast to Ares's, warm where his were cold and wary.

Ares glanced down at her, managed a smile and lifted his hand to tuck a strand of her shoulder-length chestnut hair back into place.

She was a contrast to his brother in other ways too. Her blue jeans, black-and-white sneakers and ruby jumper seemed so bright against Ares's standard black attire.

Ares finally dragged his attention away from his female and pinned it on Valen. "Are they working alone?"

"No," Eva whispered and everyone looked at her. She sat her ground, not flinching as all eyes came to rest on her. "Benares didn't seem to want to—"

She cut herself off and glanced up at Valen.

It was then he knew just how in tune they were with each other.

She knew that his brothers knowing about Benares's plans for him wouldn't sit well with him because it would reveal he had been singled out as the weak one of the herd, one who could be manipulated and turned against his family, and he didn't want his brothers to see him that way too.

But they needed to know.

He nodded.

She lingered, studying him, her blue eyes pulling him deep into them, as if she wanted to be absolutely sure that he was fine with her announcing to his brothers that Benares viewed him as a weak link.

He frowned at her.

Her lips curved into a little smile. "Message received."

He folded his arms across his chest as she turned to his three brothers and Megan and listened as she told them everything. Not quite everything. Thankfully she omitted some of the more wicked details.

Still, he hated standing beside her listening to her tell his brothers that daemons thought they could turn him to their side and use him against them.

Daimon's face darkened as he shoved a black-leather-gloved hand through his spiked white hair and looked at her.

Valen slid his gaze towards him and narrowed it on his brother in a silent warning not to judge Eva. It hadn't been her plan. She hadn't been the one to decide to seduce him. Gods, the drug had taken it out of their hands, unleashing the desire that had already existed in both of them.

He shifted as his trousers tightened, easing behind the couch so his brothers didn't get an eyeful of exactly what Eva did to him.

Daimon arched an eyebrow at him and then went back to listening to Eva as he idly toyed with the neck of the dark navy roll-neck jumper he wore beneath his black coat. He shuddered and huddled down into it, and Valen felt sorry for the bastard. He couldn't imagine what it was like for Daimon, feeling blasts of frigid cold from time to time as his power acted up.

At least Ares's power was fire, so he only had to put up with the occasional hot flush.

Ares seemed more interested in coddling Megan than listening to him, that fascination still shining in his gold-flecked brown eyes, warming them as he gently touched her face. Valen also couldn't imagine how that felt. Ares and Daimon had been starved of physical contact from the moment they had been sent to the mortal realm, the manifestation of their powers stealing it away from them. Now Ares could touch a female, and Valen couldn't blame him for taking every opportunity.

Fuck, Valen wanted to take every opportunity to touch Eva and he hadn't even been without physical contact for the last couple of centuries.

Keras stared over Eva's head at him, and Valen stared right back, not letting his oldest brother fluster him. He never had been one to back down from a challenge. If Keras wanted a staring contest, then he had one, and he would lose.

When Eva fell silent at last, Ares scrubbed a hand over his tawny overlong hair, Daimon loosed a standard dramatic sigh, and Keras continued to stare.

The concern in his brother's emerald gaze put Valen more on edge than facing a legion of daemons with a few gods thrown into the mix.

"I'll deal with the daemon siblings." Valen kept his tone firm enough that it should have eased his brother's concern and the worry steadily building in Ares and Daimon's eyes too. He pushed his long blond hair from his eyes as casually as he could manage and shrugged, trying to let their concern roll off him. "Don't worry. They aren't that powerful. The succubus tried to seduce me and her kiss was hardly anything to write home about."

Eva tensed, nothing more than a small tightening of her shoulders but he noticed it.

A feeling arrowed through him, one he found he hated.

A cold chasm suddenly opened between them and it felt as if she was withdrawing from him, distancing herself without moving from her spot on his sofa.

He had said something wrong.

It didn't take a genius to figure it out, or any of the oh-so-helpful pointed looks from his three brothers.

He inwardly grimaced.

Maybe casually mentioning how Jin had stuck her tongue down his throat hadn't been his smoothest move. In fact, in the annals of moves, it was somewhere down the bottom, hovering between killing a favourite pet and flirting with a family member.

"Ah, we uh… yeah," Ares said and disappeared with Megan, leaving a swirl of black smoke behind him.

Bastard.

He looked to Daimon but he was already gone.

Keras wouldn't ditch him. Big brothers took care of their kid ones in situations like this, didn't they?

Valen threw a pleading look in his direction, a first for him, and hoped that the novelty of him asking for assistance for once would gain him some favour and make Keras stay and help smooth things out with Eva.

Keras pinched the bridge of his nose, shook his head.

And disappeared.

Sons of bitches.

Still, there was one good thing to come of him putting his foot in his mouth with Eva. If he ever wanted his brothers out of his apartment, he knew just what to do to get rid of them.

"Eva." He looked down at the back of her head, willing her to look at him.

When she remained staring straight ahead, diligently keeping her eyes off him, ignoring him, he sighed and moved around the black leather couch.

Valen squatted in front of her but she still refused to look at him.

His earlier words came back to haunt him.

He was a massive dick.

Under normal circumstances, that was a good thing. Females liked big dicks. Right? He wanted to smile at that but feared Eva would punch it from his face and not understand if she saw it.

Females might like large appendages and the pleasure they could give them, but they did not like men acting like those appendages.

Or acting as if those appendages controlled them.

He sighed again.

She still refused to acknowledge him.

"Eva," he whispered and toyed with his words, trying to get them perfect.

This was new to him, uncharted territory. He had never cared about a female enough to give a damn about what she thought, or whether he had hurt her, or any of that shit.

It was a steep learning curve.

It didn't help that he'd had the sinking feeling all night since finding her at her apartment that he wasn't the only one who had been kissed by a daemon in the last twenty-four hours.

The need to ask her if Benares had kissed her, or if she had kissed that bastard daemon back, burned in him but he tamped it down and stamped it out of existence, because he might be new to handling females in this way, but he wasn't that big of a fucking idiot.

She had a right to be pissed at him, and he had a right to be pissed at her too, but one of them had to be the one to take the first step to move past it.

"I didn't want her to kiss me," he said to her knees, hating the way she had placed her hands between her thighs because it made her look small, hurt, and he felt responsible. "I made her stop. Actually, I tried to kill her but then she said if I did… I would never see you again."

Her hands tensed, palms pressing harder against each other.

"She said Benares—" He cut himself off when she tensed further, her entire body going rigid, and cursed himself for bringing up Benares when she was still struggling with what had happened to her.

"He kissed me," she whispered, so distant that he wanted to catch hold of her shoulders and shake her out of whatever dark thoughts were pulling her away from him. "He turned into some sort of monster when I hit him… and then he…"

She closed her eyes and lowered her head, and gods, he needed to butcher the bastard.

When the time came, he was going to take immense pleasure from slowly killing Benares.

"He didn't," Valen murmured softly with conviction, not wanting to startle her. All he wanted to do was comfort her and make her believe him.

He wanted to make her forget what had happened.

He wanted to make her smile again.

She opened her eyes and they locked with his, her internal struggle reflected in them. So much hurt. So much fear. She wasn't sure what to feel, what to think, and he hated it and how it clearly tore at her, made her flip between overly bright and darkly melancholic.

There had to be a way to ease her mind and settle her heart, and give her some peace so she could find her balance again.

Whenever he was troubled, he went to his hill and found comfort in being alone with his thoughts there.

He wasn't sure Eva would find being alone comforting though. Giving her more time to think might only make her worse, giving her fears a stronger hold over her.

Being alone wouldn't help her.

But would being alone with him?

He almost laughed at that. He wasn't sure anyone had ever found his presence comforting.

It was worth a shot though.

Not here though. It had to be somewhere removed from her job if it was going to stop her from thinking about her wretched client and what he had done. Somewhere quiet.

Where they wouldn't be interrupted.

Where he could comfort her in the only way he knew worked.

By letting down his defences.

She liked it when he was unguarded with her, and that feeling went both ways. He took pleasure from her letting him see glimpses of the heart she kept locked away from everyone, hidden behind a wall of steel as thick as the one that shielded his.

He smiled as it came to him.

There was only one place where he could take her, one place that felt right, if a little nerve-wracking.

A place he had never taken anyone before.

People had interrupted him when he was there, his family included, but none of them had been invited.

She would be the first.

He stood and held his hand out to her, and she looked at it and then up into his eyes.

"Go somewhere with me?"

She looked down at his hand and for an agonising moment he thought she would swat it away and refuse him.

A thrill chased through him, leaping up his finger bones and sizzling through his skin when she placed her hand into his.

He pulled her up into his arms, savoured the feel of her nestled against him, and closed his eyes.

Focused on their destination.

And stepped.

CHAPTER 20

On the list of things Eva hadn't expected when the darkness parted, number one was her stomach not rebelling and the world around her settling in only a few seconds.

Number two was where Valen had taken her.

He eased back, but kept his arms around her, revealing their location.

The hill.

She had followed him here once and at the time she had realised this was more than just a place where he came to enjoy the stunning view of Rome.

It was his sanctuary.

Back then, she had decided not to follow him here again and she had told herself she had done so because she wouldn't learn anything new about him by tracking him to the same location more than once.

A lie.

In reality, she hadn't wanted to intrude.

This space had seemed almost sacred, a place where he had been different to the brash, outgoing man she had followed around Rome and studied in its various nightclubs and bars.

He had been quiet, introspective, lost deep in thought and completely unguarded. Vulnerable.

"I've been here before," she whispered, afraid of how he might react to that but needing to put it out there because she didn't want to keep anything hidden from him anymore.

Valen released her, rubbed the back of his head and turned his profile to her, his golden eyes fixing on the distant rooftops of Rome.

"I know."

Those words were quietly spoken, but they offered a comforting balm to her unsteady heart.

"You're not exactly subtle." He slid her a sideways glance that teased her and heated her at the same time.

He was trying to cheer her up.

She realised that now.

He had brought her to this sacred place to share it with her, to give her a reason to feel closer to him and further away from her fears. He wanted her to find the same peace in this place as he did.

Eva looked out over the city. "I'm subtle. I think you cheat."

She could almost feel him frowning as he said, "Cheat?"

She nodded, wrapped her arms around herself to keep the chill off and wished she had brought her jacket. Spring was still struggling to arrive, and the morning air was crisp. It was hardly t-shirt weather.

"I think you have super senses or something," she muttered and Rome turned hazy in her vision as she thought about that, and everything else.

"And if I do?" he said and she wasn't surprised to hear it.

She shrugged and looked across at him, smiled when she found him looking at her rather than the city. "It's cheating."

He jammed his hands in his trouser pockets and huffed. "Not as if I can switch it off."

His golden eyes roamed back to the city. A breeze chased up the hill, ruffling his blond hair, making it dance around the other side of his face, and a flicker of surprise did go through her now.

He had stood to her right, revealing the scarred side of his face to her.

A side he usually tried to keep away from her.

Did he know he had done it, or was it a subconscious decision?

A sign that whether he knew it or not, he was growing comfortable around her.

Silence fell between them, but the chirping of birds heralding the dawn kept it from feeling tense or uncomfortable. It felt natural. A pause in their conversation.

Eva glanced at him again. His gaze slid to her but he didn't move to face her. The corner of his lips quirked.

She turned towards him and he ran his eyes over her. They went round when he reached her feet.

"Shit." He kicked his boots off and she frowned.

What the hell was he doing?

It became clear when he crouched in front of her, lifted her foot and she almost fell on her backside. She leaned over, pressed her hands against his shoulders to steady herself, and watched as he put his boots on her bare feet. She had forgotten she had no shoes on.

Eva stared down at his army boots on her feet. Warm. She lifted her head and smiled down into his golden eyes.

"Thank you… but your feet will get cold…"

He rolled his shoulders. "Not really a big deal. I won't get sick and it takes a lot for me to feel the cold."

"You never get sick?"

He shook his head and the longer strands of his golden hair brushed his right cheek. "Call it a perk of being a god."

Eva's mouth flapped open.

Her eyebrows shot high on her forehead.

"God?"

He looked wonderfully awkward as he rose to his full height and floundered, struggling for words.

"God," she murmured, shock sending a ripple of numbness through her as she tried to grasp that.

"Not like *the* god or anything. Just a god." He shrugged, but there was nothing casual about it this time.

"But a god… you're a god… oh my god… your brothers…"

"Well, it sort of stands to reason that they would be gods too." He raised his hand to rub his neck, tensed and lowered it again. "I might get into a little trouble for this."

"For what?" She was still stuck on trying to wrap her mind around the fact he was apparently a deity.

She supposed it explained why he had powers.

"Well… you're kind of mortal. It's a no-no."

"Oh." She stared at him, the shock subsiding as worry replaced it. She didn't want to get him into trouble. "But, I mean, the gods apparently appeared to mortals all the time back in the day. Jupiter was always at it… if you know what I mean."

The touch of colour on his cheeks and the way his eyes heated said that he did.

That flash of desire was gone a moment later, a frown replacing it. "Jupiter is a pussy."

It was her turn to frown.

He huffed and looked down at Rome. "The whole pantheon sucks."

The ground trembled. Valen grinned.

When he looked across at her, that grin widened and his eyes sparkled with mischief.

"They fucking hate it."

Eva wasn't following. "Hate what?"

Valen sighed, tipped his head back and stared at the lightening sky. "Having a Greek on their turf."

A Greek.

"So I would do better to mention the fact that Zeu—"

His head snapped down, his eyes bright gold in the low light, and he snarled, "Don't mention that fucker."

She tensed and shifted back a step.

His demeanour instantly shifted, the darkness lifting from it and an apology entering his soft eyes. He did scrub a hand around his neck now.

"Bastard," he muttered and spat on the grass.

Lightning rolled across the cloudless sky.

How odd.

She blinked, feeling dazed as that one tried to sink in, wanting to laugh at how crazy it was.

Or how crazy she was.

"Uncle loves it when I call him that." Valen grinned at her and then his face fell again. "Something wrong?"

She shook her head, even though everything was wrong. It was all messed up.

Valen laughed, a nervous edge to it. "I suppose you're right though. The bastard can hardly punish me for revealing myself as a god when he was always off shagging mortals."

He didn't sound sure.

The ground trembled again, more violently this time, and she eased closer to Valen, afraid the earth was about to split and swallow her.

"The, uh… Roman pantheon gods sound angry," she said, and wished she hadn't, because saying out loud that there were gods ended her ability to pretend that she had imagined everything she had seen, including the freak cloudless lightning.

Valen kicked at the grass with his right foot. "That wasn't them."

It definitely hadn't been an earthquake.

So who had made the ground shake?

She lifted her head to ask but Valen's expression warned her not to do it. There was wariness in his eyes that hadn't been there a moment before, a hint of fear that had her holding her tongue. Mentioning that he was a god had set him on edge, why?

It struck her that it was because he thought she would run away, or reject him or do something to leave him because she was afraid of him now.

It wasn't the case at all.

If gods were real and he was one, then it explained a lot.

"Electricity," she whispered and caught his frown as she dropped her eyes from his face to his hands. She reached for them, stopped herself before she could touch them and withdrew. Her gaze leaped to his face.

He stared down at his hands, a distant look in his eyes and a sombre air surrounding him.

She hadn't meant to hurt him by stopping herself from touching him, but clearly she had. If he thought she was afraid to touch him now, he was wrong about that too.

She edged her right hand towards his left one and brushed her fingertips over the back of it and down his fingers, a thrill tripping through her as they touched.

"Lightning," he said and when she looked up at him, added, "technically. I can control electricity... but when I was born, that sort of contained lightning-type energy hadn't been invented. So... lightning."

"Lightning," she whispered and gasped as tiny white-purple arcs crackled between the fingers of his other hand. She released his left one on instinct.

He sighed. "I wouldn't hurt you."

It was easy for him to say that, but it was human nature to fear electricity, and how difficult would it be for the hand she had been holding to suddenly conduct that electricity too?

"When I was 'seducing' you, you needed a time out... I saw your power then." She looked between his bright golden eyes and his hands.

He sighed again and grimaced.

"Fine. Sometimes it gets the better of me." His tone turned sombre again and he looked off into the distance at Rome. "Sometimes I let it."

He didn't sound proud of that.

He raised his hands in front of him and little bolts of lightning chased between his fingertips.

Eva studied his noble profile in silence, deeply aware of what a big step this was for him. It touched her that he was doing this for her—sharing this place and himself. All in an effort to set her mind at ease. She had the feeling that he would answer any question she asked right now, because he wanted her to feel better and it was all he felt he could do for her.

She would do something for him too. She would take that same big step and tell him about herself if he asked, would hold nothing back from him, letting him be the first person to know the real her.

"What did happen at the club that night... when you reacted to the drink?"

He smiled, tipped his head back and groaned. "Not quite what I had expected, that's what happened. I thought maybe it would throw me a little off balance, strip away a few too many inhibitions. I hadn't anticipated it would strip away my control like that instead."

He tilted his head towards her.

"I don't know the why of it. Me and my brothers are just more sensitive to some things. Alcohol, some drugs, caffeine. It makes fuck all sense to me since I can drink in a bar in the Underworld and all I do is get drunk."

Eva stared at him.

He grimaced, turned to face her and blew out his breath as his hands landed on her shoulders and he crouched so he was eye level with her.

"Let's just toss some shit out there and then I don't have to worry about it anymore, okay?" he said and she dumbly nodded, still reeling from him talking about the Underworld. Hell. He drew in another deep breath and expelled it hard. "Here goes nothing. I was born in the Underworld. You've probably heard of my parents. I have six brothers, all pains in my arse. I was banished here two centuries ago by Dad to protect gates between the Underworld and this one. Daemons like Benares and Jin are trying to shatter those gates and if they do, the worlds we love merge and it all goes to shit. Still following?"

Eva nodded again, her ears ringing and head spinning as she raced to follow him.

"I'm in charge of Rome, which is why you met my fine arse, and we think Benares and Jin are part of a group of daemons who are behind the calamity the fucking bastard Moirai... uh, Fates I guess you would know them as... foresaw."

She nodded, and kept nodding, her gaze glued on his face but her mind sweeping her away from him, down a vicious rapids that she wasn't sure she would survive.

"Take any of that in?" Valen whispered and looked between her eyes, his narrowing as he searched them.

She kept nodding. "You're from the Underworld. You have brothers. Daemons want to destroy everything. You *really* don't like the Moirai."

"Because they're bastards," he muttered and his face darkened, reminding her of the way he had looked when she had almost said Zeus.

He hated Zeus too.

Had something happened to make him hate the three Fates and the king of Greek gods?

She wasn't going to ask, because he had that look again, the one that said she would regret it if she dared to voice that question.

"Still with me?" he murmured, voice a low rasp that was far too sexy.

She latched onto that and the wicked thoughts it stirred, using it to escape the vortex of craziness of everything he had just said.

Eva stopped nodding and stared at him. She had to focus on something small, something she was comfortable with if she was going to take any of this in and believe it was real, not a figment of her warped mind.

Or his warped mind.

She looked down at his hand on her right shoulder. "You control lightning."

He nodded.

She lifted her eyes back to his. "Do your brothers too?"

"No." He eased back, released her shoulders and put his hands behind his neck, clasping it. The action raised the hem of his black t-shirt, flashing a strip of toned stomach at her that had her wicked thoughts escalating, multiplying rapidly. "We all have different ones."

His expression soured.

"Except Keras. Being the firstborn he got the job lot because he's special."

Eva had the feeling he hated Keras most of all out of his six brothers, and that it was because he believed Keras was special for some reason.

Keras wasn't at all special in her eyes.

Valen was.

She had the feeling she could fall in love with him.

She crouched, pressed her hand to the grass and smiled when she found it wasn't too damp. Good, because she needed to sit down. All of this would be easier to take in if she wasn't standing.

She planted her backside on the ground and grimaced as her jeans were instantly wet.

Maybe not such a grand idea after all, but she was committed now.

Valen sat down beside her, so close she could smell his aftershave and feel the heat radiating off him. He placed his hands behind himself and propped himself up, his long legs stretched out in front of him, his gaze fixed on Rome.

She dragged her eyes away from him and looked there too.

Dawn was coming, painting the sky with ribbons of gold and pink.

"It's beautiful." She sighed as she took it in, gave herself a moment to absorb the view and how good sitting here enjoying it with Valen made her feel.

She had never watched a sunrise with a guy before.

"Was just thinking the same thing," he murmured throatily and she frowned across at him, wondering what had gotten into him to make him sound so sexy again.

He was staring at her.

She shoved him in his left arm, making him sway sideways, and his smile was wicked and unapologetic.

"Watch the sunrise," she said, putting her best effort into sounding as if she was scolding him even as she blushed inside at the fact he had called her beautiful.

He sighed but did as she asked.

God, this was comfortable though.

Sitting on a damp hillside, watching the sun rising over Rome, next to a Greek god.

Not exactly how she had pictured her life going.

But she wasn't going to complain about it.

She looked down at the city stretching before her and Benares crept back into her thoughts, but rather than feel shaken by his presence, resolve filled her and she set her jaw as Valen's words swam in her mind.

Benares and Jin wanted to destroy Rome.

Like hell she was letting that happen.

This was her home, and she was going to fight to protect it, just as Valen did.

CHAPTER 21

"Do you have any guns at your place?" Eva said and felt Valen's eyes leap from the city to land on her.

"Guns?"

She nodded, not taking her eyes off the rooftops, seeking out all of her favourite buildings. She could see everything from up here. The Colosseum and the forum area, the Vatican and the weaving snake of the Tiber as it swept through the city.

"I have a few in my bag, but I don't want to go back to my apartment for the others. I left my favourite guns there." She swore his gaze grew more intense, drilling into the right side of her face.

He was definitely frowning at her now.

"One or two. I mostly have knives. Why, you thinking of starting a war?" he said, his tone measured and calm.

Assessing.

He was trying to figure out what she was up to even when he already knew the truth of it. A truth that he didn't like, so he was looking for another reason, one more palatable to him.

Eva glanced across at him. "They already started it for me. I'm just going to finish it."

He looked dumbfounded.

Not quite the reaction she had hoped to get from him.

He turned his face away from her, his expression losing all the warmth she had been enjoying, his eyes narrowing and glowing molten gold again. The air around him grew dark, tense in a way she didn't like because she felt as if he was shutting her out, and she frowned at him.

"Let it go," he said, his tone as dark as his aura. "It isn't going to happen. I'm not letting you fight."

She folded her arms across her chest. "You don't get a say. I'm involved in this, and nothing will change that."

"I'm changing it. I'm not going to stand by and let you get yourself killed, Eva." His voice cracked at the end and he turned his head away from her, and her arms fell back to her sides as she sensed the pain in him.

The fear.

He didn't want to lose her.

"I've spent over a decade as an assassin, Valen. I know how to handle myself. You don't have to worry." She reached out to touch his shoulders but they tensed and then he turned on her.

"But I do," he barked and she flinched, her hand hovering in the air between them. "I do. Eva… you spent a decade eliminating mortals. You're dealing with daemons now. They're too strong for you to fight."

Her lips flattened and she scowled at him. "I bet guns make them bleed just like a mortal."

His expression remained dark, his eyes devoid of emotion, cold and hard, the way she hated seeing them. "What use is a gun going to be when they move faster than you can track?"

True. An image of Benares suddenly being in front of her flashed across her mind and she couldn't argue against Valen's point. One second Benares had been before her, and when she had turned he was right there, blocking her path.

"Knives are better," he muttered and she had the feeling that he was starting to relent, his defences weakening as he looked at her. "Maybe a sword."

"A sword?" She couldn't quite believe he had just suggested that. "Who uses a sword?"

He glared at her.

Clearly, he used a sword.

"I thought you liked knives." She must have sounded as unsettled by that thought as she felt because his frown hardened and he canted his head to one side and studied her.

"Not good with knives?"

Eva shuddered and shook her head. "Too personal."

He clucked his tongue and huffed, "Women."

Eva punched him in his left deltoid and he glared at her again. "Stronzo."

He grinned. "Love it when you talk dirty."

She hit him again.

"How can you kill with a knife though?" she said and he turned serious again, a sigh escaping him.

"I'm used to it... but there was a time when I thought like you do, back when I was young... before my powers had fully manifested and stabilised, and I had mastered them." He dropped his gaze to the patch of grass that separated them and picked at the blades with his fingers, and she gave him a moment to collect his thoughts and the courage to keep talking to her, opening himself to her. He twirled a blade of grass he had plucked between his fingers and stared at it. "A knife seemed too intimate... and the thought of stabbing or slicing into someone's flesh turned my stomach."

Exactly the way she felt.

"What happened to change that?" She didn't want him to stop talking now that he had started, because she finally felt she was coming to know him, that the final pieces of the puzzle were falling into place and completing the picture of him.

"I went through my trial when I hit two hundred... pretty much a teen in mortal terms. Fucking voice hadn't even broken then. I looked like a scrawny little bastard too." He tossed the blade of grass and sat straight again, crossing his legs.

Two hundred.

It didn't surprise her to learn that he was far older than he appeared. If he had looked like a teen at two hundred, he was probably around three times that age now, maybe more. He had been in her world for two hundred years too. He slid her another look, one that silently asked her not to probe into his age. She wouldn't. Not yet anyway. He had been uncomfortable after telling her a little about himself earlier, clearly concerned that the things he was admitting would drive her away.

They wouldn't.

She was here to stay.

And he would tell her in his own time.

He yawned, flashing his tongue stud and stirring wicked thoughts that tried to distract her from their conversation.

She shoved them out of her head and focused on his eyes instead as they locked with hers. "What's a trial?"

"A rite of manhood." He waggled his eyebrows but the dark edge to his golden eyes said it was nothing to joke about.

He wanted to lighten the mood, but she wasn't sure it was possible if he was talking about what she thought he was—being forced into combat in order to prove himself a man. He scratched his left ear and shrugged, as if wanting to shift the heaviness of what he was saying from his back, but it didn't seem to work because he remained stiff, his eyes still dark and haunted.

His lips parted on a deep sigh.

"It's a Dad thing." He tried another shrug. This one didn't work either. "We get taken off to some remote corner of the Underworld and have to get back."

It didn't sound so bad, if she ignored the fact that the word Underworld conjured images of daemons more terrifying than Benares and those creatures that had been sniffing around her apartment building.

"I had a knife to defend myself... I managed to steal it on the third day, and the owner wasn't happy about it."

Third day? How far from home had his father taken him? She got the feeling that he hadn't exactly been given a map to find his way home either. She was surprised he didn't have abandonment issues. His father sounded like a real piece of work.

Probably not worse than hers had been though.

"I quickly learned it was kill or be killed, and I didn't want to die, so I gutted my opponent and moved on."

"You make it sound easy," she said and he shook his head, a solemn edge to his eyes.

"It wasn't. I didn't sleep the night I took my first life... I couldn't close my eyes without reliving it in vivid... gory... detail... but I did what I had to do to survive and I still do now." He looked down the rolling slope to the fields and beyond them to the city.

The sun had crept higher, bathing everything in a golden glow, including Valen. If she said he was handsome, he would laugh at her, would try to let it roll off his back together with the hurt he tried not to feel.

She found that sad in a way.

It made her want to take hold of him and say it until he believed it, until he believed it was possible for people to like him, and he realised that his brothers were arseholes, just like their father, and Zeus and the Moirai for whatever they had done to him to make him hate them too.

"I killed over fifty warriors of the outer regions before I completed my trials, and lost track of the number of beasts I added to that count. More than any of my brothers had to." He closed his eyes and hung his head, his longer lengths of hair falling forwards. "I can still remember every kill. They're branded on my mind… seared there for eternity."

Eva's heart went out to him.

Her father had been a bastard, violent and cruel, and she was beginning to believe Valen's father had been cut from the same cloth.

What sort of man would force their child to fight for his life?

To fight to come home?

Her eyes slowly widened.

He was still fighting to go home.

"You said your father banished you here."

He smiled briefly and glanced at her. "You noticed that slip, huh? I try not to think about it that way, but none of us can go back to the Underworld until the calamity the bastard Moirai saw is averted and won't come to pass."

"And I thought my father was bad." She turned her cheek to him, drew her knees up and rested her chin on them, studying Rome as morning light flickered over it and reflected off the windows, so it sparkled.

"How did you end up as an assassin?" he asked in a low voice, one filled with caution. "You mentioned your family before… was it because of them?"

She smiled to let him know she didn't mind him asking. He was answering all her questions, completing her picture of him, so it was only fair she did the same.

"My father was one of those men who try to control everything… and who are weak enough to resort to violence if they don't get their way."

"He hurt you?" Valen growled and she turned her face towards him, placed her hands over her knees, and leaned her cheek against them.

He had that look in his eyes again, the one that told her he wanted to kill for her sake.

"He's dead already."

Valen's eyes widened.

"No, I didn't do it," she said quickly, before he got the wrong impression. "I hated him for how he treated my mother, how it was fine for him to sleep with other women and betray her, but if a man so much as looked in her direction she was punished for it while he lied to her face about his mistresses, saying he only ever looked at her and was only with her."

His face darkened, something surfaced in his eyes and he looked away. Why?

"I'm sorry," he whispered and his shoulders slumped, his hands falling into his lap. "I shouldn't have let her kiss me."

"God," she snapped, half shocked, half dismayed. "Don't go comparing yourself to him. If that bitch was anything like Benares, she cast some weird spell on you. It wasn't really your fault."

"You don't have to call me god. Valen will do." He smiled, but it was strained, and she hated it.

She didn't want him to blame himself for what had happened.

She lowered her right hand to his lap and placed it over both of his, stared at them as she wondered whether he would ever stop pulling up his defences around her or being so quick to believe he had done something wrong.

"Don't blame yourself, Valen," she whispered and stroked her thumb across his fingers. "I hope you don't blame me."

He turned his hand beneath hers and seized hold of it, squeezed it so hard her bones ached. "Never. Bastard daemons have some sort of wicked mojo that addles the brain. I'm not even immune to it."

But he had told his brothers he didn't need their help and he could handle it. Was he sure that he could resist if Jin turned on the charm again?

She wasn't sure she would be able to break free of Benares's spell if he tried to cast it on her again. She felt weaker now, shaken by events, and she feared it would make it easier for him to pull her under his control.

"I won't let him hurt you," Valen whispered, dragging her back to him and out of the mire of her thoughts.

He raised his other hand and feathered his fingertips over her cheek, his eyes on hers the entire time, overflowing with determination, affection, and dark with a promise she knew he would keep.

"You were telling me about another bastard in your life." He looked as if he wanted to grimace.

She had to admit, it wasn't the greatest change in subjects, but it was the one they had been talking about before he had foolishly compared himself to her father.

Valen was nothing like him.

He couldn't see it, but he was noble, and passionate, and loyal, and possessive but not in a bad way.

He was possessive in a way that screamed he would do everything in his power, whatever it took, to keep her eyes on him and her heart belonging to him.

Hurting her wouldn't even cross his mind, because to his sort of possessive nature it would be a crime, something he couldn't stomach doing.

His sort of possessive nature showed itself in a desire to protect, and a deep need to cherish.

Maybe it was because he had a strong heart, filled with love for others, not love for himself.

"My father got into bad dealings with some men and got himself killed." Did she sound as sour about that as she felt? "I wanted him to suffer… eternally if possible… for what he did to my mother, always lashing out at her, always hurting her. I'm sure in the end he was the reason she killed herself."

"Eva." Valen laid his palm against her cheek, and she closed her eyes, stealing his warmth as it flowed through her and eased her pain.

"Her death drove me away from the family. It was my breaking point. I had it out with my father and brother, and I walked out the door and never looked back. I was so mad. I wanted to kill them." She rested her head more heavily against her knees as memories of those dark days filled her mind. "I had little money, not enough to last more than a few months. I ended up in a bad part of town, working wherever I could, and then I ended up on the streets."

Silence weighed down on her and she opened her eyes, needing to see Valen to lift it from her and ease her heart.

Those days were long gone, nothing more than a distant memory now. She had a home, a safe place to sleep, and enough money to last at least a decade.

"It was rough." She smiled but she didn't feel it, and the edge to Valen's eyes said that he knew it, that he wanted to pull her into his arms and hold her, but was afraid.

This was new for him too. She toyed with his hand in his lap, unsure of herself, but she had to keep moving forwards, no matter what. They could learn everything about being in a relationship like this together.

"I ended up trying to pickpocket the wrong man, and suddenly men in suits were on me. I fought them as best I could and ended up disarming one, and knocking another one out before they managed to capture me."

"What happened?" Valen brushed her hair from her face and swept it behind her ear, his gaze following his fingers, a touch of fascination in it that warmed her and made her want to tease him for being so surprised that she allowed him to do something so intimate with her.

His eyes drifted to hers and he shot her a glare.

"Message received," she said, letting him know she wouldn't say a word about it. She poked the end of his index finger with her thumb, letting her focus drop back to them and her past. He had large hands, callused, but she supposed the hands of a warrior would be worn and rough. She turned her hand in his and frowned at her own calluses. They weren't so different to each other, even if he was a god and she was human. "I thought I was a goner, but it turned out that my fighting spirit had impressed the man I had tried to steal from, who just happened to be the most powerful man in Rome at the time."

"Tough gig." He flashed another smile that sent heat pulsing through her.

God, he was devastating when he smiled like that.

"He offered to train me. I was meant to be security for his daughter, but it turned out I had a natural talent with guns and my years of sneaking around my family villa trying not to be noticed by my father and brother had made me rather good at following people without being seen and blending into my environment."

"So he swapped your job description."

She nodded.

"I was security for his daughter for a while, but then he didn't want to pay the running cost for a professional hit on a competitor so he sent me to do it." Eva raised her eyes back to his. "Let's just say that you weren't the only one who had trouble sleeping the night after your first kill. I think it took me a week to get some sleep… and then it was only because I collapsed from exhaustion."

"But you kept doing jobs?" His golden eyebrows dipped low and his irises blazed like fire.

She shrugged. "You don't really get a choice. Once I started down that path, I had to keep walking it. The alternative was leaving, and you don't just leave that world and Rome's most powerful boss."

Valen's handsome face blackened. "He would have killed you."

"He's dead too," she said before he could offer to kill him.

He arched an eyebrow at her. She shot him a look that challenged him to say he wasn't going to say it. He huffed and looked away from her, a definite pout to his lower lip.

"It didn't take me long to get used to it." She prodded his fingers but he refused to look at her. "I guess I'm like you after all."

He sighed. "We're a pair alright."

He slanted his gaze down at her and smiled.

Eva smiled back at him, silently thanking him for trying to lighten the mood.

"You'll be fine." His smile dropped, his expression turning so serious all of a sudden that hers fell with it, and his voice lowered into a dark growl. "I won't let that daemon and his bitch hurt you. Next time I see the bastard, he's going to pay."

She didn't fail to notice the way his hand rose to his face and his fingers came to rest on his scar as he said that, and couldn't stop the feeling that went through her.

There was a meaning behind his actions.

A story behind that scar.

And she needed to know it if she was ever going to understand him.

CHAPTER 22

Valen tensed as Eva's slender hand came to rest over his and her fingers brushed his scar. He wasn't sure how she could bear to touch it. Why didn't she think it was ugly, or frightening, like every other person he had met?

"How did this happen?" she murmured, voice low and cautious, as if she had sensed the tension mounting inside him, the need to push her away and tell her not to look at him, not to look at the mark of his sin.

A mark he had to live with forever.

He pulled his hand from under hers, dropped them both into his lap and curled them into fists as he looked away from her, turning his head to his left to hide his scar.

Her touch softened, the light sweeps of her fingers over the puckered ruined skin tearing at him, pulling down his defences and weakening him.

Making him vulnerable.

The tension building inside him twisted tighter, pushed harder, and he closed his eyes to shut her and the world out.

"Not going to tell me?" she whispered, her warm voice coaxing him into doing just that, bewitching him and making him want to tell her.

He couldn't.

She had looked horrified enough when he had told her about his rite and the things he had done then.

If he told her about how he had killed the Moirai in cold blood, and tried to give his uncle the same fitting end, it didn't bear thinking about how she would look at him then.

If she would look at him at all.

He wouldn't blame her if she walked out of his life.

He didn't want that to happen though, so he kept his mouth shut and pushed away the side of him that wanted to tell her, because it foolishly hoped things would turn out differently from how he knew they would and she would stay.

"Tell me how you got it." Her voice was stronger, almost demanding.

She pressed her hand against the scar and tried to make him look at her.

He growled and knocked her arm away.

Her beautiful blue eyes held a flicker of hurt as she flexed her fingers, conflict dancing across her delicate features, as if she wanted to try to touch him again.

She lowered her hand to her knee instead and muttered, "Sorry I asked."

Was he being a dick again?

It certainly felt like he was, and that strange gnawing feeling was back, eating away at him and making him want to tell her that he was the one who should be apologising to her.

It also made him want to tell her why he didn't want to share that part of his sordid history with her, but memories of that day were beginning to crowd in the corners of his mind, and he didn't want to go there. Not today.

He wasn't strong enough today.

He felt too uncertain of everything, and his demons were back, whispering in his ear that no one could love him.

Especially if they knew he had gone on a bloody rampage to slay four gods in the name of revenge.

Valen glanced across at her, gaze tracing her profile and heart memorising how she looked in the morning light, the golden glow of sunrise bathing her clear skin with warmth and the light breeze teasing the straight strands of her jaw-length hair, making the blue streaks dance amidst the black.

He could sit for hours just watching her like this.

But he needed to say something to clear the air between them and make her look at him again.

He needed to snap her out of her thoughts before she got mad at him. He didn't want her scowls and her sharp words. He wanted her smiles and her laughter.

"Want to see a magic trick?" he said and her blue eyes slid his way.

"You can do magic too?"

He hadn't meant it quite like that, but the bright shine in her eyes told him she was interested.

"Not magic like you're thinking…" He smiled slowly. "Although I can pull a rabbit out of thin air."

He thought he could anyway.

Not a real rabbit.

He studied the sky, and then Rome, charting all the positions of the lightning rods he had installed, trying to figure out if it was possible. It would take a little effort on his part, but it would be worth it.

He just hoped he didn't fail dismally.

Valen stood, brushed his damp backside down, and focused.

It started as a small dark patch in the sky over Rome that quickly grew and then clouds spilled from it, rolling across the blue canvas. He hated rain, but he wasn't meant to make lightning without clouds.

An order from those bastards on high.

Funny how Zeus was allowed to do it though.

Eva's eyes landed on him, sending a hot shiver dancing down his spine and along his limbs. He looked down at her, grinned as he caught her staring at his backside, and she tensed and blushed, her gaze zipping away from him. Gods, he loved how she reacted to him like that, not the cold merciless assassin but a shy yet alluring female.

"You're wet," she muttered.

"Yeah, yeah. Good excuse. Now pay attention because I'm about to create something far more spectacular for you to look at than my arse." He hoped.

He sucked in a few breaths, flexed his fingers and stared at the clouds, psyching himself up. He could do this. He had made dragons. He could master a bunny.

He just had to do a rabbit perched on its back legs with its ears on alert.

Simple.

Right?

He flexed his fingers again and cursed the way they shook and the uncertainty racing through him. It had been a long time since he had felt this nervous about using his power.

He glanced at Eva again.

She sat with her long lean legs stretched in front of her and crossed at the ankles, her hands planted behind her to support her as she waited, and an expectant look on her face that told him to amaze her.

Performance pressure sucked.

"You sure you want a rabbit?" He gave her a hopeful look.

She frowned up at him. "You suggested a rabbit, not me."

"Can't interest you in something else?" He smiled and cursed again as it trembled, probably flashing his uncertainty at her like a neon sign.

"I thought you were some big, powerful god?" She smiled wickedly. "If you are, then I'm sure you can handle a little rabbit."

He narrowed his eyes on her, silently cursing her this time. No damn way she was going to get away with questioning his prowess as a god.

"You want a bunny," he snarled. "You'll get a fucking bunny."

He whipped his head around, forced all of his focus to his hands as his power accumulated there, and pointed out all the places in the city he wanted the lightning to strike.

He raised his right hand in front of him.

Pressed his thumb and index finger together.

Clicked.

White-purple lightning shot from the boiling black clouds, a little faster than he had anticipated. Blame his mood for that. He quickly snapped his fingers again, adding a second to join the first bolt, and focused to command them. They split and then split again, laced together and shot through each other, forming branches across the sky.

Taking on a shape above the city.

Valen groaned inwardly at the sight of it.

The lightning connected with the rods on the buildings and the air rumbled with the force of each strike, the ground trembling with it as thunder rolled across Rome.

The image he had created stuttered and died, and he wanted to do the same.

Silence fell.

Thick, oppressive, nerve-destroying silence.

And then Eva spoke.

"I didn't expect that."

He huffed. "I was unfocused, distracted by someone teasing me. My mind got a bit off track."

"Well… it was sort of on track…" She sounded as if she was going to laugh so he scowled down at her. Her lips trembled as she fought to contain the smile that was already in her eyes. "I mean… you did say *fucking* bunny."

He grimaced, aware he was never going to live this one down and hoping she was the only one that had seen a startlingly explicit image of two bunnies going at it appear above the sky of Rome this morning.

He didn't want to even consider the rumours that would spread about him, or the nicknames he would pick up, if any gods had witnessed it.

"Can you make other shapes?" She beamed up at him.

He glared at her. "Don't say it like that, as if screwing bunnies is in my repertoire of images I enjoy forming with my powers."

That laugh that had been building inside her escaped.

His frown melted under the intense heat that spread through him, rolling outwards from his chest, on hearing it and seeing her face lighting up, all the shadows lifted from it.

He supposed he had succeeded in his desire to cheer her up, even if the method hadn't been quite what he had intended.

"I can make a few." He thought about what she might like to see next. If it kept her smiling and laughing, he would take a shot at creating whatever she suggested, and he wouldn't stop until she was done or he was utterly drained of strength. "Any requests?"

"An eagle." She looked up at him. "Can you do that?"

An eagle was close to a dragon, and he could do that, so it shouldn't be too much of a challenge.

"Sure." He shot her a smile and absorbed the way she turned all female and cute again. His little killer. He found this side of her almost as alluring as her warrior one, possibly more so because she showed it only to him.

Valen focused and snapped his fingers, calling the lightning from the clouds and conducting it so it created the image of an eagle with its wings spread above Rome. Fitting he supposed. It had been the seat of the Roman empire and they had loved their eagles.

Eva laughed again, the light sound filling his mind and his heart, warming him as the rain began to fall and keeping the chill off his skin.

She ordered another animal, and then another, not seeming to care about the rain as it fell on her.

He hadn't done this in a long time.

The warmth in him died as that thought invaded his mind, dragging up memories that still hurt. Calindria had always loved it when he had made shapes for her in the Underworld. Dragons had been her favourite.

Back then, he had loved creating shapes with his power, amusing her and giving those gifts to her, whatever she requested.

Since her death, he had only made images when his mood had taken a nosedive, using them to shake the earth and rattle the heavens, and unleash all of his pain.

It was strange to take pleasure in doing this again, the good sort of pleasure, the sort he had found in it before Calindria's death. Afterwards, he had taken a darker sort of pleasure from it, giving his power control over him and feeding off it and how strong it made him feel, invincible, dangerous, and terrifying.

A god.

"Valen," Eva whispered and he realised he had stopped and was standing like an idiot in the rain, his hand outstretched in front of him, frozen in time.

Transported back through it to relive those better days that still scraped at his chest, hollowing it out whenever he thought about them.

He snapped himself out of the past and focused on the present, because there was no point in looking back. What was done, was done, and he couldn't change it now. He hadn't been able to change it back then either.

He hadn't been strong enough.

He looked across at Eva, found her standing beside him with warmth in her blue eyes, concern that was for him and he cherished it, held it to his chest and refused to relinquish it even as that dark voice in his mind chanted that she would never be his.

No one could love him.

Zeus had made sure of that.

"Valen." She lifted her hand to his face and placed it gently against his scar, as if she had sensed it was the source of his pain, the mark of the sin he had to bear for eternity.

He fell into her eyes, into the affection they showed him, fear snaking through his veins to stir other emotions, to create a strange sense of urgency and panic that he couldn't control, a crushing need that consumed him.

A sense that if he could just keep hold of Eva that he could break this curse and she would fall in love with him.

Like he was falling in love with her.

He grabbed her shoulder, yanked her into his arms and kissed her, desperate need driving him, pushing him to do whatever it took to make her feel something for him, to make sure she didn't leave him.

She responded instantly, but her kiss was brief and he wanted to snarl when she pushed her palms against his chest and broke away from him.

No.

Cold swept through him, the fear that gripped him rising to sink its claws into his heart as it whispered that it was already too late—he was already losing her.

He dug his fingers into her shoulders and tried to pull her back to him, convinced that if he just kept kissing her, if he kept making her laugh and smile, and kept her to himself for long enough, that she would love him. She wouldn't leave him.

She wouldn't turn against him like everyone else.

He couldn't bear it if she did.

It would end him.

She resisted him, and fear birthed anger in his veins, the darker side of his blood awakening and demanding that he bend her to his will.

She would be his.

"Valen," she whispered, stopping him dead as he tried to pull her back to him and kiss her again.

He lifted his eyes to hers and the haze filling his mind, seizing control of him, dissipated as he stared into her striking blue ones and saw not hate, but deep affection in them. There was hurt there too, and fear.

He eased his grip on her shoulders and cursed himself for holding her too tightly, for trying to force himself on her. He was no better than Benares.

He went to withdraw but she caught his arms, her hands warm against his biceps, and shook her head, causing the damp strands of her jaw-length dark hair to stick to her cheeks.

"I'm not done with you," she said, a sharp commanding edge to her voice that was too damn sexy. The determination that had flashed across her features faded and her grip loosened, her voice losing its hardness, softening with shyness that was equally as seductive. "I can feel your power... flowing under your skin. What if... your tongue stud is metal."

Sweet gods, everything about this woman tied him in knots and pulled him deeper under her spell.

That's what had made her pull away from him and had put fear in her eyes?

Not his behaviour, or her feelings for him, but his power?

She was afraid his tongue stud might spark and hurt her.

He grinned, the weight lifting from his heart and the darkness in his veins fading as he brushed her hair behind her ear and thought about that.

"It won't hurt you. It's titanium." His grin widened as she looked up at him, right into his eyes, hers dark and hungry, and filling him with a need to make them even darker. Even hungrier. "It doesn't conduct well, but it might tingle if you're lucky."

Her eyes went a little wider.

A little darker.

Valen growled and pulled her back into his arms, slanted his head and kissed her hard, letting her know in the only way he could right now that she was his, and he was never letting her go.

He would break this curse.

He would make her love him.

CHAPTER 23

Eva rubbed a towel over her wet hair, every inch of her relaxed and sated. Valen had made sure of that. He had tried so hard to cheer her up, and set her mind at ease, both about Benares and about him and this crazy new world she had fallen into, and then he had shown her just how incredibly beautiful his power could be.

He had done it all for her.

She paused with the towel against her head and stared into the mirror.

Something had happened though, something that had stopped him in the middle of making a shape for her out of lightning and had hurt him.

Something that she wanted to know, but she hadn't had the chance to ask him about, and now she felt awkward about mentioning it because he seemed so much brighter, the darkness and pain that had been in his eyes lifted because of her.

She had kissed it out of him.

Or he had kissed it out of himself.

She touched her lips, swore they still tingled from the force of that kiss, one that had held a note of desperation and filled her with a sense that his thoughts were leading him down dark paths again.

He had been quiet when they had returned to the apartment, and had made her sleep to recoup her strength, promising to watch over her.

She hadn't thought it would be possible for her to sleep, not with all the thoughts about him and Benares, and that daemon's plans for him ricocheting around her mind, but she had closed her eyes anyway.

When she had opened them again, the sky beyond the windows of Valen's bedroom had been laced with the colours of evening, and he had been sitting beside her on the bed, watching over her just as he had promised.

She had kissed him for that.

A kiss that had led them into the shower together.

Now he had disappeared into the other room without a word to her, leaving her alone to dry off.

What was weighing on his mind?

If she asked, would he share it with her?

She wanted to draw him back to her, because it felt as if he was drifting away, and she didn't like the chasm that was opening between them.

She finished drying her hair, tossed the white towel on the floor with his one, and combed her fingers through her hair, styling it as best she could without her usual products.

Eva glanced along the wood-panelled corridor towards the living room, thought about sauntering in there naked to seduce him all over again, and then thought the better of it.

She wanted him to talk to her, to open up to her as he had on the hill, and getting him all hot and bothered wasn't going to achieve that.

She went into the bedroom instead, grabbed her duffle bag from near the door, and put it down on the bed. She rifled through it, reassured by the sight of her guns and the spare clips and boxes of ammunition, and chose a simple dark green halter-top and a fresh pair of black jeans.

She fished out the spare black lace bra and a pair of matching shorts, and slipped into them, and then into her top and jeans. Socks followed, and then she sighed as she pulled out her only footwear.

Black running shoes.

Not her taste, but they were compact and fitted into the bag, a bag that was meant to be used in an escape. Running shoes made sense in that scenario, more than her favourite boots anyway.

She tugged them on and laced them, zipped the bag closed and placed it back near the door.

Music drifted into the room.

She paused leaning over the bag and frowned into the corridor. Classical music too. It was soothing, calming, and so unexpected.

She would never have guessed Valen liked such music.

She drifted out into the corridor and along it to her left, following the mellow sound into the living room.

Sure enough, Valen was reclining in his wingback armchair beside the unlit fire, his black t-shirt and combat trousers making him blend into it. His eyes were closed, his chin dipping low towards his chest as he sat there.

Listening to classical music.

She had figured he would like something harder, a fast pounding beat of the rock persuasion.

It seemed so odd seeing him like this.

Was he asleep?

She started when he spoke.

"Sometimes, it's only the music that holds me together and stops me from crossing the line."

It was? She listened to it as she studied him, finding the soft string melody as soothing as he clearly did.

What would happen if he did cross that mental line he had drawn for himself?

He had admitted that he wasn't proud of how he let his power control him at times. She recalled the bar and the devastation he had wrought without using his lightning, and found she didn't want to imagine how bad things might have been if he had unleashed it.

"Mother gave it to me. Esher too. She says that it soothes Dad's rages and that she sees a lot of him in me." He pulled a face that said he didn't like that.

"You hate him." Although she wasn't really sure that was the case, because he always used a shorter name than father for him, one that spoke of affection rather than coldness and distance.

He finally opened his eyes and looked at her. They were molten gold again, glowing fiercely in the fading light of evening. The pain that had been in them since he had fallen quiet on the hill was still there, lurking in his eyes.

"Not hate," he muttered and pushed his fingers through his hair, sweeping it back so it streaked straight over the top from his brow to the back of his head. "Mutual dislike... maybe."

"Mutual?" She frowned at that. "He doesn't like you?"

It would explain the awful rite he had put Valen through.

"Not anymore." He looked away from her, gazed out of the window to his right and his whole demeanour turned uncomfortable, silently telling her to drop the subject.

For once, that wasn't going to happen. She wanted to know about him, and if that meant poking at sore spots, then she would risk his wrath by doing just that.

Besides, there was a question she had wanted an answer to since he had told her his short-and-shocking breakdown of important points about himself.

"You said he banished you from the Underworld, and now you protect gates to it, just who is your father?"

She had a theory, but she wanted to hear him say it.

His eyes slid back to her, a dark edge to them that was more than just a feeling. Black ringed his irises, eating away the gold.

He had looked that way before, when she had fought him. At the time, she had thought she had imagined it, but as she watched the black swallowing the gold, she could no longer deny it had been real.

"Say it," she whispered, suddenly unsure whether she wanted to know.

His black eyes narrowed on her.

Elongated canines flashed between his lips as he spoke.

"Hades."

The god of the Underworld.

His father was the boss down there, the Greek equivalent of the Devil she supposed, although she wasn't sure how close that was to the truth. Her mind latched onto it though, ran with it and pulled her along for the ride, making her envisage a dark and terrifying man, a cruel and vicious ruler fitting for that domain.

Valen clucked his tongue at her. "Already made up your mind I see."

She froze, shock rippling through her as she realised she had backed away from him. She hadn't meant it like that. It wasn't Valen she feared.

It was his father.

Benares was only a daemon and he terrified her. She couldn't imagine how frightening Hades was.

She didn't want to.

Valen muttered something and looked away from her again, and the darkness in his eyes faded, allowing gold to break through.

"You're not like him," she blurted and he arched an eyebrow, but didn't shut her down. She crossed the room to him, navigating her way around the black leather couch, and stopped beside him. He refused to look up at her. "I've seen you do good as well as bad."

His handsome face blackened, the darkness obliterating the gold in his eyes, and he turned sharply to face her.

"I'm not a hero, Eva… stop expecting that of me," he snapped and she eased back a step, reeling from that blow.

Where had that come from?

She hadn't meant it like that. He was overreacting.

The pain was back in his eyes, fiercer than before, and he abruptly turned his face away from her again.

The soles of her feet warmed in her shoes.

A feeling bloomed in her chest, a strange sensation that seemed to link her to him and revealed something to her.

Her words had touched a raw nerve. She wasn't sure how she knew it, or where the feeling had come from, but she suddenly understood him.

On the hill, pain from the past that was still raw for him had returned, awakened by what he had done for her, and that pain was still eating at him.

Pain that was born of great loss and the devastating consequences of it.

Her head lightened. She swayed on the spot as it seemed to pull her downwards. Her knees gave out.

"Eva," he roared and she moaned as he caught her, his strong arms supporting her, stopping her from hitting the tiled floor.

She blinked to clear her blurry vision and breathed hard, all of her strength leaving her as her feet cooled and the weird lightness drifted away.

Valen loomed over her, no trace of black in his golden eyes as they searched hers. There was only fear and concern, worry that flooded her with warmth.

"What happened?" he murmured and slowly righted her.

She didn't fight him as he checked her over, one hand remaining against her waist to keep her upright.

"I don't know… I can't explain it." She squeezed her eyes shut and prickles blazed down her spine and over her arms. What was wrong with her?

"Try," he snapped, a little harsh, and then softly muttered in a more apologetic tone, "please."

She had frightened him. It had frightened her too.

"I felt… this is going to sound crazy… but I felt… connected…" She pushed the words out when he looked up at her, the warmth and worry leaving his face, morphing back into something dark. "To you."

Valen growled, shot to his feet and stamped them against the terracotta tiles. "No meddling."

Her eyes widened. Had he gone mad?

She looked down and her eyes went even wider as she spotted the blue cornflower he was crushing beneath his boots.

Where had that come from?

She was sure it hadn't been there when she had crossed the room to him. She would have noticed it.

Eva squatted and caught his boot, stopping him, and he froze, his gaze landing on her and heating her.

She plucked the broken flower from the tiles and gasped as the damage to it reversed before her eyes.

Valen snatched it from her, stormed across the room to the set of windows to the left of the fireplace, opened it and threw the flower out. He slammed the window closed again, turned to face her and halted.

"Don't look at me like that. She was meddling."

"Like what? Bewildered? Because that's all I'm feeling." She looked down at where the flower had been and touched the floor. It was cold now. She was sure it had been warm. "What the fuck just happened?"

"Meddling," he muttered, as if that was an explanation.

He strode over to her, long legs making short work of the distance, and stopped right in front of her. He looked pissed. She wasn't sure why, and she didn't feel she had done anything wrong so he couldn't be mad with her. He was mad with whoever had apparently meddled.

He huffed and held his hand out to her. "Resist her next time."

Eva wasn't sure she wanted to resist whoever had linked her to Valen, because she had been trying to give her answers to the questions burning inside her. She had been trying to reveal the parts of Valen he wanted to keep hidden from her for some reason, parts she knew she needed to understand.

"I don't even know who I'm meant to be resisting." She placed her hand into his and let him help her onto her feet.

He sighed again and turned his cheek to her. "Mother."

So his mother, Persephone if she had her goddesses right, had tried to reach out to her to give her insight into Valen. His mother wanted her to know the things he wouldn't tell her.

Did that mean she approved of her?

Eva wasn't sure how to take that. A goddess approved of her. A goddess wanted her to make this thing with her son work.

She smiled as it dawned on her. Persephone wanted Valen to be happy, and she thought Eva could do that for him.

She had half a mind to say thank you to Persephone out loud so she would know to ignore Valen's efforts to stop her and would keep trying to help her unravel her son's defences and see the part of him he was still guarding fiercely, unwilling to show it to her.

"I think I like her," Eva said and he growled at her this time. She refused to do as he demanded, wouldn't say that she would try to resist Persephone if she reached out to her again.

If his mother wanted to meddle in their relationship, Eva wasn't going to stop her.

It went against her Italian blood, because mothers were meant to be her nemeses, the ones who stood between her and claiming all of their sons' love, but she was dealing with Greeks now, not fellow Italians. Different rules applied.

It seemed Greek mothers wanted to help the women who tried to claim their sons' hearts.

Or at least Greek goddesses did.

It still felt crazy thinking that, but she was slowly coming to terms with this world she had stepped into the night she had taken Benares's job.

She shifted her gaze to Valen.

He scowled at her. "Don't look at me like that."

Her eyebrows rose. It was the second time he had said that, but she still wasn't sure what was wrong with the way she was looking at him. "Like what?"

"I told you... I can't be what you expect of me." He ploughed the fingers of his left hand through his hair and pulled it back, tugging at his scalp, and frustration mounted in his eyes, making them flash gold at her. What had started this war in him? He ground his teeth, looked as if he would turn away from her and shut her out again, and then barked, "You look at me like I'm going to save you somehow... like I'm your only fucking hope... and I don't want that responsibility. I just can't do it. I failed the last time someone trusted me to protect her."

Eva's heart ached, the sight of him as his strength visibly left him and the pain came rushing back into his eyes pulling her to him, filling her with a need to comfort him.

He was wrong. He was hurting and he was trying to pin it all on her in order to cope with it, because he honestly believed he would fail in protecting her too.

He was afraid.

He sank into the wingback black leather armchair and hung his head forwards, his elbows resting on his knees and his blond hair falling to obscure his face.

He was afraid that he wouldn't be able to protect her as he had promised, that Benares would hurt her because of it, possibly even kill her.

Where had the brash, confident and almost cocky male who had vowed to keep her safe gone? The man who had offered to destroy Benares for her?

She slowly padded across the tiled floor towards him, her heart answering that question.

There was something inside him, a dark and terrible monster, born of his past, and it had awakened on the hill, had risen up to devour his strength and feed on his fears.

She wasn't sure she could vanquish such a monster, because she couldn't defeat the ones that lurked inside her, created by her past too, but she was going to try, because she hated seeing him like this.

She wouldn't let him push her away.

"I never asked you to be a hero, Valen." She kneeled between his feet, lifted her hands and cupped both of his cheeks. He tried to look away from her but she held him firm, keeping his golden eyes on hers. "I don't expect that of you."

He stared into her eyes for long seconds, and then leaned back, sinking into the chair and leaving her sitting between his knees. His eyes remained on hers, and she cursed how good he looked as he sat there staring down the length of his body at her, the honed muscles of his torso visible beneath his tight black t-shirt and the heat building in his eyes calling to her. She managed to keep her eyes fixed on his, not allowing him to distract her with his delicious body or that wicked promise in his eyes, because she felt close to getting answers.

"I don't need you to protect me." She didn't really believe that, but if it eased his mind and weakened the hold his fears had on him, she would say it a thousand times until he believed it.

"Good," he said, a sharp edge to his tone that cut through the air like a blade.

He didn't mean that.

She could see it in his eyes.

"Who was she?" She searched those eyes, wanting to find the answer in them, because she knew he wouldn't tell her.

Had it been a lover?

It had clearly been someone dear to him, and failing her had wounded him deeply, carving a scar in his heart that had never healed.

It had left him with the feeling he wasn't qualified to protect anyone, that he would fail if he tried again.

Yet, he still wanted to protect her.

He wanted to try.

For her.

Calindria.

That delicate name echoed in her mind in Keras's voice.

In this very room, when Keras had confronted Valen after the incident at the bar and Valen hadn't defended himself, that was the name Keras had thrown at Valen.

That was the straw that had broken him and he had left without a word.

Ares and Marek had been shocked to hear Keras throw it at Valen with so much venom.

"Who was Calindria?" she whispered.

Valen tensed.

Looked away from her.

She shook inside as she waited, needing to know whether she had been his lover, afraid to know the answer now because suddenly it felt as if she would never compare to the woman Valen had lost and still grieved.

Still loved.

He closed his eyes, his chest heaved as he sighed, and his lips moved, almost soundlessly.

Almost.

She barely caught the two words.

"Our sister."

When he opened his eyes, they were locked on her, intense and focused, sending a shiver down her spine and spreading heat along her limbs.

"Let it go now."

She nodded, because she didn't want to drag up any more bad memories for him and cause him more hurt.

He had failed to protect his sister, and he blamed himself for it.

Did his brothers blame him too?

His father?

It would explain the animosity he felt towards them, their strained relationship, but then there was also another way to explain all of that.

Valen blamed himself for their sister's death, and it had led him to believe that everyone else blamed him too.

Eva rose onto her knees between his, wrapped her arms around his waist and ignored the shock that rippled across his face as he looked down at her. She pushed up on her toes and kissed him, so he would know that he wasn't alone, that not everyone in this world was against him.

Someone believed in him.

He wouldn't fail her.

She knew that in her heart.

He tensed, lips freezing against hers, and then kissed her on a low growl. His arms snaked around her and he hauled her up onto his lap, making her sit on his left thigh. She lost herself in the kiss again, wanted to wriggle on his thigh as heat built inside her with each wicked stroke of his tongue that made her feel the stud in it.

He stopped again.

Another growl.

Eva tried to pull back to ask him what was wrong, but he dragged her against him and kissed her harder, and she forgot all about it.

Until his lips paused a third time.

"What's wrong?" she murmured against them.

"Fucking gate," he snarled.

Hardly an explanation.

"Ignore it." He claimed her lips again, and she tried to do as he had said, but it was impossible when he kept tensing beneath her as if someone was prodding him in the ribs.

"Seriously." She pulled back and he let her this time.

He scowled at her, but she had the feeling his anger was aimed at the gate and not her for stopping kissing him.

"Explain." She wanted to pepper his cheeks with kisses, but he looked as if that might be nothing more than torture, and she had the sinking feeling he was about to say something she wasn't going to like.

"I have to go out," he muttered, voice a dark growl of disappointment and fury. "Stupid gate is calling me. I have to go open it."

He kissed her again, so hard and demanding that she sank into him and came close to begging him to ignore it, just as he had said.

The gates were important though. She had gathered that much from what he had told her.

"If you don't go... and daemons opened it... would that be enough for something terrible to happen to this world and the Underworld?" She brushed her lips across his with each word and he groaned, tried to kiss her again but she stopped him.

His scowl was definitely for her this time.

He snorted. "No."

"Explain." She was getting tired of this. "Just tell me what happens if you don't go."

"A very annoyed Hellspawn who wants to travel either to the Underworld or from it tells my father what a failure I am. Nothing he doesn't already know." He smiled at her blank expression. "Hellspawn are what I like to think of as acceptable daemons. Dad hates all daemons, but over the centuries he's given the green light to some of the purer breeds that weren't involved in the uprising and allows them to come and go between the Underworld and this one. Of course, other species of Hellspawn have slipped the other way, falling out of favour and finding themselves banished."

"So Hellspawn are like good daemons?" The more he told her, the more questions she had.

He grimaced. "If you want to think of them like that. Sure. They didn't try to destroy the palace and everyone in it to seize the Underworld, so they get a pass."

But the other daemons didn't. They weren't allowed in the Underworld now. By the sounds of things, it hadn't stopped them from wanting to go there.

One day, she was going to make Valen sit down and tell her everything from start to finish, and she wasn't going to let him move until he had answered all of her questions.

Today was not that day though.

"So this gate thing is calling to you because someone wants it open?" she said and he nodded. "No one else can open it?"

He answered that one with a shake of his head.

It seemed to her that things were always more complicated than Valen made them out to be.

He did more than just protect the gate in Rome from daemons. He was responsible for allowing people to pass through it too. A gatekeeper. Without him there, whoever was waiting to use it wouldn't get through.

"So you have to go?" She hated the way her voice wavered as she asked that, betraying her nerves as they began to creep back in.

Having Valen around her every waking and sleeping minute had comforted her so much that now she was afraid to be without him. Damn him. Damn her for being so weak too, but she was dealing with forces far more powerful than she was, and she was beginning to believe that Valen was right and guns wouldn't prove useful against a monster like Benares.

She glanced at the window, into the darkness.

What if Jin was still watching them? What if she reported to Benares that Valen had left her alone?

What if Benares came for her?

Valen's palm came to rest against her left cheek and he slowly eased her head around towards him.

His eyes locked with hers, a silent promise in them, one that contradicted his earlier outburst and the demands he had issued, telling her not to rely on him to protect her.

"You'll be safe here." He swept the pad of his thumb across her cheek, his eyes falling there to track it, a hint of fascination filling them and smoothing their hard edges. "I have wards around this building, and this apartment. If anyone tries to break through them, I'll know. I'll come back... I'll keep you safe."

She nodded, trying to take comfort from that but her mind had latched on to the part where he had made it sound possible for someone to get through these wards.

She didn't let him see the fear that still lingered inside her. He would refuse to leave if he did and it was time she stood on her own two feet again and moved on with her life. It was time she stopped being so weak, so afraid. She was strong.

He slid his hand around the back of her head, pulled her down to him and kissed her hard, his roughness screaming of desperation that rang through her too, a fierce need to take all she could from this moment and never let it go.

He broke away, growled something and then forced a smile. "Be right back." He disappeared.

She dropped to the seat of the armchair and wafted her hand in front of her face, dissipating the black swirling ribbons he had left behind him.

He would be right back.

She had no reason to fear.

She would be safe here.

Benares needed her alive. She kept telling herself that, slowly coming to believe it, as she moved around the apartment, stealing a can of lemonade from the refrigerator in the kitchen beyond the living room and peeking behind all the pale wooden doors of the cupboards.

Valen apparently liked pasta with a vengeance.

She was fairly sure she had spotted it in every cupboard. He had a variety of sauces too, together with a shelf stocked with every imaginable herb and spice, and stacks of passata bottles.

Did he like to cook?

She poked her nose back into his tall silver refrigerator. There were some vegetables in the bottom drawer. Her stomach growled. Maybe she could knock herself up some food while she waited for him.

She looked at the door of the apartment.

He would be back soon.

She could make them some dinner to surprise him when he returned.

Eva busied herself with finding all the pots and pans she needed, and rifling through the cupboards and refrigerator for ingredients. She filled a large pan with water and put it on the hob, and set about dicing onions and vegetables for the sauce as the water came to a boil.

She lost track of time as she focused on her work.

The sound of her phone ringing rose above the quiet classical music that still filled the apartment.

She set down her knife, wiped her hands on a towel, and left the kitchen. She hummed to herself in time with her ringtone as she crossed the living room to the bedroom where she had left it on the side table. A quick glance at the display had her frowning.

A former client.

At least it wasn't Benares phoning her for a report.

She turned away, not interested in anything he might have to say. She wasn't looking for work. Not now, and not for a while to come. She needed a break.

A long one.

Maybe somewhere warm and sunny.

Like Greece.

She kept humming the tune as she headed back towards the kitchen, her thoughts returning to making dinner. She couldn't wait to sit down at the heavy wooden table in the dining side of the kitchen with Valen. Although she wasn't sure whether it was because she wanted to eat dinner with him, amaze him with her cooking, or just wanted to eat.

Her stomach growled again.

Maybe it was the latter.

His company was just a bonus.

She smiled at that, and how he would scowl at her if she said such a thing to him.

Eva gasped as she walked into something.

Something not furniture.

Not Valen.

She stumbled back a few steps, pulling herself together, sure that it was just one of his brothers and there was no reason to panic.

She would tell them he was out, and they would leave and she could keep cooking dinner.

Her words died on her lips as she looked at the man.

And didn't recognise him.

He ventured a step towards her, his short white robe shifting against his bare thighs beneath his golden armour, armour that made her think of one of those tacky gladiators outside the Colosseum.

Only this man wasn't looking to make a quick euro off an unsuspecting tourist.

She was fairly certain he wasn't human, not a man in the conventional sense of the word.

He was a god.

She backed off, keeping the distance between them steady. "Valen is out."

He smiled, causing wrinkles beside his golden eyes, but there was no feeling in it. "I know."

He moved faster than she could track, suddenly before her with his right palm pressed between her breasts. Her heart thundered and she tried to escape, but her back hit the wall and she froze there, trapped between it and the god looming before her.

Waves of dark brown hair threaded with gold fell to caress his sun-kissed forehead as he leaned towards her.

Her stomach twisted, heart labouring as she struggled for air, her entire body quaking but not from fear. Something pressed down on her, some pressure in the air that made it impossible for her to move and sapped her strength, stealing it from her even as she fought to keep hold of it.

"Why?" she whispered.

Bright golden light flashed between them and she screamed as fire blazed through her, devouring the last of her strength.

She slumped into his waiting arms, and as she was fading into the darkness, she caught his answer to her question.

"I need to keep my promise."

CHAPTER 24

Valen blocked the fist that flew at his face, catching it in his right hand, and grinned as he sent his lightning into it. The daemon shrieked and struggled, writhing as he desperately tried to pull his hand free of Valen's unrelenting grip.

It only made him pump more of his power into the wretch, driving him to his knees.

He released the male when he slumped, going limp and hitting the dirt.

Dead.

One down, five to go.

It seemed someone had arranged a party at the gate.

He scanned the gathered males. A couple of shifters, one of a more demonic persuasion, and the other two he couldn't place from their scent. Might be bloodsuckers of some sort. They always had a muddled scent due to their disgusting feeding habits.

A challenge, but one he would relish.

The gate shimmered between them, the flat disc hovering a couple of foot above the dusty floor of the Stadio Palatino, the circles and glyphs slowly turning in opposite directions. The air hummed with its power, distracting him, but as much as he wanted to close it, it wouldn't happen while he was near it.

He could close it if he focused, but he didn't think the daemons would happily consent to giving him a couple of minutes to do so if he asked.

The gate was the reason they were here after all.

They had been waiting for him and the moment the gate had appeared, reacting to his presence, they had jumped him. He was pretty sure he had broken the arm of the fair-haired shifter. His friend hadn't fared so well.

He looked down at the smouldering corpse and nudged it with his booted foot.

The tension in the air grew thicker, warning him that the daemons were gearing up for another go.

He held his ground, showing no fear, no trace of doubt, even when he felt a trickle of both of those things. He had come to the gate unarmed, and unprepared. Not his wisest move.

But he had wanted to deal with it quickly and get back to Eva.

He should have grabbed his knives as well as his amulet from the room he used as his armoury.

Damn it.

Sense told him to back off and leave. Without him here, the gate was safe.

He couldn't do that though.

It was his mission to protect it, and these daemons had clearly been tampering with it, because there sure as hell wasn't a fucking Hellspawn waiting for passage, not on this side or the other.

How the fuck had the daemons made the gate call him?

There wasn't a Hellspawn among them. Was it possible there had been one, but the arrival of the daemons had scared them off?

It made a damn lot more sense than the alternative—that these daemons had made the gate reach out to him.

"We should make this quick," he said, his voice breaking the tense silence, and looked around the ancient site again. "The human security guards tend to get a little tetchy about me being here."

He couldn't count the number of times one of them had tried to interfere, chasing him from the Palatine Hill as if he was a mere intruder or someone looking to steal from the ruins. Really pissed him off too.

Sometimes he wished they could see the gate.

At least then they would know why he was there.

"We'll make it quick. Hand it over and you can go." The dark-haired one in the middle, Demon-boy, pointed to his chest.

Valen frowned down at the amulet sitting against his black t-shirt, the silver portion of the black disc reflecting the colours of the gate as they shifted.

They wanted his amulet.

He laughed at that.

"Fuck, no." He shoved his right foot into the dead daemon and kicked hard, sending the corpse flying through the disc of the gate and into his friends.

The gate blackened where the daemon had passed through it, sparks of white erupting from it as it repaired itself, and then it was if the interruption had never happened. The colours returned and it continued to await his command.

The five daemons launched at him.

Valen grinned and blocked every attack, moving faster than they could. Two fell with ease, one shifter and one bloodsucker. Demon-boy managed to get close to touching his amulet in the fray and he snarled as he snagged the bastard's wrist and twisted it hard, sending him slamming into the ground. The male grunted and rolled onto his side, and Valen stuck a boot in his gut, knocking the wind from him.

The second bloodsucker used his distraction against him, slamming a fist into his right kidney and then bringing his arm up to loop it over Valen's. He pulled it back, hauling Valen away from Demon-boy, and Valen growled at him, flashing his own fangs.

He shoved his left hand against the bloodsucker's pretty face and let rip.

The male howled as lightning leaped from Valen's hand and into his head, and jerked backwards, out of Valen's grip. He huffed and launched towards the wretch, unwilling to let him escape that easily.

Demon-boy grabbed his ankle, sending him tipping forwards into a fall.

Darkness swallowed him and he appeared in the air above them, dropping out of it to land on his feet.

Black ribbons caressed his skin and he casually brushed them away as the three males stared at him.

Valen lifted his right hand, pressed his index finger and thumb together, and clicked.

A thick white-purple bolt of lightning shot from the sky.

Bloodsucker number two barely had time to look up before it hit him, vaporising him in an instant.

Shifter number two ran. *Pussy.*

Valen huffed as the daemon disappeared into the night.

Slowly turned his focus to his opponent.

And then there was one.

"You want this?" He toyed with the amulet around his neck, lifting it from his chest and letting it sway from the chain. Taunting the daemon with it. "Wanna go through the gate?"

The male's eyes narrowed on him and blazed red, and horns curled from his forehead, the points sweeping back over his hair and then curving upwards. He growled and slowly lumbered onto his feet, his body growing, stretching his dark clothing tight. It ripped at the seams as he hit seven foot.

Eight foot.

Nine.

Was the bastard going to stop?

His skin darkened to burnished red and he growled through huge canines.

He held his hand out, his black talons glistening in the light of the gate coming from behind him.

"Mine," he grunted and pointed to the amulet.

A man of few words. At least when he was in his demonic form.

Valen sighed. "I'm afraid not. You see… I don't like to share. But if you promise to tell me who sent you here, I promise to send you through the gate."

His rough features pinched, and Valen figured he was thinking. Either that or he was taking a crap.

He swayed the amulet again, capturing Demon-boy's attention with it. Longing filled his red eyes. He wanted to go through the gate, but did he want it badly enough to give up who had sent him?

He wasn't sure.

Demon-boy gave him his answer.

He kicked off and thundered towards him, cloven feet ploughing the dirt and shaking the ground.

Very well.

Valen stepped just as the male reached him, reappearing on the other side of him, and turned on his heel to track the wretch. He grinned and threw his left hand forwards, and lightning shot from it, five small bolts that twisted together to form one that struck the daemon hard in his back and sent him flying across the ancient arena.

The big brute landed hard and skidded, leaving a track in the dirt behind him. He was still for a moment, not even a heartbeat of time, and then pushed his hands into the earth and eased up onto his knees.

Fuck.

Valen had figured he would be just as weak as the others had been. It seemed he was stronger when his demonic side was unleashed.

The male growled and launched into another charge.

Valen easily dodged this one too, rolling to his left across the dusty ground and back onto his feet. It appeared the male was stronger, but his intelligence hadn't grown along with his body and that strength. Brute force wasn't going to claim him a victory here.

Even if he had grown more intelligent, Valen still wouldn't have let him win.

He had vowed to protect the gate, and he wouldn't fail in that mission.

He was damned if he was going to put it at risk as Ares had.

The daemon ran at him again, shaking the ground, and unleashed a roar that echoed across Rome.

Valen readied himself, calling his lightning, letting it flow through him and grow stronger, surrendering to it. His grin widened as it coursed through him, lit him up inside and sent a dark, addictive thrill through him.

Demon-boy wasn't going to know what had hit him.

A sharp pain shot down Valen's spine and he stiffened.

His wards.

Demon-boy slammed into him, sending him flying through the air, but he wasn't aware of it as one thought ricocheted around his head, mocking him.

He was just like Ares after all, letting people break into his apartment while he was occupied.

He grunted as his back slammed into solid stone and the back of his head smacked off it a second later, the force of the blow sending stars spinning across his vision.

"Fuck," he snarled and lumbered onto his feet, clenched his jaw and growled at Demon-boy.

Bastard would pay for managing to land that blow on him while he had been distracted.

Much as he had been enjoying himself, he didn't have time to play anymore.

He lifted his right hand to the sky. "Laters."

Demon-boy looked up. Frowned when no bolt of lightning came at him.

Screamed as it shot up from below him, running straight through his cloven feet and lighting him up.

Valen frowned, made a few quick calculations to make sure it was enough juice to get the desired results and stepped.

Just as the daemon exploded from the amount of electricity coursing through him and a blackout rolled across Rome.

Sometimes it was nice to mix things up.

Lightning came from both earth and sky after all, connecting somewhere in the middle.

He landed hard in his apartment, that lightning chasing around his hands and crackling as it snaked up his arms, ready for his command.

"Eva!" He hurried through the apartment, his lightning illuminating his path, and checked the bathroom first and then the bedrooms.

Empty.

He raced across the dark living room and into the kitchen.

A pan of water on the stove boiled over and hissed.

He turned it off and stared at it, and the cutting board beside it.

She had been making dinner.

Had she gone out to get more ingredients?

He hadn't told her that she couldn't leave the apartment, that it would cause the wards to trigger.

He let out a long slow breath to steady his pounding heart as his shoulders sagged, the tension draining from them, and flicked his hands, shaking his power from them as it settled.

She must have gone out and triggered the wards.

Gods.

His chest hurt and he rubbed it through his black t-shirt, trying to soothe the ache and the fear behind it. He didn't know what he would have done if someone had been in here, trying to take her from him, but it would have been bloody.

He couldn't lose her.

It hit him hard, almost knocking him onto his knees.

He couldn't.

Gods, it really would kill him.

He walked back into the living room as the lights flickered back on, close to laughing at himself for panicking like that, rushing to her rescue like some white knight.

Idiot.

He stilled as a familiar scent reached him through the sharp tang his power had left in the air.

Lightning.

Not his own.

This was Zeus's brand.

His heart stopped in his chest.

The bastard had Eva.

CHAPTER 25

Valen didn't hesitate. Not even when he knew the consequences of breaking the rules and daring to enter Mount Olympus again, a place Zeus had banished him from on penalty of death.

He stepped.

Darkness whirled around him, the sweet comforting embrace of the Underworld, and then it parted to reveal the bright white and gold city of Mount Olympus as it climbed towards the endless blue sky.

He growled and stepped again, focusing on the location at the top of the mountain where he knew Eva would be and ignoring the voice screaming inside him that told him to go back to the mortal realm, that this was all a trick designed to make him break the rules.

Zeus wanted him dead, and had found the perfect way to make it happen.

Because Valen couldn't leave Eva here, wouldn't let her remain in Zeus's hands and suffer whatever plans he had for her.

Eva was his.

He had vowed to protect her and he would.

With his life if it came to it.

He appeared in the middle of the pristine white marble temple high on the mountain and rushed through it, hitting the ground running. Maidens screeched and scattered, dropping their golden bowls of fruit and other offerings. He growled as he passed them, his black leather boots heavy on the white floor, and ignored their swift glances of fear.

Fear that stemmed from his appearance.

He had no doubt that his eyes were black as night, his canines transformed into short fangs, and his fingernails little more than claws.

One of the maidens near the grand doorway at the back of the temple dropped her wide shallow golden bowl, spilling water across the marble. He hit it at a dead run and skidded through the doorway, fighting for balance, his arms flailing as he struggled to remain upright.

His boots squeaked as he reached the dry marble and he kicked off again, propelling himself forwards.

Driven by the urgent need to find Eva.

His eyes leaped between rooms as he passed doorway after doorway in the corridor, heading deeper into the temple. His heart thundered against his chest, the hard painful rhythm sending blood rushing through his temples, making his head throb. He had to find Eva.

Ahead of him, the corridor opened out into a bright white space.

Valen snarled and ran for it, awareness prickling through him and igniting a fire in his veins that consumed him.

Zeus's bedchamber.

He pushed harder, forcing himself past the limit, desperate to reach her.

He was damned if she was going to wake to find herself in another strange place, the captive of another man bent on hurting her.

He growled through his short fangs. She had been so afraid when Benares had kissed her and knocked her unconscious, and he couldn't bear the thought of her going through that again, not when she hadn't even recovered from that mental blow yet.

His boots squeaked on the marble floor as he ground to a dead stop in the middle of the room, his eyes on the enormous four-poster bed opposite him, draped in sheer layers of white and gold that formed curtains across it, hanging from the solid gold frame.

Eva lay in the middle of it, sprawled across the white sheets, her dark green halter-top and black jeans and trainers a sharp contrast against them.

"Eva," he whispered and kicked off again, launched forwards with his heart in his throat and fear crawling through him.

Fear that she would be aware of where she was, would be afraid that Zeus had done something to her.

He wouldn't allow it.

He would take away all those fears for her. Somehow.

"Eva." Valen tore at the white and gold material blocking his way, ripping through it to get to her, leaving the layers in tatters and spilling scraps of them across the floor.

He finally broke through.

Stilled.

Relief swept through him, strong and fierce, overwhelming him and stealing his strength.

She was asleep.

That relief gave way to fury again as he spotted the dark mark on her chest between her breasts and realised that she wasn't merely sleeping.

Zeus had knocked her out.

"Fucking bastard," he spat and mounted the bed, his blood boiling with the dark need to avenge her.

His uncle's death would be a good starting point.

After how distressed she had been by the thought of Benares touching her, the idea that Zeus might have been out to do the same thing sickened him.

Gave the darkness that lived within his blood free rein.

It consumed him and he snarled as he gathered her into his arms, rose onto his feet on the bed and turned to step back to his apartment, vowing he would return to end his uncle.

That uncle stood before him in the middle of the bedchamber, the bright light reflecting off the polished gold plates of the armour he wore over his short white robe.

Valen snarled, flashing fangs, and stalked towards Zeus, the fury mounting in him, drawing the darkness to the surface and giving it more control over him.

"You are banished from this realm." The fact that his uncle sounded so calm grated on his nerves and stoked the fury higher, until it blazed white-hot in his veins and pushed him to react, to lash out at the male who had dared to try to take Eva from him.

There was no fucking curse.

He knew that now.

Zeus had always planned this, had intended to make the curse seem real by taking whoever he fell in love with, or whoever fell for him.

He looked down at Eva in his arms, her face soft with slumber, untroubled now but all that would change if she woke.

Part of him wanted to get her away from this place before that happened, but the rest fixated on needing to know which it was—had he fallen for her, or had she really fallen for him?

Could she love him?

He had imagined that his feelings for her were the reason Zeus had taken her but what if he was wrong? What if she did love him and that was why Zeus had stolen her, aiming to turn her against him or seduce her over to his side?

He snarled through his clenched fangs.

He would never allow that to happen.

Eva was his.

Valen slowly lifted his eyes back to his uncle and held Eva closer to him, so her cheek pressed against his chest and shoulder, and her black hair tickled his neck. She was so warm.

So his.

He narrowed his eyes on Zeus.

"I was happy to obey that banishment too… but this… taking Eva… you crossed the line and you know it. You wanted me to come." He flashed fangs again as his temper frayed, his fury getting the better of him, and took a hard step towards his uncle, showing him that he wasn't going to back down like a good little boy and do what was expected of him. "You're a spiteful old bastard. This is entrapment. You wanted to make the curse look real… but I'm not going to stand for it."

"So you will fight me?" Zeus countered him, moving a step closer, and Valen wanted to punch that smug look off his perfect face.

But he wouldn't.

He was done doing everything people expected of him.

"I hate to disappoint, but I didn't come here for a fight. I came here to take Eva home… and then you can punish me."

Zeus's golden eyes widened almost imperceptibly, but Valen noticed it. It wasn't often someone managed to surprise the god of gods, but he had the feeling he had done just that.

"You knew coming here meant your life was forfeit, yet you came anyway. Why?" Zeus looked down at the precious cargo Valen carried, nestled close to his heart where she belonged.

Valen dropped his gaze to her too, softened to pathetic mush inside as he gazed at her peaceful, beautiful face.

"Because I love her," he whispered and a chill swept over him, spreading across his back and down his spine, and up over his skull as it sank in that he really did love her, as he had never loved anyone before. "And I swore to keep her safe."

He lifted his gaze back to Zeus and narrowed it on him.

"If you've laid a finger on her, I will not go quietly. I will fight you when I return."

Zeus's right eyebrow rose slightly, another reaction Valen hadn't expected from the bastard. "What makes you think I will just allow you to leave with her?"

Valen looked around him at the white marble bedchamber and pictured the city beyond it, a sprawling metropolis of temples that was densest at the base of the mountain where the minor gods lived and the markets were held, and the servants' quarters had been established, and rose up the mountain, the number of temples growing fewer and their size growing larger as the importance of the god or goddess escalated.

"You'll do it, or I might be tempted to unleash a little of my anger on your precious city." He smiled as Zeus scowled at him, showing him that he intended to do it, he dared to wreak havoc on the city like that, regardless of the consequences to it and to him. "This mountain is a tad steep... makes the positions of the buildings precarious at best. All I really have to do is shake the mountain and many of those temples will fall."

"You think you have that sort of power?" Zeus sneered at him and golden lightning crackled around his hands.

Valen grinned. "You know I do. I'll tear this fucking place apart... everything you love in ruins."

Zeus clenched his right fist and a short jagged bright golden bolt of lightning formed in it like a spear.

"It's your choice," Valen said, ignoring the threat. "Let me take Eva to safety and I will come back and you can mete out your punishment for disobeying the ban you shoved on me centuries ago when *you* let my sister die. Whatever you see fit. I'll take it without protest."

He looked down at Eva, swallowed hard as his heart hurt, and then pushed all the sombre and stupidly sentimental thoughts out of his head and faced his uncle.

"Even death."

Zeus's eyes did widen now and the golden bolt in his grip stuttered. "You would die to protect her?"

Valen nodded.

Gods, he would. He loved her that much. If it was the price he had to pay for her safety, then he would gladly pay it.

His uncle's expression darkened, his broad mouth flattening and his dark eyebrows dipping low, forming wrinkles on his sun-kissed skin.

Valen frowned right back at him, trying to make sense of the sudden shift in his mood.

It was what Zeus wanted wasn't it?

He had taken Eva in order to lure him here and therefore give him a reason to kill him at last.

Hadn't he?

Maybe the bastard was just disappointed because he wasn't going to fight him.

Sick fuck.

That had to be it. Zeus had wanted him to come and fight for Eva, and he was pissed that Valen had chosen to calmly surrender himself in exchange for her.

Maybe he was growing up after all.

Before meeting Eva, he would have taken this opportunity to fight Zeus without even blinking, launching himself right into the fray and relishing the chance to land some blows on his smug face, and the shot at taking him down.

Now? He looked down at Eva and sighed. Now all that mattered was Eva, getting her to safety and protecting her as he had promised. She was more important than his need for revenge, more important than a feud that had been raging for centuries.

More important than anything.

He didn't want to leave her. Gods, he wanted to be with her forever. The thought of going to the blessed isles without her and never seeing her, never looking into those tranquil tropical blue eyes or hearing that bite in her tone when he had done something wrong, ripped his heart to pieces and made him bleed inside.

But if he had to do it in order for her to live, for her to be free, then he would make that sacrifice and he would wait and pray for a day when they were reunited in the blessed isles.

"You do love her," Zeus whispered.

Valen wanted to scoff at his uncle and call him a fucking idiot for taking this long to notice. "I value her life more than mine, but if it's enough for you… then take it and let her live. She deserves it more than me. She deserves to be happy."

"And you don't?"

He glared at Zeus. "You don't give a fuck about me, so drop the act. You took Eva because you wanted me here, you wanted me to break the rules so you could punish me. You wanted to take away the one person in this world who cares about me, all because of some stupid curse."

Zeus sighed. "I never cursed you, Valen. I only possess the power to say such a thing, not the power to make it real. You do that for yourself by believing in it."

Valen growled. The bastard would pay for that, for playing with his head and making him suffer all these centuries. He took a step towards his uncle, his boot striking the marble hard, and Zeus held his hand up.

"I did not take the mortal female in order to hurt her, or you, either."

Valen rocked back on his heel and eyed Zeus, trying to figure out whether he was telling the truth, because Valen sure as hell couldn't believe him capable of anything altruistic. Not anymore.

"I am doing it to keep a promise to your mother."

That shook him to his core, to his soul, and he could only stare at Zeus as it pinged around his head and his heart, filling both with conflicting feelings. His mother?

"What promise?" he snapped and Zeus arched an eyebrow at him. Valen didn't give a flying monkey if his tone was disrespectful. He only gave respect where it was deserved, and Zeus had given him no reason to believe he deserved it from him.

"After you had been returned to the Underworld, Persephone made me swear to keep whoever you loved safe so you would never lose a loved one again… but I could not believe what Helios reported to me."

Fucking Helios. The boot-licking bastard was always spying for his beloved master, reporting everything to Zeus.

"I was not sure of your feelings for her, but I took her regardless, and now I am glad that I did because I am certain you do love her."

"You were testing me by taking her? You wanted to see what I would do so you could see that I loved her." Valen wanted to gouge his uncle's eyes out with his thumbs so he would be as blind as he clearly already was. He had to be if it had taken him this long to see the depth of Valen's feelings for Eva, only realising they were true just a few moments ago.

"No." Zeus shook his head, causing the waves of his dark brown hair to shimmer with gold in the bright light. His expression turned grim. "I took her because daemons were about to take her from you… a ploy to turn you to their side in order to save her… and that I could not accept."

Because Zeus was the only one who got to fuck with his feelings like that.

He looked down at Eva in his arms, heart clenching tight at the thought he might have been trying to save her from a monster far worse than his uncle right now.

Zeus conjured a marble plinth and on it appeared a shallow golden bowl of water. The water the maiden had been carrying into this room. Valen frowned at it and stepped closer, curious about what his uncle was up to and slowly beginning to believe him.

That belief became solid and unbreakable as Zeus waved his right hand over the surface of the water and it shifted to reveal his apartment.

The succubus bitch was inside it, tearing it apart as she looked for something.

A heavy weight settled on his chest, directly over the centre of it, and he looked down at the amulet that hung there, the dark disc sitting above his heart and the silver piece in it shining brightly in the ethereal light of Mount Olympus.

Unable to find and take Eva, Jin wanted to take the next best thing back to her brother—the amulet.

Benares had sent the group of daemons to attempt to take it from him after all.

They had to be working with whoever had arranged the attack on Ares in New York. Had to be. The desire to steal the amulet was all the proof he needed.

The daemons thought the amulets were the keys to the gates, that possessing one would allow them to open them and enter the Underworld, or hold them open so they could destroy the gates and begin to merge the planes of the Underworld and the mortal one.

Keras had revealed he and his brothers had all been duped by their father though, made to believe the amulets were the keys when in reality the key was in their blood.

Hades had created the amulets as a ploy, a method of drawing out the daemons who would be responsible for the calamity the Moirai had witnessed. Everyone but Keras hadn't been stupid enough to try to open a gate without one.

Mostly because there was a creature who guarded the other side and the amulets were designed to protect them from those gargantuan monsters, the power in them placating the normally violent creatures and rendering them safe and calm.

Valen didn't fancy being squashed under their feet like a bug.

Or eaten alive.

So he had never tried to open his gate in Rome without his amulet.

The daemons had seen him always wearing it when the gate was open, and had fallen for Hades's ploy.

He watched Jin turning his apartment upside down and grinned. She was going to have to return to Benares empty handed.

Valen shifted Eva in his arms and looked across the bowl to his uncle.

Soft golden eyes watched him, no trace of anger in them, only something Valen didn't want to study too closely because he had been fooled into thinking Zeus had feelings before and it hadn't ended well for him.

Valen stared at him, a strange numbness encroaching to push out the warmth of Eva in his arms and sending him back to centuries ago when he had last stood in this temple.

"Why did you let her die?" Those words slipped from his lips and seemed to shake Zeus, because he recoiled and averted his gaze.

He sighed. "I was not able to save her."

Valen blinked. "Why?"

Zeus raised his gaze back to meet his, and remorse shone in it, making Valen want to be the one to avert his eyes now. "She died in an area where no Olympian can see."

Cold stole through Valen as he realised that was true.

Calindria had died in the area their father used for his trials, and all of it was off the grid, so no god could interfere in proceedings.

"You could have brought her back though... you did it for those bastard fates," Valen barked and his voice echoed around the enormous room, mocking him with his own words, igniting the blood in his veins again and making it burn with a need for vengeance.

For justice.

Zeus calmly shook his head. "You know that was not possible, Valen. The manner of her death—"

Valen looked sharply away from his uncle as he cut himself off, hurt spearing his heart like one of Zeus's lightning bolts, and his eyes stung.

He did know.

He had known then, and he knew now, but it didn't stop the pain or soothe his need to make someone pay for what had happened to her.

It only made it infinitely worse.

It was a living thing, gnawing at his soul, constantly torturing him and tormenting him with how he had failed her.

How he continued to fail her even now.

The manner of her death had meant her soul had never been found, had never crossed over into the Underworld.

It was still out there somewhere, lost and waiting, or worse.

Captive.

Tears lined his lashes and he blinked them away, refusing to let them fall, and fought to master his emotions as they threatened to sweep him under and rouse the darker side of his soul again with a bloody need for vengeance.

He closed his eyes and reached for the connection they had always shared as siblings, one that had allowed him to communicate with her across vast distances, as he could with his brothers.

That connection that was cold now, nothing but a void left behind inside him.

A void left inside them all.

It had been centuries, but her soul was still missing, held away from the Underworld.

From her home.

He wanted her to find her way back, and he knew his brothers felt the same. They all wanted her to reach Elysium and pass her days there on the island, where they could visit her.

Eva moaned and stirred, and he hushed her, brushing his lips across her brow and willing her to remain asleep a little longer. He didn't want her waking on Mount Olympus. She had already been through too much, was barely holding on, and he didn't want waking in the realm of the gods to be the final blow to whatever was happening between them.

Eva knew about him, but he wasn't sure she had accepted the truth of him yet, or the world he walked in.

Everything between them was so fragile right now.

He breathed her in, that scent of roses and sin he loved so much, and prayed to whatever gods would listen to him that she would stay with him, that she felt something for him that ran as deep as his feelings for her.

"Go," Zeus said.

Valen looked up at him, cold stealing back into his veins as he remembered where he was and what he had done. He held Eva closer, the cold turning to ice as it froze his heart. Zeus had taken Eva to protect her, to keep a promise to his mother, but that didn't mean Valen was off the hook.

He had still broken the rules of his banishment.

"Go, and do not come back… unless you have an offering." Zeus huffed when Valen stared blankly at him, fighting to make himself believe what he was hearing. "Do not look at me that way. Hades would kill me if I laid a finger on you."

True.

But he still couldn't believe he was being allowed to enter and leave Mount Olympus without being punished.

And he had been given the green light to come back too.

Valen scoffed. "Getting soft in your golden years, Old Man."

Zeus's dark eyebrows dipped low and his golden eyes shone, the softness that had been in them a second ago obliterated by the anger rising inside him.

A lightning bolt crackled in his hand.

As much as Valen wanted another shot at his uncle, he had more important matters that needed his attention.

Valen grinned. "Maybe next time."

Stepped.

Golden arcs of lightning chased him into the darkness of the teleport to the Underworld and then out the other side into the mortal realm, but they merely danced around him, not touching him or Eva.

He landed on the hillside in Rome and that lightning struck the rods in the city, and thunder rolled across the land.

Eva.

He looked down at her in his arms as she moaned and wriggled again. He needed to take her somewhere safe but he couldn't take her to his apartment.

The only place open to him, the place where she would be most protected because the wards surrounding it were impenetrable and ancient, created from the combined power of him and his brothers, was also a place where she might not be safe.

Or she might be.

It was a risk he had to take.

He just hoped Esher wasn't in the mood to murder mortals today.

CHAPTER 26

Esher pressed the power button on the remote, calmly set it down on the low coffee table nestled in the centre of the couches, and looked over to his right, towards the door of the mansion.

Someone was coming.

Someone not of his blood.

He curled his lip, rose onto his bare feet and started towards the door.

It slid open and Valen walked in.

If it had been only his brother who had shown up on his doorstep, he wouldn't have cared, would have welcomed the company in fact.

But Valen had brought something into his home with him, something wretched.

The mortal female.

He narrowed his blue eyes on her where Valen cradled her to his chest.

"Temper," Valen snapped.

His gaze leaped up to meet his younger brother's golden eyes. They glowed at him, warning him to tread carefully.

Valen was the one who needed to be careful.

He was the one in danger.

Esher flashed his teeth on a snarl and crossed the long room to his brother.

"You dare," he hissed and flung his arm to his right, towards where the doors into the courtyard had been parted to reveal the night. His hand shook as he pointed at the full moon, not needing to look at it to know exactly where it was, because it hung heavily over him tonight, pulled at him in ways he was too weak to fight. "You dare bring that filth into my house on this night?"

"Calm yourself, Esher." Valen set the mortal down near the door, slid it closed and rose to his full height as he turned to face him. "Last I checked, this was still *our* house. It belongs to all of us. You just get to stay here because you're daddy's precious little boy… because you're more fucked up than I am."

Fucked up?

He snarled and advanced on his brother. "You want to see how fucked up I am right now?"

Valen stood his ground, chest heaving beneath his black t-shirt, the fight to control himself as visible as the one Esher waged.

"Back off," Valen snarled.

He couldn't. Not tonight. Valen should have known that.

His brother's golden eyes flicked towards the door to the courtyard, a brief glimmer of remorse crossed them, and then they were cold again, hard and unrelenting.

"She stays." Valen folded his arms across his chest and placed himself between Esher and the mortal.

Protecting her.

Esher's top lip curled back off his emerging fangs. "She only gets to stay if we are interrogating her now, and that look in your eyes... that disgusting way you dare to block my path to her... says it is not the case."

He sidestepped so he could see the wretched creature, trying to discern what had gotten into his brothers recently to make them turn into pathetic males, so eager to please those who should fear them.

Those who would hurt them.

No one hurt his family.

He flashed his fangs at the wretch.

He would make sure this one couldn't harm Valen.

Valen appeared in his path, pressed his hands against his chest, and shoved him back. "Calm the fuck down."

He couldn't.

Not tonight.

On a snarl, he launched himself at Valen and stepped at the last second, disappearing and reappearing on the other side of him, in front of the sleeping female.

He raised his right hand, growled as he felt his nails sharpen, and brought it down in a vicious arc aimed at her throat.

Valen grabbed his arm and hauled it backwards before he could strike her, spinning Esher to face him.

Esher grunted as pain exploded across the left side of his skull and Valen's punch drove him to his right, sent him sprawling across the tatami mats. He growled and shoved himself up, was on his feet in a heartbeat and on his brother in the next.

He slashed his claws down Valen's front, ripping through his black t-shirt, and Valen hissed and stumbled backwards, evading his next blow.

"Calm down," Valen snapped and blocked the rest of his attacks, their forearms clashing hard, sending dull pain echoing along his bones. "Calm down or I'll call Keras, because you're being a dick and I thought you were stronger than this!"

Esher staggered from that blow, his hand dropping to his side as it registered and hit him hard.

He stared at Valen, at the blood that trickled down his chest and soaked into his black t-shirt, and the cuts that littered his face.

He had done that.

He shoved his hands into his black hair, clawed it back and pressed his palms to the sides of his head as he unleashed all his rage and pain in a roar.

The mortal female gasped.

Valen was by her side in an instant.

Not to shield her from him, but to coddle her.

He could only stare as his brother tended to her, his actions soft and gentle, more than tender.

The sight of him acting that way brought painful memories to the surface of his dark mind and he didn't want to entertain them, didn't want them invading his life again, not when he was struggling with the sway of the moon and the havoc it wreaked on him, and the darkness that pushed inside him.

He edged away from them, each step more difficult than the last when the darkness wanted him closer to the female, his fangs in her flesh and his claws tearing her to pieces. His hands shook against the sides of his head and the sound of water running outside stopped as the darkness rose within him, pushing harder and breaking through his carefully constructed barriers.

Seizing control of him.

Valen froze and slowly turned to look at him. "Get a lid on that right now."

He couldn't. Not even when he knew that his power would hurt his own flesh and blood if he didn't get it back under control.

Even Valen wasn't immune to it.

There was water in him.

Just as there was water in the filthy mortal.

Water he would command to do his bidding.

He fought against his hands as they lowered from his head, warring with himself as he tried to stop his body from moving, the darkness from taking shape inside him and unleashing the other side of himself.

The side he loathed.

But couldn't defeat.

"Take her away." Because he could see that she meant something to Valen, and that hurting her would hurt his brother. His blood. He couldn't bear it if that happened. "Take her away!"

It was hard enough to control himself around Megan, but he did his best because Ares was clearly in love with her and he wanted his brother to be happy.

He wasn't sure he had enough willpower to contain his darker side if Valen added Eva to their group.

"She stays," Valen said, his tone brooking no argument, and Esher snarled at him. Valen huffed and eased back onto his feet, coming to face him. "The wards are strongest here and she has daemons after her. They want to hurt her in order to turn me to their side, and the gods only know I would do it, Esher. I would do anything for her."

Esher reeled from that blow too, took another handful of steps backwards as it sank in swift and fast, making his head spin.

Valen was already in love with her.

Darkness surged, obliterating the happiness he wanted to feel for his brother on hearing he had finally found someone to love, devouring it as it demanded he sated it with blood and violence.

Because the wretched mortal might hurt Valen.

He stared at her.

Weak, but toxic. All mortals were the same. They were treacherous. Cruel. Vicious.

He shook his head as his darker side whispered in it, words that tried to seduce him into surrendering to it, giving in and giving it control. He wanted to do it. He wanted to punish her for the hold she had over his beloved brother, turning him into a male willing to risk death and ruin for her.

If he dealt with her, Valen would be safe.

He had to protect his family.

Didn't he?

He could not allow anyone to harm them.

A flash of his reflection whisked across his eyes, there and gone in a heartbeat, an image of his face daubed with blood and his eyes blazing crimson.

He clenched his fists, felt them trembling and the blood in his veins vibrating with his power. The very air around him shook as the urge to unleash it grew fiercer.

"Esher," Valen whispered. "You okay?"

Esher tore his eyes away from the female when Valen stepped in front of her, shielding her with his body.

Making it clear that in order to eliminate the danger the mortal represented to Valen, he would have to go through Valen himself.

He could not hurt his brother.

If he remained here, he would end up doing just that, whether on purpose or not. The pull of his power was too strong, controlling him too easily tonight. It would take only a slip in his control for him to do something terrible.

Using their own blood against them.

He took another step back and teleported, disappearing just as Daimon appeared in the mansion, his pale blue eyes filled with concern as they landed on him.

Darkness engulfed him and he welcomed it, the brief connection it gave him to the Underworld taking the edge off and helping him claw back some control.

He hoped Daimon wouldn't follow him.

He knew his brother had come for his sake, not Valen's, their bond so powerful that they could sense when each other was in pain, but he wouldn't go back.

Daimon could deal with Valen in his stead, and call in their brothers.

Hopefully, by the time he returned, the mortal would be gone.

He landed on a rooftop overlooking the Shibuya district of Tokyo, a short distance from the mansion where it stood in extensive grounds near Yoyogi Park.

He wasn't sure why he had picked this spot.

Because it was close enough to his brothers that he would be able to sense if they needed him, or because he was testing himself?

Hundreds of mortals milled around below him, waiting at the lights at the busy intersection, some watching the giant television screens on the buildings overlooking the crossing and others busy talking to friends. Cars sped along the wide street, heading beneath the building below him that formed a bridge over the road. More mortals spilled out of the section of the building to his right, from the train station there, some heading towards the famous meeting spot near the statue of Hachiko, a faithful dog, and others hurrying for the crossing as the lights changed.

Neon illuminated the entire area, including the pedestrian street to the left of the building opposite him, affording him a clear view of everyone below him.

He couldn't remember the last time he had dared to leave the mansion when the moon was full.

The temptation to leave the rooftop and venture into his favourite Starbucks in the lower section of the building opposite him tugged at him, but he resisted it.

It would be too much.

The sweeping front of the building was glass on the level where the café seating was situated, revealing just how busy it was to him.

Too much.

He had never tried to enter the coffee shop and order a drink from the mortals when the moon was out on his side of the planet, let alone when the moon was full.

It would be disastrous.

Besides, it felt good up here, more relaxing than he had thought possible, everything rushing around him distracting him from the pull of the moon.

The wind buffeted him as he stood on the roof, carrying the scent of snow and chilling him through his pale grey-blue shirt and dark jeans.

It was peaceful to stand above the world like this, looking down on it like the moon that hung above him, casting its warm light on him and soothing him even as it tore at him, lured him into sinking into his power and unleashing it.

The crossing lights changed again, and the mortals swarmed, forming a tight ball in the centre of the road that broke apart a moment later as they went on their way.

Ants.

Hideous creations of the gods.

He sneered at them all.

Esher closed his eyes, drew down a deep breath and expelled it slowly, seeking balance again and restoring some control over himself.

The wind picked up, whipping through his black hair, and he stretched his arms out at his sides and stepped up onto the edge of the building, letting it chill and shove at him.

He opened his eyes, tipped his head back and fixed them on the moon suspended overhead against the inky sky, faint stars shining around it. It pulled at him, full and beautiful, entrancing him and holding him under its sway.

Mesmerising him.

He lost himself in it, the sounds of the mortal world falling away from around him, and reached his arms up, stretching them towards it, part of him aching to take hold of it and bring it down to him.

Heat spread across his left side.

A metallic tang flooded his mouth.

His hands dropped and he flinched as his left arm hit something, and warmth bloomed over his hip.

The odour of blood filled the air.

His blood.

Esher looked down at his side.

And the blade protruding from it.

A violet haze wobbled around the edges of his vision and he frowned as he reached a trembling hand towards the black hilt of the dagger. Dark purple smoke swirled around the blade, writhing like a living thing, angry and agitated. Hungry.

He swallowed hard and gritted his teeth against the fire spreading through his side, sinking into his flesh and creeping into his veins.

A hand appeared in view before he could reach the dagger.

Wrapped around the hilt.

Yanked it from his flesh.

Esher flung his head back and screamed.

Water exploded from the streets below, geysers shooting high into the night air as the pipes burst one by one, spreading outwards with him at the centre.

A deep voice echoed in his ears as he went down.

"Give your sister my regards."

CHAPTER 27

Valen scooped Eva up into his arms, stifling a wince as the cuts across his chest stung, and carefully manoeuvred her into a position where he wouldn't get blood all over her. He carried her over to the TV area on the right side of the long rectangular room and eased her down onto the couch, shutting out the way Daimon was glaring at his back, as if he was responsible for Esher's outburst and disappearance.

Maybe he was.

He had forgotten the moon was full.

"What's up with her?" Daimon ended his call to their brothers and pocketed his phone as he edged closer, but didn't pass the barrier of the couches in the TV area.

The whole damn section of the house seemed ridiculously out of tune with the rest of it, which Esher had kept more traditionally in line with old Japanese houses. The dining area at the other end of the long room had a low rectangular wooden table and seating more fitted to the mansion—butt-numbing cushions. He never had been able to get comfortable with the Japanese way of things.

Sitting on hard floors just felt like punishment to him.

"Nothing." He finished settling Eva on the couch, stifling another wince as he stuffed some cushions around her so she would be comfortable, his focus wholly on her well-being rather than his own.

Little frowns flickered on her brow, her eyes still a bit too glassy for his liking as she stared at him, miles away and locked in her own body.

He hoped to the gods that she hadn't come around at any point on Mount Olympus and that was the cause of her current stupor. He was banking on it being just the after effects of being hit with Zeus's power to render her unconscious.

"Nothing?" Daimon scoffed and moved a little closer. "Nothing my arse."

Valen looked over his left shoulder at his brother, rose back onto his feet and came to face him. "Nothing."

Daimon shook his head, and it was a wonder the soft white spikes of his hair didn't collapse. How the fuck he managed to style it that way, Valen had never figured out. It was either some sort of magic, or Hong Kong and Japan had incredible hair products.

"Don't lie to me, Brother." Daimon pulled his long black coat off, revealing his standard dark navy roll-neck long-sleeved top, and a pair of black jeans, together with a set of very wicked silver throwing knives and shuriken strapped into the holster he wore over his shoulders.

His brother shared his love of imbuing steel with his power and letting it fly. While Valen delivered a nasty shock that way, sometimes enough to end the daemon if they were weak and young, Daimon delivered a blast of ice the equivalent of a sudden onset of frostbite.

Valen had witnessed daemons lose limbs to it in the blink of an eye.

The slashes across his chest burned and he couldn't stifle the grimace this time. Shit. He gritted his teeth and tugged his black t-shirt up, his entire torso blazing as his muscles shifted. Fucking damn. He hissed through his clenched teeth as fresh pain rolled through him and gathered a clean section of the t-shirt into his right fist.

It stung like a motherfucker as he dabbed at the wounds, using his ruined t-shirt to mop up the blood and reveal the slashes.

More like grooves.

They were pretty fucking deep.

Esher needed his claws clipped.

He scowled down at the wounds, trying to see whether they were healing yet and struggling to keep a leash on his mood.

He couldn't hold them against his brother.

Esher had only given him what he deserved for daring to bring Eva, a mortal, into his home on tonight of all nights.

"What happened to her?" Daimon said again, softer this time, and jerked his chin towards Eva.

Valen stopped prodding at the healing cuts on his chest and glanced down at her, found her staring up at him with that blank look in her eyes, and sighed as he smoothed his clean hand over her hair, hoping it would soothe her and bring her back to him.

"Uncle." He knew he didn't need to say any more than that when Daimon's face darkened and he folded his arms across his chest, causing his muscles to flex beneath his tight top.

Still, he had expected his brother to blame him for upsetting Zeus, to make out that he had done something wrong. It seemed even Daimon had his limits when it came to what he would try to blame on him, and his uncle taking a mortal and hurting her had crossed that line.

"Why would he do that?" Daimon studied her, a cold edge to his pale blue eyes that Valen didn't hold against him.

It was rare for Daimon to look any other way.

Valen blamed his power for that, and the fact it had manifested when they had entered the mortal world, the same as Ares's fire, cutting them off from everyone in a way. What Valen now felt was the worst way possible.

Not being able to touch others would certainly suck.

Although, the Carrier that Ares had fallen for, Megan, could withstand their power. They still hadn't figured out how, but Valen suspected it had something to do with her ancestors and whoever her power to heal had come from.

Maybe that god or goddess was a little closer in the family tree than they had thought, and she was nearer to Hellspawn in status.

Or higher.

Was it possible she was a close descendent of a demi-god?

If she was, it would explain how she could withstand Ares's fire and Daimon's ice.

"He hates me," Valen said at last, pulling himself back to Daimon and pushing the little Carrier out of his thoughts.

"It was more than that," Daimon shot back, not missing a beat.

It was, but Valen was damned if he was going to tell his brother that he loved Eva and that was the reason Zeus had taken her.

There had been another reason though, one that he was more than happy to mention.

"I was out at the gate and the daemons were coming to snatch her from my apartment, so Zeus beat them to it."

Daimon looked as if he was having a hard time believing that.

Valen shrugged.

"It's true. The old fart made a promise to mum that he would protect whoever I… ah…" This was going badly. Normally he could think of excuses at the drop of a hat and make his brothers believe them, and now he was on the verge of admitting the one thing he had just sworn he wouldn't. He grunted, "He just made a promise, alright?"

Daimon's slow smile said he wanted to press the subject and get the truth out of him.

Valen shot him a glare, daring him to do it, and felt his eyes shift, the gold growing brighter as his temper went from mellow to a need to lash out at Daimon and make him shut up.

Daimon opened his mouth.

Snapped it closed.

His eyes burned bright white and frost glittered over his gloved hands, and then he jerked to face the main door of the house.

"What's wrong?" All thoughts of brawling with Daimon fled as Valen's senses rang alarm bells and he was around the couches in a split second, heading towards him.

"Esher."

Daimon disappeared.

Fuck.

Valen looked back over his shoulder at Eva, torn between following his brother and remaining with her. She stared at him, her blue eyes still distant and haunted.

"Fuck," he barked and growled, and she didn't even flinch.

"No thanks." Ares's deep voice rolled over him, laced with warmth for once, and a female giggled.

He whipped around to face his older brother, and Keras appeared just beyond him, with Calistos landing a second later in a swirl of black smoke.

"Esher," Valen snapped and all three of his brothers tossed him blank looks. "Daimon… he felt something… Esher is in trouble."

"Remain here." Keras stepped, the haste of his teleport disturbing the black vapor trail that he left behind.

Marek appeared in the middle of it, looked around at everyone and ran a hand over his tawny wild hair, a confused crinkle to his brow that echoed in his deep brown eyes. "Did I miss something?"

"Esher flipped his shit at me and left and now Daimon has gone after him, but… I think Esher is in trouble. Keras has gone too." Valen looked back at Eva and then at Marek. "The daemons after Eva… do you think they can teleport?"

Marek shook his head, approached him and held out a thick wedge of paper. "It's all the information I have on their species."

Valen stared at it, and then his brothers, torn between remaining in the mansion with them now he knew Eva would be safe from Benares and Jin, and going after Esher with Keras and Daimon.

This was all his fault.

If he hadn't brought Eva here, Esher wouldn't have left and he would have been safe.

He glanced at Ares, who shook his head slightly, a warning not to do it.

Gods. It was his fault though. He should be the one out there trying to locate Esher. What if something happened to him, something he couldn't heal?

What if something happened to him that stirred up the past?

He flicked a glance at the door, the need to go after Esher and bring him home safe pounding in his blood, but another desire pushed back against it, keeping his feet planted to the tatami mats.

Keras had ordered him to remain here, and disobeying him would land him in trouble.

And he was done being a pain in his big brother's arse.

Who the fuck was he kidding?

He focused to step.

Keras landed hard in the middle of the room, shaking the wooden structure of the house, and Valen whirled to face him. He laid Esher down on the golden tatami mats and the room collectively tensed. Keras looked down at his blood-stained hands and then up at Daimon as he appeared.

Blood covered him too.

Valen was by their sides in an instant, his brothers joining him to surround Esher.

Esher's eyes snapped open and he snarled as he lurched off the floor, his back arching. His mouth opened on a roar of sheer fury as Keras pinned his shoulders, keeping him in place. Valen grabbed his ankles, fighting to keep him contained as he struggled, kicking at him and catching him hard a few times. Esher could kick him to death and he wouldn't let go.

"Calm down," Daimon whispered and kneeled above Esher's head.

Esher didn't listen. His fight grew more frantic, his snarls more desperate as he tried to break free of Keras and Valen. His boot connected hard with Valen's jaw as his leg shot up and Valen grunted as he fell backwards, his head spinning from the blow.

Marek was on Esher's feet before he could kick out again, nodding to Valen. Valen nodded back to let him know he was fine. He glanced at Esher's face as Calistos joined Keras in holding his shoulders down. None of them dared to speak, but it was clear all of them wanted to bring Esher back from the dark place that had consumed him.

"Esher," Daimon whispered, his voice low and soft, the only damn thing that could calm their brother now.

Valen felt more than useless as he tried to help Esher, aware of just what little power he had in this situation. He glanced around his brothers and their sombre faces said it all, relaying how he wasn't alone in his feelings. They all felt useless, unable to do anything but hold Esher down and wait for Daimon to reach him.

"Esher." Daimon ghosted his hands over Esher's head and Esher snarled and snapped at him, his eyes shooting open.

"Shit," someone whispered and Valen seconded that.

Esher's eyes were verging on red.

"Esher!" Daimon snapped and Esher jerked to a halt, stared up at Daimon as he leaned over him, so Esher could see him. "Come back."

For a heart-stopping moment, Valen thought that he might.

Esher lurched up and snapped fangs in Daimon's face. The action sent blood pumping from the wound in his left side, and crimson seeped across the golden mats, spreading fast.

He was losing too much blood.

Valen stared at his face as he fought to keep Esher's legs contained with Marek, willing his brother to respond, to shake the darkness and come back to the light.

Gods help them all if he didn't.

It would be a massacre.

Valen sensed Eva moving closer and held his right hand out behind him, warning her to keep back.

Too late.

Esher lashed out, his fight growing fiercer, and slashed sharp claws across Keras's arm, ripping through the sleeve of his long black coat. Keras huffed, grabbed Esher's wrist and shoved it down hard, pinning it to the mat. It only made Esher fight harder, and his eyes shifted to his left as he bared his fangs.

Eva.

She gasped and Valen felt her move back.

Ares moved Megan away too, taking her as far as the dining table.

Esher growled low in the language of the Underworld, causing the ground to shake beneath them and tearing pained gasps from Eva and Megan that only drew his focus to Eva even more. "Mortal must die… they all must die… vile bitch. Start with her. Make her pay. Tear her apart and feast on her screams, and show the others what will become of them. She will be my standard in this war."

Valen flashed his own short fangs at his brother.

"Fucking try it." He couldn't hold it against Esher, because the pain had pushed him into his memories and now all mortals were threats to him and his family, but he wasn't going to stand by and let him say shit about hurting Eva. He glared at Daimon. "About time you did something, don't you think?"

Esher kicked harder, catching him in his gut, and he grunted as his breath left him.

Twisted the bastard's leg and tore a satisfying grunt of pain from him.

Keras tossed a black look over his right shoulder at him. Like hell he was going to apologise for it. Esher was on a warpath and his woman was the first target.

Fucking Keras would have done the same thing if it had been a certain goddess in the room being threatened by Esher.

Daimon growled, his eyes shone bright white, and remorse flickered across his face a second before it hardened in determination.

He pressed his gloved palms against the sides of Esher's head.

Esher roared, jacking up off the mats again, his skin paling as Daimon's ice spread glittering frost across his cheeks and his black hair. His lips turned blue and he slowed, still snarling but his fight was leaving him, his actions weaker as the cold sapped his strength.

"Enough," Keras barked and Daimon yanked his hands away.

Esher collapsed against the tatami mats, lying in a pool of red.

Too still.

Had Daimon overestimated how much Esher could take in his weakened state?

Valen held his breath, staring at Esher and willing him to respond now, to give them all a sign that he would be alright, because they couldn't lose him.

He couldn't lose another sibling.

He lifted his head and looked at Calistos, keeping an eye on his youngest brother as he stared at Esher, hope flooding his sky blue eyes and his blond hair hanging in long tangled threads around his shoulders and cheeks, pulled from his ponytail by Esher's frantic struggling.

Black warred against the blue, Calistos's struggle visible in his eyes as he fought for control.

Valen risked taking one hand off Esher's left leg and pressed it to Cal's shoulder, squeezing it through his black t-shirt, needing to let his youngest brother know that Esher would be fine and they weren't going to lose him.

Not as they had lost Calindria.

Cal sniffed and cleared his throat, and nodded as he closed his eyes. Valen kept his hand on his shoulder, offering him the only comfort he could while they waited for Esher to respond.

"Come on," Daimon muttered, tension bracketing his mouth in deep lines as he stared down at Esher. He grabbed Esher's shoulders and shook him hard. "Come back, you bastard."

Esher gasped, his chest expanding rapidly to stretch his grey-blue shirt across it, and then sank back against the mats.

"Fucker," Valen whispered.

Marek shot him a look that said he seconded that one and sat back on his heels, his hands still clutching Esher's right leg and his strength visibly leaving him as he sagged.

Keras followed suit and Cal's trembling subsided beneath Valen's hand and he curled forwards, muttering curses aimed at Esher.

Valen stared at Esher's left side. Blood still trickled from the wound.

Something was wrong here. Esher should have been healing by now, even with all the struggling. His body should have started to repair and seal the wound, stopping the bleeding.

He pushed Esher's soaking shirt up and the dark grey t-shirt he wore beneath it.

Cal gasped.

Keras swore.

It was that bad.

The wound was nothing more than a two inch puncture, a clean cut.

It was the skin around it that had them all cursing and the air growing heavy again with the fear they still might lose Esher.

Black surrounded the wound by at least another two inches in all directions, slowly turning into purple at the edges and transforming into tendrils that spread across Esher's body.

They writhed and shifted like a living thing, growing as they all stared.

Ares bit out, "Wraith."

A chill went through Valen.

He tore Esher's shirt open and shoved his t-shirt up his chest, needing to see how far it had already spread.

The tendrils snaked across his stomach, past his navel, and up his chest to his left nipple.

"Fuck," he snarled.

Megan appeared between him and Calistos, pushing them away from Esher. "Give me room."

"Sweetheart," Ares said, a note of caution in his deep voice, and she shot him down with a glare.

"I'm doing this. Just back off and give me room!"

Valen didn't know what to say. Ares had explained that healing them drained her and left her weak, that she had come close to death once when trying to aid him.

Valen admired the fuck out of her as he knelt beside her, watching her assessing the wound, knowing that she was about to risk her life to save Esher's.

Ares moved around behind her, sank to his knees and placed his hands on her shoulders, rubbing them through her light black cotton jacket.

She pulled her chestnut hair from her face and secured it with a black band, her fingers shaking as she struggled to tie it in a ponytail at the nape of her neck.

She was afraid.

Valen couldn't blame her. Using her power wasn't the only risk she was taking. She was taking a huge one just being close to Esher when none of them knew when he would come around. If he woke with her near him, a mortal in his eyes, he was liable to kill her.

Valen wouldn't let that happen. The grim look on Ares's face said he wouldn't either.

Megan reached a trembling hand out and placed it on Esher's stomach just above the wound. When she added a second, below the wound and close to Esher's hip, Ares growled and she tensed.

"Sorry," he muttered against her hair and pressed a kiss to the back of her head. "Knee-jerk reaction."

Valen understood why. If it had been Eva touching one of his brothers in front of him, he would have lost his shit too.

He looked over his right shoulder at her. She stood near the couches, her bottom against the back of one, and had her right hand tucked against her chest. Concern filled her expression as she looked at the group. Her blue eyes shifted to meet his, and relief that she looked normal again now flowed through him and straight out again as his worry for her was replaced by worry for Esher.

Valen pulled his focus back to his brother.

Megan closed her eyes and hung her head forwards.

The room filled with an air of expectation as everyone stared at the violet tendrils, waiting to see a change in them.

Their writhing slowed, but they didn't stop spreading.

Fight.

Valen willed Esher to hear him, to do as he pleaded.

Fight harder.

Because it was his soul on the line.

A wraith's blade was deadly to all creatures, a method of slowly extracting a soul through an excruciating death.

This was all his fault.

A wraith wouldn't have been able to do this to Esher if Esher hadn't been preoccupied with calming himself, and he knew that was exactly what his brother had gone to do. He had driven his brother out by bringing Eva here, and had placed him in grave danger.

"Do not blame yourself," Keras said, as if he had read Valen's mind.

Maybe he had. Keras was a pain like that, always sticking his nose in where it wasn't wanted.

He shrugged it off, but couldn't deny the relief that flooded him as Keras's comforting words sank in and the tendrils spreading across Esher's body finally began to reverse, shrinking back towards the patch of black around the wound.

Ares kneaded Megan's shoulders. "You're doing great, Sweetheart."

She nodded and swallowed hard, sweat beading on her brow and her skin draining of colour as she kept going.

Healing Esher.

Valen couldn't believe it.

He had never seen her heal before, and while he had heard the stories from Daimon and Ares about the times she had healed them, part of him hadn't quite believed she possessed that talent.

But it was true.

He stared wide-eyed at her hands on Esher's side and the black as it began to shrink towards the wound.

When it was all gone, violet smoke rushed from the wound on a hiss and dissipated.

Megan collapsed back against Ares, breathing hard and trembling. Ares wrapped his arms around her, tucking her against his broad body, and petted her, whispering sickly sweet things to her.

Gods only knew how Esher was going to process what had just happened when he came around.

He looked down at his brother.

Esher owed a mortal, and he owed her with his life.

That was a shit storm brewing on the horizon if he had ever seen one.

Keras carefully lifted Esher into his arms and walked towards the corridor on the right side of the room that led to Esher's bedroom.

Daimon stood and didn't look at any of them, his eyes remaining locked on the dark crimson patch on the floor.

"I'll pay penitence in his stead." He stepped before Valen could stop him and take his place.

It should have been him receiving punishment from Nemesis for Esher speaking the language of the Underworld in the mortal realm, not Daimon. What had happened to Esher had been his fault.

Megan moaned, and he looked across at her.

"Is she okay?" he said.

The whole room stared at him, shock etched onto all their faces.

Valen flipped them off one by one. "Fuck you all."

They didn't have to make such a big deal about him being concerned about someone else.

"I'll be peachy again soon." Megan sounded a touch too bright. She sagged against Ares's chest. "I could use about thirty years of sleep though."

"Sweetheart," Ares murmured and stroked her hair. He looked as if he wanted to chastise her, but then he forced a tight smile. "Thank you, Baby."

She nodded and snuggled closer to him, closing her eyes and sighing out her breath.

Ares scooped her up into his arms and stood.

"Take care of her, Old Man," Marek said as he came to his feet. "We have things here."

Ares nodded and stepped.

Calistos muttered something, pulled a sour face, and shoved onto his feet, issuing a glare to all of them. "Damn gate is calling. You say anything interesting while I'm gone, and I'll murder you all in your sleep."

He disappeared, revealing Keras as he emerged from the corridor, his too handsome face set in a dark expression and his green eyes verging on glowing.

He was on the warpath.

Valen pitied whoever was in the firing line of his oldest brother.

"Tell me everything," Keras barked, his green eyes glowing now as they narrowed on him. "Starting with what the fuck you were doing on Mount Olympus."

Valen's stomach dropped.

He swallowed hard.

He was the poor bastard in the firing line.

CHAPTER 28

Eva's head was killing her, which was making taking in everything that was happening all the more difficult. She stared at the dark patch of blood on the floor, soaking into the straw mats. Something had happened, something awful, and she had come around in the middle of it, roused by a sound that had made her think of monsters.

Of Benares.

The relief she had felt on realising he didn't have her had fled the second she had discovered she was in a strange place, but it had come back a little when she had stood and spotted Valen.

Fighting to save one of his brothers.

Valen stood a short distance away, scrubbing a hand over his face. He was a mess. There were long rips in his black t-shirt that exposed angry wounds beneath, cuts that looked as if someone had slashed at him with claws, and bloodstained skin. She wanted to know what had happened to him, felt a deep and consuming need to go to him and tend to his wounds, but remained silent and still, frozen in place by the way his brother had looked at her, red eyes shining with a hunger for her blood.

Whatever he had said in her direction, it had pulled a fierce reaction from Valen, leaving her in no doubt he had intended to hurt her.

He had done enough damage with that language he had spoken. It had felt as if her eardrums were going to burst, every word he had spoken sending searing pain piercing her skull.

Valen stared down Keras as he stopped in the middle of the room, his golden eyes haunted but gaining a hard edge as he steeled himself for his brother's wrath.

Marek, the one with tawny wavy hair and sun-kissed skin and a love of dark linen clothing and sandals, tensed and backed off a step, giving Keras and Valen more room, as if he feared they might suddenly explode and catch him in the crossfire.

She tensed as a flash of another man matching his description shot across her mind and sank against the couch behind her.

"Eva." Valen was by her side before she could open her eyes and tell him that she was fine.

She looked up into his golden eyes and saw different ones looking back at her, and a voice echoed in her mind.

I need to keep my promise.

"Promise?" she whispered, her eyebrows dropping low as she tried to understand. "What promise?"

Valen's hands came to rest on her bare shoulders and he gently squeezed them. "Nothing for you to worry about."

She shook her head, kept struggling to remember what had happened even though she knew he wanted her to stop and let it go.

If he wanted that, then something had happened, something he thought would frighten her.

She looked down at her chest, touched the spot over her heart as it throbbed. It was hot beneath her fingertips.

Valen captured her hand and held it in both of his.

"Valen," Keras snapped.

His head whipped around to face his brother and he snarled, "Give me a minute, will you?"

"No. I want answers." Keras stripped his black coat off, folded it in half and placed it on the back of the couch at the other end of it to Eva.

It was strange that he always dressed so formally when all of the brothers were more casual. Didn't he fight much? His crisp black tailored shirt and slacks, and neat black shoes were far too impractical.

She looked from him to Valen, whose tight black t-shirt and combat trousers, and heavy boots were better attire for fighting.

Even Marek's loose black linen trousers and dark brown shirt were more suitable. She wouldn't even begrudge him the sandals.

She had that weird feeling again, that sensation that he looked like someone else.

Valen growled, grabbed her arm and pulled her to her left, blocking her view of Marek.

What had the big guy, Ares, said after he had positively growled at Megan for touching Esher?

It was a knee-jerk reaction.

Had Valen's been one too?

He didn't like her looking at his brothers.

"He just reminds me of someone."

"Me?" Marek jabbed a finger at himself and his rich brown eyes turned thoughtful. He rolled his broad shoulders. "Father always says I look like our uncle."

"Your uncle?" She looked to Valen for the answer to that one.

He didn't look as if he would give it to her.

"Let me take you to somewhere you can rest." That sounded a lot like he was avoiding saying it for some reason, which only made her want to know even more.

Coupled with the fact he obviously didn't want to discuss things with Keras in front of her, and not because she was technically working for their enemy because Keras certainly didn't seem to mind talking about things around her now, suspicion formed as a seed in her mind and took root, growing as she stared at Valen.

He tried to tug her away from the couch.

She snatched her arm from his grip.

"It's fine. It's okay." She raised her hands and cupped his cheeks, holding his gaze. "I'm stronger than you think, Valen. I'm not made of glass."

He sighed. "That isn't the problem. I know you're strong."

"So what is it then?"

The way he looked at her gave her the answer.

He was the one afraid.

He feared that whatever she might hear in his conversation with his brothers would drive her away.

Not likely.

She'd had her outburst, her moment of crazy, and she was over it now. Valen, his brothers, her clients, and the man who had taken her from Valen's apartment, were all the stuff of dreams and nightmares, of fantasy, but she had finally found her feet and the ground beneath them was stable again.

She'd had the time she needed to take it all in and process it.

And deep inside, she knew that it had happened while she had been asleep. Unconscious. She remembered the man, and then there had been a bright warm light, and she had heard two voices echoing through it.

She had caught snippets of their conversation, fragments that she couldn't remember now but the warmth they had stirred and the comfort they had given her lingered like the light inside her, leaving no room for fear.

"I'm not going anywhere," she whispered, wishing they were alone and he was the only one to hear those words, because they were private, meant for only him, along with the rest of what she had to say. "The safest place is with you, right?"

His golden eyes lit up, the warmth in them a strange thing to see, because all the times she had seen him around his brothers he had kept a lid on his feelings, concealing them from his family.

"So sweet," Marek muttered.

That light vanished. Darkness replaced it. The Valen she was used to.

He glared over his shoulder. "Fuck off."

Eva stepped up beside him and took hold of his hand. His eyes instantly leaped back to hers, a flicker of shock in them. If he looked shocked now, he was going to look blown away in a second.

Because she had just remembered something.

"So why did Zeus take me to Mount Olympus to keep a promise?"

His golden eyes shot wide and he blinked at her.

Keras and Marek stared at her, stunned expressions making her smile.

"I think snippets of it are coming back. I remember you there, like a shadow in the light... I think you wanted to fight."

"We have a history." His free hand lifted, fingers absently grazing the scar on the left side of his face as he stared down at her.

"Not a good history?" She frowned and he shook his head.

The way his two brothers looked at his back with pity in their eyes spoke to her. She knew Valen now, had finally completed the picture of him. He had a temper, a very short fuse, and his power was seductive because it was so strong and violent, playing on that temper and teasing it to the fore.

She could imagine that not even the alpha god of their world would be immune to his wrath if he had pissed off Valen.

"I remember hearing your sister mentioned."

Keras took a sudden step forwards. "Calindria?"

Valen's golden eyes grew dark and haunted, and he nodded. "I'm glad Cal had to leave, because I have a few things to say that I don't think he could bear hearing… and a theory that my gut says is the answer to the question that has plagued us for centuries."

"Go on," Keras said, but Valen didn't continue immediately.

He stood next to her in silence, and she could see the struggle in his eyes and feel it in the way his hand trembled in hers. She remembered how his shadow had flickered in that bright world, red at times and black at others. She remembered his pain.

She squeezed his hand.

He clutched it tighter, squared his shoulders and looked at Marek and Keras.

"The wraith we keep encountering was involved then. We all know that they can capture and store a soul, and that… hers… is missing." His voice shook, revealing his emotions to her, feelings that crossed his brothers' faces too as they paled. "Wraiths weren't banished from the Underworld until only a couple of centuries ago, after they had pissed off Dad. It makes sense that if it was a wraith who did it, it was this bastard… and… maybe that means we can find Calindria's soul and free it."

Her soul? His sister had lost her soul?

Ares had mentioned a wraith earlier, when they had been trying to help Esher.

This wraith could kill Valen and his brothers.

But they were gods.

A foolish part of her had thought that meant they were immortal, unable to die, even when Valen had mentioned he had lost his sister.

Valen squeezed her hand now and glanced at her. "No wraith is getting the jump on me."

She nodded, wanting to believe that.

"Do not pin your hopes on being able to find it, Valen," Keras said, his fine black eyebrows pinching together above his clear green eyes and his lips flattening, the corners of them turning downwards as he started to pace. "It has been a long time. It might not be possible to find it now… or it might be—"

Marek and Valen fell silent and grim, as pensive as Keras.

She didn't want to ask what it might be, because the way Keras had cut himself off said that whatever it was, it wouldn't be good.

Was it possible something might have happened to Calindria's soul to change it? Could a soul turn evil?

Could she become a daemon?

"I cannot deny the thought that the wraith might be involved in her death hadn't crossed my mind, even played on it, since Ares and Daimon witnessed him killing Amaury." Keras rubbed his right thumb across his lower lip, his left arm wrapped around his waist and supporting his right elbow.

Marek stepped forwards. "Could he be the leader?"

"Whether he is the leader or not," Valen said and Keras and Marek looked at him, "we have to find him and capture him, and not only because it might end the plot to destroy the gates and save our world and this one. We have to try to save Calindria's soul."

Resolved filled Keras's eyes and he nodded.

"I will hit our database and see what I can find on wraiths." Marek had barely finished his sentence before he disappeared.

The young blond brother appeared next to Keras and casually brushed the black ribbons of smoke from his bare arms. If it wasn't for the blue eyes, and the slight difference in years, she would have hazarded a guess that he and Valen were twins. They even had the same taste in clothing, dressed exactly alike.

"Miss me?" He beamed at Keras and Valen, his blue eyes bright with his smile.

There was a streak of something black across his cheek.

Keras curled a lip at it, took a handkerchief from his trouser pocket and wiped it away, more like a doting father than an older brother.

"Damn daemons, always bleeding all over me." Calistos scrubbed at the spot with his hand and gave everyone an expectant look. "So, what did I miss?"

Keras's expression shifted towards sombre as he pocketed the handkerchief. Valen remained silent so long she wondered if he would ever speak again. It seemed neither brother knew what to say, which was strange.

She opened her mouth.

Valen shot her a glare, the one he always used when telling her to remain quiet.

"We think the wraith might be the leader." Valen left it at that and she frowned at him.

His golden eyes slid down to hers and he shook his head, just enough for her to notice.

Why hadn't he mentioned his theory about their sister too?

Eva had wanted to know more about her, but it was obvious that conversation wasn't going to continue now that Calistos had returned. He looked between his brothers, a blank edge to his expression as he waited for them to tell him more. She felt sorry for him.

Why were they keeping things from him?

"We need to deal with your daemons first," Keras said, dragging her focus back to him, and she shivered as she thought about returning to Rome where Benares and Jin awaited her.

Her three days were almost up.

And if the snippets of her time in the weird warm light that were coming back were right, Jin had already tried to take her to Benares to lure Valen into a trap and over to his side.

She wanted this over now, so she could be in Rome again without fearing for her life, without looking over her shoulder every second of the day expecting that monster to come after her.

She wanted him dead.

His bitch sister too.

"Do you have a plan?" Keras said to Valen.

Eva stepped forwards and all eyes came to land on her.

"I have one."

CHAPTER 29

"Fuck no," Valen barked and ignored the pointed looks Calistos and Keras gave him, and the way Eva planted her hands on her hips and glared in his direction. "Not going to happen."

What she had proposed was madness.

He couldn't allow her to do it, not only because it placed her in danger, but because every fibre of his being, every drop of his soul, screamed that he wouldn't be able to protect her.

He would fail.

Eva huffed, the sharp action causing her chest to rise in a way that was too damn distracting in the green halter-top she wore. The wicked glimmer in her eyes said that she knew it too, that she was using her best weapons against him.

He flashed his teeth at her. "Not going to happen. Deal with it."

"Listen to reason," Keras started but fell silent when Valen shot him down with a glare. His big brother held his hands up at his sides and sighed. "I know it goes against your blood, but if the daemons had planned to take her and use her as bait for you, then it stands to reason they will try again."

"And if they kill her?"

"They won't kill me." Eva didn't sound sure, in fact she sounded almost convinced that they would and it frightened her. No, she *was* convinced. She had been convinced Benares wanted her dead for a while now, which made it even harder to go along with her plan.

Stupid plan that it was.

"Valen, this might be our only way of getting to them." Keras again, trying to play the voice of reason.

Calistos mercifully held his tongue, the look on his face saying he wasn't going to risk his neck by courting the darker side of Valen's temper with suggestions that he just let Eva place herself at risk, as if she meant nothing to him.

When she meant everything.

"I can't," Valen rasped and dragged his hands over his hair, clawing it back and digging his fingers into it. "You know that."

The soft look in Eva's blue eyes said that she did know. She knew how difficult this was for him, and she knew the risks, and she was still willing to do it.

For him.

And for herself too.

"How else are you going to get close to them? Benares is fast."

"I'll just have to be faster," he said and she rolled her eyes, earning a growl from him. "I can outstrip that bastard, don't worry."

"And all the men he employs?" She scowled at him. "There are at least two dozen of them... and I get the feeling they aren't human."

"If their boss is a daemon, it stands to reason they are too," Keras said, and Valen wanted to punch him.

Luckily for his brother, he was making sense, and so was Eva, and Valen wasn't in the mood to lash out at people for no real reason tonight.

He looked down into Eva's eyes, weighing his options, and finding both of them sucked. If he tried to go in alone, he would be facing at least two dozen daemons, their strength and age unknown factors that might lead him to his doom. He could be overpowered by less than ten strong daemons if they were coordinated, and of the right species. What sort of daemons would follow an incubus?

He didn't know.

But the only other option was to let Eva do things her way. Jin would take her from his apartment, and he would track them to the villa. Once enough time had passed, he would walk right through the front door, a welcomed guest.

Although, he would probably end up taking out a few of the daemons along the way, and not only for show.

The thought of Eva being taken by Benares, a captive of a monster she feared, and held at his mercy had him wanting daemon blood on his hands already and he was only thinking about it.

If he did let Benares take her, then he would want more than daemon blood on his hands.

He would want a war.

He would want to tear apart the villa with his lightning until every damned daemon in it was dead.

He stared down at Eva.

Gods, he couldn't do it.

Zeus had taken her to protect her, because the Moirai must have foreseen something bad happening to her.

Valen couldn't stand by and let that happen, just so she could lure the daemons into a trap for him.

"Tell me where they live and we'll launch an all out assault on the place," Valen said, his voice a deep snarl that shocked even him, his darker side roused by the need to protect her at whatever cost.

She shook her head. "They'll be expecting that from you. It's your MO. I wouldn't be surprised if Benares had increased security since I was last there. They have guns, Valen. If a knife can hurt your brother, I'm fairly certain bullets can hurt you."

That wasn't going to stop him.

"I'll deal with them," he snapped.

She folded her arms across her chest and her lips compressed in a mulish line. "It only takes one of them to raise the alarm and then Benares and Jin are gone. Is that what you want?"

He glared at her.

"She does have a point."

Valen shot Keras another warning look but this time he didn't back down. His brother narrowed green eyes on him that glowed in their centres, shining brightly around his pupils. He was testing Keras's patience, but he couldn't stop himself, not when the thought of putting Eva at risk was screwing with his head, making him want to step right now and obliterate the mansion so she didn't have to do something crazy.

"Tell me where the mansion is."

"No," she barked and shook her head, making her black hair sway across her jaw. "I will not... because you aren't listening to reason... you'll go off and... and get yourself—"

Valen's anger flatlined.

His shoulders sagged as it all drained out of him as if she had pulled a plug rather than simply cut herself off, stopping herself from saying something that she didn't want to voice.

Something that told him everything.

She really did care about him.

And he was being a massive dick again.

He only wanted to protect her, but he hadn't considered that he would end up hurting her by trying to do it. She wanted to help, because she was afraid that if she didn't, he would get himself killed.

"Hey," he murmured and she refused to look at him, kept her eyes fixed on his chest. He closed the distance between them, smoothed his right hand along her jaw, and brushed his thumb over her cheek. "It isn't going to happen."

She still wouldn't look at him.

Keras's gaze bore a deep hole in the side of his skull.

Fine.

"I won't do it," he muttered and she lifted her eyes to his, and gods, the relief in them hit him hard in the chest, punching a hole through it to his heart. "But answer this... what's to say Benares isn't already on to us?"

"All he knows is that I wasn't at your apartment when he sent Jin there. I'll check in and say things are going according to plan, and I'll be ready to hand you over soon. He's bound to send Jin to take me again if I say that I'm just waiting at your place while you deal with some business at something you called a gate." Eva looked sure as shit that her plan was flawless.

Valen wasn't convinced, but he didn't say it, didn't even let her see it in his eyes. If things went south, he would find a way to save her. He had told her not to expect him to be a hero, but it seemed he couldn't help himself where she was concerned. It would always be this way. The second she got into trouble, he would be there like some cliché white knight to rescue her arse.

"You'll feel the wards trigger, and then you'll come after me, and they'll welcome you with open arms."

"When I go to them alone," he said what she wouldn't.

"No," Keras snapped, a powerful command behind that word that made the air around Valen tremble.

Valen looked across at his older brother, shock rippling through him as he registered what had just happened.

Keras hated the idea of him walking into danger alone, and he hated it so much he had almost lost his temper.

Almost.

Valen had seen the things that happened when Keras lost his temper, and that widespread destruction was half of the reason he kept a lid on it. The other half? Valen didn't know, but something held back his negative emotions and kept him mellow.

"So you'll hang around at a distance as back up." Valen grinned at him, aiming for his usual charming and cocky self to soothe his brother's temper, because Esher would be pissed if he came around to find Keras had levelled half of Tokyo.

"We need one of them alive." Keras curled his hands into fists and clenched them, and the vivid green-gold in his eyes faded to emerald as he got his emotions back under control. "Do you think you can manage that?"

He wasn't sure. Just the thought of them hurting Eva had him close to the edge of losing control already. He couldn't guarantee he would be able to keep his head when he knew they had her.

"I will have Marek come too. We will track you and wait in the shadows for a sign you need help." Keras took his coat from the back of the couch and slipped it back on, the hem swaying around his ankles before it settled.

There was a lot Valen wanted to say in response to that—he didn't need help, it was dangerous for Keras to use his command over the shadows to conceal him and Marek, and this was his moment and he would kill his brother if he stole his gig as white knight.

In the end, he settled for saying, "Thanks."

Keras nodded and disappeared.

Calistos blew out his breath on a low whistle. "You really know how to push his buttons, Brother."

Before Valen could respond, Calistos stepped. Little bastard.

But he was right.

Keras's temper had flared. Only a little, but it had happened, and he couldn't remember the last time their fearless leader had been affected by anything that happened to them, or anything they had proposed to do.

Esher must have shaken him deeper than everyone had thought.

Or he was finally reaching his limit, and everything he had bottled up during his time in the mortal world, every negative emotion he had contained, had him close to bursting.

Valen didn't want to be around when that happened.

He fished his phone from his pocket, the handful of small innocuous charms that hung from it rattling, and sorted through them, searching for the right one.

"What are you doing?" Eva moved closer, peering at his phone.

"Sending a message."

She frowned. "You do that with the screen, you know?"

He smiled. "Not this sort of message. There are no phones on Mount Olympus."

He pressed the simple sword and shield metal charm against his palm and closed his fingers over it. It was warm. Metal of the gods.

Valen closed his eyes and sent the message.

He just hoped her brother didn't pick it up.

He stuffed his phone back in his pocket, shutting out the voice at the back of his mind that whispered about how much he hated people meddling in his affairs and now he was doing it to others.

He shrugged that off.

It wasn't meddling.

He liked to think of it as saving the world.

He held his right hand out to Eva.

"Walk with me?"

CHAPTER 30

Valen didn't realise how much he needed to be alone with Eva, how fiercely he wanted to spend every last possible second with her before they kicked their plan into action, until she placed her hand into his.

He clutched it tightly. She frowned down at their joined hands, and then up into his eyes, and placed her other hand over his.

"I'll be fine," she said and he nodded.

But he didn't believe it.

He couldn't when every possible scenario was running through his head, weighing down his heart.

"Come on." She tugged on his hand, leading him towards sliding wood-framed white panels that had been pushed back to reveal the covered wooden walkway that ran around the three sides of the building facing onto the courtyard. She looked back at him, a smile in her eyes. "You never told me you knew a place like this."

Why did she look so fascinated?

He smiled when it hit him. The nightingale floors in her apartment.

"We don't have any." He shrugged when she looked disappointed. "We don't really need them. The wards around the mansion stop anyone from entering."

"You keep mentioning wards. Are they like a barrier?"

He nodded and took the lead as they stepped out onto the covered walkway. He tugged her to the right and followed it around a bend and along that wing of the ancient house.

"We all lived here once, so the barriers are strongest, reinforced by our father." He stopped at the two decorated paper panels that formed a door to the room at the end of the wing, over the koi pond. "As the world developed, we all ended up leaving this place to be closer to our gates. Only Esher stays here now, but Daimon stops over from time to time."

"They seem close," she whispered and he nodded again.

"They share one hell of a bond." He released her hand and carefully slid one of the doors back, revealing the room on the other side.

A single square paper lantern illuminated the almost naked space, situated on the tatami mat floor a few feet from his brother's head.

Valen stepped into the room and kneeled beside Esher on the floor. He was still too pale, his breathing laboured as he fought to heal the wound. Valen drew the thick blue blanket down to reveal Esher's bare chest and folded it over his hips. He leaned over and studied the wound.

Sank back on his heels as he saw it was healing and let out the breath he had been holding.

Esher would be fine.

Physically anyway.

He would have to wait to see what sort of mental shape his brother was in when he came around.

He closed his eyes, drew in another deep breath, and took hold of Esher's hand, issuing a silent apology to his brother.

"Will he be okay?" Eva whispered and he let go of Esher's hand, covered him again and rose back onto his feet.

She stood in the doorway, partially hidden behind it, and he couldn't blame her for keeping her distance after the way Esher had reacted to her.

Valen nodded, stepped out of the room, and gently closed the sliding door. "He'll be fine... up and around in no time and probably tearing us all new ones for walking around the house in our shoes."

He took her hand again and led her to the broad stone step, and down into the courtyard, following the path that snaked through the gravel and the manicured small trees.

She stopped, forcing him to stop with her, and he glanced over his shoulder at her.

"Will you?" she said, and when he frowned at her, added, "Be fine?"

Her blue gaze dropped to his chest.

He smiled to alleviate her worry and fingered the slashes in his black t-shirt. "Esher lost his temper when I arrived with you, but I'll be fine. The cuts are healing and they'll be gone in a few hours."

"Incredible," she murmured and lifted her eyes to meet his. "You healed quickly from the wounds you picked up in the bar fight in Rome too."

He shrugged it off. "Perk of being a god."

A hollow clacking sound echoed around the peaceful garden, sending a jolt down his spine, and he glared at the water feature responsible for that harrowing noise. He hated the damn thing.

It was nothing more than a simple construction involving a bamboo pipe and a water course that fed it, filling it up until it tipped on its axis and spilled its contents into the square pool of the thick stone disc on the gravel near the pond, but he hated it. He hated the sharp wooden sound it made when the empty bamboo pipe swung back the other way, the sealed base striking the stone.

It royally pissed him off whenever he stayed at the mansion, keeping him awake for hours.

Esher loved the damn thing though.

Valen stalked over to it, scooped up a handful of the spring water from the pool and used it to wash his chest. Shuddered. Fuck it was freezing. He scrubbed the blood from his body as quickly as he could and then stilled as moonlight shone down on him, allowing him to inspect the wounds. They were healing well now. A few more hours and they would be little more than pinkened skin.

Eva studied him, so fiercely he could almost feel her concern.

He shot her a smile over his shoulder. "All good. They'll be gone before you know it."

He held his hand out to her. She slipped hers back into it and he led her along the path past the water feature to the small bridge that arched over the pond.

Eva slowed at the apex of the curved red wooden bridge and he looked back at her.

Stopped.

Sweet gods, she was beautiful.

Moonlight bathed her skin, making it clear and milky white, and transformed her eyes, so they shone almost like his did at times, hers bright blue in the strong light.

She tensed and he swore a blush of colour rose onto her cheeks as she looked away, but then her eyes met his again, and the determined look in them almost swept his legs out from under him.

She hemmed him in against the arched wooden balustrade of the bridge, lifted her hand and touched his cheek.

His left one.

"Does this have something to do with your sister?"

He wanted to shut her out, bring up the barriers and not let her see that part of him, but he was tired of always hiding it from her. She would find out one day, and he would rather that day was now, when he was only falling in love with her.

In order to spare himself greater pain in the future, he had to put himself through the agony of telling her now.

"It wasn't my finest moment." He tipped his head back, looking up at the moon in the clear sky. Stars twinkled around it, faint but visible, struggling as their backdrop lightened. It would be dawn soon. He planted his hands on the balustrade and sighed. "When she died, I went off the rails... and I killed the goddesses who had sworn to protect her."

He lowered his eyes back to Eva's.

"I butchered the Moirai."

Her eyes widened. "The Fates?"

He nodded and turned his cheek to her, watched the koi sleeping in the pond, peaceful and unaware of his pain.

Lucky bastards.

"I went after Zeus, blaming him for not stopping what happened to Calindria. Gods, I burned with that need for vengeance and it consumed me. I was so convinced I could both avenge her and get her back at the same time. I wanted to defeat Zeus so he would bring my sister back." He closed his eyes and sighed again. "Even back then part of me knew it wasn't possible... that Zeus could do fuck all for her without her soul."

"What happened?" Eva pressed closer to him, her warmth chasing some of the cold away, and he draped his arms around her bare shoulders and pulled her closer still, needing the light weight of her body against his and the scent of her soothing him.

"Zeus defeated me and gave life back to the Moirai, and he would have killed me if my mother hadn't shown up and pleaded for my life." He gazed down at Eva and stroked her short hair behind her right ear. "Instead of killing me, Zeus banished me from Mount Olympus and decreed that I would no longer know the gods of that realm, and they would no longer know me. He took his favour from me."

He brushed his fingers across his scar.

Her eyes fell there. "Favour?"

He nodded. "Each of us were blessed with the favour of a god or goddess when we were born. My brothers still bear the marks of those who favour them. You've probably noticed the writing on the underside of Cal's forearm, and that stupid black heart below Keras's eye."

"I didn't realise it was a heart." Her eyebrows rose.

"Aphrodite thought it would be funny, apparently."

Eva smiled. "It does make him look a little…"

"Girly?" Valen had always thought so, and the twinkle in Eva's blue eyes said she thought it too.

Her expression turned serious and she pressed her palm to his scar. "What was yours like?"

She just had to ask, didn't she?

He hated thinking about it. It was a constant reminder of what he had done and that his sister was gone.

But there was hope now, a chance that they might be able to save her, if her soul hadn't become corrupted.

He cleared his throat. "Like purple lightning. It was beautiful. I used to stare at it so much as a kid, convinced I would be as strong as my uncle one day because he had given me his favour… and in the end I was weak. I let my power control me, let my anger consume me, and I still keep doing it."

She swept her fingers across the distorted skin of his scar, her touch tender and gentle, and a soft light entered her eyes.

"Don't look at me that way." He pushed her hand away. "I don't need your pity."

"It isn't pity, Stronzo," she whispered and tiptoed, and he stilled as her lips pressed against his.

Gods, her kiss was so soft and light, so tender it overwhelmed him and he wasn't sure what to do, didn't know how to behave.

Because no one had ever kissed him like this.

He was used to roughness, to passion pushed to its very limit, consumed by desire and driven by need. If she had kissed him hard, bitten his lip and given him pain, playing as rough as they had before, he would have been able to handle it.

But he couldn't handle this.

It was too new, too powerful.

He had thought that the way they had been together the last two times had been everything he craved, everything he needed.

How could he have been so wrong?

How could she undo him so thoroughly with nothing more than a light brush of her lips across his?

He told himself to move, to do something before she thought he really was an idiot, but he couldn't convince his body to obey him.

Her kiss destroyed him, tore down his strength and made him weak, but it built him back up too, piecing him together in a new way, one that felt stronger.

Because this kiss was meant to tell him something.

Her feelings.

He had waited so long for someone to love, and someone to love him, that he hadn't thought it possible, had become convinced that Zeus's curse had been real.

Now he could see how blind he had been.

All that time he had been waiting for her.

He hadn't wanted to get involved with the females in the Underworld in any lasting way because they hadn't been the one.

They hadn't been Eva.

Her kiss grew uncertain, spurring him into action, and he took the leap, returned it as softly as he could as everything overwhelmed him, hoping she would know that he felt the same way.

That he loved her.

He drew her against him and kissed her softly, losing himself in it as it warmed him right down to the marrow of his bones and filled him with a lightness that carried away all his doubts and fears, leaving only Eva and this moment.

Her hands came down against his chest and he groaned against her lips, his mind leaping forwards.

She whispered against his lips, "So if you used to live here, does that mean you have—"

He cut her off by teleporting her into the room she wanted to see.

She pressed harder against him, but her kiss remained light, gentle and teasing. He moaned and gathered her closer still, but his little assassin resisted, pushing him back and breaking her lips away from his.

She glanced around the room.

Other than two wide sets of drawers against one of the walls, and a low wooden table that had been pushed back against the opposite wall, it was empty.

Esher had kept the bed down though. Valen didn't miss the unforgiving hardness of Japanese sleeping arrangements. Not even the thick blanket that acted as the mattress beneath the duvet was enough to stop him waking with an aching back in the morning whenever he slept over.

Still, he didn't intend to do much sleeping.

He was going to make love with Eva.

Gods, that shouldn't terrify him as much as it did.

Eva seemed to sense it, because she flashed him a wicked smile and pressed back against him, and her mouth claimed his again, a little rougher than before.

He groaned and pinned her against his body as he lost himself in the kiss, stroking his tongue along hers and teasing her with it. She moaned and wrapped her arms around his neck, and leaped. Her legs snaked around his waist and he grabbed her backside, holding her in position, her weight nothing in his hands.

He supposed she was right, and making love was just a matter of the feelings that went into it, the emotions they both felt.

It didn't have to be gentle all the time, as long as it was slow.

Which was good, because the way she nibbled his lower lip pushed him way past being gentle with her.

He growled and paid her back, nipping her plump lower lip between his teeth, tearing a quiet moan from her as she trembled in his arms.

Wicked little assassin.

He dropped to his knees and lowered her onto the bedding, covering her body with his as he continued his assault, alternating between kissing her softly, and being rough with her lip. She mewled beneath him, her hands coming down on his shoulders and fisting his t-shirt.

"More," she breathed against his lips and he groaned and surrendered to that command, bringing his body down into contact with hers.

He ground against her, driving his hard cock between her thighs, but rather than giving him the pleasure he needed, it only frustrated him. He needed her naked, bared for him.

He kissed down her chest, over the swells of her breasts, and savoured the way her heart beat frantically against his lips.

Sweet Eva.

She arched as he tugged aside the right cup of her green halter-top, pulling her bra with it, exposing her nipple. It tightened in the cool air, calling to him, and his cock ached and throbbed in response, driving him into obeying that call.

He groaned and lowered his lips, wrapped them around the sweet bud and suckled it. Eva moaned and writhed beneath him, tangled one hand in his hair and clutched him to her. Delicious. He would never get enough of how she reacted to him.

He shoved at the other side of her top, freeing her breast, and toyed with the tight bead as he suckled her other one. She jerked and moaned as he tweaked it, squeezed it between his fingers and plucked at it.

"Valen," she breathed, voice low with need.

Gods, he would never get enough of that either.

Hearing how much pleasure he gave to her almost undid him.

He growled and released her nipple, and shifted across to latch onto the other one. She arched against him, pressing her breast into his mouth, and he hungrily devoured it as he skimmed his hand down her side. She giggled as he traced his fingers over her bare flesh beneath the hem of her top and then moaned again as he found the fly and began working on it.

He needed her naked.

Bared to him.

He undid the button and lowered the zipper, and pushed his hand inside, a groan escaping him as he found her moist centre. So warm. Wet. Aching for him as he ached for her.

He sucked hard on her nipple, tugging it as he pulled back, and she shuddered on a moan as he let it go and loomed over her. Her eyes opened, dark with need that echoed inside him.

But need wasn't the only feeling shining in them. There was acceptance there too, and a hell of a lot of love.

That shot him past sweet, straight into wicked, filling him with a fierce hunger that demanded he sate it, a need to be one with her again, buried deep in her and claiming her as his own.

He growled and that hunger in her eyes only grew more intense, beckoning him.

She moaned as he yanked her jeans down to her ankles, taking her knickers with them, and didn't resist as he removed her trainers and then them, tossing them to one side. His t-shirt followed it and he rolled onto his backside and kicked at his own boots. He needed to feel her skin on skin with him again.

Needed to claim her.

It seemed she was on the same wavelength, because she yanked her top off and tossed it aside to join the rest of her clothes, and he could only stare at her, his fingers paused against his fly.

Eva grinned wickedly, shifted onto all fours and crawled over to him.

He scowled at her. "I'm meant to be making love with you."

A blush stained her cheeks. "This is making love."

It was?

He stared at her, unsure about that. Making love was meant to be slow at the very least, and the look in her eyes said she was proposing something markedly different from that.

She crushed his ability to think by running her hands over his thighs and up to his hips, and he sat there staring at her like an idiot, on fire with a need that consumed him.

A need she seemed all too happy to fulfil.

She pressed her hands against his bare chest and gently pushed him back, and he hit the mats but didn't feel it as she kissed down his chest, lavishing the healing wounds with attention.

Gods, that felt good. Wonderful in fact.

Another first for him.

He had never had a female fuss over him like this.

She swirled her tongue around his left nipple. He grunted as she bit it, sending hot tingles racing across his torso, and then melted into the floor as she continued downwards, trailing her lips over his stomach. She moaned low in her throat, a murmur of appreciation that stoked his male pride, rubbing it the right way.

Her hands reached his trousers and he waited as she opened his fly, holding his breath as his hard length throbbed with need, aching to feel her hot little hands on it.

Cool air washed over his cock.

Warmth followed it, slick and moist, driving him out of his mind.

He groaned and tipped his head back into the mats, his entire body going rigid as she licked down his length and back up again, and took it in her hand. He grunted as she fisted it hard, a few rough pumps that had his knees shaking, and then released him and took him into her mouth.

Sweet gods.

The feel of her mouth on him, her warmth surrounding him as she sucked him, slowly taking him as deep as he could go, unravelled him.

He lay at her mercy, panting hard as feelings collided within him, swirled together and flooded him so fiercely he feared he might drown in them.

Gods, he hadn't lied that first night, when he had told her he could die right that moment and he wouldn't care.

That same feeling swept over him now, the bliss of her touch so intense that only it mattered.

He shuddered as she stroked a hand over his balls and then grunted as she tugged them, rolled them and found a new way to drive him out of his mind.

Too much.

He fisted her hair and pulled her away from him, dragged her up for a kiss that he had hoped would give him time to get himself back under control.

His little assassin had other plans.

She rubbed her body against his and let her legs fall away from him so she was straddling him.

Issuing a startling reminder of just where they touched.

He groaned and grabbed her bottom, trying to force her into contact with his cock.

She denied him, rolling off him on a giggle.

Valen growled, rolled onto his side and caught her around the waist. He dragged her back to him, plastering his front against her back. She moaned and wriggled in his arms, her protests just a little too weak to be real.

She liked this.

Wicked little assassin.

He caught her throat with his left hand and kissed the back of her neck as he lay on his side with her, trailing his right hand over her curves. She moaned again, lower and softer now, revealing her need to him. She stilled as he lifted her right thigh and slid down her body, and sighed as he fed his cock into her slowly, easing it as deep as it could go, until he met with resistance.

Eva arched her back, taking him deeper still, and he groaned against the back of her neck and grasped her right thigh, holding it over his legs.

"Valen," she moaned, a soft plea.

He shifted his left hand up to her face, twisted her head towards him and kissed her as he pulled out of her, swallowing her moan as he made her feel every inch of him and what she did to him.

What only she did to him.

She moaned again as he drove back in, and he tried to keep the pace slow and steady, managed it for a few strokes before the feel of her and the way she responded to him hijacked control of his body. He kissed her harder as he plunged deeper, more forceful strokes as the need to claim her took over. She moaned with each one, arched and pressed back against him, encouraging him.

As if he needed it.

He tightened his grip on her throat and her thigh and drove deeper, hard thrusts that had her groaning sweetly, whispering pleas for more that intoxicated him. She reached a hand down and he grunted as she fondled his balls whenever they came into reach, tugging on them and then stroking her fingers over his shaft as he withdrew.

Sweet gods.

He broke away from her lips and pressed his mouth against the back of her neck as he plunged into her, harder now, drinking down her moans and how she was touching him as he took her, lighting up all of his senses until he couldn't take any more.

He dropped his hand from her thigh and fondled her bundle of nerves, pushing her closer to the edge with him.

She tightened around his cock, her voice strained. "Valen."

"Eva," he moaned against her neck and squeezed her bud.

She cried out, her body going rigid against him as he thrust into her, and then shattered in his arms, her legs shaking violently and core milking him, quivering around his cock.

He lightly bit the back of her neck and screwed his eyes shut as he joined her, release blasting through him as he felt her shaking, heard her heart pounding and listened to her panted gasps of pleasure.

Gods.

She completely undid him.

He held her to him, shaking with the force of his release, trembling as violently as she was in his arms, barely able to breathe.

Eva placed her hands over his, holding him gently, and he sank against her, pulled her closer and refused to let her go. She stroked his hands, her touch light and tender, a message to him.

She wasn't going anywhere.

That touched him deeply, soothed his heart and calmed his mind.

Even when he feared that she was.

Even when he feared he would lose her.

CHAPTER 31

Eva sat in the black leather wingback armchair in Valen's apartment, staring out of the window at the moonlit rooftops of Rome, waiting for him to come back. Her heart beat unsteadily, loud in her ears, and it was hard to focus her mind and stop it from conjuring images that unsettled her.

Visions of Benares.

She pulled down a deep slow breath, held it for a second and then released it just as slowly.

It was only a matter of time before he came for her.

And he would come.

Every instinct screamed that it was inevitable, and although it was all part of the plan, her plan, it still had her on the edge, fighting a losing battle against fear.

How many lives had she taken as an assassin? How many times had she faced odds stacked against her so strongly that she had been convinced it was the end? She had always emerged the victor though, scraping through somehow, living to see another day.

How many of those days had she squandered?

Now it felt as if she should have done something with them, should have saved them somehow to use them with Valen, as if they were a resource she could hoard and use as she wanted, when she wanted.

Hell, she wanted more time with him.

She could have it if she survived the next twenty-four hours.

She just had to fight for it.

And she would.

She would fight for it with all of her heart, every drop of blood in her body and breath in her lungs. No matter how frightening things got, she would keep on fighting for what she wanted.

Valen.

She closed her eyes and blew out her breath, wishing he was here with her. He had been reluctant to leave her alone, and she had been afraid of it too, knowing what would happen when he stepped away to the gate.

The way he had savoured every last second with her, as if it were their last, had left her feeling empty and bereft when he had teleported, as if the connection that had been blooming between them had been severed by the distance.

As if she would never see him again.

She pulled her legs towards her and pressed her feet into the edge of the seat, and leaned back into the chair, resting her forearms on her knees. Her eyes opened and she fixed them on Rome, aching with a need to see Valen.

She would see him again.

She only had to fight for it.

Just one more fight, the biggest of her life.

She could do it.

For Valen.

A noise off to her left had her gaze shooting in that direction, heart rising and warming as she looked for Valen.

Purple-black smoke curled outwards from a single spot around four foot above the tiles, spreading until it was around five foot wide and eight foot high, and had formed an oval that flickered with green and violet sparks.

Not Valen.

Eva shot to her feet as an immaculate black Italian leather shoe emerged from the shimmering smoke, the crisp leg of tailored dark silver slacks following it. Her heart lodged in her throat as her mind screamed that this was it.

Benares had come for her.

She steeled herself and shook away her fear and her nerves, set her face in a scowl and considered reaching for the blade strapped around her ankle beneath her black jeans. She forced herself to remain away from it, because it would be her only weapon, and Benares would easily disarm her. She needed to keep it a secret.

He emerged from the portal, blush lips stretched in a warm smile that reached his green eyes, making them shimmer as brightly as the flashes of light that danced across the smoke at his back.

Marek had said that they couldn't teleport.

This wasn't good.

Valen was expecting to feel the wards trigger, and return in time to follow her as Jin took her to the villa via the roads.

Instead, Benares had come for her through what looked like a portal.

If he took her, there was a chance Valen wouldn't be able to find her. She had only given him a vague location of the villa, because she had feared if she told him the exact one, he would go off half-cocked looking for a fight to avoid Benares taking her.

Benares advanced and she backed off, but there was nowhere to go. He stood between her and the door, preening his sun-kissed hair, a smug air about him.

As if he had already won and Valen turning to his side was a sure thing now.

He didn't stop when he was close to her. He kept pressing forwards, driving her back, and she gasped as her bottom and shoulders hit the wall between the window and the fireplace.

His smile widened and he slowly lifted his right hand towards her face. She flinched as he stroked her cheek, the light touch repulsing her and making her stomach squirm, even as it warmed her and drove all thought of running from her mind.

"That's good," he murmured and she stared up into his eyes, thoughts blurring together and slipping out of focus. "My angel."

Not his. Never his.

He lowered his head and pressed his lips to hers, and the haze in her head grew thicker, swamped all of her thoughts and replaced them with new ones, with a desire to step into his arms and give herself to him.

He smiled against her mouth when she did just that, her body moving without a command from her, her arms rising to loop around his neck. He bent at the knee and scooped her up into his arms, one beneath her knees and one against her back, his mouth still fixed on hers. She sagged against him, leaning heavily against his chest, his black shirt soft against her bare arms.

When he finally released her lips, she stared up at him, only able to focus on him, everything else around him a blur that meant nothing to her.

"My angel," he whispered and a frown flickered on his sandy eyebrows before it melted away, but the sharp spike of anger that had entered his glowing eyes remained.

Jealousy.

A vision of the monster he was inside overlaid onto him, ringing his eyes with black laced with blue lightning and dark lips that concealed vicious fangs, and she pushed against his shoulders.

He clucked his tongue and held her closer, kissed her again and drove her thoughts away, leaving her fighting to remember what she had been afraid of just a second ago.

When he pulled back and turned with her, carrying her towards the portal, he was just a man, handsome and charming.

A man who wanted her.

She sighed and settled her head against his chest, aching for him too.

A warm breeze laced with the scent of metal and wood flowed over her as purple and black mist danced around them, and then light pierced the veil and she found herself in a familiar room.

His office.

The haze that had been filling her mind dissipated with the portal, clearing slowly as the warmth flowed from her body and thoughts began to return.

She was in his office.

She looked up at Benares.

In his arms.

She scowled and shoved at his chest, and twisted free of his grip, landing on the grey marble floor at his feet in a crouch. She rose to her full height and glared at him.

"What is the meaning of this?" She was surprised her fear didn't show in her voice, but it gave her the confidence to continue. She took a hard step towards him but he stood his ground. "I had a few more hours."

"Your work is done." Benares neatened his appearance, preening his blond locks and smoothing his hands over the point where his black shirt met his dark silver trousers, tucking it back in. "I do hate portal jumping."

"A necessary precaution." A male voice she didn't recognise filled the room and she pivoted to face the owner of it. "Would you rather I allowed you to drive so he could stop you before you reached here? Failure is not an option this time. Do you understand, Benares?"

Benares nodded, and looked as if he wanted to kill the man for daring to issue orders to him.

Eva stared at the newcomer.

He stood off to the left of the huge ebony desk, near the bank of three windows that intersected the black wall, wrapped in a fitted black coat that was buttoned from his neck to his waist, and flared from there to reach his ankles, revealing a hint of black trousers and knee-high riding boots.

The man stared at her, his pale skin a contrast against his wild black hair, and those eerie purple eyes.

Had to be a trick of the light.

She wished she could believe that, could fool herself into thinking he was just a man, and not another monster.

He smiled at her, thin-lipped and cruel, and a cold shiver ran down her spine, chilling her blood.

"What happened in Tokyo?"

It took a moment for that question to register, but when it did she barely contained her reaction, schooling her features at the last second so he didn't see her shock.

Wraith.

This was the man who had tried to kill Esher, the one who might have killed Calindria too.

She had to delay him until Valen arrived, because she knew how much the thought of saving Calindria's soul meant to him. Valen wanted to give her peace, and this man was the key to making that happen.

Eva tipped her chin up and kept her cool. "They thwarted your plan, that's what happened. Esher is fine."

His smile turned colder, his purple eyes brighter.

"Fine is not a word I would associate with that god." He sighed and flicked a piece of lint off the breast of his black coat with the air of a man trying to let something roll off his back and not bother him, when it was annoying the hell out of him. "Never mind. It would have been my head on the butcher's block if I had succeeded. She would have been a little annoyed with me… the god is to be her pet after all."

Esher was meant to be someone's pet?

"Whose?" she said without thinking, and he laughed coldly as he looked from her to Benares.

"Deal with her before she gets you into trouble, Incubus. She seems to have forgotten her place as a member of our side. Are your skills so lacking that you cannot even hold sway over a weak mortal? I have never understood why she favours you so much."

Before she could ask another question, Benares had his hand over her mouth, his arm across her chest pinning her back against his, and the wraith was gone.

Damn it.

She had the feeling that the 'she' the wraith had spoken of wasn't her, but this woman who was meant to make Esher her pet.

Or another woman entirely.

How many people were in their organisation?

"Insufferable bastard," Benares muttered and huffed as he released her and stepped back.

She turned to face him, a thousand questions flooding her mind, but fear stole her voice.

Benares towered over her, taller than before, white embers sparking in his green eyes and his pupils narrowed into thin slits. He glared down at her, the black around his eyes spreading and cracking, bright blue shining through the fissures.

"No one lectures me on how to handle my females." He shot his hand out and captured the nape of her neck, dragged her against him and had his mouth on hers before she could react.

Fire blazed through her, burning away all the questions, all of her fears, replacing them with a fierce need to be closer to him, to do whatever he wanted. He kissed her deeper, making the inferno burn hotter, and she clawed at his black shirt and writhed in his arms, restless with a need for more.

He broke away from her lips and breathed against them.

"You are mine now, Angel... and I will make sure of it."

He feathered his lips across hers, teasing her as he whispered.

"I will take you from that god."

Cold swept over her skin, extinguishing the fire, and everything that had seemed so urgent a moment ago was inconsequential as she stared up into Benares's eyes.

Eyes that glowed with a dark and terrible need.

Hers widened.

He was going to kill Valen.

CHAPTER 32

It hadn't been difficult to find the villa based on the information Eva had given to him, or at least it shouldn't have been. Feeling the wards on his apartment trigger and returning to find her gone, and no trace of the scent of daemon in the area, had sent him off the deep end a little, and screwed with his senses.

The need to take her back, to protect her and keep her safe, and to destroy whoever stood in his path, was strong, commanding him against his will to shake the earth and the sky, unleashing his fury on this world.

It had taken him twenty minutes of going in circles, draining his strength by frantically stepping from one spot to the next across the valley, before he had finally calmed enough that he could focus and use his senses again.

The moment they had cleared, he had caught the coppery stench of daemons in the air, and had known exactly where to go.

He lingered in the shadows against the perimeter wall, tracking the daemons patrolling the other side of it and waiting for a break in them so he could pass through unnoticed.

Lightning flickered around his hands, and he scrubbed it away. He needed to be covert, and that wasn't helping. He was lighting up the whole godsdamned area.

He tensed as his senses spiked and looked off to his left, away from the gate, into the darkness down the wooded slope.

Keras had arrived as promised. His older brother had frighteningly sharp senses, able to pinpoint any one of them no matter what distance separated them.

He just hoped his brother kept back until he needed him.

This was his show.

He supposed he had better make it look good.

After all, he was meant to be here to take Eva back, and that was the perfect excuse to dispatch any wretched daemon foolish enough to cross his path.

No need to engage all of them though. The ones in the house would suffice.

In a single leap, he cleared the stone wall and moved through the shadows at speed, crossing the grass and following the tree-lined drive of the house. It glowed in the distance at the peak of the hill, all elegant and flashy, a fucking palace compared to his apartment.

He hoped to the gods Eva wasn't impressed by such material things.

He doubted that hope with a prayer when he passed the black Lamborghini parked next to a yellow Ferrari on the gravel in front of the yellow-ochre mansion.

A shriek pierced the night.

Eva.

All attempts to be covert shattered and lightning forked from his hands, cracking and snapping as it struck the ground around him.

He was coming.

Two daemon males at the grand entrance of the villa peered around the perfectly trimmed topiary, stared at him with disbelief written across both of their faces, and then sprang into action.

The bastards opened fire.

Not what he had expected given that Benares wanted him here.

Bullets sprayed everywhere, ploughing up the gravel and the grass beyond it, and shouts came from all directions as an alarm sounded.

Valen snarled and stepped, appeared on the roof of the porch above the two daemons and let loose. The lamps that hung from the underside of the roof shattered and the males screamed as electricity arced from them and hit them in the back. Smoke curled from their black fatigues and he called more power forth, funnelling it all into them. They fell to the ground, convulsing violently.

He grinned.

A bullet ripped into his right thigh.

His grin faded as he looked down at the dark wet patch spreading across his black combat trousers and then up at the male who had dared to shoot him.

The daemon's handgun shook as he stood on the other side of the elegant stone balustrade that formed a border around the huge paved area in front of the house.

Valen clucked his tongue and lifted his hand, causing the daemon to tense.

When nothing happened, the male relaxed.

Big mistake.

Valen clicked his fingers.

A thick white-purple bolt shot down from the sky and hit the daemon.

He didn't stop to watch the fireworks. He leaped down to the gravel, landing with a grunt and a grimace. No fucking way he could fight with a bullet lodged in his thigh. He growled from between clenched teeth and checked his surroundings, pinpointing all the daemons in the vicinity. There were more inside, but they weren't moving, were obviously waiting for him. The ones outside were still at a distance, but they were heading towards him.

He had time.

He stuck his finger in the tear in his trousers and widened it a little, just enough for him to see the hole in his thigh. He curled his lip, hesitated for only a heartbeat, and then jammed his index finger into the wound. White-hot pain blazed outwards from it, chasing up and down his leg, turning his stomach.

Had to be done.

He swallowed hard, closed his eyes as the world pitched and rolled in time with his stomach, and kept on digging, pushing deeper.

His finger hit something solid.

Metal.

It started as a low growl in his chest as he called on his power, focused it so it wrapped around the bullet and drew it to him, and came out as a roar as he yanked his hand away from his leg, tearing the damned thing free of his flesh.

Heat spilled down his thigh and he breathed hard as he pressed a hand against it.

Motherfucker.

He fumbled in his side pocket with his other hand, found a wad of material he always kept there, his own version of an emergency medical kit, and quickly pressed it against the wound. Pain throbbed through his bones but it slowly abated, falling to a level he could manage.

Valen undid his belt, whipped it free of the loops, and secured it around his thigh, using it to keep the wad of black cotton in place.

He straightened and tested his leg, placing some weight on it. It burned with each step, but it was better than before.

Satisfied that it wouldn't slow him down, he turned as casually as he could towards the mansion and walked up the steps, forcing himself to move without a limp.

Damned if he was going to show these bastards that he was hurting.

He was a god.

He prowled through the huge door and into the building.

The brightness of the foyer stung his eyes, the light from the crystal and gold chandelier reflecting off the white marble floor, and he raised a hand to shield them as they adjusted to it. Movement on his senses had him tensing, preparing.

Any second now.

A hail of bullets rained down on him and he growled as he shoved both of his hands forwards. A web of lightning exploded from his hands, forming a net in front of him, and the bullets dropped from the air as they connected with it, their momentum and their metal feeding the barrier. He pushed his hands forwards again and the web spread, rushing towards the two daemon males that stood on the balcony at the top of the twin staircases that curved up the pale yellow walls, and the two bastards beneath it on the same level as him.

The male in the lower left dodged behind the wall, and one at the top escaped into a room, but the other two weren't so fortunate.

The second daemon on the balcony screamed as the lightning wrapped around him, and the remaining one below kicked off to his right, but the web caught his leg and he shrieked as he went down.

Valen closed his eyes and focused on the mansion and tracking Eva. She was here somewhere. Where? He had to find her.

His internal radar was still.

Why couldn't he sense her? She had to be here still. All he could sense were daemons.

He growled through clenched teeth and focused harder, shutting out the two daemons as they ran, the third as he crumpled into a heap, and the fourth as he dragged himself away, along a corridor.

Valen frowned.

Drew down a deep breath and thought about Eva, about her scent.

It was hard with the stench of daemons and the tang of his lightning filling the air.

His frown flickered.

Roses.

And sin.

Eva.

He launched forwards, towards the corridor the injured daemon was taking, and bolted down it, despatching the daemon with a flick of his right wrist that sent five small arcs of lightning shooting towards him.

The male bellowed and then silence reigned.

Filled with the sound of Valen's rapid breathing and racing heart as he checked each room that led off the pale green corridor.

The sound of a struggle came from ahead.

His eyes fixed on the wooden door there.

He stepped and appeared in front of it, and kicked it open so hard it flew off the hinges and shot across the room.

A male with hair that faded from black at his roots to crimson dodged it, ducking to his right as it flew over his left shoulder and slammed into the black wall behind the ebony desk that took up a large section of the room. A daemon. He turned glowing green-white eyes on Valen and sneered, his black lips peeling back off all-sharp teeth, and the blue lightning that forked from around his eyes shone brighter against its obsidian backdrop.

Benares he presumed.

Valen's gaze sought Eva, which earned him a snarl from Benares. The bastard didn't have to worry. Valen would get to him soon enough.

Relief swept through him when he spotted Eva sitting on the floor beside the desk on the left side of the room, her blue eyes fixed on him, as round as full moons.

Jin stood behind her, dressed like a slut as always, wearing a tiny dark crimson dress and thigh-high matching red boots, her blonde hair draped over her breasts. Her blue eyes locked on him for a second before they slid to Benares.

Valen curled his fingers into tight fists and gave the bastard the whole of his attention.

"Let her go," he barked.

Benares smiled wickedly. "I cannot do that... but I will offer you an exchange. Your life in exchange for hers."

"No!" Eva screamed and shot to her feet.

Benares backhanded her and she collapsed to her knees, hitting the pale grey marble tiles with a harsh thud.

"Son of a bitch," Valen growled and stepped forwards, arcs of electricity twining around his arms and snapping against his skin as his rage boiled back to the surface. "You lay a fucking hand on her again and I will end you."

Benares had the audacity to laugh at that. "I would love to see you try... but we are not here to fight... we are here to do business. Pledge yourself to us, and she will be spared."

The relief in Eva's eyes said that she had been convinced Benares meant to kill him, and that had his mouth moving before the fragment of sense that remained in his thick skull could speak up and convince him to stick to the plan.

"She'll be safe if I kill you." Valen shot his hand forwards and lightning arced from his fingers, six bolts twining together to form one, aimed at Benares's chest.

Benares didn't move to block or evade.

Valen grinned.

Piece of cake.

That grin died as his lightning hit an invisible barrier and shot back at him, and he had to throw himself on the ground to avoid the blast. White-purple arcs scorched the walls as they hit it, leaving smouldering circles in the black plaster.

Valen looked across at Benares as he pushed back onto his feet.

Hexagonal glyphs shimmered across the air between them, pale blue and lasting only as long as it took for the ripples created by his attack to pass over them.

The damned barrier stretched the width of the room, and from the floor to the ceiling.

Fuck.

Eva was on the other side of that barrier.

He tried to step through it, but when he reappeared he was stood against the invisible wall.

He couldn't get to her.

Rage curled through his blood, setting it on fire, and he snarled and banged his fists against it. Eva stared up at him, fear shining in her eyes, fear he wanted to take away but he couldn't.

He couldn't do anything for her.

He shifted his gaze to Benares and growled at the bastard.

Benares shook his head and sighed. "Did you really think it would be that easy?"

Valen shrugged, but it was stiff, his body coiled tight with a need to attack. "I had kinda hoped it would be, yeah."

He looked off to this left, to the windows there. If he went outside the building, could he teleport back into it on the other side of the barrier. He eyed where it was, tipped his head back and checked out the ceiling.

"I can assure you, there is not a crack you can exploit. My sister is very good at what she does."

Jin blushed and stared at Benares with the same moon eyes that Ares gave Megan.

Sick.

He curled his lip at the bitch, and she just smiled at him.

Her laugh grated down his spine.

"We have something you want. All you have to do is work for us," she said, her smile holding, her blue eyes shining brightly as she swayed her hips and flicked her fall of blonde hair over her left shoulder. "You do want her, don't you?"

Valen looked down at Eva where she still knelt on the floor, locking eyes with her. "More than anything in this world."

Benares growled, and Eva flinched, and Valen shot him a glare. Something was going on, something he wasn't aware of and wanted to know about right now.

Because from where he was standing, it looked as if Benares wanted Eva for himself.

Over Valen's dead body.

Even then he wouldn't let Benares have her.

He would make his father release his soul from the Underworld so he could kill the bastard from beyond the grave.

"What about more than anything in your world?" Benares hissed and pushed away from the desk, coming to stand opposite him. Gods, Valen wanted to punch him. Stupid barrier. He was going to find a way to get rid of it and then it was lights out for Benares. The bastard smirked at him. "Do you want her more than say… your sister's soul?"

Valen had to take a step back to brace himself as that hit him, and he saw in Benares's eyes that he was being serious.

"You fucking son of a bitch." Valen flew at the barrier, raining blows down on it that sent sparks of lightning flying in all directions. He felt his teeth shift, and his eyes join them as his fury got the better of him, the need to find Calindria's soul seizing control of him and demanding he beat the location out of the bastard.

That need warred with the need he felt to do anything to save Eva, to take her back from Benares and keep her safe, protecting her as he had promised.

But Calindria.

It tore him in two, ripping his heart straight down the middle as he battered the barrier, hammering it so hard that his hands hurt.

"We could get that soul for you," Benares whispered, not moving from his spot on the other side of the invisible wall that separated them, not even flinching as Valen rained unholy hell down upon it, desperately trying to break through.

Gods, that was so tempting.

His punches slowed as that temptation swept through him, whispering seductive words in his ear and to his heart.

If he could get Calindria's soul back, if he could save her, the redemption he had always desired would be his.

"Don't do it," Eva hollered and pushed forwards, coming to the barrier and pressing her hands to it.

He looked down at her, his ears ringing and shoulders slumping as his fight left him.

"Don't do it." Eva's eyes narrowed with her frown and she shook her head. "We will help her somehow, but not this way… she wouldn't want it this way."

Valen stared at her.

She was right.

"Shut up," Benares snarled, grabbed hold of her black hair and hauled her onto her feet, twisting her to face him. "Good angels know when to be fucking quiet."

Valen lost it when Benares backhanded her and she screamed, falling for a moment before the daemon pulled her back onto her feet and struck her again, and again, until her lips were bloodied and her left eye began to swell, a cut near it pouring blood down her cheek.

"Get the fuck off her!" He pressed his hands to the barrier and put all he had into it, unleashing as much power as he could in his limited state.

Limited.

He growled and reached for the band around his left wrist, and froze with his fingers against it, duty and desire pulling him in two opposite directions. He couldn't. If he did, his brothers would never forgive him.

His father would never forgive him.

His mother too.

"Godsdammit!" he bellowed and hit the barrier again, lighting it up with more juice this time, cracking a few of the bright blue hexagonal glyphs.

But it still didn't break.

He sank to his knees, breathing hard, his heart labouring as pain devoured it.

His brothers would never forgive him for this either. His father would never forgive him. His mother too.

But he had to do it.

He shook his head and pressed his hands to the barrier. "Stop… I'll join you… just don't hurt her any more."

Benares released her and she collapsed in a heap on the floor, her left eye swollen and dark, and blood covering that side of her face. It dripped from her lips onto the marble tiles, forming a stark crimson pool.

"Eva," he whispered and shuffled so he was in front of her. "Look at me, Eva." She continued staring straight ahead, her right eye glassy and empty.

Damn it.

"Eva!" He banged his fists against the barrier. "Look at me."

Please.

He sagged and leaned against the barrier, pressing his forehead to it, his rage draining from him together with his strength as he stared at her, willing her to respond.

Because he couldn't lose her.

Eva weakly lifted her head and her lips moved silently.

He growled and shot to his feet, flashing fangs at Benares. "Let me through. Let me get to her. I need to see she's going to be okay."

Benares sneered at him, flashing his own sharp teeth, and that look entered his eyes again, the one that said he wanted Eva to belong to him. Never. She was his, and she always would be.

He would kill anyone who stood between them or tried to take her from him.

He growled again as he remembered he had promised Keras that he wouldn't kill Benares.

Fucking damn it.

Fine. Benares got a stay of execution, and he would be a good boy for once.

And then as soon as they had all the information they could get out of him, he would kill him.

Benares would die for what he had done to Eva.

"Eva," he rasped and she frowned, moaned and tried to get up, but she collapsed back against the floor. Her cheek landed in the blood. He returned his gaze to Benares. "Let me in."

"Why don't we sweeten the deal? Say the words to pledge your allegiance to us, and you can have Eva, and me too." Jin moved to stand between Eva and Benares, her red lips curved in a sultry smile and blue eyes promising all the pleasure he could ever desire.

It made him want to vomit.

Benares stepped forwards, towards the barrier, but either Valen's head was more screwy than usual because he was barely keeping a leash on his temper, or the daemon was slowing down, moving through the air as if it was molasses.

The hairs on the back of Valen's neck prickled and rose on end.

Keras.

His power flowed over the building and it should have brought everyone except those Keras had made exempt from it to a halt, yet Benares and Jin were still moving.

Eva too.

The prickle danced down his spine as her face darkened, her eyes on Jin, and she reached for her ankle. She was on her feet a moment later, a war cry leaving her lips and rage burning in her eyes. Something flashed in her hand as she brought it up.

A blade.

Valen threw his hands towards the barrier to pound on it and stop her.

Eva brought the blade up as Jin slowly turned towards her, blue eyes enormous and red lips parting in shock.

The knife struck hard, plunging deep into Jin's side.

Valen's hands went straight through the barrier and landed on Benares's chest.

Jin screamed as she toppled and Eva went down with her behind Benares.

Benares stared down at his chest, at Valen's hands, and roared as he shoved his own hands forwards, catching Valen hard in his own chest before he could unleash even a tiny bolt of lightning into the bastard.

Valen flew across the room and grunted as he slammed into the wall and dropped to his knees.

Jin had created the barrier, and she must have been maintaining it by focusing on whatever power had called it forth, constantly nurturing and repairing it.

Eva had shattered that focus.

She had found a way to let him in.

Eva pushed up and pulled the blade out, and Valen felt a little hot all over as she tossed her head back, her blue-streaked black hair flying in slow motion as Keras's power increased in strength and began to slow even her, and she unleashed another battle cry and brought the blade down again, thrusting it to the hilt between Jin's breasts.

Sweet gods.

He shouldn't be as aroused as this on the battlefield, it was wrong on so many levels, but he just couldn't help himself as he watched her fight.

It wasn't only her prowess as a warrior that had him flustered though.

It was her fury at the succubus's offer to be his lover too.

His little assassin wanted him all to herself.

Would kill anyone who stood between them.

Damn.

He loved her.

He grinned and kicked off, launching himself at Benares. Once they had him subdued, Keras could question him.

Valen stopped mid stride, grinding to a halt just a few feet from Benares.

Benares stood in the middle of the room, green eyes wide as he stared down at his chest.

At the wet patch spreading across his black shirt.

Valen's eyes leaped to Jin and the blade sticking out of her chest.

Fuck.

They were more than brother and sister.

They were bound.

No.

Benares laughed, black blood trickling from his obsidian lips as he touched the wet spot on his chest and brought his hand away, and stared at his black-stained fingertips.

He lifted his green eyes from them to Valen.

"It wasn't meant to end like this... we were meant to rule this world," he whispered and the black around his eyes faded, the blue lightning disappearing, and his green eyes dulled. "She promised."

He collapsed, landing hard on the marble floor, and grunted as he twisted onto his back and reached for Jin.

Jin reached for him, stretched her arm as far as it would go, and her fingers twitched and then stilled as her hand dropped to the floor.

Benares took hold of her hand and clutched it. "She promised."

"No. Fuck it. No!" Valen's knees hit the marble tiles next to Benares and he took hold of his shoulders and shook him, staring down into his fading eyes. "I need answers, you fucking bastard."

Benares sank back against the tiles and exhaled on a sigh.

No heartbeat reached Valen's ears.

"Fuck!" He shoved away from Benares and growled as he paced the room.

"I didn't know," Eva whispered and he stopped and looked down at her, and let all of his rage drain away. Her right eye was wide, a flicker of fear in it, remorse and guilt, and he sighed as he sank down into a crouch beside her. "I'm sorry."

He shook his head and wanted to growl as he touched her cut cheek just below her swollen left eye and she flinched. "I know. I didn't know either. None of us did."

But now he had no daemon to hand over to Keras, and they had no leads to go on.

"The wraith was here," Eva said, dragging his focus back to her, and he stared at her, reeling a little as that sank in.

"You saw him?" he said and she nodded. "Clearly?"

"He was in this room."

"You could describe him... like a photo fit thing mortal police do?" When she nodded, the ache in his chest eased just a little, because at least they had something they could work on, something that might help them uncover who was behind the plot to destroy the gates.

She eased closer to him, and he tore a strip off his black t-shirt and used it to carefully clean the blood off her cheek.

"There's another thing too." She flinched when he dabbed a little too hard in response to that and he issued a silent apology to her. "The wraith mentioned a woman too… and… I have the feeling she's higher up the command chain because he was worried he had killed Esher."

"What does Esher have to do with this?" His blood ran cold at the thought of anyone targeting his brother.

Esher was a ticking bomb on the best of days, and when he came around from recovering from the wraith's attack, it was not going to be a good day.

Eva winced as she touched her split lip. "The wraith said Esher was to be her pet."

Pet?

What the fuck did that mean?

It conjured images of this mystery woman holding Esher captive, chained, and like hell he was going to let that sort of thing happen to his brother again.

"We need to tell Keras. Gods, he's going to tear me a new one for this though." Valen stood and held his hand out to Eva.

"Tear you a new one for what?" Keras's deep voice rolled through the room.

Valen tensed as Eva placed her hand into his, and slowly pulled her onto her feet, turning a sheepish smile on his older brother at the same time.

Keras looked from him to the two dead daemons, rolled his eyes and pinched the bridge of his nose as he sighed.

"They were bound," Eva said before he could even try to explain, and stepped in front of him. Fighting in his corner? Gods, it had been a long time since anyone had done that and it felt so good that he wanted to grin at his brother and then kiss her. She folded her arms across her chest. "I did it… so if you're going to be angry with anyone, be angry with me."

Fuck, he did love this woman.

Keras shot her an irritated look that melted away as he really took a look at her and spotted her injuries. "We need to take you to Megan."

Valen frowned at that. He was pretty sure that if he had been the one in Eva's position, and had killed Jin, and accidentally Benares in the process, that his big brother would have been close to losing his temper, not fussing over his injuries.

He glared at Keras.

Plus, fussing over Eva was his job.

"Temper," Keras murmured, and Valen reined it in just this once.

"We did get some new information about the wraith, and that there's a female targeting Esher." Valen pulled down a breath to steady his heart and considered not mentioning everything else that happened, but he couldn't hold it in.

He didn't want to keep things from his brothers anymore, no longer wanted that divide between them. It had almost cost him everything.

He glanced down at Eva.

Grew some balls.

And put it all out there.

"Benares said he could get Calindria's soul." Valen raked a hand over his hair as Marek walked in just in time to hear that, wiping black blood off his hands. "He offered to get it for me… and I couldn't do it. I could have saved her."

Keras crossed the room to him, placed his right hand on his left shoulder, and squeezed it gently. "You did the right thing, Valen. We will save her one day, but not like that."

The warmth in his green eyes, the relief that shone there, told Valen that he meant every word.

"We will find the wraith who killed her and we will free her soul, but we will do it together. As brothers." Keras gave his shoulder another squeeze. "As family."

The only reason there were tears stinging Valen's eyes was because Keras was a dick and squeezed too hard, hurting him. It had nothing to do with what he had said. Absolutely nothing.

Really.

His big brother hadn't just made him go all teary-eyed by spouting shit about them being brothers, and family.

Not wanting to look like a sentimental prick, he cleared his throat and played it cool, even when Marek shot him a sly smile that he knew was meant to be teasing. Fucker.

"We should gather everyone to discuss this, because it has become clear we are facing an entire organisation, and we are yet to meet its ringleader." Keras looked back at Marek, whose brown eyes got that twisted glow they had whenever he was being told to scour their database and do research. Marek nodded. "Let us meet in Tokyo."

Valen nodded.

Keras and Marek both stepped, and Valen went to gather Eva into his arms and follow them, intent on getting her to Megan so the Carrier could heal her wounds.

Eva placed a hand against his chest, stopping him, and looked up into his eyes. "I need a moment… alone… with you."

His heart pounded hard and he told himself not to read into it, that it wasn't going to be anything bad and he wasn't going to lose her, but old habits died the hardest and fear trickled through his veins, chilling his blood.

He nodded stiffly, gathered her into his arms and stepped, landing on the hilltop overlooking Rome.

She didn't help matters by pushing out of his arms the second they landed and pacing across the grass.

Gods.

He swallowed hard and tried to steel his heart, but it was already falling apart, that dark voice at the back of his mind spreading poison through his blood that weakened it and pushed him to the verge of breaking.

Her job was done, contract fulfilled, and Benares was dead, no longer a threat to her.

But she loved him, didn't she?

Didn't she?

He stared at her, breathing hard as he fought for air, desperately trying to calm his mind so he could think rationally and not let his fears sweep him along.

They were too powerful though.

He couldn't lose her.

"Eva—"

She cut him off. "I'm sorry."

Gods, she really was going to leave him.

He growled and lightning struck hard all around them, tearing up the earth and filling the air with the scent of it. Rain lashed down, saturating them both, and she recoiled and turned in all directions as more lightning strikes connected, shaking the ground beneath their feet.

"Valen," she shouted and did the most wonderful thing. She ran to him and cupped his cheeks in her palms, the fear shining in her eyes not fear of the lightning, nor fear of him. She feared for him. "What's wrong?"

He couldn't bring himself to say it, because he was no longer sure it was true, and he didn't want her to laugh at him if it wasn't. He wasn't sure he could take her laughing at him. She wouldn't mean to hurt him with it, but it would cut him deeply nonetheless.

He glared down at her.

She smoothed her left fingers across his brow, easing his frown away, so much concern in her eyes and all aimed at him, when she was hurt, her left eye swollen and cheek bruised, and lip split. She should have been more concerned about herself.

Gods, it hurt to look at her, to see her injured and know if he had been stronger, smarter, she might have been fine, spared the pain and the fear she must have felt.

He narrowed his eyes on her wounds and cursed himself.

"Why do you always make yourself look that way? Why must you always try to look so frightening? There is a good heart in here."

She dropped her right hand to his chest.

He sneered at her as that heart she had spoken of so softly ached a little fiercer and fear brought his barriers shooting up around it, centuries of shielding it controlling him and making him snarl at her even when he only wanted to hold her and make her love him.

"I don't have a heart," he growled, and in part it was true, but not in the way he wanted her to believe. "Haven't you figured that out yet?"

His soul whispered the true meaning of his words to hers.

Hadn't she figured out that he had no heart because he had given it to her?

She spread her fingers outwards, covering more of his chest, and that heart pounded against her palm, desperate to reach her.

Her blue eyes held his. "Yes, I have figured you out. I just don't quite understand you yet. I don't understand why you act the way you do, why you pretend to be something you aren't and why you push people away like you're trying to push me away. That isn't you."

Gods, he didn't want that.

He wanted to fall to his knees, wrap his arms around her waist and do whatever it took to make her stay, but the fear of losing her was too strong. It was fear that had been carved in that moment centuries ago, given form and control over him, and it had festered inside him ever since, eating away at him.

He was so tired of it, but he wasn't sure he had the strength to take that necessary but difficult first step towards overcoming it.

"It is," he said when all he wanted to do was tell her that she was right, and long ago he had been a different man, and he wanted to be that man again. "It is me, and it has been since—"

"Stop punishing yourself," she whispered but she might as well have shouted because he rocked back on his heels, shaken by the force of her words. "Valen, you don't have to keep punishing yourself. You reacted the way anyone would have."

He looked away from her. "Not my brothers… or my parents. None of them would have done what I did. None of them… and I'm not sure they can forgive me."

Gods, that had been hard to say, because he had threaded it with a hope, a need he was sure she would see.

He wanted their forgiveness.

"For killing the Moirai?" She frowned at him.

Valen shook his head. "I should have stopped her. I knew what she was going to do and I should have stopped her. I never should have let her go."

Her blue eyes softened and he didn't pull away when she raised her hands back to his face and held his cheeks. He took all the comfort she offered, pulled it deep into his soul and tried to patch up his heart with it.

"You can't think like that." Her eyes searched his and she sighed. "The fault lies with—"

"Don't you blame her," he snapped and lightning struck all around them, harsh flashes illuminating her wet face.

Another sigh escaped her. "I wasn't going to. I was going to say that it lies with whoever killed her, not you. You can't carry the weight of this alone, Valen… and you don't have to."

He clenched his fists when all he wanted to do was reach out and take hold of her, to apologise for being so messed up that he was lashing out at her when he didn't even know why she had brought him here. Everything about her actions said it hadn't been to dump his arse as he had thought.

Now she was trying to piece his heart back together for him, gently encouraging him to take that first step towards crossing the divide between him and his brothers and healing their bonds.

She was giving him all of her strength.

Fuck, he loved her for that.

"Who's going to carry it with me?" He ignored how his voice shook, uncertainty and hope mingling in it to make him sound pathetic.

"Your brothers."

He snorted. "They blame me too."

Eva planted her hands on her hips and scowled at him, frustration darkening her eyes and warning him he was pushing too hard, needed to rein it back before he did end up driving her away.

"You want them to blame you, but they don't. Your brothers do love you." She caught his cheek when he went to look away, her touch firmer this time, and brought his head back around so his eyes met hers again. There was that temper he found so damn alluring. She looked ready to tear him a new one, or kiss the hell out of him. "They love you, and they worry about you. I worry about you. Stop punishing yourself… stop seeing what you want to see. I didn't ask you to bring me here so I could turn against you, Stronzo."

Ah. She did have him figured out after all.

He got the feeling that he would never be able to slip anything past her, that she would always read him like an open book, no matter how well he tried to hide his feelings. She had possessed that talent from the night their paths had first crossed in front of the Pantheon, and he felt blessed that whoever had created her for him, they had made her perfect in every way.

A woman who could see through him, straight down to his heart, and didn't take any shit from him.

Or his brothers.

"Open your eyes, Valen, and see the truth for once." Her soft voice coaxed him back to her and he looked down into her eyes, trying to spot what she was talking about.

"The truth?"

She nodded, and faltered, and did she look nervous now? Godsdammit, if she was going to leave him after all, Rome was about to get hit with a cataclysmic storm.

"Why did you bring me here?" He couldn't hold on any longer without knowing, because he wasn't going to be able to get a hold of his temper and clamp down on it until she just came out with it.

Her eyebrows rose. "To apologise for not being able to detain the wraith long enough for you to get there while he was still around. I didn't want to mention it in front of your brothers… because there's that thing where none of you seem to want to mention your sister in front of Calistos."

Oh.

That was why she had wanted to be alone with him.

"And…" she said and tailed off, looked away from him and fiddled with her lip, suddenly fascinated with the cut in it.

He wanted to take her to Megan whenever he looked at her cut lip and swollen eye, but he knew Eva, and she would fight him if he took her anywhere before she was ready.

Before she had said all that she needed to say.

"And?" he parroted her, and wasn't sure he could wait to hear it, because a tight feeling had settled in his chest, squeezing his heart, and he might die if she kept him waiting.

Or if it was just another apology.

"The truth is… Valen," she whispered but her voice slowly gained strength, and volume as she turned back to face him and lifted her eyes back to his. "The truth is your family loves you, which is more than I've ever had, and you're a good man… and I… I…"

"You what?" he said, maybe a little too harshly judging by how she glared at him.

He wasn't trying to rush her.

Much.

Her pretty faced screwed up, frustration flashed in her eyes, and she grabbed his cheeks, pulled him down to her and whispered against his lips.

"Ti amo."

Her mouth was on his before he could utter a word, her tongue stealing all of his focus as it traced his lower lip, and he somehow managed to restrain himself even when his heart was screaming at him to hold her tightly and make her know he felt the same way, that she was everything to him and he was never letting her go.

Rather than crushing her to his chest, he carefully wrapped his arms around her and lifted her up, and kissed her softly, tenderly, so he didn't open the cut on her lip because no way in hell he could ever hurt her.

Because he loved her.

He poured it into the kiss as he held her to him, her legs around his waist and the rain pouring down on them. Lightning chased across the sky, making the air hum with its power, but not his body this time.

That hummed with the joy Eva had given him, two simple Italian words that had pieced his heart back together and given him the strength to move forwards, towards a day when he would be the male he had once been, the male he wanted to be for her.

And on that day, when he was good enough for her, when he was the male that she deserved, he would tell her.

In a language she understood.

He was going to have to pay penitence for this, but fucking hell it would be worth it.

He smiled against her lips, carefully covered her ears to protect them, and whispered in the tongue of the Underworld.

"I love you too."

The End

ABOUT THE AUTHOR

Felicity Heaton is a New York Times and USA Today best-selling author who writes passionate paranormal romance books. In her books she creates detailed worlds, twisting plots, mind-blowing action, intense emotion and heart-stopping romances with leading men that vary from dark deadly vampires to sexy shape-shifters and wicked werewolves, to sinful angels and hot demons!

If you're a fan of paranormal romance authors Lara Adrian, J R Ward, Sherrilyn Kenyon, Gena Showalter, Larissa Ione and Christine Feehan then you will enjoy her books too.

If you love your angels a little dark and wicked, the best-selling Her Angel series is for you. If you like strong, powerful, and dark vampires then try the Vampires Realm series or any of her stand-alone vampire romance books. If you're looking for vampire romances that are sinful, passionate and erotic then try the best-selling Vampire Erotic Theatre series. Or if you prefer huge detailed worlds filled with hot-blooded alpha males in every species, from elves to demons to dragons to shifters and angels, then take a look at the new Eternal Mates series.

If you have enjoyed this story, please take a moment to contact the author at **author@felicityheaton.co.uk** or to post a review of the book online

Connect with Felicity:
Website – http://www.felicityheaton.co.uk
Blog – http://www.felicityheaton.co.uk/blog/
Twitter – http://twitter.com/felicityheaton
Facebook – http://www.facebook.com/felicityheaton
Goodreads – http://www.goodreads.com/felicityheaton
Mailing List – http://www.felicityheaton.co.uk/newsletter.php

FIND OUT MORE ABOUT HER BOOKS AT:
http://www.felicityheaton.co.uk

Printed in Great Britain
by Amazon